Echo

A Demon Hunter Romance #4

Carrie Thorne

Published by Thorny Books

Carrie Thorne

https://carriethorne.com/

Standalones

The Christmas Bet: A Double Feature Christmas Standalone.

Enjoy free books, first looks,

review team access,

and occasional hellos from Carrie?

Let's do this: carriethorne.com/newsletter

For my own nerdy veteran.

1

Midair, flying backward, chest throbbing from the blow, Archer aimed his sidearm and unloaded at the... blur? Whatever the fuck it was, he'd pissed it off, and it hit back. Hard.

Half his damn bullets ricocheted off the haze. The other half were chewed up, swallowed, and swelled into miniature mushroom clouds.

Crash imminent, no way to avoid the rocks that cluttered the path behind him, he clicked on his safety and tucked for impact. Ass first, he slammed into the gravel.

Breathless, the wind knocked solidly out of him, he gasped a recovering breath. A sharp crunch stopped him cold, his sternum throbbing from the blow.

Shards of shale dug into his skin. Bruises flowered on impact, probably already a purple backside.

No time to think about it. Archer gritted his teeth and pushed through the pain. He pivoted behind the nearest boulder.

Hazy, blurry static swarmed the space he'd just evacuated.

Archer ducked low and crouched out of sight.

Razor blades sliced into his lungs with each inhale. He braced his sternum, cautiously drawing in air. That hit, whatever the fuck that thing was, it was like a goddamn hazy fist as big as his head. At first, he'd thought it was a trick of the light, but his bruised ribs said otherwise.

Sidearm aimed steady, he peered around the edge of the rock.

Nothing except for the cloud-diffused sunlight glinting off the littered shrapnel where his shots had landed and burst at twice their magnitude, far from the target.

The target that was gone.

He blinked to focus, but it didn't help.

"Archer? Talk to me. You alive?" Chan's voice, steady as ever, came through the com in his ear.

"Yeah." Each breath sliced into his sternum. Hand braced against his chest, he masked the breathlessness and ordered, "Echos, report."

A series of check-ins from his squad chimed in. Walker's voice was low, hoarse. "Lost consciousness for a blink, hell of a goose egg, but I'm good."

"Walker, you're on lookout. Hold your position."

"Roger."

In sequence, the squad confirmed consciousness, at the least. He sucked in a sigh of relief, recoiling as the movement aggravated the pain.

"Kerse. Sauer. Report from on high?"

From her sniper's position atop a towering outcrop outside the mouth of the canyon—one of many odd formations in the shale talus they were hiking up—Kerse answered, "Before that blast, it was hazy, but now I can hardly make you guys out through the smoke."

Across the mouth of the canyon, from a similar perch, Sauer rumbled through the com, "Same. What am I aiming for? All I saw was a blur of shadows."

Pulse pounding under his veins, he creeped further around the edge of the boulder, but couldn't make out shit. Aborting wasn't an option, not yet, not without some clue as to what this was and how to take it out. But they sure as hell weren't going in far enough to die like all the others.

Too many soldiers' lives had already been lost trying.

Archer tried to explain what he'd seen, knowing his squad would give him shit. If they made it out alive. "This hazy fist thing swung at me, so I fired at it, but it... Fuck. I don't know. Don't shoot at it, or we're more likely to get hurt than... it."

"Fist?" Chan hissed from her position a few meters back.

"Um, sort of," he admitted, rubbing the crust of dust off his eyelids. Across the rubble of the canyon floor, he searched for the whatever the fuck that was that ruined his damn day, but the thing seemed to...

Okay, maybe he was losing his damn mind, but it seemed to blur like an unfocused photograph of Bigfoot. Then it dissipated as quickly as it had appeared.

"Forget your reading glasses?" Sauer teased, chortling at his own joke.

"Fuck off." He held the eye-roll, but fully intended to nail him with a comeback later. Once he could see straight. "I'm moving closer."

A thunderous crash echoed ahead, like a stack of boulders tumbled into the basin all at once.

A shadow, nothing more, oozed closer. Muggy and roasting like a North Dakota summer, the heat emanating off the figure filled his lungs, choking him with the viscous wind that permeated the paper-thin air.

From her post above, Kerse whispered steadily, "I see something. I'm taking the shot."

"Hold your fire," he hissed. "I don't think it likes being shot at."

Brock kept his voice low and said over the com, "I've got a clear path."

"Go. Eyes only," Archer agreed. Shooting at shadows was likely to leave him with more than a bruise on his ass and a few cracked ribs.

Whatever this thing was, it had to be massive. Some sort of defense system he'd never encountered.

"I'll come around the other side," he said. He shifted his hand off his chest and let the splintering pain lash through each breath, raising his sidearm—out of threat and habit, more than an intent to risk using it again.

At the opposite side of the canyon entrance, Brock held his weapon ready and wove upstream from boulder to boulder.

Archer glanced back and saw Walker moving to the base point Brock had vacated.

Silence over the com. The squad held their breath, waiting.

A stream babbled down the center of the canyon. It could almost feel like a pleasant day in paradise.

But the somber, bone-dry rocks all around, the matching gray clouds above, felt more like a gateway to hell. Or maybe it was the realization that it wasn't some secret weapon protecting this canyon, but something far more terrifying. Fuck, his report wasn't going to make a lick of sense.

As they moved closer to the mouth of the canyon, the heat intensified. The hairs on the back of his neck stood on end, static crackling over his skin.

Archer crossed closer to Brock. He caught his eye and nodded ahead. Locked and loaded, both stepped into the middle of the canyon.

Thunder without a storm roared, vaulting from wall to wall.

Shifting his gaze, he scanned the gray nothingness.

Two, maybe three figures. Or maybe nothing at all. Shadows. Dust. Haze. The threat loomed just out of sight.

Rising like a phantom, chilling his blood, a darkness oozed over them.

The trickle of a stream babbled louder underfoot.

Bigger than his head, yet not more than a blur. That fist swelled and swung at Brock.

Archer rushed to knock him out of the way, but the wind from the blow knocked him back.

Too late. Too fast. The fist caught a piece of Brock and sent him tumbling down the canyon floor.

On the move before it could swing through again, Archer holstered his weapon as he sprinted for Brock.

The stream rose higher and deeper with each passing second.

Out cold, Brock lay motionless. Water rushed over him, his blond hair and beard rinsing clean.

Archer heaved him over his shoulder. "Evac. Now," he hollered over the com.

"Abort? We haven't even—" Kerse hissed.

"Run," Chan roared, eyes wide as she turned and took off, blurry clouds chasing after her.

The rest of the squad didn't hesitate and sprinted downslope toward the Hummers. Half were limping and bleeding, the other half were either nursing head wounds or worse, but they didn't hesitate.

Whatever the hell this was, it was pissed. And it wasn't some new tech, no matter what Army intelligence wanted to believe.

Loose rocks shifted under his boots. Cool water rushed over at his ankles, growing deeper with each step as the stream grew to a creek.

Gusting behind him, he felt the wallop of shadowy wind reaching for him, as if the canyon was pissed as hell to let anyone leave alive.

The air rumbled in protest as they escaped from the mouth of the canyon. Approaching a six-foot ledge in a series of terraces down the talus, Arche maintained his brutal pace and launched over. Dread burned in his mind. No way of landing soft on wet, jagged shale. Midair, he tightened his grip on Brock so his friend didn't land head-first.

Archer dug the thick heels of his boots into the loose rocks to break the fall. Brock jostled in his grip and the pair slammed backward into a pile of rocks, rising water from the creek rushing over them.

Walker and Kerse appeared seconds later and grabbed the unconscious Brock from Archer's protective hold.

Archer ignored the searing throb where his backside had hit the ground and leaped to his feet, bracing his sternum, and followed close behind.

Walker loaded Brock into the backseat of the nearest Hummer before running to his own transport. Archer dove in next to Brock as Chan took the driver's seat, slamming on the gas before even closing the door.

Bracing against the rocking of the Hummer as they sped away over rough ground, Archer held his friend.

A gash over his forehead, already black and blue, his ankle puffing to the size of a grapefruit, Brock looked like hell.

Archer held his fingertips over his wrist. Stable enough. Pulse was strong, his breathing labored, but effective. While Chan drove like a demon, Archer checked Brock out as best he could. As best as he could tell, no major neurologic damage.

Sucking in a razor-sharp breath, Archer closed his eyes and whispered, "Hang in there."

Nothing more he could do. He buckled Brock in as secure as he could, shrugging off his jacket and cushioning it under his head.

He climbed up front next to Chan. Behind them, the blur seemed to darken, the clouds rumbled and swelled, satisfied to have maintained its boundaries as it flipped them off, scared little bunnies running from the big bad blur.

"Did you get a good look?" Chan asked as she steered them down the rough terrain. "What are we up against?"

He gritted his teeth and checked the side mirrors. "No fucking clue. It was like a blur of..."

"What?"

"Fury," he admitted. "Like we were trespassing on its territory, and it wanted blood."

Chan's voice was hoarse, her grip tight on the steering wheel. "That was a thing? I thought it was a funnel cloud or something."

Archer shook his head and rubbed his mud-caked hands in his hair. "Definitely a thing. Or a few things. Or... Not. I don't know."

"Break it down. What *exactly* did you see?" Chan asked as the Hummer bounced over another rocky berm, her knuckles white as she gripped the wheel to keep them from spinning out at the breakneck speed.

"Nothing. Something. I don't fucking know. It was like a blurry, cheap snapshot of... a troll or something. And this massive blob of darkness coming at us. Or maybe it wasn't so big. Like it could have been the size of the canyon or shorter than you. It was like some blurry image that only conspiracy-theorizing fucks would admit to having seen." He grimaced as the rig jarred down, his ass and chest throbbing with each tiny bump in the path.

Brock winced as he lurched against the seat. Relief welled under Archer's gritty eyelids.

Chan kept her eyes on the road. "It's got to be what killed the Rangers."

"Intelligence said they were killed by some new weapon the insurgents came up with, something that creates a fog and heat."

"That wasn't a weapon."

"No, it wasn't." But someone had to describe it in credible terms.

He reached back and checked Brock's wrist again. His fingers twitched, then clung to Archer's hand.

"Hang in there," Archer murmured. "We'll be back home, sharing a pitcher at Tumbleweed before you know it."

No one knew what this was or how to describe it, and few had gotten close enough to feel the threat that emanated from the canyon itself. Which was why they'd been sent in. When an entire platoon of Rangers goes missing, the nearest known insurgent encampment miles away at the opposite end of the canyon, and intel from satellite imagery said the canyon in between was dark as night and the camera couldn't seem to focus on it?

Intel said the head of insurgents was hiding out in a northern branch of the canyon. Despite a failed Echo mission a few years back to infiltrate Batvinia from the southern mouth of the canyon—right before Archer had joined the squad—things were heating up fast, the Army decided to try again, and sent in Rangers.

The Army blamed the Rangers' deaths on some new weapon.

"Archer? I can hear those wheels cranking from here. What's on your mind?" Chan kept her tone light, but he knew she was equally worried.

Best of the best, his special ops unit was one of a kind. No identifiers. They were unofficially referred to as Echo, but on the books, they were just another Ranger squad. Most of them had been Rangers at one point anyway, but they were their own entity, and not even the Deltas knew about them.

He pinched the bridge of his nose and puffed out his cheeks. "What do we have on the history of that canyon? Geography, politics, geology? There's something we're missing."

Chan rattled off the facts, working out the problem with him. Again. "The escarpment marks the border between Otrivka in the south and Batvinia to the north. The region surrounding the canyon is a rare pocket of desert. Before the attempted coup a few years ago, the Batvinia end in the north was pretty quiet, and is still home to a number of rural villages. Prime place for the insurgents to recruit and train, as the canyon is the only access point and it's desolate as fuck and poorly mapped."

Something wasn't adding up. Why was this end of the canyon so impassible? Sharper, narrower, different rock formations. Around the canyon, the weather was eternally cloudy, bone dry, and a constant dust cloud of ground-up shale.

When trouble began brewing in Batvinia, the UN wanted to quietly infiltrate the southern point of the insurgent's stronghold by securing the canyon.

He withheld a breath and braced his chest to draw air in. "Which is why the Army sent infantry in, but they were wiped out, no survivors, no witnesses. Echos were sent in to investigate, and only two walked away. Mission failed, canyon impassible. Peace talks were making headway, so military efforts eased. Fast forward five years, and the insurgents bombed the shit out of the capital and turned tail when Batvinian military, with UN support, pushed back hard."

Ribs starting the ache as swelling set in. He glanced back and checked Brock again. Still breathing.

Chan turned the wheel sharp to avoid a tire-sized rock in the road, and continued his thought for him, "The border's a goddamn mess. The insurgent leader is said to be holed up in the encampment at the north end of the canyon, so Rangers are sent in through the south end of the canyon. Eighty percent casualties, only those farthest from the canyon having survived."

Mission fail. Again.

Insurgents were changing their strategy, recruiting heavily from disgruntled rural areas and blocking aid.

As it always seemed to end up, the Echos were pushed into the middle of things. While the higher powers patted themselves on the back for protecting the economic center of Batvinia, the rural border regions were ready to boil over. So, sneak special forces in through the southern end of the canyon and take out the insurgent leaders in their sleep. Covert as fuck. No one even knows who took care of the little problem.

But these decisions were above his paygrade. So Archer worked the problem.

Teeth gritted tight, Chan glanced in the rearview at Brock. "You said only two Echos walked away before. Did you know them?"

"Yeah, I knew them. I was one of the replacements for the Echos that died in the canyon. Connery and Simmons were the only survivors."

"Never heard of them."

"Yeah, well, they made us look like a bunch of pansies. Classified legends. Then they both died in a training op back home."

As the path finally flattened, the combat outpost coming into view, Chan flashed him a look, her dust-encrusted brow drawn tight. "You don't buy it."

"All the Echo squads were at that training, and a dozen of them were killed. I was supposed to join them after my brother's wedding." The terrain evened out as they turned onto a dirt road. He checked behind to see the other Hummer still followed close behind. "Fuck, I don't know what I'm getting at. I want to know why Connery and Simmons are the only two who have survived that canyon.

2

Hands wrapped around a cup of coffee so strong she could stand a spoon in it, Lana curled into the library sofa and took a slow, savoring inhale. From the plush velvet sofa, watching the morning mist begin to dissolve through the picture window, she could see exactly why Astrid spent so much time in this very room. Although their taste in books was vastly different.

Not that Astrid would get to sit still enough to read a good book anytime for the next eighteen years. Astrid was upstairs snuggling her newborn while Bodie took his usual morning wolfy run before the sun engulfed the summer Montana sky.

Early mornings were the best, when she had the opportunity to savor the mountain air tickling the curtains in the isolated ranch house. There was nothing like the serenity of solitude, when the rest of the world was still asleep. Her book was not the leather-bound demon hunter journals that Astrid had stocked the library with, nor the anthropological analyses of paranormal origins that Bodie enjoyed, but a romance novel.

Lost in steamy and sappy fiction was her preferred way to spend her leisure time, particularly when it came to the vivid descriptions of how the heroine licked the Navy SEAL's tight abs.

Okay, so it pissed her off that the descriptor "heroine" was akin to false advertising. The meek bitch simpered the moment anyone so much as considered dropping an F-bomb, until the hero showed her the ways of the world. Ugh, the worst, was when the delicate flower experienced a sexual awakening thanks to the lessons from the gruff rogue. Lana powered on, as this writer could write an appealing man, the sort that dove headfirst into the fight, had biceps that even the simpering bitch wanted to bite, and was as adept at oral sex as he was at saving the world.

Ha. If he actually existed? Lana might consider that dreaded marriage thing that her father continually reminded her was her duty.

Duty could wait. Another century or two could pass before she needed to pop out some offspring to continue the fight long after she met her own end. Okay, so Quinn—her favorite cousin and teammate—had found a muscle-bound, demi-god-demon-hunter-Coastie worth a lick or two. And, well, okay, Astrid knew what she was doing in settling down with the well-built shifter. As werewolf clothing didn't magically disappear and reappear when they shifted, as they did in PG movies, Lana was lucky enough to know exactly what Astrid saw in the man.

Ryan and Bodie had been great additions to the team. How awesome was it, that her fellow female teammates had found men worthy of fighting alongside, rather than that weird, toxic masculinity sort of relationship that had haunted female demon hunters for centuries?

Seriously. Bennett's parents were great. His mother was badass mixed with elegant lady and had married a man of leisure. Sweet and adorable, and neither lacked bravery, but they didn't share a dynamic that appealed to Lana. They didn't seem the sort to throw each other on the bed, mount up, and rock their world. Like the lickable Navy SEAL in this morning's book.

The creak of the back door interrupted what was turning out to be a yummy scene. Really, why couldn't she meet a guy who was so capable with his mouth?

As the bare footsteps padding over the worn wooden floors drew nearer, she glanced up from her book to say "good morning" to the sleepy new dad.

But it wasn't Bodie.

"Noah. Hey." She grinned and set her book down. "You made it."

Damn, he was as tasty as his brother. With a past so much darker than hers—than any of theirs—he typically kept to himself in the remotest regions of Northern Canada. But a family man at heart, as werewolves tended to be, he came home to visit his pack a few times a year. And Lana never tired of looking at the broody shifter.

Too bad she knew he was fated for one of her favorite people on the planet. Not that he'd figured it out yet, and Lana didn't want to break it to him. He had at least another twenty years before he needed to worry about it.

"Hey, Lana." He smiled, teasing his hand in his hair. His joggers were slung low over his hips, his chest bare. "Are Astrid and Isla still asleep?"

She nodded. "You must have passed Bodie?"

"I caught his scent."

Lana set down her book and rose to her feet. "Let's get some breakfast going."

"Where's Grammy?"

"Utah."

"Utah?"

"Felicity, Jessie, and Grammy are on a road trip," she said as she sashayed past him and into the country kitchen. "Coffee?"

"Mom always did love hiking," he said with a resigned shrug, scratching his hand over the back of his neck in a nonchalant position remarkably similar to some of her favorite romance novel heroes—the one that shows off the biceps, pecs, *and* abs, in one glorious pose. Made more appealing by being entirely unintentional.

Lana chuckled under her breath and topped off her coffee. "Jessie is equally adventurous."

"That she is," he said with a sweet, huff of a laugh.

She was a little envious of the werewolf family. Her own was great. She adored them.

But the Connery women were tough as nails, whether they married into the pack or were shifters themselves. Her own grandmother had passed away when Lana was too young to remember, but Bodie and Noah's Grammy was a force of nature. Three-hundred fifty-four, and still as fierce as ever. A bit more arthritic and wrinkly each year, and sometimes you couldn't tell if she was dozing or dead, but she was still undeniably fearsome.

Noah disappeared to the laundry room and reappeared, pulling a t-shirt over those edible abs. Okay, dang, she needed to start dating again. Dearth. That's what she'd been drowning in. A dearth of appealing men lately.

As, statistically, it was likely that attractive, humorous, charming, intelligent, badass, self-effacing men probably existed among the plethora of them on this planet—case in point ten feet from her—it was likely *her* problem. But that hot pink little battery-operated toy she kept in the bedside table in her Sitka apartment was running out of steam. As was her imagination.

"Wait..." He rubbed his eyes before pouring himself a cup of coffee strong and deep enough to knock a human on their ass. "Did they miss the birth? I can't imagine Mom would—"

"Of course not. They left yesterday. I think they were trying to step back and give the new family some space."

"Oh. I didn't think of that. Maybe I should go—" He glanced around, his aquamarine eyes scanning for an easy exit.

"No." She grabbed his arm and pulled him back. "You are going to help me throw together one of Grammy's famous breakfasts that Astrid talks about whenever we're far and gone from civilization and home-cooked meals. And then, you are going to rave over your niece and spend the next week being the uncle Bodie is counting on you to be."

A sheepish glint flashed in his aquamarine eyes. "You are tenacious."

"Get slicing," she said, winking as she pulled the eggs from the fridge.

"Are you all coming?" he asked as he set out the cutting board and started slicing the dense loaf of homemade bread Felicity had left for them.

Coated in egg white thanks to the shell that shattered mid-crack, Lana scowled at her gooey hands and asked, "The team?"

"To meet Isla?"

"Mostly. Bennett and Adair are in England babysitting his little siblings while his parents are taking an overdue vacation, but they'll be here in a few weeks."

He glanced around. "I see why Grammy ditched. Full house. Guess I'll crash in the library."

"I'm sure you want a nice cozy bed to curl up in."

"I thought I was the only one that preferred the library."

"Get a fire going, curl up all night with a book, easy access to coffee in the morning, with that view of the mountains? It's my favorite spot to crash. Besides, you got it for Grammy's birthday party." She grinned hopefully, raising her eyebrows for good measure. "My turn."

His parents babied him—excessively, terrified he'd go feral and run off again, so he tended to stay in the tamer, no-pressure home of his brother and grandmother.

The front door swung open and a four-year-old, lava-red-haired, dark-eyed force of nature came sprinting in ahead of her parents, while they carted in hefty boxes of supplies to stock the remote home for the new parents.

Lana laughed and held her arms out. "Hey, Skye, where's my hug?"

Sprinting past her, Skye launched straight into Noah's arms. She leaned into him and nuzzled. Grinning and holding the little girl cozy in his arms, he carried her into the kitchen, grabbed a piece of crispy bacon, and handed it to her. "How's my best girl?" he asked.

Lana rolled her eyes. "Dog meat. That's what I turn into when you're around."

"Wolf meat." Skye giggled and snapped a bite of the bacon.

Lana rustled her hand in Skye's hair and poked her in the belly button. "When are you going to come hang out with me in Sitka again?"

"Ooo, take me out on the boat again like Gamma does." She grinned with her tiny, toothy grin.

"It's a date. Maybe we'll do a little shopping and get you some new cowgirl boots."

Skye giggled and stole another piece of bacon from Noah's hand.

"Hey." He teased a snarl and grabbed it back. "Even for that snarky grin, I'm not sharing *my* bacon."

Unfazed, Skye hopped down and headed straight for the garden, as all of Grammy's grandchildren—biologic or not—were fond of doing. Ryan waved hello and followed her out the door.

Quinn poured herself a cup of coffee and dropped to the table. "Hi," she said with a sighing smile as soon as she got the bitter brew to her lips. "You guys see Isla yet?"

While setting the pair of overflowing casserole dishes into the oven, the heat blasting her in the face, she tipped her face away from the heat and said, "I got to hold her last night before they turned in. She's incredible. Tiny and sweet. She's got Bodie's glowing eyes with Astrid's light hair."

Vann came in the door a moment later, carting another box of goodies. "Hey," he said softly, the familiar rumble in his voice stirring the air with the subtle greeting.

Sporting jeans and nothing else, Bodie strolled into the kitchen. He pulled a t-shirt on and rubbed his hand over the back of his neck. "Mornin'."

As if on cue, her pin-straight blond hair damp from the shower, Astrid eased down the steps with the snuggly bundle in her arms. Bodie greeted her halfway up the stairs and sank into a melty kiss as he took Isla and propped the infant against his shoulder.

Okay, Lana had to admit, they made a pretty picture that maybe, just maybe, tugged at that envious heartstring. But she'd never admit that in front of her parents.

They all settled in for breakfast, chatting and catching up. The last few weeks had been uneventful, so the conversation stayed pleasantly benign.

Thank fuck. Another biggie had found a good-sized tear in the veil and decided the people of Barrow, Alaska had looked like a tasty bunch. Since their demon ancestor had imbued their team with a boost of power, said demon ancestor seemed to enjoy passing along hot tips, directing them toward the tougher missions.

Eight months pregnant, Astrid had delivered the final blow to the horned lizard thing. If that wasn't badass womanpower, Lana didn't know what was. What was that they said about Ginger Rogers? Something about doing everything Fred Astaire did, but backward and in high heels?

After a lazy day around the ranch, helping the new parents catch up on chores and rest, evening closed in. With Isla on her chest, Lana curled into one of the leather couches in the library. The sleepy bundle flooded her with melatonin vibes until she felt an overwhelming need to hit the sack early tonight. The sun lowered in the sky, and the fire roared in the hearth as the high elevation Montana air cooled the evening.

Ryan and Quinn had disappeared upstairs. Vann stretched out with a book on the porch swing outside, taking advantage of the chill of the evening and the vast solitude. Bodie and Astrid were stretched head-to-foot on the opposite sofa, Bodie's eyes at half-mast over his book and his hand wrapped around his wife's foot, Astrid's eyes long-since closed.

Skye's eyes were near rolling back in her head as she sat with Noah on the chair next to the hearth. In her sweetly confident voice, she read from the story, "Then the tuh... tull..."

"Troll," Noah said patiently.

"Then the troll gave her a blanket and the vuh... vol... vil..."

"Village."

"Village was warm all... winter... long." By the time she reached the end of the story, her eyes eventually crossed, and she fell asleep mid-sentence.

With one hand on the baby on her chest, Lana muffled her chuckle. "I didn't realize trolls were so kind and made such good bedtime stories."

Keeping his tone soft so Skye didn't wake, Noah said, "Yet there is an unshakable trend among humans to dress up like feral werewolves for fun, fantasize about romancing one, and decorate their homes with moon themes and wolf rugs. Bodie's the professor. Maybe he can explain why people get it so dead wrong."

More asleep than awake, Bodie said in a gravelly voice, "Not totally wrong. Those stories come from somewhere. Werewolves are actually protective and doting spouses, so that's not too far off. Trolls, however-er. Never seen one, and maybe they don't exist. But there are an awful lot of stories about them."

"Do they regularly make people blankets? If they were so friendly, I'd imagine we'd have seen them before," Lana said.

"That's where we need to look past the glorification. Trolls are consistently lumbering hermits, so probably something to that. If they're truly friendly, yeah, we'd know something about them. Which leads me to believe—if they exist on this side of the veil—they're probably very *unfriendly*." Bodie pretended to look back at his book, but his eyes slackened.

Bodie's phone buzzed on the coffee table. He forced his eyes wide open, as if reminding himself he was awake. Astrid stirred and sat up. She leaned across and grabbed the phone, glaring at the unknown number before handing it to Bodie.

Confusion drawing his brows together, equally puzzled, Bodie finally answered. "Yeah?"

"*Hi. This is Major Archer Belak. Is this Boden Connery?*"

"Yeah..." Bodie responded as he sat up and lowered his feet to the floor.

"*Sorry to bother you, but, um... I knew your brother, Noah.*"

Bodie sat bolt upright.

Noah stiffened, guarding Skye so she didn't wake.

"Oh." Bodie held his breath.

"First, I want to say, I'm sorry for your loss. I didn't know him more than a few months, but he was a good friend."

"Thanks," Bodie said, sniffing the air in a rare wolfy gesture while in human form.

"If you don't mind, I have a few questions I'm hoping you can help me with."

"Sure, um, what can I help you with?"

"This is a total shot in the dark. Shortly before I joined his squad, he was in a fight like nothing else..." The caller seemed to draw out the pause. Lana strained to hear, knowing something was very, very wrong with this conversation. *"I hate even calling to bug you with this, but I'm running out of ideas. I've read all the reports on his death, and it's not making sense."*

Bodie let out a slow exhale, eyes locking with Noah's. An entire conversation passed between them in the single look. "I don't know what you think I can help with. My brother's gone."

"Let me put this frankly, and if you can shed even the dimmest of lights on this situation, I'll be grateful. I have no interest in opening any files or changing history. This conversation is between us. Off the record, so to speak. I'm sure you know Noah's unit wasn't an ordinary Ranger unit."

"I do."

"Noah's last big op was... covert. After heavy casualties in his unit, the government looked for other ways around the problem, but we can no longer avoid the... dangerous route."

The room was dead quiet. Skye stirred and stared up at Noah with her dark eyes, but she didn't say a word.

"I don't know how much he told you, as there's not much he could say. A few years back, only he and another guy survived this canyon, the same

spot where most of a Ranger platoon was wiped out about three weeks ago. My squad was sent in for recon only, to see what we're dealing with. We hardly even breeched the perimeter, and thankfully no casualties, but we took some... surprising hits."

Lana's ears perked up at what he implied. Astrid sat up and scowled at the ground in front of her, listening intently. Demon hunters were the first to say they had no extrasensory powers, but there was *something*. Habit, experience, intuition... something.

Vann appeared in the library doorway moments later.

"What are you getting at?" Bodie asked.

"I'm desperate, or I wouldn't have bothered you with this. This canyon is dangerous, and it's critical. Did he say anything about... what he saw? Anything about that last op? I mean, fuck, it wasn't long before that training incident took so many lives, including your brother's, and if there's a connection..."

Bodie looked to Noah, their matching aquamarine eyes confirming what they all suspected. Noah shifted Skye on his lap and motioned for the phone, closing his eyes and taking a long, measured inhale before saying in a crisp military accent, "Belak?"

Long pause. *"... Connery?"*

"I'm still dead. Tell me what happened."

"Fuck man, I knew something was wrong with those reports. Simmons make it, too?"

Noah ground his teeth and his expression darkened. "No."

"Sorry. I know he was a good buddy." Archer paused, a heaviness to his voice that Lana suspected was due to the *something* they'd found. *"Thirty Rangers were wiped out trying to get into the canyon that took most of your squad. Their gear was charred, torn to bits, and scattered to the wind. From all accounts, no enemy nearby. The survivors' stories don't make much sense."*

"Survivors? They can't have made it far in."

"Only those who kept their distance, holding the perimeter."

"So they sent Echos in, again. Colonel Jameson won't appreciate you having this conversation."

"As I'm talking to a dead man, I don't think anyone would believe me anyway."

"And it's to stay that way." Noah's tone was light, but the meaning behind it heavy with certainty.

"They won't ask how I know what I know."

"What do you know?"

"It was like a hurricane brewing from the middle of the canyon. We took it slow and got as close as we could. All I could see were vague shadows in this blur. Not like it was too fast or too overwhelming, like a literal blur."

"I'm familiar with the blur." Noah sat calmly, brushing his scruffy hair out of his face. "Get about twenty feet into the blur and it's not just a windstorm, but a goddamn thermonuclear blast."

"With a fist the size of my head. Or it looked like a fist. I don't know what it was. This is going to sound crazy. It wasn't a real fist, more like a trick with wind and smoke, but it hit hard."

Archer scrunched a hand in his hair and stared out the darkened window. "The blur got denser and denser the further in we went, the sky darkened, and out of nowhere, it was like a damn bomb went off. That fist took out half the squad in one hit. Wind and rain. An avalanche came down on top of us. Simmons and I barely made it out of there."

"How did you survive? What can we do about it? That strip of territory is all that stands between us and..." Archer stalled, as if what he was about to say was going to break all the rules.

Nearly as much as his rumbling voice, Lana enjoyed knowing that whoever this was, he was a rebel.

As if the situation was devastatingly personal, Archer finished, *"There's no other route in, and the insurgents holed up in the north end of that canyon are planning some nasty shit. I need to get through there, before they do something stupid and more people die."*

And his determination to come to the rescue. Call her old-fashioned, but a special forces guy determined to save the world from a power-hungry, genocidal militia, and save as many lives as he could while doing so? And searched outside the box for the tools to defeat a mysterious enemy that didn't fit into what he would have been taught? That was the kind of guy she wouldn't mind fighting alongside.

And other things alongside. And on top of. Underneath. In front of. Any manner of positions. If he was as appealing as his voice.

Damn, she needed a little more nonfiction action in her life. Isla stirred in her arms and Lana soothed her back to sleep with a soft shushing sound.

Noah rubbed his hand over his face. "I'd heard they are rooted even deeper into the villages on the north rim. That's what we were there to stop. The military called it a tragic loss, brushed it under the rug, and fortunately, diplomacy was making headway." He scanned the room, the team of demon hunters all knowing exactly what was up.

Well, not exactly. Lana had never heard of anything like this.

Quinn and Ryan appeared in the doorway next to Vann. Quinn tiptoed to Skye, scooped her into her arms, and carried her up to bed.

Noah bit his cheek and said, "With or without official support, we knew the canyon needed clearing, and we'd planned to go back... more prepared, so to speak, but the training accident changed everything. You're not going to beat this without help. I know some people that... have experience in this sort of thing."

"I shouldn't even be talking to you *about this."*

"You're not going to beat this without them. Don't go back to the canyon without them."

Quinn reappeared in the doorway and hissed, "Tell him to back off. We got this."

Noah covered the speaker with his hand and said, "There are too many parties watching that border. You won't get close without a military escort."

"Not an option. Just tell me what we're up against."

"You won't believe me if I said. I'm not entirely sure what it is, but I know they can help. At least meet with them."

Lana raised her hand and motioned to herself. Relaxation could wait, especially if her contact was as hot as his rich voice that rivaled the stimulating rumble of her vibrator.

"Fine. Send me a name and number, and I'll give your friends a call. Maybe they can give me some ideas of what this might be, or how to get through it."

"Lana is a friend of mine, and I trust her completely. She knows everything, so don't hold back. She'll fly out tonight and meet you in Tucson. Trust me, you're going to want to meet her."

"I guess I don't have much choice. Tumbleweed Pub. 1900 tomorrow work okay?"

Noah agreed and disconnected the call.

Astrid leaned forward and pushed her pin-straight blond hair back. "This isn't something I've come across. Blur? Shadows? Heat storm?"

Arms folded over his chest, Vann shook his head. "Nothing I've ever heard of. Not a hybrid, that's for damn sure."

Ryan tipped his head and said, "Canyon. Sounds like an old tear in the veil, so something must either have slipped through, or has been hiding out in there. How big is it?"

Noah shrugged and pushed his hair back out of his face. "Hundred fifty miles long, roughly."

"I'll head into the demon realm and see if my dad knows of a tear in that area. Maybe I can check it out from the other side, see if it's still active, and if I can get a sense of who's on this side."

"Be careful," Bodie said as he stuffed his phone in his pocket. "We'll hit the books."

Checking her watch, Lana realized she wasn't going to get much rest tonight. And she did love to sleep. Or, at least, she looked forward going to bed so she could wake up and enjoy her lazy morning in the mountains. "Where am I going? Who am I meeting? Sitrep please."

Noah rose from the chair and kneeled in front of the fire, shifting the unburnt part of the log before adding another. "Captain Archer Belak, or I guess Major now. Belak's a decent guy. Special forces, so to speak. After the canyon, we had a few openings, and Belak was one of the top choices to replace them. He was, uh, on leave, when Simmons and I dosed the other Echos with the serum. Anyway, my squad, Belak's, we're the guys they send into impossible situations. Classified, off-the-books sort, without an official title."

"Guys?" Lana snorted.

Noah flashed her a wink and adjusted the wood. "I meant *guys* gender neutrally. Plenty of women in Echo. Other units might have a sexism problem, but Echo is where the best go."

"Thought they didn't have a name," she fired back with a mirroring wink.

"Instead of saying the special-ops-unit-with-no-name, unofficially they're referred to as Echo."

Ryan laughed out loud. "As in, one more than Delta?"

"You got it." Noah pointed and rose to his feet again. "Hand-picked by Colonel Jameson. No application, no tryouts, only the best of the best."

Vann crossed one foot over the other and smirked knowingly. "Bet werewolves like you and Simmons were top picks."

"Yeah. Not that they knew why we were always a step faster and a push-up stronger than the others. Back then, it would have been a perk to have access to the canyon, but Belak's right, and it is the only way in. Belak's not afraid to break the rules to do the right thing. And, like all of Echo, he's tougher than tough, but not stupid. He knows he's got good reason to be scared."

Voice hoarse with sleep deprivation and, Lana suspected, a wallop of worry, Bodie's fists clenched together. "Whatever's in that canyon, it's the reason you and Simmons made the serum?"

"Not even two werewolves were tough enough to take this thing—we were lucky we made it out alive. One whiff, and I knew this wasn't from our realm." Noah cracked his knuckles and nodded subtly. "Wish I'd known you guys back then. Would have saved us the trouble of trying to control the feral side and upgrade a few Echos to be like us, so we'd be strong enough and have enough numbers to go back."

Ryan tipped his head and said, "Come with us. We'll bring you back if you go feral."

He puffed out his cheeks and stared down at his hands. "I've got a lot to pay for, but I'd fuck it up. Again."

Bodie's brow dropped as he studied his brother, and slowly shook his head. "If you want in, just say the word, but I'd rather not risk losing you again."

"We got this," Vann rumbled. "And I don't want any humans near this thing. How do we convince your squad to step back?"

"You're not getting in there without a military escort."

Lana leaned back and propped her feet on the coffee table, a wicked grin spreading across her cheeks. "I haven't made a new friend in ages. I'll go, play along, and most importantly, I'll find a way in. You guys figure out what this is and how we can crush it. I'll play diplomat."

Quinn leaned into Ryan as he tugged her against him. She snorted and said, "Lana the Diplomat. Take it easy on him."

"Of course," she answered with an eye-roll.

Ryan raised an eyebrow. "Don't take it too *easy* on him."

"Hey, this is work. I don't mix business and pleasure," Lana huffed. "Usually. Unless he's really hot."

3

Holy shit, it was toasty in the Sonora Desert. So much for the tolerability of a "dry heat." Ovens are a "dry heat," yet no one wanted to vacation in one.

Rain or snow, sunny or overcast, Lana rocked the boots and denim skirt look. Today, she regretted that personal adage. Apparently, even dry heat wove heavy and sticky into the thick fabric. Although that was probably her sweat. Thus, her boots and denim skirt universal ensemble was no longer going to be universal.

She stripped off her leather jacket and stuffed it back in the rental car. No need for that today. Alaskans layered, but it might not be socially acceptable to strip down to her underwear, however tempting.

Should be. She tugged at the hem of her skirt and wished she'd worn flip-flops, but she breathed a sigh of relief that she'd worn a breezy linen tank.

Laughter, hoots and hollers, and thundering music echoed up and down the hopping 4th Ave. Tucson was bigger than Sitka, yet still sported a small-town feel. With the year-round nice weather, outdoor seating was aplenty.

Although she couldn't imagine why anyone would want to sit out in this furnace, with or without the hose-delivered mist under string lights surrounding most of the patios. Groups of diners munched on pizza in the shade of the alcove eatery where she paid for street-side parking, while many of the sidewalk tables were closing up umbrellas as the sun diffused in the western sky and granted a welcome cast of shade.

Heels tapping on the sidewalk, in pace with her growling tummy's complaints, she hurried to get inside to air conditioning and pub food.

Nice. Her kind of place. Not a dive bar, exactly, but seasoned with care. A different sport on every screen. People, lots of them. Happy and laughing and carefree under the amber glow of low hanging lights and weathered plank ceilings. Tumbleweed had the similar rustic feel of her family's place, but it was newer by at least a century, and with more TVs and taps.

And one lonely looker in the corner. Pitter patter. Hop, skip, and a jump.

Lana's libido tripped over itself and melted her like a snowman in the desert. Noah's description had been bang-on—not that he'd mentioned how edible Major Archer Belak was—but Lana knew this was her guy.

Or, well, she hoped so, or this hottie was going to be very confused in a few moments.

Tucked into a booth by himself, immune to the rest of the roaring bar, her contact was buried in books. She couldn't decide which she liked best: the furrowed brow, the black-rimmed glasses, or the thick chiseled arms and tight abs under the athletic tee.

Strutting across the bar in her own civilian attire, the air conditioner thankfully de-sticking the frayed denim skirt from her skin, she tugged her dark hair into a loose pony and slipped into the booth across from him.

Brow furrowing even deeper, he slid his glasses up to the top of his head like sunglasses and eyed her suspiciously. And what nice eyes he had. Sizzling cobalt, like a boiling sea.

No wonder the team ragged her about her one-track mind.

"Hi. I'm, um…" He trailed off, looking adorably befuddled.

Okay, she might have to knock him on his ass for being a sexist, presumptive jackass that assumed she was here to hit on him, rather than to tell him to leave the big bad monster to her.

He cleared his throat and sat up straight. "Are you Connery's friend?"

Okay, maybe not sexist. Speechless, maybe? Befuddled over a mutual checkout? That was absolutely acceptable. "As much as anyone can claim to be so." She rested her elbows on the table and settled in.

Tousling his fingertips through the start of a curl in his short hair, he knocked his glasses off and juggled them a moment before catching them. With a sheepishly sexy smile, he said, "Archer Belak."

"Lana."

The server appeared a moment later and skipped the notepad, sliding a head-heavy porter in front of Archer, her gaze lingering longer than was appropriate, before finally sparing a glance for Lana. "Thirsty?"

"Stout, please. I just got in and I'm starving. How are your burgers?"

The server shrugged and settled her attention back on Archer, her rosy lips glossy and kissable—and notably unnoticed by Archer as he gnawed on the end of his pen, staring at a wordy library book in front of him. "Ask our regular, here. Spicy nacho burger for you tonight?"

Distracted, he mumbled, "Yeah, thanks."

"I guess I'll have the same," Lana said, leaning back in the booth and eyeing the awkwardly one-sided checkout. As the server disappeared, Lana gestured to the books and asked, "History?"

He shook away the hyper-focus and nodded. "Yeah. The region. I'm hoping local history will shed some light on what's going on in that canyon. That thing wasn't like anything I've ever come across. Did Connery fill you in on everything he knows?"

"Thing, like, you actually saw it?"

"I saw something, enough to say it's a thing and not bad weather or bad luck, and definitely not a weapon. But I couldn't begin to say what it was."

"Like four-legged or armored or humanoid?"

He scowled and finally looked fully at her since the initial gawking surprise hello. "Connery didn't exactly say much about who you are, or why I should trust you."

"No, he didn't." Her beer appeared. She sat up straight and took a long pull, the heavy brew filling the cavernous void of her empty belly.

"Care to shed some light on that for me?" he asked, a subtle lilt in his question.

"How long have you been in?"

"Why?"

"You've got that military cadence to your voice."

"Fourteen years."

"Straight out of high school?"

"The day I turned eighteen."

"I see." She settled into the booth and took a slow sip. "Hero to the core, huh?"

He shifted his glasses off the top of his head and hung them from the neck of his shirt before leaning back into his side of the booth, his long legs extending across the narrow space and resting on her side. A spark of amusement quirked at the corners of his mouth. "I'm the one with security clearance. What makes you think you can interrogate me?"

"You may have your eyes-only, confidential, top-level, classified, don't-fuck-with-me clearance, but I know more about this *thing* than you do. So yes, I need to know if I can work with you, or if I should be finding another way into this canyon."

"Scientist or something?"

Lana raised an eyebrow and folded her arms over her chest. "Do I look like a scientist?"

"Wow. There is no way I'm walking into that one." He grinned over the rim of his beer and shook his head. "If I say yes, I'm implying that you're homely. If I say no, I'm saying you don't look smart enough."

Tipping her head back, she let a laugh bubble up in her throat. "Can't I be an attractive, smart-looking nerd? I genuinely know plenty of those." Including the one in front of her.

Leaning forward, those yummy cobalts watching her with a fascination that sent tingles over her skin, he said, "As do I. I'm thinking you are all the above, plus something else you're not going to tell me. But still, none of that answers why you think you are an expert about this canyon."

"I'm not an expert about *this canyon*."

Raising his glass, he took a swig and seemed to ease his shoulders back. "Fine. Interrogate me first, then I expect you'll answer all my questions."

"We'll see," she said with a wink. "Background check. Go."

"No criminal record."

"I figured. Give me the good stuff. How did you end up in the Army? Aspirations for heroism?"

"Not exactly. Beanpole dork. Couldn't pass a written test to save my life, hadn't been out on a date or even kissed a girl besides Jenny Kiplinger on the bus in kindergarten, and I'd played way too much *Halo* and *Rainbow Six* in high school. Middle child of seven. It was Army or find something I wasn't terrible at back home in Low Plains, North Dakota, population one thousand thirty-two."

She looked at the massive pile of books on the table, the thick glasses tucked in his shirt. "You look pretty studious now."

"Turns out, I needed reading glasses and have raging dyslexia. It's a challenge, but I've learned some strategies to get by." He looked up and nodded as the server brought their baskets-o-burgers.

The painfully obvious flirty server asked if there was anything else she could do with him, adding a quick correction that she meant *for* him, and topped it off with a fluttering laugh.

"This is it, thanks," he said, his voice gruff and distracted, as if completely oblivious. Or was he intentionally ignoring the come-on?

"Can't be easy," Lana asked as the server gave up and drifted to the next table.

"Huh? Oh, the reading? No. But, not everything is on audiobook or text-to-speech. So I muddle through and try to glean the key points."

"How'd you end up in... your unit? From what Noah implied, it's invitation only."

"What else did he tell you?"

"As much as I needed to know to decide that I *might* be able to trust you enough to coordinate." She nudged her legs against his and raised an eyebrow. "Quit with the tangential. I'm still doing the interrogating."

He chuckled, nudging her back. "And I expect the same in return."

"It's only fair to take turns."

"Fuck." He shook his head and grinned. "Connery's got a hell of a sense of humor, making me think he was sending me help. I'm beginning to suspect I'm the tool here."

Biting her lips together, she choked on that one. Too easy of a target. Hell, she could go either way, calling him a tool or referencing his tool.

Or maybe both. Their waitress would choose the latter, no doubt.

"I'm not any man's tool," she snarked instead, daring him with an eyebrow raise.

His smile didn't falter as he held her gaze. "I know damn well I'm a tool for the government. But at least I acknowledge my depersonalized implementation."

"I don't work for anyone."

"Don't you? You're on this mission for recreational purposes?" Tongue parked between his teeth, his swimming cobalts were locked onto hers without a hint of a blink on the horizon.

Lana hadn't lost a stare-down... ever. Missy had been a tough competitor, but once Lana had taken on the demon hunter traits, her sister didn't stand a chance. Archer was giving her a run for her money.

Catching a shadow of the server in her peripheral, Lana said loud enough for her to hear, "You must be desperate, looking to throw your *tool* around recreationally?"

An eager grin on her face, the server responded to the call and took Archer's half-consumed glass straight from his hands and promised to bring him something fresh.

Archer glanced away and watched his drink disappear, wincing as the server licked her lips like he was a tasty treat. Without responding, he nodded and turned back to Lana. "Well played."

"Likewise. Now finish it."

He reached for her beer and drained it by half before passing it back. "Thrilled to be doing *something*, I practically begged to be placed in whatever infantry unit would get me on the front lines as soon as possible. No way in hell was I getting sent home because I couldn't cut it, so I dug deep. I had a hell of a sergeant, saw something in me, but knew I was as green as my cheeks the first time I jumped out of an airplane.

"He kicked my ass until I bulked up. I was a late bloomer. Good guy." Archer's voice rolled like velvet over her skin, but more than that, the amused thrill in his look as he told the story, he passed into another world, and carried her along the journey with him. "Our first deployment was... well, let's just say it made the news, and not in a good way. I, uh, got a few medals, and Colonel Jameson decided to send me to college and make an officer out of me. I bombed the entrance exams—as I had tried to warn him—and he was humiliated. Stubborn ass, he sat me down and rapid-fire asked me a bunch of questions from the practice exam, and I did okay. Next thing I know, he's got this learning specialist drilling me like I was some billion-piece puzzle."

"I'm guessing you did something heroic and daring and re-markable for him to go to all the effort. What happened?"

"Classified," he said with a wink.

"Ha. Is everything about you classified?"

"Tit for tat."

A fresh beer slid onto the table between them. Lana snatched it first and took her half, then passed it across. "You got lucky, getting noticed like that."

"That remains to be seen." He shrugged and finally picked up his burger, taking a massive bite that would impress Ryan, who was famous for eating a burger in four bites. Politely wiping the corner of his mouth, he swallowed and said, "Are you satisfied?"

"So far." She grinned and took an oversized bite of her own before she inadvertently described exactly the satisfaction she was experiencing as she listened to him. Very unprofessional.

The corner of Archer's lips quirked up as he watched her devour the burger.

At the gooey, savory goodness, she groaned, pleasantly surprised by the jalapeños and nacho cheese sauce that blended perfectly with the salty soft pretzel crust. "That's a good burger. Nice choice." She downed a swig of beer before tearing into the next bite.

"The place is loud, the service is... interesting, but the burgers are epic." He grinned before finishing off his dinner.

"Almost as good as my family's tavern in Sitka."

"I've never been. Nice place to live?"

"The best. But I'm biased."

"You fish?"

"Always." She winked and took another bite of burger.

Chuckling under his breath, he shook his head. "Okay. My turn. Who the hell are you?"

"Lana Fischer."

"Got that. Lana Fischer of Sitka, Alaska. Imbiber of dark beers and devourer of spicy burgers. And some expert that Connery says can figure out what top military experts—including Connery himself—couldn't?"

"Don't play the brainless woman in a short skirt card." She glowered across the table, ready to kick him in the shin with her pointy-toed boot.

"Don't get me wrong, the skirt's... nice, and has nothing to do with your brain or brawn. Two of the six in my squad are women."

Easing her foot back, she smiled. "Okay. I apologize for assuming you were a sexist ass. I run into it too often."

"I get it. I trust the women and men in my squad equally, and a hell of a lot more than the rest of the entire military, but I know a lot of women had to work twice as hard to get where they are to prove the plethora of sexist asses wrong."

"You said plethora." She grinned and nudged his legs with hers.

He nudged her back. "Now who's being judgmental?"

"Not judgment. I'm fond of the word dearth."

"Pessimist?" His grin widened.

"Not usually, I just think it sounds cool and your use of another favorite bombastic word reminded me. I'm generally not considered bombastic, but I enjoy dabbling. Guilty pleasure." Lana crumpled the wrapper from her empty burger and set it in his, then stacked the baskets together and slid them to the end of the table.

"Look, let's pretend we both happen to need this canyon cleared, me for my reasons, and you for whatever vague reasons yours may be. But if I don't know who you are and why you're involved, I'm not sure we can be of much use to each other."

"*I* don't need *you*," she snarked, leaning back in the booth and folding her arms over her chest.

He pinched the bridge of his nose and exhaled. "The canyon is a fucking hotspot, and any civilian caught near it will be killed or captured by both sides. I need to know what I'm working with. To start, Connery was one of the baddest asses I've come across, and that's saying something, considering the people I work with. Are you... how much do you and he have in common?"

"A bit," she said. "Like cousins, but... not at all related."

Close enough anyway. Both were demon-human hybrids. Where she descended from a demon ancestor that created a line of demon hunters to protect the earth from the violence-intending monsters that cross from the demon realm, Noah and Bodie came from an ancient demon shifter who fell in love with a human and spawned the original werewolves. Well, after said-shifting-demon nearly killed his love while feral and saved her and their unborn child from certain death by giving her a mystical heart transplant with a wolf.

But that was a long winded mouthful of history he didn't need to know about. Or he would run screaming, and she would be back to square one on finding a way into this canyon.

"And his brother married one of my best friends." There. Much simpler.

The server scooped their baskets and slid a check onto the table. Archer snatched it, but Lana held tight onto the other half. He raised an eyebrow and shook his head. "You're here because I asked, and I'm not near finished with you. I'm buying."

"What else did you have planned?" She traced her tongue over the crease of her lips and released the slip.

Biting his tongue with a cheeky blush, he pulled a card from his wallet and slipped his glasses on to read the check.

Forget the charming rogues from her regencies. A hot, badass nerd? Way yummier.

While the server ran his card, Lana stuffed her phone back in her pocket and said, "Is there somewhere more... private, that we can talk?"

"I promise I'm not coming onto you when I say: want to come back to my place?"

"And I promise I'm not making a move when I say: Yes." She grabbed half of his stack of books and walked alongside him out of the bar. "If it helps, I do have a vague code of ethics and won't do more than flirt. For now."

"As I'm discovering your flirting skills surpass mine anyway." He laughed under his breath as he shifted the books under his left arm and extended a hand. "Business only."

"Business."

4

ARCHER FIRED UP THE engine to his truck and called Brock, moving as slowly as possible so he could find an edge before he faced her again. Unarmed and unprepared when it came to Lana Fischer, he was epically flailing and needed more ammo and armor.

"What's up?" Brock's voice was distracted as a giggling voice hooted in the background. Muffled, his hand probably over the speaker, he said, "*Nice try, Munchkin. Get back to bed. I'll come read you another story when I get off the phone with Archer.*"

He chuckled, picturing the boisterous toddler peeking out from her bedroom. One by one, the Echos were settling and doing the family thing. Brock was ahead of the bunch, with four under age six. "I need a stat background check. You have five minutes."

"Hang on." Brock groaned as he answered. "Who and why?"

"Lana Fischer. Lives in Sitka, Alaska where her family owns a tavern. Dark hair, green eyes."

"Shitty way to start a date. A little mystery is a good thing."

"This is business. Tight timeline."

Brock's keys clicked rapid-fire in the background. "Keep your panties on. Although, with the losers you've dated lately, maybe you should consider having me look into them first."

Archer turned down Campbell, aiming to take the long way to buy some time. "Four minutes. And you wonder why I'm picky?"

"Parents are Ross and Julia Fischer. Sister Missy is married to Vince Hellstrom and they share a two-year-old son Kai. Family owns Fischerman's Tavern. Lana is listed as a bartender. Clean driving record, no criminal record. Passport's got a lot of stamps on it. Shit, in the last four years, she's been to Bangkok, Greece, Paris, Chile, most every port in Western Canada, but spends most of her time in Seattle, Eureka, Sitka, and Montana."

"Montana? Any more on that?"

"Private airfield. Flies herself usually. A pilot? Damn."

"Three minutes."

"I'm getting the feeling she's not just loaded, but really loaded. Massive inheritance from the looks of it, no chance it's all from the tavern. Looks charming, but not a gold mine."

"That airfield in Montana. Any idea who owns it?"

"Connery Ranch."

At least that aspect checked out. Connery had so many stories about growing up in rural Montana, and his brother was listed as living on the family ranch. "I need more. Something. Anything." Like what in the hell made some hot friend of Noah's an expert on the most terrifyingly vague and kinetic hotspot he'd ever faced.

His driveway was coming up on the right. Fuck. Out of time.

"Graduated University of Alaska, geology major, mediocre grades. Nothing special there either. Did you know she's forty-one? A little old for you."

"Forty-one? She looks mid-twenties."

"You didn't mention she's fucking hot. Nine years older is fine when she looks like *that*."

Archer pulled his truck far enough into the narrow drive so Lana could fit her rental behind him. "Business."

"You said green eyes, but I'd call them crisp apple or dew-kissed grass. And damn, those lips redefine pouty," Brock crooned, then muffled his voice as he covered the receiver and hollered, "*One more sec, Munchkin. I'm trying to find Archer a nice woman to marry.*"

"Time's up. You find anything else, text me, okay?"

"Will do. Archer?"

"Yeah?"

"She may be hot, but her background is... odd. I'll keep digging, but there are a lot of gaps and a lot of things I wouldn't have guessed about an heiress geologist bartender from Alaska."

"So far... actually it's making a lot of sense." He hopped out of the rig and hauled his books out. The summer evening air was roasting. Didn't matter that it hadn't rained in a month and a half, that it was technically a desert, Tucson still didn't feel as dry as his hometown, and not nearly as desolate.

Lana hopped out of her rental and... there was no way to describe her walk, but it had struck him the moment she'd walked into that bar. Somewhere between a strut, a sashay, and a kick-your-ass power walk. A swing to her hips and a knowing smirk said she'd either knock-you-on-your-ass with her right hook or tie your tongue in knots with a kiss hotter than the metal fastener of his seatbelt on a hundred-degree day. She was a force of something, and he had no idea what. Whatever it was, she wasn't giving him an inch on any front.

She tugged the tie out of her thick hair, and as she hopped over the barrel cactus to join him on the stone walkway, she teased her fingertips in the unruly waves. Without asking or offering, she gently took the books from his arms so he could unlock the front door.

Hesitating in front of the adobe structure, he held his breath, hoping to hell he'd tidied before he'd left. With all the time he'd spent researching, exploring everything from little green men to mirages to even vampires, he hadn't done much of anything else. Cleaning had taken a distant backseat. Fuck, the kitchen was probably overflowing with dirty dishes.

The storm door opened with a squeal, and he jammed the key into the front door lock next, grimacing as he anticipated the mess beyond.

Yup.

As he'd expected.

Laptop open on the dining table. Stacks of open books and crumpled notes. Scrambled egg debris dotted the plate he'd left on the coffee table, with throw pillows deposited everywhere *except* the couch. Water glasses of unknown age sat out on about every flat surface between the living room and kitchen.

He flicked on the light switch, and a pair of standing lamps cast a warm glow on the dark furniture and weathered tile floor. Scrunching his hand in his hair, he felt the blush heat his cheeks. "Sorry, I, uh, wasn't planning on company and haven't had time to…"

She laughed out loud and stood next to him. "That's why I hire a cleaning service. I hate housework."

"Yeah…" He trailed off with a wince and quickly cleared the coffee table. Lana didn't bat an eye, and set the books on the entry table, then picked up pillows and tossed them on the black leather couch. She set the Xbox controller in the basket with the remotes and pulled the blanket over the arm of the couch.

"Bathroom?" she asked as he reappeared from the kitchen—after clearing plates, before quickly bussing another load of half-consumed water glasses and coffee cups to the sink.

"It's probably worse than the living room, just warning you. But there should be toilet paper and soap. Not so sure about a clean towel."

"I've survived worse," she teased and followed his directions through the arched doorway on the right.

Leather creaked under him as he dropped onto the couch in the cozy living room. The house wasn't big enough for entertaining, and his family and guys from the squad knew he wasn't one to cook or clean or... well, do anything a host might do. He'd rather curl up with a movie or a video game on his nights off anyway.

And female company? Yeah, dearth—Lana's favorite word—perfectly described his sex life the last... nope, not considering how long it had been. Brock was right. Some pre-date recon might not be a bad idea.

Not that he was home enough to commit to a serious dating life. How the hell some Echos managed the separation from their spouses and kids, he didn't have a clue.

Lana reappeared a few moments later, her hair down and swept behind her shoulders. All curves in a tiny package, her confidence was bigger than she was. Hottest woman he'd invited over... ever, and he had to stick to business. Yup. Dearth.

"You going to tell me who you are?" he asked, leaning forward and resting his forearms on his knees, studying her powerful moves, her carefree arrogance. Like her background check. Normal on the outside, but... something wasn't exactly standard issue.

"That remains confidential, even in private. I can tell you that whatever is in the canyon is within my area of expertise. I'll need my team, as it's probably beyond what I can take care of alone."

"What sort of team?"

"The sort that takes care of things that can't be explained."

"Like Mulder and Scully?"

"No," she said with a lilting laugh, and lowered to sit next to him on the couch. Not at the opposite end. Close enough to tempt him into pretending this wasn't business. She teased her fingers in her hair and angled her knees toward him, not quite touching. "You know, I've gotten into a lot of places I shouldn't. What makes you think I can't get into that canyon without you?"

"It is literally the most dangerous place in the world right now, and not just because of the blurry fist thing. You can't come in from the north, as intel says the insurgent leaders are encamped at the north entrance. Come in from the south, and our forces will be on your ass in a heartbeat—or, if you're lucky, you'll be shot by insurgents nosing into Otrivka. Either party will call you spies and blame the other side, and what is currently a bitch of a conflict will inflate to full-out war."

She tucked her lip between her teeth as she flashed him a snarky grin. "Well, that doesn't sound very safe."

Archer shook his head with a laugh under his breath and leaned back. Without a doubt, she'd happily stroll into the middle of any conflict without batting an eye. He gripped his hands in his hair and glared up at the spackled cracks in the century-old ceiling. "It's bad. Which is why I've spent the last nine months of my life over there more often than I'm home. But if we can clear this canyon, maybe, just maybe, we can take them apart from the inside."

"So you need the canyon for, shall we say, important reasons, and it's my... responsibility, to address this sort of threat." She kicked off her boots and peeled off a fluffy pair of pink ankle socks. She pulled her bare feet onto the couch next to him, her toenails painted a vibrant blue. "When are you going back?"

"Day after tomorrow."

"I'm going with you."

"Not possible."

Lana folded her arms over her chest and companionably leaned her shoulder against his, her wiggly toes contrasting her grave tone. "Noah and Simmons survived what no one else has. Trust me, you need us, or your squad will be flattened. This is what we do."

Suspicion boiled in his gut as he imagined what made Connery and Simmons different, and why Lana was so confident about the op. Breath rushing from his lungs, he glanced over at Lana and settled in next to her, his gaze heavy as he anticipated the inevitable. "I can't bring a civilian across enemy lines."

"Seven."

"What?"

"You'll need all seven of us. Well, Astrid probably won't join us as she's on maternity leave, but Adair will probably sub in for her. I wish Bodie could stay home with the baby longer, but after everything I've heard, this isn't exactly a routine op for us either."

"Hey, wait. That's not happening. You tell me what to do, and my squad will take care of it." Slap on the wrist if he got caught smuggling seven civilians into a combat zone, if he got lucky and Jameson backed him and fudged some retroactive approvals. Court martial, at best, if they died on his watch.

Lowering her feet to the floor, Lana reached under the coffee table for her boots. "Then I'm done here. Noah can point us to the canyon, and we'll find a way in without you."

"Wait." He held his hand on her arm. Stilling at his touch, she turned to him, her jaw taut in frustration. "Answer one question for me, and I'll make it happen. But not all of you, not from here. I'll help you to get your team in—without risking either side getting hot tempered."

"I'd rather do this without attracting attention."

"Ditto. If you sneak across, and it gets out that you were at my place tonight? I can kiss my career goodbye." He bit his cheek, wracking his brain as he considered tracking Connery down to see why he'd shackle him with the tenacious expert who was more possessive of her secrets than all of Echo.

"Depends on your question," she said with a lip-biting smile and tension over her brow.

Teeth gritted tight, he flexed his jaw and held her green eyes with a look. "What sort of team? Why do you think you can take this thing?"

"That was two questions." Her eyebrow lifted synchronously with the corner of her mouth.

He laughed under his breath and settled back into the couch. Lana rotated toward him, as if they were old friends catching up. Her skirt shifted up with the movement and he could just see the curve of her upper thigh, a jarring distraction he wasn't ready for. Inhaling sharply, he shifted his gaze up. "Who are you?"

Gaze steady, apple green eyes alight with determination, she seemed to be silently ordering him to shut the fuck up and listen close at the same time, yet that hint of amusement teased at her cheeks. "I really can't tell you, or I'd have to kill you." She winked and gave him a saucy grin.

"Who do you work for?"

"I can tell you that Noah and I have a lot in common, but I'm more... equipped, for this sort of work. It's a rare case when we can tell anyone, and even what you have probably gleaned already, you need to keep our existence to yourself. You can't even tell your own mother."

"Mom will get it out of me no matter what, so no deal on that one," he teased. Mostly. His mom was a frightening woman and should have gone into intelligence work. Neither he nor any of his six siblings ever got away with shit. Still didn't.

The corner of Lana's lips turned up. "She wouldn't believe you anyway."

He extended his hand and waited for her to shake on it.

Palm touching his, hand wrapping in solid connection with him, her delicate fingers wrapped around his. Holding on longer than a handshake should be, she didn't release him when she said, "As far as anyone is to know, my team and I are freelancers. Mercenaries." There was an incomparable power in her grip, a strength that shouldn't be possible, yet she appeared as casual as if they were passing strangers politely shaking and moving on.

"You're more than that." Tongue swelling to twice its normal size, he forced a swallow as she traced his hand with her fingertips, adding an electricity to the connection that had nothing to do with strength and everything to do with a mounting urge to shift her onto his lap and trace every curve of her. Voice hoarse, he managed to find the words to respond, "Let's call you scientists. You're a geologist, right? The others have special skills, if my squad has questions?"

"Speedy background check. I'm impressed."

"I don't invite just every woman I pick up in a bar back to my place." Nope. Just the one who had more secrets than he did.

"Nice try," she snorted. "You ran the check after we were on the way here. Did you panic that you were inviting over a serial killer?"

"Not exactly. I needed a little more than a vague reference from a dead man."

"And? Did you learn anything good?" Thumb tracing the contours of his hand, her grip loosened as her handshake turned into a simple, blazingly distracting flirtation.

"You're well-traveled," he said as his gaze unconsciously dropped to her lips.

"I am," she said with a devious smile.

"What's in Seattle and Eureka?"

"My teammates. Where are you from?"

"It's my turn to interrogate." He quirked up an eyebrow, waiting for her to counter again. Instead, she released his hand and leaned shoulder to shoulder against him. Sensation still radiating from the memory of her touch, he folded his arms over his chest. "Did you find the fountain of youth in Greece?"

5

"I AGE WELL."

"What about your teammates, do they age well, too? And Connery? Simmons? Not a wrinkle or a gray hair on either of them, and I'm not sure I ever saw either of them break a sweat."

She glanced at him and raised an eyebrow, her look daring him to push further.

"Any superpowers?" he added.

"Are you done with your interrogation?"

"You're not really answering anyway, so I guess I am."

"Look. Archer. I know your squad is the best, but my team isn't even on the same ranking system. We are stronger, faster, and better trained to deal with this." As if reading his mind, she added, "I don't want you involved any more than you want to bring me over there."

"How strong?" he asked, his mouth curving into a full smile.

"Maybe you'll get lucky and I'll show you sometime." She flashed him a devilish wink. Fuck, he was toast. "We've got more stamina, too."

He laughed desperately and shook his head, meeting her look and letting the sensation sizzle into his veins. "What do you think we're up against?"

She exhaled forcefully and puffed her cheeks out. Once she released the long breath, she curled into him, as if they'd passed the flirtation stage and had landed in long-term relationship territory. Resting her feet on the coffee table next to his, her knees tipped into his. As if the desert heat wasn't intense enough, the contact was like an inferno radiating into his skin. "I don't know," she admitted, her flirty look long gone and she dropped her cocky posture in frustration.

"If you don't know, why am I supposed to bring you into the middle of a war-zone, exactly?"

"Because I can guarantee it's something in my area of expertise. That's why I'm on board with not sending in the whole team right away, as it sometimes takes time and subtlety to finesse out what the threat may be. We're short on time, but we're not going in without a plan." Chewing her cheek, she considered for a moment, then said, "If we can figure out how long it's been there and what all it's capable of, I'll feel a hell of a lot better, rather than walking up and knocking on its front door. We're not easy to kill, but it happens often enough."

"From what I've found, that canyon's been uninhabitable for about four hundred years."

"How'd you work that out? Your mountain of books?"

"Pretty much. It's… information's not very reliable and scanty at best, probably because no one can get close enough to find out."

"We need to talk to the locals."

"I agree." He rubbed his eyes and glanced at his watch. Nearly nine. Forty-eight hours until go-time, and he didn't know much more now than he did when that damn fist cracked his sternum. Oh, except Mulder here might tell him it was a damn alien or something. "Beer?"

"Yes please." She grinned and squeezed his knee before pushing to her feet ahead of him. Probably nothing more than a pat on the shoulder to her, but, damn, she was… going to be the death of him.

Like the glutton for punishment that he was, he watched her make herself at home and strut into the kitchen and lean into the fridge, that shredded skirt of hers inching halfway to heaven, and those adventurous toes wiggling on the tile floor.

She appeared with a pair of Barrio Brews and started opening cupboards until she found glasses.

Curious, he leaned against the arched doorway. "Are you always this… comfortable, in other people's houses?"

Rising to her tiptoes to grab a pair of pint glasses, her skirt slid just high enough to ruin any shred of hope for a decent sleep tonight. His imagination went wild and made him wish he'd put the glasses on the uppermost shelf.

Mission accomplished, she turned back toward him as she lowered back down, a sly grin curving at the corners of those devilish lips. "Maybe. I like your house. It reminds me of my apartment."

"In Sitka?"

"My parents own a fishermen's tavern that's older than the town. As I travel so much, it's not worth getting my own four walls, so I live in the apartment above it."

"Convenient location?" Biting his tongue, he managed to avoid adding, "to catch those fishermen you mentioned?" Yeah, that wouldn't have gone over well. No wonder he hadn't had a date in… way too long.

Special forces operative ought to come with perks, but when you were so specialized you couldn't advertise your status as a certified badass? Or when you pulled out the reading glasses to pay the check, worse, admitting you read at the pace of a kindergartener? Or when a gorgeous woman flirted like Lana did and your tongue lolled out and you lost the ability to speak.

"Ideal. I get to see my sister often as she pretty much runs the place now."

"She runs the tavern while you… solve problems?"

"Pretty much. She chose the quiet life. Not that it's quiet; she's got a husband who's laugh can shatter windows."

"Wow, tell me how you really feel."

"No, seriously, she's the best. It's just not what I pictured for her when we were kids. The normal life thing. We were supposed to grow old together."

He hesitated, parking his tongue between his teeth before he said something stupid, or shattered the thin layer of trust they desperately needed to get through this op. Pushing her on why she couldn't grow old with her sister wasn't going to help. "You didn't want to join her behind the bar?"

"I do when I get restless. I mean, I can vacation like the best of them. There is nothing like putting my feet up and reading a good book for a week solid." She poured their beers with the efficiency and expertise of a seasoned bartender and carried his to him, stopping inches away and looking up at him like she was ready to end the business meeting if he so much as leaned her direction. "But I prefer to stay busy."

Breath caught in his throat, he nodded and downed half his beer. Although he was tempted to lean in and take her up on the unspoken offer, he wanted a steady head and control over his libido before crossing any lines. Speechless, he followed her to the dining table, remembering the detritus that buried the third-hand table, and quickly dashed ahead. Without a word, she set her beer next to his on the sole scrap of bare table and helped clear. She neatly stacked books behind the couch while he piled up dishes and dumped them in the kitchen sink.

Lana pulled a blank notepad from the depths of the pile and tapped a pencil on the pad. "Think you can draw me a map?"

He snatched the pencil from her hands and pointed the eraser end at her suspiciously. "Going to sneak in when I'm not watching?"

"Never." She winked, a breathless grin blossoming on his lips that sent his imagination whirling.

"Seriously."

"I won't. You might come in handy." She watched him over the rim of her glass. Brock was right, those lips gave pouty new meaning. More like amused lips, with every emotion in her head filling that bitable lower lip. "I'll wait and ditch you after I get what I need."

"Ditto," he said, parking his tongue in his teeth and waiting for her to counter.

She shrugged lightly.

He reached to the top of his head for his glasses, patting and realizing he had no idea where he'd left them. Not seeing them on the table, he turned to see if he'd left them on the couch.

Lana subtly slipped the glasses from the neck of his shirt and handed them over with that amusement dancing in her look. Yeah, that wasn't an ordinary green. They were... poetic. And he was officially under her spell. Shit, what if he actually was? There was something about her. Magical, beyond human.

"Thanks," he murmured, his breath shallow and his brain wiped of any useful banter he may ever have been capable of. Knowing he was a lost cause, he put pencil to paper. He started slow, outlining the surrounding rivers and mountains, then narrowing in on the canyon, the pencil scraping faster as he added details and shadows. An ankle-deep stream trickled down the center of the canyon, angular boulders lining the base like the latest debris flow had been massive and recent.

"Scale?" she asked, studying the paper as he brought the sketch to life.

"I'm getting there," he muttered, the corners of his mouth turning up. Leaning back, he chewed the edge of his tongue, then leaned in and drew a rough legend. "The canyon's roughly two hundred kilometers in length, width varies with a maximum of two kilometers at its widest, but at the egress in the south, it's roughly fifty meters wide. Walls can be fourteen hundred meters high in places. On average, the northeast ledge is thirty meters higher than the opposite side. Five to thirty percent grade northwest to southeast, average about eight percent."

"What's this?" Lana pointed to a tortuous branch about a mile in from the egress that terminated without an outlet.

"Satellite imagery indicates it's a cave-in."

"Earthquake history?"

"Nothing I could find."

"Huh. Why the cave-in?" she asked vaguely, looking up as if the wall beyond was equally able to answer her question.

"No idea. I want to know why there isn't more of a river at the base."

She glared at his sketch, then pulled the larger printed map out from underneath. "There could be an underground aquifer, but I'm not an expert. What's the social history?"

He leaned back in his chair and pulled off his glasses to see her better.

She flipped her wildly wavy hair back out of her face and tapped her fingers over her crossed arms. Turning toward him at the small table, her legs interlocked with his, one knee wedged between legs. Yet she didn't even seem to notice the intimate proximity. Or it wasn't a big deal or her.

Groaning inwardly, he tensed and tried to focus on the conversation. "Nomadic until the last couple of centuries. The south side has changed hands numerous times since then. The north side, thanks to the terrain, is pretty isolated, the canyon being the primary link between the north and south, without a long-ass drive through populated areas if you want to go around it. The canyon divides this escarpment that runs for miles in either direction, unpassable even for an experienced climber."

"That's why the insurgents are holding so strong in the north? There can't be any way to reach them without scaling mountains or a nautical jaunt across Lake Kvalin."

"Exactly. The people there have been so sheltered from the outside world for generations. Until now. The insurgents have drafted a lot of the north siders into their forces, and it's tough to tell who the bad guys are versus the good."

"That's a loaded concept anyway."

"True. But there are honest people up there that need our help. We need that canyon."

She looked up from the sketch and squinted a curious smile. With a subtle shake of her head, she muttered something incomprehensible under her breath, but he was pretty sure she said something about a damsel and a Navy SEAL.

Somehow, and he hadn't even thought it possible, she scooted a fraction of a millimeter closer, her knees a whisper away from pressing into the goods. What were they talking about? He opened his mouth to talk, but realized he'd been waiting for her to respond.

"Archer?" she asked, her eyes set dead serious, but the corners of her mouth twitched with an inside joke.

"Yeah?"

"What's your plan to get me over there?" She clenched her jaw, reading right through his façade.

He leaned back in his chair.

Amusement dancing in her fairy green eyes, Lana inched closer, her knee agonizingly close to his balls. Unable to breathe, he froze, terrified and aroused and utterly enjoying the torture either way.

At his hesitation, she applied the slightest pressure.

"Devious. Damn, I thought you were making a move." Laughing out loud, he sat up straight and shifted to relieve some of the pressure. "You're not going to trust me until I've dropped you dead center in the middle of that blur, are you?"

"Maybe it was both." She sat up and folded her arms over her chest. "Let's get some sleep, and in the morning, I want to know *exactly* what you saw in that canyon, what you felt, what you heard, down to the nitty gritty, the slightest minutiae, *everything*, so my team can get researching while you and I get to work."

He nodded.

"Great. I'll get my bag. Can I trust you to at least not sneak out of your own home in the middle of the night to ditch me?"

"You're perfectly welcome to stay at a hotel. There's a nice place a few blocks down on Speedway."

"Ha. You're cute." She snagged his glasses off his head and folded them, setting them on the table and rising to stand in front of him.

Like the idiot he was, he froze in his chair. Looking up at her, he clenched his hands tight at his sides. Cute? Would she think that if he knew how fucking bad he was aching to splay his hands around her hips and tug her onto his lap. Or stand and kiss that attitude away. Or tug up the skirt and...

The corner of her mouth quirked up, probably catching him drooling as he ran through the many possibilities in his overworked imagination.

"You're quick to trust me," he whispered.

"Noah said I can trust you," she answered quickly. Her brow furled, and she folded her arms tight over her chest. She looked almost angry about how quick she was to trust him.

He cleared his throat. "I won't skip out while you're asleep. Deal?" he asked and risked rising to his feet.

Stubborn ass, she didn't move, leaving a half a damn centimeter between them and taunting him with her nearness. "Deal," she said, tipping her head to the side as she looked up at him. "I can crash on your couch. Or we can agree that business hours are over?"

Breath rushing from his lungs, he bit his lips together and closed his eyes, hoping to hell she didn't look down and see that his brain was the only part of his anatomy declining the offer. "I've got a spare bedroom," he said with a throat-clearing hoarseness.

"Clean sheets?" She raised an eyebrow and looked around at the pigsty that was his embarrassment of a house.

"Of course. My family visits every few months. Cleanest room in the house, or my mom would have my hide."

6

Lana's eyes eased open as the sky began to glow a diffuse purple on the far horizon. A change from Sitka, the sounds of the night hadn't let up once. College bars three blocks south, a lively social scene four blocks east, and the small adobe home sat comfortably in a row of homes she suspected had been here longer than the university.

With the sprawling desert and growing tech, there were plenty of newer, suburban neighborhoods Archer could have chosen for a fraction of the cost. His choice of the quirky small house in the seasoned neighborhood built up the mystery, and wasn't helping the crush she'd developed. Last night's decline of her offer hadn't been playing hard to get.

A mama's boy, a hint old-fashioned, and sporting biceps she wanted to lick, he was not at all what she'd expected. Well, maybe the biceps.

Maybe she read too many books and heard too many stories. He probably wouldn't be flattered to know that she'd been expecting an egomaniac who wouldn't have hesitated to fool around during downtime, and she had thoroughly been looking forward to fucking between fights.

Archer was... not the worldly hero that wanted to show her the ways of the world, like the military alphas in her books. But she wasn't the damsel, either.

The way he looked at her, his jaw muscles clenched tight when he was clearly trying to behave himself. Maybe he wouldn't move fast, but when he moved...

She had no doubt he was going to be a hell of a playmate. She drew in a long, heated breath, a smitten grin curving up the corners of her mouth as she pictured it.

What was that they said about not playing a player? What about the player playing the sweet guy that happened to be hot and lickable? Sure, she suspected he'd seen almost as much combat as she had, but she gathered he was more careful with his heart than his life.

The bedsheets were clean, as promised, beige sateen cotton under a cotton-weave blanket with a crocheted orange and blue throw folded over the foot. A simple white dresser held a small flat-screen TV and a bouquet of dried flowers. Simple, cozy, and clearly decorated by his mother.

Lana flipped off the sheets and tiptoed across the cool Saltillo tile floor, smooth under her bare feet. She chuckled as she pulled back the vinyl shower certain liner—sans outer curtain—and marveled at the state of his bathroom. Nothing was disgusting, at least. Not like her first apartment, when she'd realized the black stuff growing in the toilet and edges of the bathtub weren't some mysterious evil encroaching on her home, but a maintenance issue.

As her parents had always lived simply, she'd gotten into the habit herself, but demon hunters tended to be well off. Admittedly, she suspected some of that was unfairly obtained centuries ago, as not all demon hunters fought monsters ethically. Regardless of where the money had come from, it was invested well, and she had no qualms about blowing it on cleaning services.

And boots. Skirts. Tops that were soft, lacy, or made her boobs look good. Italian undergarments. Organic, biodegradable shampoo and hair masks that smelled like a glacier.

The guilt from indulging in extravagance was alleviated by her regular donations to organizations supporting victims of domestic violence, as well as free and accessible women's health programs. After all, not every woman had the training and power to knock a monster on its ass.

Conditioner slipped slick through her thick waves as she teased out the snarls. No wonder Archer smelled so good. Where he skimped on frivolities like shower mats or hand towels, he invested well in soap that smelled of the crisp ocean breeze mated with a Pacific Northwest forest. Or that's what the bottle said. She would have called the scent "drop-your-panties-and-let-me-lick-you-all-over, I'm-a-sex-god-with-a-long-tongue-and-tight-abs."

Only one towel on the rack. And none in the cupboard. Archer better not mind sharing.

Already seventy-freaking-degrees, she didn't bother searching for a hair dryer. She tugged on a pair of joggers and a lightweight tank before tiptoeing into the kitchen as the automatic pot garbled out the final drops of the good stuff.

Orange rays radiated across the sky as the sun announced its arrival, purple and pink clouds hinting that they could accumulate and soak the earth by nightfall. No mountains or ocean to look at, but the backyard was downright charming. Lana curled up with a cup of coffee in the cushioned swing and breathed in the desert air.

Tidy and cozy, plush and inviting, she could imagine spending hours in this very spot. Bricks that were old as dirt were lined up, settled and slightly angled in the time-worn patio. A round iron table stood under a shaded pergola with a cluster of lanterns in the center and seating for six. A chiminea stood in one corner with cushy seats on either side, crying out for a small fire and marshmallow roasting.

While she indulged in her second sip and her moment of quiet, she fired off a text to update the team. Not that she trusted Archer to not ditch her yet, but she was optimistic. Maybe they could dig deeper into canyons and blurs and everything else Archer had described.

The patio doors creaked open. Scratching his head, cobalt eyes glazed with sleep, Archer stumbled outside in a snug white tee with black Under Armour joggers slung low on his hips. He plopped down onto the swing next to her and took a long sip from his stoneware mug, the steam from his coffee wafting over his face and brightening his complexion.

"You're up early. Afraid I'd ditch you?" he asked, rubbing his eyes and blinking a few extra times as he stared blankly at the ground in front of them.

"Actually, no." She smiled and resisted leaning into him, tempted to curl into him and indulge in a full snuggle. "I might actually trust you."

"Yeah? What made you decide that?"

"Like I said, Noah trusts you, and trust me when I say, that guy doesn't trust easily."

"I'd love to know what the hell happened to him."

"No, you wouldn't."

"Record says he died in a training op, alongside Simmons and... the rest of our squad. Fuck, they almost shut down the Echo program after that. To lose four to that canyon, then a dozen more in that training op? There aren't that many of us to begin with, only four squadrons in total. I'd just joined, too. Would have died with the rest of them if I hadn't been on leave." He glanced over at her, his brow furrowed in worry.

Lana reached across and smoothed the crease, then rested her palm on his cheek. "That's why."

His eyebrow lifted, curiosity boiling in his look.

"You wouldn't have allowed yourself to go the way the others did." Something about his dig-deep way of powering through challenges told her he wouldn't have taken the werewolf serum to try to get a leg up on the enemy. Good thing, too, as it hadn't turned out well for any of them. "You are good deep to the bone."

"Thanks for noticing." He laughed under his breath and added, "The guys are always teasing me that it's my MO."

"Nice guys always finish last, that's how it goes, right?"

"Apparently."

"But what if he's really hot?" she snarked. "It's not that you're too nice, and you're definitely not lacking in the looks department. Nor that badass, bitable bicep'd edge."

He gulped and his gaze dropped to her lips. "No?"

"It's because you don't want to take the risk," she whispered, wishing to hell he'd follow through on the look that said he was equally attracted.

"My job is one hundred percent risk. Just ask my parents, I am the bravest person they know." He grinned adorably, in full tease now.

"See what I mean? You're adorable. That waitress at the tavern? She was sending out some serious fuck-me vibes."

He laughed out loud and shook his head as he looked away.

"If you wanted, you could have a different partner every night."

"Maybe I could. But if that's not what I want?"

She tucked one leg under the other and rotated to face him on the patio swing. Tracing his jaw, she whispered, "You're a rare find." Leaning forward, she touched her lips to his cheek, enough to inhale his scent. That whisper of desert sand that saturated the air, coated with the pheromone-stimulating shampoo, sent her in a dizzying spiral.

He stilled, breath held, but pulled away before she could take it further. "I did a lot of thinking last night," he said.

"And?" She held her breath, hoping to hell he'd been thinking what she had, and would make that move. But she knew he wouldn't.

He rolled his eyes, his sleepy smile downright snarky. "I'm taking you with me."

"I know."

"I don't know why I trust you, but I do."

Lana took a long, slow, dark sip of cooling coffee, and snuck a look over at him.

He met her look, curious, heavy but laced with flirty interest. "Is it because of whatever it is that you are? Like a spell or something?"

"Something like that," she whispered, and closed her eyes to combat the rising panic and thrill that fueled into her veins. She was tempted as hell to call Quinn and Astrid and ask what it felt like, knowing, but... then they'd get suspicious and if she was wrong, if this was just the result of reading too many romance novels and being way too desperate to find a hot sweet sexy fighter... fucking hell, she was so screwed. "Noah's not the only reason I trust you," she whispered, and met his look again.

He rubbed his free hand over his eyes, then cradled the mug. "You do what I say when I say, not just for both our safety, but so I don't lose my job because of you."

"You trust me, and I trust you. Good. But you're still not convinced you should take me with you."

With his bare feet, he pushed the swing in a gentle sway. Lana curled her legs onto the seat and leaned into him.

"The truth would help," he rumbled with a husky tone that vibrated over her skin.

"Yeah? You're doing a great job working it out on your own. You've ruled out scientist and alien-obsessed Fed. Bet you were up all night, hypothesizing." She nudged him.

Shaking his head, he chuckled under his breath. "Half the night. How about you just lay it all out for me? I won't tell. Cross my heart and hope to die." He flashed her a wicked, boyishly charming grin that about knocked her flat on her ass.

"As I'd have to kill you, that promise would be fulfilled a little too quickly."

"You expect me to sneak a total stranger, on the vague recommendation of a dead man, onto a secure military base, fly you in a military plane to a populated base, then drive you from a forward operating base to ground-fucking-zero?"

"There are a few exceptions in which I could tell you, but we've only known each other a few hours. My identity is way bigger than you and me. I mean, I could tell you everything if we got hitched, and then you might be able to tell your mom if you're vague about it, but otherwise, mum's the word. At the very least, we need more history before I can lay it all out."

He rose to his feet and took her coffee cup, setting both on the table. A gleam in his eye, he sported a wicked smile and beckoned her toward him. "You're strong. You're fast. Prove it."

Heart pitter pattering in her chest, Lana battled a smile and raised an arrogant eyebrow as she rose to her feet. "Think you can take me?"

"I'm damn good at what I do. I can protect you. But I can't keep you safe while fighting... whatever this thing is."

Unable to resist, Lana strutted close and stopped inches away, teasing her lip between her teeth and whispered, "Maybe I'll be the one trying to keep you safe. I need to know I won't be getting a civilian killed."

Darkness coating his gravelly tone, he shook his head. "And I know when to run like hell, or I'd be as dead as the others who tried to tackle that canyon before me."

As his gaze settled, she held fast, teasing her lower lip between her teeth, daring him to take her up on the... offer. "I don't think you've ever backed down from a challenge."

"Fatal flaw." Clearing his throat, he backed up a step and said, "Take me down."

"That brick doesn't look very comfortable. I'd hate for you to break your tailbone or something."

"Scared?"

"Never. But it's your butt on the line. Literally."

Knowing he wasn't going to accept her until he understood how serious she was, Lana kicked out to nail him in the chest, ready to halt inches from impact.

Panic widened his eyes as he caught her foot an inch from his chest. "I, uh, watch the chest, okay? That fist—"

"Oh, shit, sorry. Forgot," she said, wincing and smiling apologetically at him. Shaking her head, not even wavering on her single foot, she said, "Don't go easy on me."

With gentle pressure, he pulled at her foot to throw off her balance.

Holding strong, she waited to see how far he'd pull. Hands wrapped around her ankle, he watched her, daring her to go all-in.

Using his hold for leverage, she leaped into a roundhouse kick. Swinging wide, she arced her bare foot over his head.

Free of his grasp, she landed on her feet, fists up and ready to counter.

Eyes wide, he huffed a smile rich with accepting disbelief and raised his arms defensively.

He swung lazily with the left. She easily brushed it away. When the right came blasting full speed, she ducked back, but he'd already pulled back and wouldn't have hurt her.

"You won't hurt me," she said as she braced for more.

"No, I won't," he answered.

She swung punch after punch, each jab he brushed off, each uppercut be juked.

"Not bad," she said, genuinely impressed.

"You going to come at me like you mean it soon?"

She launched into a back handspring, so close he had to lean back to dodge the kick that could have come with it.

Popped back up in a ready position, just outside his reach, she beckoned him closer.

The corner of his mouth turned up as he accepted he wasn't getting a hand on her, even if he tried for real. Playing along, he swung for a punch and halted an inch from her nose.

Anticipating the move, she grabbed his fist and launched herself into the air and hooked her leg over his shoulders. Swiftly spinning him off balance, keeping behind him, she yanked him backward, so he landed on top of her.

Wind gushed from his chest as he thudded sprawled on his back, her legs wrapped around his abdomen, and hissed, "Ow. What the fuck was that?"

"You asked for it." She laughed as she held him pinned, his backside against her as she cushioned him from the brick patio.

The moment she decided he wasn't going to fight back, he gripped his hand tighter around hers and sprang to his feet, hauling her up with him.

In the space of a blink, she was hanging over his shoulder like a sack of potatoes.

Before he could release her to adjust his grip, she tightened her grip on his hand and twisted his arm behind his back. "Say uncle," she taunted.

"No," he half laughed, half helplessly yelped.

"Now?" she asked as she squeezed tighter.

He hissed and strained to pull his arm free. "Fuck," he muttered as he seemed to accept that she had him, even in the precarious position. Voice strained, light as he trusted her to not hurt him, he asked, "How's your pain tolerance?"

"Better than yours," she snarked back.

"You going to kick my ass if I hurt you?" he asked.

"Yes."

"Good," he said with a laugh as warm as the rising sun.

Dropping his shoulder, he sent her plummeting toward the ground so she released him on instinct.

Catching her at the last second, he cradled her inches above the ground.

Before she had a chance to wiggle her way out of his grip, he tossed her onto the swing.

Laughing out loud as she slammed into the cushions, swinging wild, she shoved her hair out of her face. Once the momentum tapered, she pulled her legs up and curled into the swing. Thrill bubbling through her, she watched him grinning at her, playful and satisfied and intrigued. "Partners?"

"Almost." He grabbed her coffee and passed across as he settled at her side. "My squad comes first. The op. Civilians. If we have to run to protect them, then we get the hell out of there."

"Protecting human life is top on my priority list. That includes your squad. And you. But when it comes to the final push, when I say run, you run. You're to leave me and my team to end this thing."

"We'll see," he said under his breath. Turning to her, those dang simmering cobalt blues in full smolder, his voice rumbled melodiously, "I'll get you over there. But I'm not leaving you to the mercy of the canyon. I suspect we're going to need all of us."

"Not many can come close to knocking me down. You're human, but you're impressively tough. I almost wonder..." She studied him and shook her head. Nah. Maybe some distant ancestor had a drop of demon blood in them, but he was too human and thus far too breakable. "This is what I do. I can't risk you or your squad."

"And this is what we signed on for. Partners, or you're finding your own way in."

Extending her hand, she was surprised yet again at the shock of the connection. "Partners. But—"

"No buts. Full partners."

"Tell me everything that happened in that canyon," she said, holding that cobalt gaze.

Clenching his jaw, he glanced up at the clouds accumulating over the last scrap of blue and took a slow breath.

7

"HOW MUCH SHIT ARE you bringing?" Archer's eyes widened, his jaw slackened to a full gape, as he watched Lana load a steel-clanking duffel bigger than she was into the backseat of his truck. What sort of person carried a Tolkienesque axe, throwing knives, her own bulletproof vest with a smiley face on the nametag inside, and cowboy boots?

"As I don't know what we're up against, I don't want to skimp on gear." She shrugged and looked in at the bag, then adjusted it to lay flatter, metal clanking against metal. "Although, I suppose if you need me to cut back, I usually default to my axe anyway."

He'd drawn the line at the throwing knives stuffed into her boots. Bad enough he was sneaking her on post, but an armed, unauthorized woman with a spotty background check, on very short notice? He absolutely didn't want to bring attention to his nontraditional consultant by getting her on post through any legit channels. "What century do you think this is?"

She tossed a borrowed military pack of his on top of the load. "You said yourself, bullets seemed to make it worse. In my line of work, a good blade solves most problems."

"If I get caught smuggling not only an uncleared civilian, but a mountain of sharp objects...?"

"Then don't get caught. Don't you have some sort of extra clearance with your... role?"

"Yeah, but base security is tight with breach at the federal building last week. Part of my extra clearance comes with my discretion."

"I'll be quiet as a mouse."

He waved her into the back seat and tossed his blanket, backpack, sleeping bag, and jacket over Lana and her gear. If they ran into any trouble, he'd pull rank and, worst case, make a few calls to get a retroactive authorization for her. But he'd rather not draw attention to taking a... whatever she was, on post.

At the gate, the MP stepped up to check his badge as he pulled to a stop. "Hey, Zechmann. Pretty quiet today?" Archer said as he held up his ID.

"Nothing too exciting. Big plans for the day, Major Belak, uh, sir?" the MP stuttered.

Laughing under his breath at the overeager kid, he took pity on him as he replaced his ID. "Another boring day on my schedule, thankfully."

"Sir," the MP saluted and tripped over his words for a moment, lingering with a question tugging at his tongue.

Fuck, so busted.

"My, uh, my little sister is looking into enlisting and wants to be a Ranger. Any advice?"

He masked his relief with an easy nod. "Never give up, and no shortcuts. Officer's program and combat experience would help."

"Thanks. You know, I've always wondered, what is behind the red gate? Not many take that route, and just you and Captain Pierce are the only ones that stop to talk to us MPs." Glasses thicker than his own reading pair, the kid may as well be sporting braces.

"Offices."

"Of course, I should have thought of that." He saluted again. "Thank you. Sir. Have a good one."

Archer nodded and drove casually forward. After rolling the window up, he reached behind the seat and ruffled Lana's hair under the pile. "Okay back there?"

She grabbed his hand and hissed, "Is it social hour at the gate? It's hot under all this crap."

"I didn't want to be rude. And I told you I'd get you on post, one way or another, and trust me, this was the quickest and easiest."

"Can I come out yet?"

"Not yet." As he neared the empty stoplight, it lowered to green, and he turned down the path less traveled, slowing again as he approached the red gate that was more rust than paint anymore. An older section of the base, overgrown and uninviting, not many came this way. This next guard waved as he approached and flicked open the gate.

He hadn't lied. His office was behind the red gate, tucked away in the outdated, forgotten buildings from World War II. Most importantly, it was adjacent to the special ops airfield. "Clear. You can climb up front."

He shifted the gear off her and she sat up, looking like she'd been buried in a haystack or something. Flipping her hair out of her face, she slid over the center console and dropped into the passenger seat. Decked out in black leggings with cargo pockets, a black sleeveless shirt, black boots laced halfway up her calves, she left her hair wild, but he knew there was a hair-tie tucked away in her pocket.

"Come on," he said after hooking her absurdly heavy bag over his shoulder and motioned to the faded white and green 1940s wooden building.

She hopped to catch up and strolled alongside him.

Archer paused at the beige steel door and turned to her, "Follow my lead, okay?"

Hands on her hips, she chewed her cheek and shook her head. "That's not in my skill set."

"No shit," he muttered.

With an eye-roll, she finally nodded and followed inside. He chuckled under his breath. Smartass wouldn't last a day in basic training.

Dusty and pea green with a rickety wooden chair, the unlit, unmanned front desk served to warn off any unlikely trespassers more efficiently than an armed guard with its blunt message: no one gives a fuck about this place. The black and whites of the original officers to occupy the building didn't drop any hints as to the current tenants.

At the scuffed door behind the unlit, unoccupied reception area, he lifted the deadbolt façade and flashed his ID badge over the blinking reader. Thick bolts clinked open, lubricated steel sliding through steel, and the door skimmed open. He pushed ahead and glanced around.

Must all be downstairs. He nodded for Lana to follow along, unsurprised to find she was already inches behind him, waiting nonchalantly. Three darkened offices down, he pushed open his office door and flicked on the lights.

Overhead LEDs responded immediately, lighting up the office he kept tidier than his home. Mostly. He dumped the bag containing her gear on the floor next to his black leather sofa, and she slid her backpack off her shoulder, setting it on top. Suddenly shy, he pushed his fingers through his short hair and stepped back.

It wasn't so bad, he supposed. His computer screen was dark, no dirty dishes aside from an empty coffee cup. Crumpled on the edge of the couch, his sweatshirt was the only evidence that he'd crashed last week after giving himself a raging headache trying to read the texts the special ops librarian had wrangled for him—only to give up and call Noah's brother.

That decision had better pan out. For all her reported expertise, Lana hadn't even hinted at what was blocking that canyon. Except that an axe and throwing knives were necessary tools of her trade.

Lana rested her hand briefly on his shoulder as she passed to the window and looked out at the airfield. "Nice," she said with a snarky, lopsided grin. "And here I thought you spent your stateside hours pumping iron and practicing your aim."

"Smartass," he said, shaking his head and moving to stand next to her.

"Kidding. We spend more time planning than operating, as I'll bet you do, too."

"For the most part. Don't forget meetings, digging through intel reports and giving a few of my own, and hours on hours of research."

"I feel ya. Not the meetings, as, well, our meetings are just us. And our intel reports are typically weird news articles about murders and animal attacks. But the planning and research? Necessary, I know, but I'd rather just dive in and—" She nudged her elbow playfully into his side and grinned up at him. "You know? You've got one of those faces."

With a grimace, he asked, "Do I want to know what you mean by that?"

"It's a compliment. You're so genuine and such a good listener. You're irresistibly sweet, and I want to tell you everything."

He turned toward her and planted his hands on his hips. Brow drawn to a scowl, he feigned irritation, but the twitch of a smile at the corners of his mouth ruined the sternness of the look. "Badass. Remember?"

"Without a doubt," she said, resting her palms on his abdomen as she stepped closer. "Bet you're a good kisser," she said, tipping her head to the side curiously. "You take it slow and savor in the moment, don't you?"

Fuck. Anyone else. If he had half a brain, he'd lean closer and test if her lush lips were as soft as they looked, then bury his hand in her hair and haul her up against him to kiss her until they were both lightheaded. "Savor, yes. Slow? Well..."

A throat cleared in the doorway, Sauer's rumbling laugh shattering the smidgeon of hope his libido had clutched onto, dreaming that he was going to make a damn move. "'Bout time you showed up. We depart in under an hour."

Archer stepped back and stuffed his hands into his pockets. "Sauer, this is Lana Fischer, Lana, this is Ulrich Sauer. Lana is, um—"

"Hi," Lana said with a bright smile, strolling across the office and comfortably shaking Sauer's hand as if... as if she wasn't stuttering over a failed moment like he was. Probably would have been less painful if he'd had his tongue halfway down her throat when Sauer came in. Now he wasn't going to hear the end of it.

"Hi," Sauer said with a smitten grin.

"Archer called me in to consult on the canyon. I'm an expert in this sort of... quandary."

"Expert?" His eyebrow raised synchronously with the smile masked under his cedar-red beard, the enjoyment palpable on the six-foot-six brick of a man with boyishly curled hair. After interrupting what Archer was going to fuck up anyway, Sauer was having the time of his life. Apparently.

"Yeah," Archer said, pushing his shoulders back and daring Sauer to ask questions. "Scientist, of a sort, I think. I'll fill you in on the way over."

"Whoa, wait, she's coming with us? Like, over there?" he asked, disbelief flashing over his pale blue eyes. "Sure," Sauer said as he backed out to the hall. "Belak, I trust you more than I trust myself. But I want to witness you telling the others we're bringing a tourist."

Resigned, Archer moved into the hall, knowing Lana was close behind. "Basement?"

"Yeah. I was sent up here to see where the fuck you were hiding. Now I see why you were sneaking around."

Archer wound through the series of hallways and meeting rooms, finally opening the reinforced steel door to the basement. Music boomed up the narrow stairs. The rest of the squad laughed and riled each other, letting loose before departing to again attempt to penetrate the canyon that had already disabled one of them, not to mention the countless numbers that hadn't made it out at all.

At the foot of the stairs, he paused while Lana stepped up next to him. Arms casually folded over her chest, hip cocked out, she took in the scene with the enjoyment she seemed to find in the situations he found routine. Although, this one could be a bit unusual to those that didn't lead similar lives.

The basement had originally been built as a fallout shelter and had retained the purpose, with modernization and renewed supplies. Hell, if the end of days happened, this is exactly where he'd want to shelter. Plush sofas surrounded a high-res TV, with every game system to have been released in the last half century, plus a boot-scuffed coffee table that had served as a footrest for dozens of Echos before him. To the left, the kitchen was state-of-the art with on-demand hot water and coffee, double ovens, and double refrigerators were stocked with whatever they needed to unwind. Industrial bathrooms and bunks were attached at both ends. Plus, a storeroom full of survival equipment from food to weapons, and for the worst-case scenario: cyanide tabs.

The bulk of the place was dedicated to the training Lana had referred to. Machines, weights, benches, and a big ass open area to burn off energy and pump for the next op.

Four sets of eyes landed on his guest, and he knew the fifth set beamed behind them as Sauer was smug in presenting his find. Although faced with mixed reactions, confusion was most obvious. "This is Lana Fischer," he said, motioning as if they ought to know what he was talking about. "She's an expert and is coming along."

Unfazed, Lana waved and said, "Hey."

Crutches leaned against his chair, his casted foot up on the coffee table, and his forehead still yellow from the injury that had nearly taken his life, Brock tilted his head. "You didn't tell me I was screening my replacement."

"Fuck that. As soon as you get your lazy bones to unbreak, you'll be back in the action," he fired back. "She's a consultant."

Lips pulled tight, posture easy as she leaned against the back of the couch, Kerse sneered, "She doesn't look like a consultant."

Lana opened her mouth to fire back, but Archer stilled her, resting his hand on her shoulder and giving her a look that he hoped to hell she would follow. "I may look like an easygoing superior officer," he reprimanded Kerse. "We leave in thirty minutes. Tell me, were you all planning to walk right back in there and hope for a different outcome?" Wandering gazes looked at feet, twiddling thumbs, the ceilings. "We've had two weeks to plan. What have you all come up with?"

Walker tipped his head in a subtle nod. "What's the word on an airstrike?"

"As far as I'm concerned, that's not an option. My own bullet nearly knocked me out of the fight," he said, glancing at Brock's bruised face and casted leg. "This is an unknown enemy that we can't even get close enough to attack. We can't do this the old-fashioned way."

Sauer shrugged, brushing his hand over his overgrown beard. "I still say fuck that canyon, we're going over the top."

Chan chucked a pillow at him. "With no cover? We'd look like baby turtles booking it across the beach. Easy pickings."

Without a word, Archer stood silently and let them argue it out.

Lana stood back and watched the banter. Finally, she asked, "Exactly what happened when you shot at it?"

Chan watched her, uncertainty frank on her expression. Archer nodded that it was okay. "Pissed it off."

She nodded, arms folded casually over her chest. "Explosion?"

"Fucking nuclear storm," Walker hissed from his spot on the weight bench. Long and lean, he grabbed a towel from the rack and wiped a layer of sweat from his face and stalked closer. "Airstrike isn't an option. Nor is up and over, nor flying around."

"Something's blocking that canyon, and it's not something you've ever dealt with before." Lana teased her fingers in her hair and brushed the wild waves from her face, casual as ever.

"Just what do you think this is?" Chan stared, her brow furrowed.

"Not sure yet," Lana said with a lazy shrug. "But this is within my area of expertise."

While the others fired more questions, Archer cut through the noise with a sharp tone, "We need more intel and more time, but we don't have that luxury. Connery and Simmons are the only ones to have ever survived venturing into this canyon. Lana has a lot in common with them, and there are six more just like her. This is further outside the boundary than I've ever asked, so if you're not comfortable with that, you sit your ass down. If you're willing to take a chance, fall in."

Chan looked back and forth between Archer and Lana before nodding. "I secured a C-17 and retrofitted three civilian SUVs with extra storage, stocked with advanced medkits to keep us out-of-body bags, and triple the firepower—if we get to use any of it. Ready to depart anytime."

Kerse moved for the first time, rising to her feet and stalking like the predator she was.

Without so much as a flinch, Lana stood her ground, as Kerse stopped inches in front of her.

Shoulders back, Archer moved in behind Lana. Instinct, or something. Yeah, he had no doubt Lana could take down any one of them after the show she'd put on yesterday morning. But Kerse wasn't the understanding sort.

The corners of her lips turned up, arms gently folded over her chest, Lana may as well buff her nails while she was at it.

Tipping her head back a nudge to look down her nose at Lana, Kerse gritted her teeth and rumbled, "Who the fuck do you think you are? You may have Archer convinced you've got some sort of edge on this thing." She looked her over and sneered. "But this is our fight. And we don't need help from a civilian."

"Kerse," Archer warned, but knew Kerse needed a moment to find her footing.

She snapped a look at him and locked back onto her prey.

Lana tipped her head subtly to the side and studied Kerse curiously. "Tell me again, how'd you fare last time you faced this... blur?"

Unmoving, Kerse held her ground, her tone steady. "I've been knocked down before. But I hit back."

"And I can hit harder," Lana answered easily. "Look. I already had this conversation with Archer. You can accept that I'm coming with you, or I'll find my own way in and take care of this thing without your assistance."

Flippant, Kerse huffed and glanced a look at Archer. "Where'd you dig this thing up?"

"Classified," he said. Lana didn't seem fazed in the least, and Kerse was a natural at intimidation. Actually, Lana seemed to be enjoying herself.

"Bullshit," Kerse hissed.

"I can't and I won't say how I found her or why we need her. If you've got a problem with that, ruck up or sit your ass down."

8

Empty aside from a few decrepit hangars and their waiting jet, the runway was broad and smooth. Dusk was fully awake, but the heat still sucked her breath away and stimulated a trickle of sweat between her breasts and stickiness in her hair. It would be a shame to soak her desert air dried hair with sweat. Arizona stores probably didn't sell many hair dryers.

"Maybe don't antagonize my squad." Archer nudged Lana as they walked across the tarmac. Although better acclimated to the heat than she was, Archer had his jacket tied onto his pack, and his t-shirt clung to his damp skin.

Okay, so she'd never had a uniform thing. Like, ever. Lana would happily consider a man in or out of uniform, but it hadn't been a "thing" like some people had.

But the shoulder-hugging t-shirt gave her a spectacular hint of how defined his deltoids were. It was as if he knew how her imagination would flutter when he wore low-slung pants—whether it be him in jeans from the bar, joggers around the house, or, like now, in his dark gray and black cargos, letting her know lickable his abs were.

And the aviator glasses.

Yum. She may have whimpered.

She'd known some stacked guys in the past—demon-enhanced ones—but Archer held his own without an ounce of demon blood. If she so desired, she could resist, but why? The man was freaking adorable, his grin mixed with dead serious as he defended his squad.

Nudging him back, she teased, "I suppose they're a bunch of snuggly bunnies under the surface?"

"Most of them. Kerse, however… I'm not sure she has a soft underbelly."

"You do," Lana teased.

"What? Never. Six-pack of steel right here," he boasted with a self-effacing laugh, hoisting his pack higher on his shoulder and sneaking a look back at her over the glasses.

"You're not helping," she said. Her promise to be on her best behavior wasn't going to last long. If they hadn't been interrupted in his office, she would have happily indulged in a little playtime.

"Lana, you are completely, entirely more than I can handle."

She tipped her head back, a giggle bubbling up in her throat. "From what I've already gathered, you don't back down from a challenge."

"It's a flaw, I admit that. But, I'm already getting some suspicious looks from the rest of the squad. If I dropped my gear, right here on the tarmac, and kissed you like I want to? They'd think I'd all sense of reason."

"But you do want to kiss me?"

In the last of the day's sun, they walked into the shadow of the jet. He exhaled before speaking. "Let's focus on the canyon."

They stepped into the back of the cargo plane, pushing past a trio of ordinary SUVs that looked straight out of the cold war. The bulk of the interior of the C-17 was dedicated to the transports, nets along the sides for securing equipment, and closer to the front, there were several rows of seats in the middle that looked modular, movable, depending on the cargo needs and number of passengers, with flip-down benches lining the sides. Lana admired the layout, wondering how obvious the team would look with their own military plane. Damn, no, it would not be subtle, landing that thing at a civilian airport.

Archer nodded for her to wait, and walked ahead to meet with the pilot.

Chan came up behind her and set a hand on Lana's shoulder. "Don't mind Kerse. She'll come around."

Lana raised an eyebrow and didn't mask her eyebrow raise.

Laughing hesitantly, Chan shook her head. "Okay, maybe not right away." Tossing her duffel onto one of the seats, Chan claimed a row for herself and motioned for Lana to do the same. "Belak trusts you. If he could explain why he's bringing you along, he would. We wouldn't survive if we didn't trust each other one hundred percent. So, I'm trusting him about you."

Lana sighed and leaned against the seat in the back row. "Appreciate it."

Walker stretched out on the bench along the side and rested his head on his jacket, fluffing it one more time before settling in. "Something's fucked about this canyon, so if you know how to get in there without anyone else dying, I'm in."

Voice rumbling so low she almost couldn't hear him, Sauer gruffed, "I don't know why we can't charter a commercial jet and buy rigs while we're there. Long ass flight and we're stuck hiding out like cargo."

Terse as she claimed her spot, Kerse answered, "You want to take a civilian jet to the FOB?"

"No," he grumbled. "I'm telling you. Air. Strike. Crumble that canyon and we'll stroll in through the rubble."

Chan groaned and shook her head. "Jameson's trying to buy us more time so that precise thing doesn't happen."

Darkness swallowed the jet as the back closed up. Archer strolled out of the cockpit, already looking worn out, shirt untucked as his cargos rested lazily on his hips, his hair tousled, and his shadow of beard darker than it had been that morning. He dropped into the seat next to her and took out a book for himself, passing another to her. Without a word, he reached to the top of his head for his glasses. Not finding them, he checked the neck of his shirt.

Lana reached over and pulled the missing specs from the chest pocket of the jacket he'd strapped onto his pack.

Smiling sheepishly, he slid his glasses on. "Thanks," he whispered as he adjusted the glasses on his nose.

Each having a row or side bench to themselves, the squad had spread out and prepared for the next steps in their own way.

Except Archer had taken the seat next to her, theoretically under the guise of collaborating, but Lana got the warm-and-tinglies at the proximity. Side by side when there was an empty row in front and behind them. A heavy ache in her chest like a butterfly on steroids trapped in her ventricles, Lana resisted the urge to lean into Archer and leaned on the opposite armrest as she curled up with her book.

Out of *his* league? As if. Irresistible. Adorable. Ripped. Determined. He was in a league of his very own.

After an hour of reading quietly, the others already asleep except for the two of them, Archer rubbed his eyes under his glasses. Finally, he whispered, "The canyon was dry and barren around the 1790s, when the rest of the region was coated in snow and the sun didn't come out from behind the clouds for over six months."

"One of the cooler periods of the Little Ice Age?" Lana asked, vaguely remembering something from college. Quinn, Bennett, Missy, and she had deigned to become a team from the time they were sparring with sticks in the backyard. Missy ditched out on them and refused the life, but the rest decided to vary their educations to maximize their training.

Lana had studied geology. Bored out of her mind through minerals, petrology, and sedimentology, she tried to at least remember her geomorphology, seismology, and hydrology courses, as those were moderately interesting.

"Sounds like a children's book," Archer said, a laugh under his breath.

She chuckled softly, "Maybe I'll write one. Skye would get a kick out of it."

"Skye?"

"Quinn and Ryan—two of my teammates—their daughter is four. She is a sucker for all things cute and thinks she is the world's best reader."

"Wow, pretty young to be reading."

"I think she takes after her father and grandfather. Ryan's development was... rapid." Catching herself, she omitted the why. "You have little ones in your family?"

"Too many." He shook his head, grinning widely. "In a good way. But the holidays are... chaotic."

"My sister has the cutest little man she's raising to be just like her, already another on the way, and she thinks the world should be in love and reproducing."

"Married one of those fishermen?"

"Of course. Running the tavern, she has little else to choose from. Coasties, of course, but they're a riskier breed for one so firmly rooted in their hometown."

"I thought you enjoyed a little catch and release?"

"As often as I can, but... okay, my brother-in-law is great, and they're sweet together, but it's not the type of partnership I'm looking for. If I was in the market for something *permanent*, it would be with someone—" How did she describe the predicament? Thanks to Ryan and Bodie, Lana discovered that she had a type.

"I'm tempted to ask what *permanent* would look like, but that might sound like I'm fishing, and I'm not. No offense."

She snorted a laugh, then covered her mouth to avoid waking the others. "None taken. I have at least a century before I'm walking down that plank—metaphorically speaking, of course."

"Of course." Those cobalt eyes were thick with curiosity, and she was so tempted to drop more clues so he'd figure it out on his own. The man carried a lot of secrets, and one more wouldn't hurt. Ryan's former Coast Guard crew knew, out of necessity, and if this canyon was full of beasties in her area, well, it would become necessary to tell him.

Then see if he was still game for a little something along the way.

"This... whatever it is that you are, I was thinking it was hereditary. But your sister... isn't?"

Biting her lip, she withheld a breath and gauged him for a reaction. Nothing suspicious. No digging, just curiosity. "It's hereditary, but it's a choice we make on our eighteenth birthday."

"That doesn't make any sense. How would something like that work? Like, DNA with a manual on-off switch?"

Maybe her hints were getting too close. "I have no idea how it works, but there's a ritual with words and feelings, and the process starts. Sort of like marriage." The process had been excruciating, being rebuilt from the inside out, but even during the worst of it, when she feared she might not survive it, she knew it was the right choice.

Archer studied her with a wicked amusement, the corners of his mouth curled up in a baiting grin. "Wow, you really are a commit-ment-phobe."

She snorted a whispery laugh and leaned into him.

"So you made the choice to... be able to fix things?" he asked.

She nodded.

"What made you choose it, but not your sister?"

"I can't speak for Missy." Well, she could, but she probably shouldn't say it out loud. Bad enough she'd ripped Missy a new one when she came back from a mission to celebrate, only to find Missy hadn't gone through with it. She still kicked herself, wondering if Missy would have been brave enough to try, if Lana had made it home for the big day. "It wasn't a choice for me. This is what I was born for. What made you join the army? And not just because you were scrawny and stubborn. Why did you sign on with Echo?"

Shoulder to shoulder, his legs stretched out long and spread wide with his thigh pressed against hers, he folded his arms over his chest. Thumb grazing mindlessly over her skin, he answered, "You first."

"I was born with something unique. Yeah, it was a choice, but for me, it really wasn't. It's like being granted a power to help, and to refuse it seemed... wasteful." She shifted her hand up and traced her fingertips over his arm. "Besides, who wouldn't want to be a badass without even trying?"

He glanced and grinned at her, that curious expression rich with amusement.

"Your turn."

"Unlike you, I have to work my ass off to do what I do. But it was better than the alternative. I needed to get out. A few of my friends left Low Plains, but only managed the feat because they were gifted at something. Rocket-scientist intelligence or an operatic singing voice."

"Not you though?"

"Not me. Lanky. Not gifted at a damn thing. I had two nieces and three nephews before I even graduated. Don't get me wrong, my siblings are great. Eva just opened up a clothing shop on the main drag, right between the gas station and the motel, so it's a prime spot, considering Low Plains is a tourist leg-stretch or shut-eye stop on their way between interesting towns. Mik and his husband are buying out the antique shop. Karl seems to think he's going to make his fortune as a podcaster. Lorie has too many rugrats to work these days. Rachel seems to think she's going to make it as a writer. Nik's loving running the shop with dad, and he's a gifted mechanic. Seriously, he hears one tick and knows what's wrong with a car. But I didn't want any of that. So it was Army or..."

"You have a huge family."

"Four-bedroom house. Seven kids. Plus Baba and Ded, my mom's parents, live in a cabin behind the house. Dad's parents are across the street. Even if I wanted to find trouble, there wasn't the space to."

"Very international."

"I know, right? Trust me, our family reunions are disorienting. Insults spewed in a mash of Russian and English and broken English and broken Russian."

"And Echo? You could have served your time and found your niche in the civilian world."

"I worked my ass off to get where I am. I like it, and found I'm pretty good at it. It's nice, to be good at something."

She smiled and flicked the corner of his jaw with her knuckle.

He grinned, his smile holding as he looked closer, deeper.

The engine rumbled against the silence, a soft snore from a few rows up.

His eyelashes lowered, his gaze focusing on her lips, and he leaned toward her, a breath away.

As she let her eyes flutter closed, so close she could feel his heat, could almost taste him, and see if they torched the plane when the chemistry experiment they had going detonated...

But he hesitated, the vibration of his nearness about killing her.

She wanted to clutch him and end the torture, but he pulled back.

He leaned back into his seat, the stupid armrest a mountain of annoying separation. "We should get some sleep."

Dreamland decided to torture her as badly as the kiss that didn't happen. Archer everywhere. On top of her. Under her. Limbs entangled with hers.

Chest rising and falling as if she'd been making love with him all night, as if his tongue was caressing hers, the soft velvet massage warm and stoking a fire deep in her belly, her eyes popped open and she was genuinely surprised to discover they weren't making out, for how vivid the dream was.

Worse, he was gone. His jacket was stretched over her like a blanket. Rubbing a hand over her arm, she closed her eyes and tried to figure out what to do about... him.

Flipping her hair out of her face, she rose from the seat and made for the bathroom. After giving herself a good talking-to in the mirror, she shook it off. Okay, sure, he was adorable. Unwittingly charming. Honest. Built. Seriously, those biceps alone would make any appreciative party swoon. That grin... yeah. That was nice too.

She splashed cool water over her face before slipping out of the bathroom. Echo members were starting to get up and move around after banking sleep over the long flight. Kerse stared blankly ahead, frozen as if she refused to rub her eyes and stretch, lest she show any signs of weakness. Sauer was still snoring in an awkward position. Walker flashed a sleepy smile as he passed on the way to his own refresh.

Buried with her nose in a book on history in the region, Chan motioned to the rear of the plane. "Archer's in back."

Lana nodded and headed to the back of the first SUV.

Illuminated only by the vehicle's dome light, the rest of the jet still dimmed for the night, Archer was sifting through his gear as he loaded it into the back.

As she neared, a smile tugged at the corner of his mouth and his breath caught as he looked over at her… and she tripped a little further. "Hey," he said, not the slightest bit coy, hoarse and tempting, watching her with patient curiosity.

"What's up?" she asked, swallowing the butterfly that flapped its unsteady wings in her throat.

A stack of camo waited on the tailgate; he lifted it and sat where the pile had been. "I forgot to mention, I, uh grabbed these for you back in Tucson. Captain Pierce."

"Why do you call him Brock, but the rest of you call each other by your last names?" she asked, a curious smile on her face.

Archer's lips curled up into a sweet smile, a glimmer in his look as he glanced at the uniform and huffed a soft laugh. "First day with Echo, we're crashed in the basement for an impromptu meeting after some intense training—not hazing, but, uh, honestly, I wanted to know what I had to work with."

"Like you did with me?"

"Pretty much. Anyway, his phone rings and this adorable little voice, his oldest daughter, in kindergarten at the time, hollers, 'Captain Brock, you forgot to pick me up from school,' and rage hung up."

Lana laughed out loud and tipped her head back, imagining the fierce little thing telling off her certified badass father. "That's adorable."

"He's adorable. Seriously, he's always got some kid hanging off of him. His wife is just as sweet."

She smiled at the description, then compared patches. "I'm not sure I like that you outrank me."

He laughed under his breath. "Chan and I combined some of our gear for you. You're about her size, but they might be a bit tight in... um, they might be snug up top. And I stole Brock's name for you, which he thought was spectacular. We'll be Rangers until we get to the COP, then you and your team can be scientists."

"COP? I can't even guess what that one is."

"Combat Outpost. Not far from the canyon." A smug grin on his face as she inspected her new jacket, he added, "We'll be landing at the FOB in two hours to talk to anyone who's been near the canyon, particularly anyone from the platoon that got hit, or talked to people in the platoon after and might be able to shed some light on what happened there. Then we'll drive into this little town in Otrivka near the border, question locals and data mine along the way. Civilian airport nearby, so we can pick up your team there."

"FOB?"

He watched her and grinned, his tongue parked in his teeth as if holding something back. "Forward Operating Base."

"I'll contact my team from the FOB to let them know the ETA they should be arriving at the LZ, so we can pick them up in the SUV to go to the COP and pretend to be PhDs."

He chuckled softly. "I won't pretend to be thrilled to bring seven strangers to what's essentially a safe house in a delicate area, but I've given up pretending that I don't need you."

"Told you."

"Lana. We're in this together." His voice was thick with sincerity, but he blew it by adding, "By together, I mean, I outrank you, so I wouldn't call us partners—"

"Ha. Rank won't mean shit when my team gets here." She looked into the back of the rig and back at Archer. "These rigs aren't exactly standard issue. How many miles are on this?" From the outside, it looked like a cheap piece of shit that her grandfather would have driven, and he was three-hundred and four when he died.

Inside was equally alarming. A cracked vinyl bench seat for the driver and front passenger, plus a wide bench seat big enough to crash out on behind it, and another row behind that. Tucked in back like a soccer mom prepared for war, were cases of guns, ammo, and other fun explosives. Strapped next to the spare tire was enough fuel to drive them across all of Eastern Europe.

"Where are my weapons?"

"Second row, tucked under the seat. I have no desire to try to explain why we're carrying axes and throwing knives."

"I didn't bring any boots tall enough for daggers."

"I don't even know how to respond to that." Archer chuckled under his breath and handed her the pile of clothes. "Better get changed. We're landing soon."

She hooked her thumb over his rough chin, fully intending to make it playful, but he shifted his gaze up to her, those dreamy cobalt blues simmering again. Tempted beyond reason, she leaned in... and backed away and tugged her top off before she did something foolish.

She wasn't one to hesitate, but she had the feeling he'd stiffen up if she pushed too hard—and not the good kind of stiffening up.

Groaning, he looked like a hot, horny, fish out of water as she passed him her top and adjusted her bra.

"Hold this for me?" she asked with an innocent grin. Okay, so she didn't have it in her to take it easy on him. Nor would he appreciate her cutting him any slack.

"What...?" he garbled.

Taking the Army-issue black tee from the pile, she pulled it over her head and adjusted it over the girls. Okay, yeah, it was a bit snug. Archer didn't seem to mind, his lips pouty and his eyes hazing over, still speechless.

She grinned mischievously and reached for the pants next, the latest dark gray-green with shades of gray and black camo matching the military's Eastern European strife. Balanced on one foot, she slipped off her boot and began to tug her leggings down her hips.

Shaking his head, voice cracking, he said, "You're going to be the death of me."

"I was just checking," she shrugged, hoping to hell he didn't see right through her. Quinn would call her on it. Bennett most certainly would. Vann wouldn't say it, but he'd know. She was floundering, more unsure of her grip with him than she'd been with anyone before.

Best way to find solid ground? Take charge.

"Lana. This is... I... Fuck," He rubbed his hands over his face and tangled his hands in his short hair.

"I hope so." She winked and wiggled the rest of the way out of her leggings.

Breath whooshing, Archer watched for a brief moment, then looked up to the ceiling. "Lana, I—"

"Relax. If I was trying to seduce you, I'd be much more obvious about it."

"And taking your clothes off isn't obvious?" His voice was near shrill as he stared straight up.

"I'm wearing underwear, and not even skimpy ones."

"Trust me, they're imprinted into my brain already. If that's not what you consider skimpy—"

"Oh my. We are going to have fun." Giving him a break, she pulled on the rest of the uniform, from cargo pants and military boots—half a size too big but would be perfect with an extra pair of socks—and nudged his tummy. His rock-hard, ripped tummy that she wanted to lick. The image coming to life in her head, she bit her lip and indulged in the fantasy.

Tongue parked in his cheek as he held back a grin, Archer rose to his feet and handed her the jacket, tossing her civilian clothes on the back seat.

Lana pulled on the coat and secured it around her, posing like a melodramatic model on the runway.

He tucked his fingers in her waistband and tugged her close. Methodically, gingerly, he buttoned the jacket, and her imagination boiled over. "Is it weird that I'm turned on by you wearing my gear?" he whispered.

Ignoring the ache in her chest, she feigned a laugh. "I call that possessive."

"Whatever it is, I should probably ignore it." He finally looked down at her and held.

She melted into a puddle. Tracing her fingertips along the rough stubble of his jaw, she held her breath and tried to find the upper hand without him noticing.

But nothing was that simple.

"Thought this was business," he said with a growl rumbling in his throat.

Busted.

Breath whooshed from her lungs, the jet spinning around her as she pressed into him. "I don't care for rules." Lana teased her lower lip between her teeth. Waiting, her gaze drifting over his lips.

And she waited some more.

The corners of his mouth turned up devilishly. "If you want to play, let's play. But don't expect me to follow desperately along behind, picking up breadcrumbs."

Letting the potential energy arc between them, she traced her tongue along the crease of her lips. "Then keep up."

9

THE CORNER OF HIS lips upturned, Archer tipped his head as if to settle in for one of those languorous, testing first kisses.

Her eyes fluttered closed.

"I'll give you a head start," he murmured as he pulled away, and strode back to their seats with a casual swagger.

Fuck, he needed to gear up for a full expedition. Lana wasn't like anyone he'd met. Not even close to anyone he'd dated. Out of his league? Fuck yes. But, as she'd put it, he wasn't one to back down from a challenge.

A smile still teasing at his lips, he hooked into his seat and dug into another book. Within seconds, his eyes crossed, and the words swam together in a chaotic jumble. He patted his chest, checked his head, but he'd probably lost them again. The couch at home had swallowed at least a dozen pair, and he suspected twice as many lived in the depths of his office.

Lana rested her hand on his shoulder as she dropped into the seat next to him. Without a word, she reached into the seatback pocket in front of them and pulled out his glasses. She quietly set them in his hand and curled up with another book, her feet tucked under her, and leaned into him.

Another hour went by, his brain throbbing as he tried to puzzle together the key points he'd managed to glean. He rubbed his fingers over the bridge of his nose and tried to clear the fuzz. Tapped out, he stuffed the book back into the bag and stuffed his glasses in the neck of his shirt.

The plane shifted gears. The engine fell suddenly silent as if it had cut out.

Archer forced his eyes to stay open, repeating over and over in his thick skull that this was normal. Just starting the descent. Totally normal.

Lana put her book away and buckled her seatbelt. She looked at him like she was about to say something, but she must have seen his bunny-frightened eyes or his pasty complexion, and slipped her hand into his.

Fuck. Tight landings were always the worst. His stomach rolled, shoving bile up into his throat.

Closing his eyes, he breathed forcefully in through his nose and mouth. Silently at his side, Lana squeezed his hand.

Opening his eyes, he turned to face her.

Rather than finding her amused, she looked sympathetic, her lips turned down.

He must look as pitiful as he felt. "Hate this part," he grumbled.

"Astrid always gets seasick, carsick, airsick. And we don't… get sick easily."

Entranced, he held her gaze and the steadiness in there. "My very first landing in a combat zone, and there was unexpected ice overnight. The pilot got food poisoning or something and puked all over the cockpit, so the copilot was gagging and trying to hold his shit together, losing his lunch as we touched down onto a mess of an airstrip. Total cluster." He swallowed the burning in his throat and bit his tongue.

"CO was pissed. Took weeks to repair the plane, how remote we were."

"How about repairing the troops that were inside?"

"My hip still cracks and locks if I sit still for too long, but nothing serious."

"First big fight I was in, this… big bad dude… he was a lot faster than he looked. Took a chunk out of my neck."

He brushed her hair out of the way where she pointed, but not a trace of a scar. "Healed nicely."

"I heal well."

Lingering with his hand on her skin longer than he should, he traced where the scar should be before pulling away. "Bet it hurt."

"Like fire. My dad was pissed that I hadn't been paying enough attention."

"He's… like you?"

"Yeah. Trained me from birth, so you can imagine how disappointed he was when I almost got myself killed my first time out."

"He wasn't mad, he was scared."

Silence echoed from the engine as the pilot seemed to cut off power completely and the plane felt like it had stalled in midair. Archer repeated to himself the ground was right below them. Eyes sealing shut again, he gritted his teeth and faced forward.

Lana whispered in his ear, the heat of her breath dancing over his skin and tickling at his neck. With an amused lilt, she asked, "How was your first time? Did it hurt?"

Arousal spiked a rapid, fiery swelling in his groin. He bit his lip to tame the devious grin.

"Your first skirmish. You've got a dirty mind, Major."

Laughing under his breath, he hardly noticed as the jet slammed into the ground, the brakes clenching down hard, the Echos jolting forward from the rapid deceleration. "Only my broken heart," he murmured.

Within seconds, the oversized jet came to a halt, the passengers heaving forward. Anticipating the abrupt stop, he caught his hand on the seat in front of him so he didn't knock his head.

Leaping to their feet, the Echos scooped up gear and headed for the SUVs. Lips pulled tight, Kerse nodded. "Depart 0500 tomorrow?"

He nodded. "I want to be on the road at first light. For today, I'll make the arrangements so we can meet with anyone that was near that canyon." His stomach rolled as he imagined how much shit could go wrong just getting to the canyon. He looked at Lana and said, "Our route sucks, between here and the COP, but this is where the surviving Rangers went before heading home, so we start here. Things are really fucking hot all around here, so we'll have to drive through hell tomorrow."

"Will we get a view of the canyon before heading into town?"

"From a distance, yeah, so you can get a feel for it. We're not getting close again until we know exactly what we're up against."

Sauer followed behind Kerse and they loaded up their rig.

Chan stopped at their row and checked out Lana in the uniform. "I know Archer seems to think you're capable on your own, but stay with us at all times. This is our world."

Shoulders back, Lana delivered a practiced salute and answered, "Yes, Ma'am."

Flashing Archer a wink, Chan grinned, "Nicely done. Although, Lana, don't forget to check rank."

"It's alright," Archer answered way too quickly. "Trust me, she'll be able to fit in."

Moving in behind Chan, Walker laughed, and his amusement echoed across the fuselage. "She's a natural Echo. We're good. Besides, this way Archer can... keep an eye on her."

Archer tried to defend himself, but realized it was pointless. He'd claim he could stop drooling over her any time he wanted, but they wouldn't believe him... and they'd be right. The night he'd met Lana, the squad had tried to convince him to come out to one of the bars next to the base, and he had little doubt they'd been planning to set him up. Again.

Joke was on them. He was caught hook, line, and sinker. If Noah was doing a sort-of-posthumous setup, another Echo on his ass...

Shaking her head, Chan knocked him in the shoulder and said, "Brock always bunks with you anyway. At least this one probably doesn't snore."

Turning to face him, Lana grinned up at him, that devilish amusement rich in her expression. "Hey, roomie."

Chan stood to the side and waved Walker by, but she held fast. She rolled her eyes and gave Lana a look. "Do you mind if I have a quick word in private with my superior here?"

"Of course," Lana answered and strolled to the front SUV and climbed in the passenger seat.

Fuck. He knew what she was going to say. "I swear, she's only here because—"

"Don't," Chan warned. "We know you better than that. If any of us thought for one minute that you'd brought her along solely because you had a little crush, we wouldn't have gone along with this. There's something different about her. I know you won't say why you think she can help, but she's more than a consultant. Do me a favor?"

Hand stuffed in his pockets, he cringed and said, "I won't fuck up the op by getting involved."

Leaning against the back of the seat in the row ahead, she crossed her arms and laughed. "No one would ever accuse you of letting your dick do any thinking for you. What I was going to say, is, we've all been talking, and we agree—even Kerse—that it's time you let your dick do a little thinking."

Fuck, he needed to get out more, if his entire squad conspired to take control of his sex life. "My dick doesn't take orders from you guys."

Walker stood at his other side and knocked him in the shoulder. "But it could absolutely stand at attention for that one."

Chan agreed. "She's perfect for you."

"I'd say she's a mile and a half beyond my league."

Walker nudged him and backed toward his SUV. "Further. But she's hot, it's obvious she wants you, and even more obvious that you're a puppy at her heels. Plus, you've got easy access, and you could use any head start you can get."

A pained eye-roll blurred his vision, and he pouted under his breath. "I can't believe we're having this conversation. I do date, you know."

With a final wide-armed shrug, Walker said loud enough for Lana to hear, "Yeah? When was the last time you got your play?"

"Fuck. I'm fine—"

Chan nudged his side, "It's not that complicated. You're lonely."

"I don't have time to be lonely."

"Even worse."

He looked inside the SUV to see Lana adjusting the passenger seat to her liking. "We're working. We don't have time for this shit. See you at chow," he said crisply and squared his shoulders.

Rolling her eyes, Chan saluted and muttered, "Case in point."

He climbed into the SUV with Lana and crashed his head on the steering wheel.

"Good conversation?" Lana asked cheerfully.

He glanced her way and took his time buckling.

"What?" she laughed.

"Nothing," he groaned.

"You're blushing. What did they say?" Lana was enjoying this way too much. As his entire squad seemed to be doing. They weren't wrong, but he sucked at this sort of thing.

Biting his tongue, he fired up the engine. He rested his hand on the back of her seat and backed down the ramp, then flipped a quick turn and drove into the motor pool. She didn't say a word, but watched so closely he figured she'd already read his mind.

Finally, he let out a controlled exhale and checked his words, finally landing on, "Let's go."

DECKED OUT IN HER military finest, Lana straightened the jacket and wiggled her ankles in the leather boots. She knew it took moving mountains to update anything about military uniforms, but come on, the fabric was stiff and unforgiving. It made sense to keep the pants tucked into boots, but they bunched funny. There must be an art to making this comfortable.

Strolling up behind her, Archer shifted his pack over his shoulder and pointed to a building in the center of the small base. "I need to check in with the CO at the TOC. Chow in ten; mind saving me a seat?"

She giggled out loud, then quickly covered her response to avoid attracting attention. "I have no idea what you just said."

He nodded to the Echos and said, "Just stick with the squad and try to blend in."

The rest of the squad was already heading into a screened-off shanty, blending in with the troops already stationed here. "This isn't like any base I've seen on the news," Lana said. The place was a lot smaller than she had imagined.

"Nope," he agreed. "Too close to the front lines. No entertainment, no celebrities at an FOB. They allow occasional press, but this is mostly a central staging area before deploying to forward ops."

Mostly clustered tents and plywood structures, with a crumbling stone building at the edge, the base looked slapped together with whatever was conveniently nearby or was easy to put up and take down. Thick, makeshift fences surrounded the base in a serpentine pattern, built from interlaced fencing filled with rocks that looked to be from a nearby quarry. In the corners and scattered throughout, plywood towers guarded the base.

"How many soldiers are stationed here at a time?"

"Few hundred, tops."

He reached for her bag and nodded, "I'll drop our gear in the tent. I arranged for about as private of quarters as it's going to get around here. You'll see why the guys were messing with me about our sleeping arrangements. You'd better not snore as loud as Brock."

As she entered the chow hall, a cluster of babies, or so they looked it for how young they were, stood tall and saluted. These troops couldn't have been in long. She quickly remembered her brief training on protocols, then escaped to the tables and parked with the rest of Echo in the isolated corner. Four others were the first through the chow line, dressed in all black, out of uniform, looking completely out of place. "Who are those guys?" Lana whispered to Chan.

"CIA."

"Oh." She hadn't realized CIA spent much time on military bases. "That's why Archer said you guys sometimes pose as CIA."

Sauer spoke low across the table. "They can blend in like the best of them when they need to, but those guys are just passing through and don't give a rat's ass. But, as we don't exist, *we* are attempting to blend in."

"Rangers, right?"

"That's usually the cover. Sometimes we're engineers, other times, we're civilian contractors. Depends on the op."

Kerse folded her arms over her chest and nodded. "Which is why I'm trying to figure you out. Archer doesn't exactly spill state secrets, even for a booty call."

Walker knocked Kerse in the ribs with an elbow.

Folding her arms under her chest, Lana shook her head. "No, it's okay. I'd question me too. But you'll have to keep on waiting for an answer to that one. You know," Lana looked around and watched as more troops filtered in. "I've fought across the globe in all sorts of terrain, differing cultures and languages. Spent some time on a Coast Guard vessel a few years back. *This* is culture shock."

Chan chuckled and popped to her feet. "Be prepared for some gourmet fare then," she teased and motioned for her to join them.

At the line, she grabbed two trays, not seeing a sign of Archer yet. Chan cleared her throat behind her, and the others all grinned at each other. Setup was written all over this. And they seemed so pleased with their progress. Maybe even Kerse, her sneer belied by a dimple burrowed into her cheek.

"You know," Lana said as she scooped spaghetti onto her plate and then onto Archer's, "I'm not sure what you're hoping for. My family regularly tries to match me with guys they think are perfect for me. I can smell a setup a mile away."

Walker grinned even wider. "At least one of you can. The guy's dense. You've got to be obvious."

"I don't play coy." She shrugged and kept moving through the line. "But I also don't want to hurt anyone."

Traversing through the ravenous diners, Lana followed the others and slid the trays down, glancing back to the entrance just as Archer strolled in like he was a regular diner here. No, he wasn't dense, nor was he shy. He was picky. And didn't seem to realize that he was irresistible.

He slid into the spot next to her and dove into his meal. "I told the CO we're investigating the canyon attacks, so they're expecting us to ask a lot of questions. I've got a list of names, and he'll work on setting up meetings for us."

"Any updates on the possibility of an airstrike?" Chan asked.

"Nope, and he is not thrilled that investigators are here—us. Morale is low enough right now. Too many losses thanks to that canyon, one crackpot planning an airstrike, and now we've got some lieutenant colonel vying for promotion points and thinking he can get a special ops team up and over the escarpment. Jameson's trying to buy us time."

Sauer growled under his breath, "I don't give a damn how we get the upper hand, but we don't need any more body bags around here."

Kerse set her fork on her plate and gritted her teeth. "Scrap the canyon. It would be a death trap even without whatever's haunting it. *We* can scale the escarpment."

"And be easy pickings for the insurgents as we stroll across barren land right into their backyard?" Walker grumbled. "Count me out."

At her side, Archer ate in silence, watching the others. They all knew the risks of even attempting to climb up and over, and the danger of the canyon. It was a no win. Which was why Echo was involved to begin with. Lana could relate. Her own team tended to operate under similar circumstances. The ones to send in when there were no options.

They ate dinner quietly once the surrounding tables started to fill up. More, they all knew it was up to them to solve this, or the death toll would rise.

10

Night enveloped the base as they stepped into the darkness. The CO had offered up space in the TOC for him to interview witnesses, but Archer had moved it to a quiet rec tent and hoarded some snacks from the chow hall.

Rather than one-on-one, they'd brought in a few friends in at a time, so they'd get to chatting and reminding each other of details some may have missed. Lana had to admit, Archer turned what could have been another cold report into a casual, almost therapeutic break. Not to mention, he'd laid it out to all that nothing would be documented, so they felt free to admit to the crazy stuff they'd felt.

In the middle of the open, not a soul left to interview, Archer bit his cheek and dropped his hands to his hips. "We need to eliminate this thing before the rumors get worse. These troops are broken from even being in its vicinity."

Lana stood at his side and looked up into the murky sky. "They're rightly shaken. Even those who were nearby saw nothing more than the blur, heard nothing more than screams, but everyone seemed to think this wasn't the insurgents."

Archer buried his face in his hands and rubbed his eyes, then motioned for her to walk with him. "I can't even imagine. Even lookouts from half a mile off felt a foreboding hum in the air. Connery and Simmons were messed up after losing their squad to this thing."

Biting her tongue, Lana wished she could tell him how right he was, and how far they'd gone to try to make it right. Even the demon world had basic laws of nature, which they'd violated violently after experiencing the impassability of this canyon. Noah would never get over it, spending the rest of his life hiding away from humans, coming around only because his family made him.

As they neared one of a hundred matching tents on the edge of the barracks, Archer nodded to the entrance. "This is us."

"Cozy," she said. "Is there someplace I can shower first? Or I can wait until morning. I just want to avoid the rush."

"You're better off waiting until we get to town."

"Are you kidding? That could be days."

He shrugged outside their tent door, a *your-funeral* smirk playing at the corners of his lips.

"What?" She laughed suspiciously, hovering in front of him, keeping her hands to herself while they were in sight, in case anyone strolled by.

"You want a shower? You can have a shower. I'll stand guard."

"Maybe you stink, and I'm trying to hint that you're the one who needs a shower." She winked and ducked into the tent.

As he followed her inside, he dramatically sniffed his pits and winked. "I smell like rose petals."

"Hey, I've been out on enough missions with zero plumbing, not even a river. I can go days without food or water—not that I like to—but I really hate skipping a shower if I don't have to."

"Fine. Grab your shit, and I'll de-stink too."

Gear piled in their arms, they traipsed through the silent base until they reached a cardboard sign that was posted outside the showers. "Enter at your own RISK."

Beneath the ominous message, a slightly more official looking sign indicated it was vacant.

Lana slipped around Archer and immediately realized why he wasn't keen on showering here.

Three stalls were partitioned off with flimsy scrap metal half-walls. Steel barrels were hung inverted, with rickety faucets dangling overhead, and only one seemed to be attached properly.

"I've seen worse," she said with a shrug.

Archer scowled at the broken tanks and shook his head. He righted the one that wasn't marked off by comedically webbed hazard tape and clicked something under the shower. Without a word, he moved to the sink and loaded minty paste over his toothbrush.

Parking next to him, Lana brushed her teeth and then stacked her shampoo, conditioner, and soap onto the teetering plastic stool in the shower stall.

"I won't look," Archer said as he flicked on the water and added, "But be quick."

Before he could turn away, Lana peeled off her top and tossed it at him, covered from the shoulders down by the flimsy partition. Reflexively, he looked up at the ceiling and bit his lips together.

She laughed and said, "I'll save you some hot water."

Archer muttered, "Don't bother," as he kept his gaze widely averted and set her clothes on the "out-of-order" third sink.

Easing her head into the water, she soaked the waves that had begun to rebel after the long day of travel.

He slipped out of his jacket and added it to her pile, then unlaced his boots.

"Three more minutes," Archer rumbled.

"Until?"

"If you're lucky. Maybe two. Then you're out of hot water."

She rinsed the shampoo as she scrubbed her body, quickly combing the conditioner through her travel-mussed hair before the shampoo was even half rinsed. "I'm hurrying. You should join me in here, so you can get a hot shower."

Groaning, he exhaled and stripped off his pants and stood in a t-shirt and black slick boxer briefs, then moved to lean his back against her shower stall. He kept his gaze trained down at his bare toes and finally answered in a gravelly voice, "No thanks."

Unable to resist, Lana tilted her hands in the spray and aimed, knocking him in the back of the head with a mini deluge.

Whipping his head around, his eyes were wide, and his smile hovered between horrified and shocked.

Lana hummed as she tipped her head back and rinsed.

Grin turning into a playful smirk, Archer subtly reached around, and she could just make out the creak of a nob as he flipped her water to freezing.

Lana gritted her teeth and clamped down, pretending the temperature was bearable. Cold wasn't pleasant, but she could handle it. Better than that damn desert heat he lived in. "Nice try," she calmly said as she rinsed the last of the suds.

"No way." He peeled his shirt over his head.

Watching over the partition, Lana lost her voice—at the yummy vision more than at the shock of the temperature. He was... yeah. Lickable.

"Better hurry. There's actually still quite a bit of warm water."

Not a trace of the bashfulness she'd expected, Archer stripped the rest of the way in half a second, covering the goods at the last moment with his towel.

Icy cold water rushed over her skin, but it seemed to turn to steam on impact, thanks to the heat fueling through her at the vision of Archer in nothing but a towel and a shy, lopsided grin.

Rock-hard everything under smooth skin, he looked more like a hybrid, like her teammates and werewolf friends, rather than full human.

Lana stepped out of the water and secured her towel before coming around the partition. She gave Archer a saucy wink and strolled out.

"There should be some hot water left for you," she murmured as she passed inches away, looking up and teasing her lower lip between her teeth, adding an unconscious catch to her breath as she followed the movements of his lips.

"Thanks," he groaned, watching her while he closed himself in and hung his towel over the partition.

She watched as he stepped into the water, still dreamy eyed...

"You fucking bitch," he yelped, and leaped out of the spray with his hands guarded his over his package—or so she assumed, judging by the posture and the string of expletives.

"You can borrow my soap," she said carelessly as she strolled to the sink and checked to see how many eyebrow hairs had sprouted since she'd last plucked.

Leaning in, she frowned and realized she'd forgotten her tweezers.

Freezing water blasted across the bathroom and nailed her in the back. Mouth open in shock, she looked over to see Archer had already flipped the water back down and was scrubbing his hair, still grinning at his success.

Lana waited until Archer scrubbed the soap over his face and turned into the spray to rinse.

She snagged his towel from the partition and returned to the sink. Smug and grinning, she waited for him to notice.

Would she be treated to that arrogant, shy smile again?

She pulled on her clothes, only slightly damp with splatters, then leaned back to wait.

Archer flipped off the water and looked for his towel. He parked his tongue between his teeth and shook his head, but that grin gave him away. "Touché," he muttered, then flicked a look over at her, snarky and flirty over the sweet shyness. "You going to give me my towel, or ransom for a look at my dick?"

Lana laughed out loud, her tummy warm and fuzzy. "I figured you were going to blush and come out here with your hands covering the boys."

"If you're that desperate for a show, I'm happy to help." He folded his arms over his chest and looked around. "But I'd rather get naked together when we can do something about it."

She walked close and handed the towel over, doing her damnedest to not step close enough to get the full view. "Is that a promise?"

Reaching, sliding the towel out of her hands, he winked. For someone who claimed he wasn't adept at flirting, he easily stayed one step ahead of her.

Archer's lips were still blue from the freezing shower by the time they got back to their tent. "Eighty degrees today, but somehow that water seems to hang out at thirty-three degrees year-round."

The tent wasn't at all what she'd pictured, and certainly not what she saw on the news or in movies. No lines of bunk beds or rickety cots. Instead, there were two sturdy cots spaced a few feet apart. In a nod to daily function, there was a small table with a task lamp, and two lightly padded chairs. Some of the other tents were larger to hold more troops, but the smaller ones at the edge of the living quarters must be designed for brief lodging. An electric light hung overhead, just bright enough for changing, but not enough to read by.

Lana dropped onto her cot and scrunched her hair in the towel. "I told you to shower first. The cold doesn't bother me."

"That's the thanks I get for a little chivalry?" he muttered lightly as he tossed his bedroll onto his cot.

Lana stepped in front of him and rose to her tippy toes. "Thank you for risking your comfort for mine."

He leaned in to kiss her, but halted a breath away, biting the edge of his lip instead. Standing tall, he softened his look. "Thank you for being so understanding today. We talked to a lot of troops with some bad nightmares. I don't think I've said it, and I should have. That canyon is more than we can handle alone. Whatever you can do to help, I'm grateful."

Resting her hand on his chest, Lana watched as he switched from flirtatious to serious in a blink. "There's not a lot of thanks in my line of work. It's nice to hear. And, really, for all of my pushiness, thanks for looping in my team. I know trusting civilians with something this big is a huge risk for you. For your career."

Lana waited until he was settled and clicked off the light. Sleep didn't come easy on a mission anyway, especially when she didn't have her team around to back her up.

Archer unsettled her for entirely different reasons.

She laid her bedroll out on the empty cot. The cots were only two feet apart, maybe less. Too close.

He had borrowed her shampoo, the familiar coconut-lavender an enticing contrast from his natural, more rugged scent. Yeah, she said it. Rugged and yummy and adorable. An epic badass, but also goofy and self-effacing, and she had enjoyed discovering his sweetly sentimental streak.

And apparently, he was a great sleeper. Within three minutes, his head was cushioned on his bent arm, his cheeks were lax, and his lips were slightly parted. The dark shadow of beard was sharper in the hazily filtered light from outside. Blanket barely covering his waist, a light sheen of sweat from the humid air coating his skin, he had defrosted well after the shower. From the desert, he was probably much better acclimated to the summer heat than she was.

Lana slipped off her stiff Army attire, leaving on just her panties and a light tank top to combat the heat... but left on a layer of fabric to protect her from temptation. Sneaking to avoid waking Archer, she quietly curled into her bedroll and rolled to face him. So relaxed, like he didn't have the weight of the world on his shoulders.

The corner of his lips turned up, and he murmured, "You going to watch me sleep all night?"

"I'm considering it."

He opened his eyes and reached across the divide. Hooking his hand over the edge of her cot, he dragged her bed across the divide until it touched his. Lana may have sighed out loud. It couldn't be helped. Some things were swoon-worthy. The man was sculpted brilliantly, and the movement put his stacked arm and shoulder gratuitously on display.

As the cots collided, he rolled her away from him and tucked her backside against his front. "Now sit still and go to sleep."

"I can hear you smiling," she teased, nuzzling in tight.

Breath warm and tickling her hair, he softly kissed behind her ear.

Turning in his arms, Lana leaned in to kiss him, but he pulled away.

"Not yet."

"What do you mean *not yet*? It's perfect timing. We've had our first date, we're on our first trip, we've seen each other mostly naked, and now we're snuggling."

"Yeah, but I'm too sleepy to make it a memorable first kiss. So not yet."

"You just kissed me."

"I mean a real one. On the lips with tongue and all that good stuff. The memorable kind."

Nuzzling in, Lana pressed her lips to his neck, scraping her teeth over his Adam's apple, trailing her tongue along his collarbone, then kissed him long and slow in the hollow of his neck. The potent heat radiating off of him stirred her beyond reason. "This isn't memorable?"

Archer laced his hand around her waist and flipped her underneath him on his cot. The rush of the movement, of the strength and ease of it, set her pulse racing.

Sliding the strap of her top off her shoulder, he trailed a river of kisses along her shoulder, gliding his tongue over the ridge of her collarbone. With one finger, he pulled down the center of her top and touched his lips to the center of her sternum.

Mouth soft and warm and achingly close her breasts, he was going to drive her out of her mind.

Thick heat wafted from the contact, and she arched into him, silently begging for more.

"Memorable, yes. But think about your first kiss," he whispered against her skin, his dark lashes shading his eyes.

"Ivar Sanderssen, in the back seat of his parents' car. He was a terrible kisser. But so was I."

Archer nipped the edge of her breast through the jersey fabric and laughed under his breath. "I said think about it, don't tell me about it."

"Just saying. First kisses aren't necessarily good."

"But was it a good memory?"

"Yes, actually."

Scooping her breasts out from her top, Archer encircled both in his hands and teased his thumbs over the tips. "But do you remember the first time a guy kissed your tits?"

She laughed out loud and arched into him.

He grinned and took her deep in his mouth, suckling until her laugh turned into a gasp, and she couldn't remember what he'd asked. Liquid heat rushed under her skin and she felt nothing but his mouth on her skin.

"Do you?" he asked again.

Voice raspy as she tried to focus, she said, "No. I confess, I don't."

He laved before taking her into his mouth again, cupping her other in his hand. Back arched as she rose into his touch, her breath caught, and she whimpered in sharp, desperate pants.

"See my point?" His clever tongue teased at the adventurous and dedicated lover he would be, and that the shyness had nothing to do with his confidence in his abilities.

She bit her lower lip and grinned, asking, "Is this a thing you do, saving up for the big first kiss? Do you normally steal second before you've even hit the ball?"

"This might be a first." He took one last, long lick, flicked each nipple with the tip of his tongue, then slid her top back up, finally tucking her in against him again. Spooning snug together on his cot, he nuzzled against her neck and whispered, "Get some sleep."

"There's a lot we can do that wouldn't involve kissing."

"I don't pack condoms on deployments."

"Coincidentally, I can't contract or pass diseases, and I'm not in a fertile window, so no condom needed. Sex isn't kissing."

"Go to sleep, Lana," he grumbled, but the laugh in his voice tickled over her.

"Yes, Major."

He pinched her side. "Careful or I'll write you up for insubordination."

"I fully intend to follow that order."

"I can't picture you following orders well."

"I don't. Goodnight, Major Belak."

"'Night Lana Fischer, mystery super-powered woman."

She settled in, melting into him, comfortable despite the lack of space, unable to sprawl out as she normally would. Eventually, she'd need to stretch her legs, but the indulgence was worth it. Her eyes fluttered shut, and her breathing slowed to match his.

After sleep had encased them in a peaceful cocoon, the stillness of the night was shattered by a tremble in the ground. Clusters of explosions in drew closer like a thunderstorm over the ocean.

"Archer?"

Voice rumbly with sleep, he murmured, "It's a few miles off. They'll alarm if we need to do anything."

"Are you sure?"

He chuckled, the vibration soothing her back to sleep. "I'm sure. We've got a few hours left. Tomorrow's going to be a long day."

11

With a pair of coffees in standard white, mass-produced mugs in her hands, Lana eased back into the tent and found Archer just as she'd left him. With the crook of his arm serving as a pillow, his expression was soft and sleepy and innocent. But that rough edge of beard, the angle of that jaw, and the dog-tag chain snaking over his bare chest... she wanted to ditch the coffees and the mission and snuggle another hour with him.

She lowered onto her cot and faced him. Okay, so he might be onto something about holding off on that kiss. Not that she'd ever waited, on the kissing or any of the rest of it.

But those lips were absolutely worth waiting for, as she'd discovered last night. Not rushed. Soft when he needed to be soft. Rough when she needed the tension. He knew how to use that mouth.

"Good morning, Major," she whispered.

He shuddered, but didn't do more than stir.

"Since there aren't many troops out yet, still dark and all, I wanted to be quick, so I snuck out in my bare feet to grab us some coffees. I'm sure no one noticed. Some fancy looking guy, General somebody, he gave me the evil eye, but—"

The corners of Archer's lips edged up, a chuckle vibrating his shoulders.

"Really, I don't think he even noticed. He was wearing pink fuzzy slippers anyway. It is early, and we all need that caffeine fix when the sun is still in bed."

"You are so full of shit," he murmured, finally opening his eyes, knocking her on her ass with the dreamy, wicked gleam.

Donning a jaunty grin, she extended his coffee. The blanket—woobie, as he'd called it—dropped to his waist and gave her a full view of yummy. Biting her lips together, she didn't hide her perusal.

He didn't disappoint, and his grin warmed his blush.

Fingertips grazing over hers, he watched her as he took the cup and sipped, the steam curling around his face. "We can grab some breakfast for the road."

"Step ahead of you," she said, winking through the steam. "I ran into Kerse, and although she didn't appear enthusiastic about assisting me in my foraging venture, she escorted me to the kitchen, and we packed a traveling feast. She even laughed at one of my dumb jokes."

"You are hard to resist."

She nudged him gently and grinned over the rim of her mug. "I need to contact my team to set up the rendezvous."

"Agreed," he murmured, savoring an unhurried sip.

"Do you have any suggestions on that? No cell service. Is there a secured landline? They don't tap the phones, do they?"

He nodded to his pack. "Scrambled sat phone. Front pocket."

Lana pulled the sturdy thing from his pack and dropped back to her cot. These dang military jackets were so restricting. She slipped out of the stiff outer layer and adjusted the black undershirt.

Archer took the phone and punched in an access code, then handed it back. He rose to his feet, his hip clunking for no more than a step or two—imperceptible if you didn't know it was a problem—then pulled a fresh set of clothes from his pack.

That man was a sight. Taller than average, but not so tall she couldn't wrap her arms around him and tug him down for that eventual first kiss. But absolutely more toned than average. Sculpted. Stacked. No... swole? That was it. Newly added to her vocabulary, she had no idea where the term originated, but she liked it. Sounded less urban dictionary and more Middle English, so she was going with it.

And it suited. He belonged on a calendar with the sleek briefs and dog tags. And nothing else.

Okay, or maybe with the unbuttoned camo pants.

"You going to make the call?" He turned and raised an eyebrow.

She winked and sported a wanton grin. "Working on it. Quit distracting me." Enjoying his smug return wink, she finally punched in Quinn's number, but didn't need her eyes for the call, watching as he tugged his black tee over the delectable abs.

"News?"

"And hello to you too," Lana rolled her eyes.

"Sorry. I was attempting to make chocolate chip cookies using the recipe I stole from Astrid that she got from Molly, but apparently, I cannot bake."

"Pity. I love chocolate chip."

"Yeah, well, we'll leave it to Astrid. Mine are oddly burnt and undercooked simultaneously."

Holding her hand over the receiver, she asked Archer, "Hey, do you cook?"

"I'm an awesome cook."

"Just checking."

"That was highly suspect. Did you just ask a man if he could cook?"

"I certainly did. Archer is withholding kissing, so I may keep have to keep him around long enough for a few sleepovers once we get back to the states."

Archer took a long, pained exhale and shook his head.

On the other end of the line, she heard Ryan asking, "Already?"

Quinn shushed him and said to Lana, "As I meet so few of the men you date, I'm looking forward to actually getting to know this one."

"You sound like my dad."

"Hey, no pressure, I just haven't heard you interested enough to know if a man cooks before, so I'm curious." Quinn's tone was light, but Lana didn't miss the eagerness she tried to downplay.

"It's an honest question," Lana said, as if it were entirely commonplace to ask a man she'd made out with the night before if he could cook. She covered the mic again, knowing damn well it didn't do more than muffle, and said, "I'm a good cook, by the way."

Archer laughed quietly and shook his head, the grin lingering while he stuffed his feet into his boots and started lacing.

"She makes a kickass seafood stew," Quinn said loudly, and Archer's grin widened. "Anyway, we haven't found squat on blurs of any sort, nothing like what Archer or Noah described, and no mention of anything active that region."

"Damn. Okay. Meet us at the hotel. I'll send you coordinates, and we'll head to the COP once we're all together."

"COP? You're sounding very military already."

"Aren't I? Combat Outpost, I think," Lana said, glancing at Archer with a questioning smile.

Archer nodded a sweet affirmation, with a hint of something hungrier laced in the look.

Lana continued, "Anyway, it's the closest we can get to the canyon and has bare bones staffing. We'll snoop around town and see if the locals know anything." Lana strolled close and leaned up, hoping to steal a nibble of those lips.

Shaking his head, he backed up and winked. Brat.

"Perfect. We're grabbing some more research material, and Bodie's going to ask some of his relatives if they've heard of anything like this. Bennett will bring texts from his parents' library that might help."

"Astrid will be so bummed to miss out. She loves research sessions and stacks of old books." Astrid never missed anything. She'd research from her end, but it wasn't the same. Lana was bummed her friend wouldn't be out on this one, but little Isla was pretty dang cute and would grow up to be a badass demon hunter and werewolf, the first of her kind.

"She's having a tough time, but I reminded her it's just a few months out of a few hundred years, so stop worrying."

"I'll send our hotel info when we get there. Keep me posted. There will be cell service in town."

"It's a date."

"SMARTASS," ARCHER MUTTERED OVER the radio. Ahead, the sky was as densely gray as the rocky terrain. Trees and vegetation thinned with each passing mile, until he felt like they'd been transported to a barren wasteland that starkly declared this territory wasn't hospitable.

Sauer fired back from his position at the front of the caravan, his voice even raspier thanks to the static, "Brock is going to be pissed when he finds out Lana didn't just steal his spot on the squad and his snuggle-buddy, too."

Chan's knee-slapping laugh was audible over the radio as she added her piece, "Aw, Archer, I didn't know you and Brock snuggled."

Archer cringed. "Fuck off. Brock isn't here to be able to defend my irresistible cuddliness." It helped to keep it light, but while he messed with the others, he scanned the horizon, every puff of dust a possible unfriendly patrolling the area. The FOB CO had tried to warn him to take the long way around. A convoy had passed through here a few days back and got caught in an ambush as the insurgents grew bolder.

Whatever Lana was, he hoped to hell laying eyes on the canyon would stir something. Desperate times and all that.

Raising an eyebrow, Lana riled him as bad as the others. "Your friends are... sweet."

"Sweet, ha." He rolled his eyes and clicked the mic off. "I'm not sure anyone in history has ever referred to this bunch as sweet."

The clouds were thick, casting murky shadows on a sea of gray rock outcrops. One minute the sun could be shining and a daisy could peek out from a crack in the ground, the next the wind could gust through with golf-ball sized hail pummeling the ground in a deafening roar, visibility reduced to zilch, and then the ground seemed to swallow it all and nothing dared move again. Unforgiving terrain with sharp slopes prone to rockfalls and an unsettled mass of loose shale and dust made the drive interesting.

Archer said into the com, "Pull over here. We should be able to see the canyon from the top of that peak."

"I'm not climbing that shit," Walker squeaked over the airwaves.

"Come on, just like Prominent Point back in Tucson. This can't be more than a 5.13 R."

"One solid vertical crux," Chan muttered.

Lana looked out her window, nodding appreciatively. "I see why he'd rather keep his feet on the ground."

"I still don't trust you to choose our day trips after that one," Sauer rumbled, muttering further, "Fun, my ass."

One by one, the caravan stopped in the middle of the deserted road. Sauer and Chan popped out of the roofs of their SUVs and took guard positions. The matte black, dusty, scuffed-with-age finish on the rigs Chan had come up with blended perfectly with the terrain.

Hand already on the door and ready to go, Lana grinned as she looked up at the cliff. Archer stopped her and pulled a pair of helmets from behind the seats. She looked at him like he was nuts and raised an eyebrow.

"Please," he said, brushing her bangs off her forehead before setting the helmet onto her head. Quietly trusting him, she studied him as he gingerly hooked the chinstrap and secured it, lingering longer than he should.

Parking his tongue between his teeth to tame his dopey grin, he quickly snapped on his own helmet. Unable to look away from Lana, he felt her fascination coat him like the desert sun. He secured his earpiece then pulled on his vest, motioning for Lana to tighten hers, then asked the others, "All clear?"

Chan answered back, "Clear. Go check it out."

Confidence in every step, Lana seemed to take in her complete surroundings with little more than a glance. She strolled straight up the crumbling talus and didn't slow at the base of the rock face, but leaped and grabbed hold of a jug seven feet up with one hand and swung her body, hooking her fingers into a crack and wedging her feet into another. Watching her free climb the thing like a pro athlete, Kerse and Walker's jaws dropped.

Stone-face stunned, Kerse muttered, "Where did you find this thing?"

"Classified," he said, then followed the path Lana had taken.

He reached the top a few moments after Lana and steadied himself on the narrow ledge before taking in the bleak horizon. Standing close behind her on the peak, he wrapped his arm around her waist, finding the height wasn't so intimidating joined together, and pointed to the edge of the horizon.

"Looks perfectly ordinary," she said, a lilt of disappointment laced in her tone.

As he'd shown her in the sketch, the highland and lowland were sharply divided by a cliff that ran for miles, the only division in the stark wall of the canyon in question, which looked to be little more than a notch in an unshakable wall from their perch. Land as gray as the clouds, the earth and sky merged, the horizon imperceptible. "Even up close, it seems fine, and then you think you should put your glasses on to clear the picture or something."

"I'd almost call it a gully or small valley, for how it seems to flow with the terrain, like a river carved it out, but it doesn't look natural. The sinuosity is wrong, the elevation changes are odd."

"Up close, the incline up the hillside is terraced, so it seems more gradual, but in the canyon itself, the walls are about ninety degrees, or more, in places. A mountain goat, or even you, I suppose, wouldn't be able to scale it." He huffed a long breath and scanned the horizon, the canyon, trying to see it with fresh eyes. "It looks more like a tear in the terrain."

Lana's shoulders slumped, and she leaned into him. "Fuck. That's what I was afraid of. There's no back door to get to this thing, is there? I hate strolling right up to a demon's front door and knocking politely."

"Demon?" he asked, hoping to hell she was using another vague metaphor. A chill crawled up his spine when he saw the ferocity in her expression as she calculated.

12

"WE NEED TO GET closer." She scowled and wrapped her hands over his, securing his grip tighter around her middle. "The geology makes sense as a tear, but… It's almost like I should look right past it, as if it's camouflaged. How does it make that blur, the heat? How much is a façade and how much is conjured or tangible? Is the fist thing an offensive or defensive move?"

Heart skipping a beat in his chest, he repeated her words in his mind, questions so far outside of this reality. The casualness of her tone, the abilities she'd hinted at, he got the feeling his understanding of this fucked-up-op barely scratched the surface. "Want to run that by me again?"

She turned and looked up at him. Dead serious, her jaw gritted tight, she held his gaze. "This is definitely in my area, but I don't think it's anything I've fought before." Lana bit her lips together and took a controlled inhale.

After one last look at the canyon, she released him and started the climb down.

His radio blew up in his ear. "Unfriendlies. Get your asses on the ground. Now."

"Move," he shouted to Lana.

Too fucking late. Cracking the air, echoing from rock to rock, machine gun fire blasted from a cluster of trucks rumbling their way. Fragments of rock went flying as bullets sent rocky shrapnel raining to the ground below.

Lana let go and dropped thirty feet down, landing on her feet, ready to fight.

While he hauled ass down the cliff to join her, Chan and Sauer blasted back from their positions in the sunroofs. Kerse ducked behind a boulder and aimed her sniper rifle, firing, shifting her aim swiftly, and firing again, taking them out one by one.

Walker took Lana by the elbow and tugged her behind a boulder. In his peripheral, Archer watched Lana pull a pair of throwing knives from her boots. She brushed past a frantic Walker and ducked from boulder to boulder as she made her way closer to the fight.

Five hollowed-out trucks bounced along the path toward them, a dozen and a half insurgents showering them in a blanket of lethal chaos.

Nearing the bottom, Archer dropped and hit the ground running, pulling out his sidearm and sprinting to reach Lana.

Walker hissed as Archer tore past, "I tried to stop her."

He reached Lana as she halted behind a boulder closer to the road.

Skilled marksmen, his squad had already taken out half, dodging hit after hit themselves. Sauer popped out the sunroof SUV with a grenade launcher and fired, taking out one of the trucks and quickly arming for his next shot.

Archer aimed his sidearm as another truck drew near. As he watched, waiting for a clear shot, he hissed to Lana, "I thought I said to leave this part of things to us."

"I am," she said pleasantly over the deafening rapid-fire shots. "Just backing you up."

He adjusted his aim.

As the truck turned toward them, crashing down into a gully and back out again, Lana pulled her arm back and sent one knife flying. Eagle-eye aim, the blade whizzed faster than any knife-throw he'd ever seen, and embedded into the front tire of the lead truck.

The tire burst, the truck instantly out of control on the rough ground.

The driver cranked the wheel hard, nearly flipping over.

Narrowly avoiding a collision with another rig, the truck plowed into a ditch and slammed to a halt.

Breath held, steady, Archer squeezed the trigger as the insurgents bailed out.

Without hesitation, he marked the next, moving on and taking another out. Four more down.

Echo snipers took out those farthest out.

Archer ducked and spun in a squat to Lana's other side. Insurgents snuck around wreckage.

Lining up the shot, he snapped three more rounds.

Another grenade whistled through the air from Chan's post, and the last truck ignited, flipping off the road in a fiery blast.

From behind the rubble, the last man standing pulled out a grenade and launched it in their direction.

Kerse took him out seconds too late. Her pissed off growl resonated across the cliffs.

Instantly on the move with lightning-fast instincts, Archer grabbed Lana and they dove out of the way.

The grenade hit right where they'd been moments before. Exploding on impact, the grenade sent shrapnel launching at them as they sprinted away from the blast.

Piercing the back of his leg, he felt a shard of metal slice into his skin. Without releasing her hand, he hollered as they ran for the SUVs, "Let's move in case they called for backup."

Situation stable for the moment, they didn't hesitate. Not their fight, not today anyway.

Lana piled into the SUV after him and they took off down the road. In the rearview as they took the lead, he watched the trail of dust from the other SUVs, ensuring no one else followed.

"No more sightseeing, I hope?" she asked, her voice light, but there was an edge of tension that matched his own.

Seeming to hit every damn pothole on the shitty road, he felt the chunk of shrapnel dig further into his flesh. He clenched his jaw and gripped the steering wheel tighter, leaving it for later. He wanted to get her the hell out of the hot zone. When he'd first joined Echo, he'd been warned how hard that would be, running away from fight after fight, knowing his mission was to end the war itself.

After another three-hundred miles of deserted, rocky nothingness, the road finally began to smooth out, and they passed a few leafless trees, then clusters of gnarly shrubs. After another hour of driving, vegetation thickened, greener the farther they got from the canyon. He radioed to the others, "Everyone good?"

"Yeah, we're clear. See you at the rendezvous." The other Echos drove ahead to see what they could dig up from locals in the region, separating into pairs to go undercover and do some good old-fashioned intel work before meeting Lana's team and storming the canyon. Not his favorite part of the gig, but a necessary evil. At least for this op, research involved a hot shower, dinner out, and a cozy bed.

Pulling down a quiet road, he stopped under the shelter of the forest. He drew in a controlled breath and braced his leg as he climbed out and tried to not hobble as he walked to the back of the rig.

"Are you okay?" Lana asked as she followed him, her brow drawn low with concern. "You look a little pasty."

"I'm fine," he answered through gritted teeth. He flipped open the back gate and pulled out the medkit, finally turning to see how bad the back of his leg looked once he had the tools to deal with it.

Lana appeared at his side and dropped to the ground behind him. "You get hit, you say something," she admonished, a fury to her tone he'd never heard from her.

"It'll be fine. I just need to get it out and slap on a bandage."

"Get it out? Get what out?" she roared, glaring up at him.

Jaw tensing, lips pulled into a grudging scowl, he held his tongue before he snapped again that he was fine. Fuck knew he'd been through worse.

But she wasn't wrong; he was ready to pass out or puke thanks to the jarring drive and hours of pretending he wasn't hurt until it was safe to deal with it.

The corner of her lips twitched as she sat back on her knees and said in an entirely different tone, a gleam in her eye that said she knew he'd respond better to a laugh than a lecture, "Take your pants off."

The pain eased as he looked down at her wicked grin and he laughed hoarsely. "Um..."

She laughed so hard she snorted. "You do suck at flirting. I'm on my knees and asked you to take your pants off. I gave you plenty of ways to run with that one."

"There was no way to respond without sounding like a complete jackass. If you were actually offering... I mean, of course not, as I'm gushing blood and flirting with infection here, but... um... I'm going to stop talking."

"Hey, once I get you all patched up, I'm open, as long as we're taking turns. Unless you consider that kissing. Surely you remember the first time a woman kissed your dick."

He groaned, tightening as he imagined taking her up on the offer, in the middle of this forest, the evening sun dappling through the trees around them, birds chirping like a fairytale. "Just rip the fabric," he muttered. "There's no way I'm taking my pants off *now*." The heavy fabric was about the only thing keeping things reasonably masked.

Not hesitating, she ripped the pant leg and her tone softened, "Oh, ouch."

"My thoughts exactly." He laughed, grimacing as he anticipated what she had to do next.

She stood and opened the medkit, sanitizing her hands and then squirting saline over the wound. He hissed at the burn, but knew it was necessary.

Hand steady, she held forceps ready as she studied the wound and gently murmured, "Sorry," before she buried the tips of the tool into the wound.

Hissing, he bit his tongue. So much worse than the way in, the metal ripped at his inflamed wound.

Voice steady as she focused, she said, "I didn't know you were a rock climber."

Turning his head back to watch, he realized he shouldn't have when he saw the quarter-sized piece come out of his skin. "Ditto," he said. A little woozy from the procedure, he took a controlled breath and braced his hand on the car.

Staring at the wound, still down on her knees behind him, she said, "Not done yet. This is gnarly. You need stitches... and I didn't see any lidocaine."

He nodded, his breath shallow. "Slap some steri-strips and a thick bandage on. I don't mind the scar."

"It's not about a scar. We've got a lot of work to do, and you're useless if this rips back open or gets infected. I can do it. Just wanted to warn you."

After ripping the cap off another tube of sterile saline, she squirted the cleansing fluid over the wound. He squealed helplessly before biting his tongue to keep from whimpering.

"Hey, tough guy. It's okay to shed a few. I would."

"You climbed that rock like Spiderman and jumped thirty feet off. I can't picture a little gash getting to you."

She uncapped another sterile saline and, as she poured it over, she said, "Big smelly guy ripped a big hole in my leg once. It hurt like a son-of-a-bitch and I cussed and cried while Vann patched me up."

Tongue pierced between his teeth to keep from crying out as she doused the wound again, he asked, "One of your team?"

"Yeah. Thinks he's the serious one, but he's got a smartass quip for every situation."

"And when the... 'big smelly guy' with something sharp got you..." he hesitated, wondering what she was actually talking about, imagining some jailbird named Bubba, then continued, "Was Vann mean enough to douse salt water on your wound like you're doing to me?" He looked back and winked, already knowing she was enjoying playing doctor a little too much.

"Want to lie down?"

"I'm planning on passing out once you're done anyway, so just finish it." Still, he braced both hands on the SUV and bit the edge of his tongue as he swallowed a few dozen expletives.

Each needle pierce worse than the last, he stood steady while she stitched him up, then lathered on some antibiotic ointment and bandaged him up. Finally done, she rose to her feet and grinned at him, hands proudly behind her back. "Tougher than the average human."

Shaking his head, he packed up the medkit and stowed it back inside. He leaned against the tailgate.

Not a scar on her, but she knew her way around a gnarly wound without batting an eye.

"We're about eight hours out from town. There should be a few forests like this we can crash in. We can stay here, knowing this is probably a secure site, but there's always the risk of being spotted and having to run like hell. Or we keep driving through the night."

Lana hopped and sat next to him on the tailgate, her feet dangling over the back. "I can go a week without sleep, so it's up to you."

Arms folded over his chest, matching hers, he tipped his head and nodded. "For someone that doesn't need sleep, you've been awfully protective of your bedtime rituals."

"Need versus want. I am not bothered by a lack of sleep, but I do enjoy a good night's rest."

"Like cold."

"Precisely. Not a fan, but not a problem."

"And you can climb up and jump off high places. And heal without a scarring. Oh, and you're freakishly strong. Lana. Demons? What the hell are you?"

Staring at the ground, she pinched her lips between her teeth and shook her head.

"You know all my secrets."

"It's not that I don't want to share. Secrecy is key to our survival," she whispered. "Could you imagine what the government would do with people like me? Or worse, my enemies?"

"Lana, there are few people in the world with clearance higher than mine. Because I handle the shit no one else can. What if I can help?"

"Noah isn't like me, but... he is. You have no idea how hard he worked to keep his origins secret. And the consequences when he combined worlds."

"Look. You can't say, I get it. Connery's secrets will go to the grave with me." Archer pushed off the SUV and turned to face her.

She wrapped her legs around his, drawing him close and rested her palms on his chest.

Holding her gaze, he murmured, "As will yours. No matter what."

"I know." She offered a sad smile. "But I don't make the rules. There are only a few hundred of us, and we can't afford to be hunted, by humans or by our quarry. Sometimes, when it comes down to the wire, we can talk about it under very narrow circumstances, because we need help. So, I'm sure you'll know by the time this is over."

Fuck. He was so gone. Pouty wasn't the right word, her lips exuded the passion she felt for everything, ready to smile or sneer or kiss with all the power she bore. In the dappled light of the evening forest, her eyes were a million shades of curious green, dark lashes framing them and adding drama to each long blink as she searched him for acceptance. Fearless and loving it, she was like no one he'd met.

Nor was there a chance in hell she'd stick around when this was over. Desperate to hold on in the only way he knew how, he leaned in and nuzzled into her neck, inhaling deeply, realizing she smelled like nothing at all until he was this close. When his lips touched her skin, he caught the faintest scent of wild and revitalizing, like a rare mist in the desert.

Shifting and framing his jaw with her hands, she whispered, "Will you kiss me now?"

A smile teasing at his lips, he turned to kiss her palm and answered, "Nope."

Touching her forehead to his, breath lacing with his, she murmured, "I can't tell you how infuriating I find you."

A laugh caught in his throat, choking him with frustration, of his own doing. He hesitated a fraction of an inch from her mouth, wanting this to be that moment. The ache burned under his sternum as he pulled back.

Not yet. For all her flirting, she wouldn't hang around long enough to get attached. "I'm dead on my feet. Your turn to drive." He opened his pack and pulled out jeans and a t-shirt.

"Now you're going to take your pants off?" She folded her arms over her chest and stepped back as if to enjoy the show.

Laughing under his breath, he shook his head and said, "I'll change back here, you over there. I might explode if we attempt a repeat of last night. As I'd rather feel like I can come close to impressing you, let's wait until I'm less woozy."

"Spoilsport," she grumbled with a grin, grabbing her backpack and pulling out jeans and a gauzy top with a knot in the front.

Back on the road, she wolfed down an MRE, but his stomach was still complaining over the shrapnel extraction. Lana was as awake as she'd been when she'd delivered his coffee that morning. Like a machine—a perky one with every thought written on her face—she followed the map he'd made without a glimpse of hesitation. Not entirely astonished to discover he had no problem trusting her with his life, Archer folded his sweatshirt into a pillow and closed his eyes, sleep washing over him in seconds.

13

Nightmares of the shadowy canyon clashed with visions of naked Lana riding him like a goddess-cowgirl, the contrasting images strobing faster and faster until his eyes slammed open. Pulse thundering in his ears, he puffed out his cheeks, and reminded himself where he was.

Without a word, Lana slipped her hand in his and gave a gentle squeeze, seeming to remember he was slow to re-enter the real world. Breath flowing in and out, letting the sensation of her fingers laced with his center him, he watched the road ahead, the scenery gradually coming into focus.

As they neared town, the green forests became fairytale lush, as if attempting to compensate for the bordering bleak terrain. Brightly colored houses began to dot the landscape, and the town itself was like something on a postcard. Not many tourists with the fighting so close, but enough that they wouldn't draw too much attention.

This town was a wildflower in the rough. Surrounded by strife, harsh terrain, and unpredictable weather, yet the bright culture was a breath of fresh air in an otherwise desolate part of the world.

They parked behind a charming hotel, and he met her on the sidewalk. As if they did this all the time, she slipped her hand into his and smiled up at him. "Nice spot for a honeymoon." She grinned with pure snark and enjoyment.

"Newlyweds? That's our story?"

"How about I'm trying to escape my evil husband, who is the king of a small nation further south, you're my sexy bodyguard, and we're on the run?" Her eyes danced with enjoyment.

"Or we could go with the honeymoon thing." They hooked their backpacks over their shoulders and walked toward the front of the hotel. "Are you ever in a bad mood?"

She considered for a moment. "Of course. But there's enough negativity in this world, so I save that for special occasions."

He released her long enough to open the door.

Like the town, the hotel lobby was something out of a tourism commercial. Floral brocade chairs sat in front of a fireplace—no fire this time of year, but instead a bouquet of silk gardenias brightened the space. Aged wood trim framed the wallpaper-lined walls of the cozy space, with walkways to a steep set of stairs, rooms in either direction, and an office behind the cream-colored desk. On the desk, a computer older than he was blinked with a green icon on a black screen.

"Mr. and Mrs. Belak. Hello. You had a fair journey here, I hope?" asked the rattling voice of a paper-skinned host in thickly accented English.

Archer answered in Russian, "This town is a diamond in the rough. I can't wait to explore and learn some of the history. Have you lived here your whole life?"

With a glowing chuckle, the host nodded and responded in Russian. "As did my children and their children, and my parents before me."

Hand still laced with his, Lana leaned into him and smiled sweetly.

"Where would you recommend we start our tour?"

"The museum of course. It's not more than a few rooms, but you'll get a wonderful feel for our roots."

"We'll do that, thanks. We're thinking of going for a drive tomorrow. Which direction would you suggest?"

"You'll want to head toward the lake," their host answered easily, as if it was the only option.

"It looks like there's quite a forest and some mountains beyond, perhaps a nice picnic spot?"

The host shook his jowls and adopted a stern scowl. "Not that way. Nothing but drab stones and harsh wind beyond the forest."

Archer pondered and scratched his hand in his hair. "I wonder, why do you think it's such a difference? It's so lovely here."

"It's always been that way. Inhospitable by nature, I suppose."

"Interesting. I'll have to see if I learn anything about that in our museum tour." He pulled out his wallet and slid across their payment. "Thanks."

"Have a lovely stay."

Each step creaked under their feet as they climbed to the third floor of the tallest building in the area. Loose in the lock, the key easily opened the thickly painted wooden door that jarred open as he pushed it through a swollen frame. The room was generously sized, and hopefully big enough to fit the Echos and Lana's team tomorrow morning for the rendezvous.

A wide sofa bed and two side chairs framed a painted brick fireplace with a delicate coffee table in the center. The kitchenette was simple, only a sink and minifridge, but they wouldn't need more than that. Fresh flowers topped a little round dining table, and four mismatched wooden chairs surrounded it.

When he came out of the potpourri-scented bathroom, Lana was at the window, looking over the town and glanced back toward him. "How are we going to celebrate our honeymoon?"

A lopsided smile tugging at his lips, he chuckled and shook his head. "Business, remember?"

"Oh yeah, that," she said with a mischievous grin as she moved closer. Toe-to-toe, she stopped in front of him and looked up, then trailed her fingertips over the corner of his jaw. "Take me out for dinner tonight?"

"Of course," he murmured, unmoving. "Multitasking. We can stop in the shops on the way to dinner to ask about the canyon, then the restaurant staff."

"Third date. I think that's a milestone worth a kiss."

In a pathetic attempt to mask his grin, he feigned a serious face. "Second."

"No way. The night we met. Then the shower. Hell, if you count our road trip, we might as well count this as date number four."

With a teasing shrug, he stuffed his hands in his pockets and said, "The shower doesn't count. It might have, but that ice cold water softened the mood real quick. I was bleeding or passed out for most of the road trip, so that absolutely doesn't count. And I'm more of a tenth date guy."

"We could meet in the middle."

Cracking, he backed toward the door as he baited her and said in a thick rumble, "We'll meet in the middle. And on top. And everywhere else. I take my time getting started, but do you realize how much time that gives me to work out exactly how I'm going to take you? Creativity takes time."

Head tipped back, she grumbled and followed him toward the door. "You're killing me," she said, her tone lilting with humor when she caught up to him and wrapped her arms around his middle. "I need a preview to tide me over."

Breath heavy in his chest, his body aching as desire surged over his skin, he gripped her hips and scooped her up. His control threatened to shatter as she pressed against him. She may have everyone convinced she was casual about sex, but the honest, loving look, her eyes soft and lips parted as she searched his gaze, said this wasn't a game to her either.

He lifted and braced her against the wall. Hands wrapped around her thighs, he was rapidly hardening and aching to give in. His resolve wavering, he pressed tight against her.

She leaned in to kiss him, but he shifted and licked a narrow line up her neck.

She squealed playfully and ground hard against his cock, the pressure sending him throbbing.

He framed a hand around her jaw, then traced her pouty lower lip with his thumb. His voice was hoarse as he struggled to maintain control. "I'm going to take you slowly and methodically. The first time I fuck you, before I even touch you, I'm going to push up your skirt and lick you until you scream. When you're burning up and grinding against my mouth, I'm going to turn you over and come in from behind."

As he went to release her, she squeezed him close and nipped his earlobe, sucking him in before releasing him. "What if I'm wearing pants on our fifth date?"

The edge of his mouth turned up. "Wear a skirt. I don't care what else you wear, but skip the panties. I don't want anything getting in my way."

Lana laughed with utter delight sparkling in her tone as he lowered her back to the floor. "Museum is date three. Dinner tonight will be date four. What are we doing on date five?"

"I just told you," he said, backing away to steal one last glance of her equally expression, then headed straight down the stairs before he could let his brain catch up.

Boredom would never be a factor when Lana was around. As far as third dates went, this one was making the hall of fame. She seemed to find everything interesting, from raving over the raspberries and champagne flavored ice cream they'd indulged in on the walk to her heartbreak in the darker section of the museum that told of the region's history of strife and loss that never seemed to end. And her wholehearted enthusiasm, the depth to which she experienced everything, was infectious.

Hundreds of stories and relics were on display in the museum, but anything pertaining to the canyon was markedly not among them. An older couple was paying for matching t-shirts and chatting with the cashier. With a rural and western accent more like his grandparents, although in a Ukrainian dialect similar enough to the localized Russian he'd grown up with, the woman said conspiratorially, "We'd wanted to drive east further, but hear it's too dangerous."

Hunched and frail, wrinkled and arthritic, the gray-haired cashier nodded and answered, "Even without the fighting, it's not safe to drive east of here."

"Why is that? The geology of the area is incredible from what I understand." The man's head bobbed as he talked, intrigued by every little detail.

"The weather is terribly unpredictable," she answered cautiously.

"We can handle bad weather," the man said with a snort.

"It's... outsiders wouldn't understand," the cashier said as she bagged up their souvenirs and handed it across.

Archer tucked his arm around Lana and pretended to show him a brochure. She seemed to be calculating in a struggle to listen. He smiled and pecked a kiss to the top of her head.

The cashier finally continued. "There's something... dark... that way. Go far enough, and you won't come back."

"That is a good tale." The man chuckled as he tucked the bag under his arm.

"It's no tale," the cashier answered, her tone no longer meek, her expression dark.

The couple finally left, seeming unconvinced and thinking the tale was a ghost story to intrigue tourists.

Archer slid some local books on history and culture onto the counter. Lana added a silver charm bracelet and stood at his side while he asked in fluent Russian, adding a local dialectical inflection, "I couldn't help but listen in. We have lost some friends because of... that darkness. What do the stories say about it?"

Lana glanced up at him with sappy admiration, as if he'd won an oversized stuffed unicorn from the fair for her.

Searching to ensure no one was watching, the cashier leaned in and said, "My brother and I tried to find out in our youth, trekking to the base of it, convinced it was all lies to keep us from leaving home. The stories are all true. We got scared the closer we got and ran back. But there's something not right about it. No one that goes near comes back again. It's said that a demon created that canyon as a door to the other side, so he can unleash other demons to our world. Werewolves are spawned there and unleashed as a plague on this earth."

Lana politely slid cash across and smiled. In broken Russian, she said, "My werewolf friends are actually from America." She thanked the clerk as she took the necklace, and headed outside to wait.

Archer thanked the cashier and took the books, following Lana outside. Despite the sunny afternoon, the wind was chilly. He pulled his jacket tighter and adjusted the books to take Lana's hand. "Impressive," he said.

"Me? I only know enough Russian to... make new friends at the tavern. You sound like a local."

"I'm half Russian, which is why the Army keeps assigning me to this region. Baba and Ded refuse to learn English just to piss off my other grandparents, so I grew up with it. Werewolf friends?" he asked.

"I was speaking metaphorically," she said flippantly, digging into her pocket for a hair-tie.

"Hey, don't take it out on me. Not my myth."

"It's shit like that..." she began, then clamped her mouth shut.

Once they were closed in their hotel room, she kicked off her boots, snagging one of the books from their shopping bag, and started flipping through like an uninteresting magazine.

"Want to talk about it?" he asked, sitting down in the opposite chair with one of the other books.

She chucked her book back to the table and grabbed another, glaring at it. "It's not a door. Trust me, we'd know."

Patting his jacket pocket, he looked around to find his glasses. The corners of Lana's lips turned up. She leaned across and pulled his glasses from the neck of his shirt, then settled back in and fiercely flipped through another book, the pages slicing across each other with each turn.

The book that had caught his attention from the window before they'd even entered the shop was a poorly hand-sketched, unremarkable book ripe with grammatical errors that sent his dyslexia down a confusing spiral, yet he landed right on a drawing of the canyon. Focusing to read the letters in order and understand each as he went, not caring that he was painfully slow at it and sounded like a first grader attempting to read Joseph Heller, he translated, "*Like a black hole, the canyon sucks in life, releasing it with a hellfire blast.*"

She set her book down and moved next to him.

"*Some say it has been there since the dawn of time, but my people have been here longer. The river, once a source of life, later raged and flooded our crops. Clouds engulfed the sun, so no recovery was possible. Attempts to reclaim our homes were blocked like a bad dream come to life. Those daring enough to venture into the shadow disappear, the rest of us comprehend the message loud and clear. The canyon does not allow visitors.*"

Lana traced the sketch with her fingertip. "This drawing looks like yours. When was this written?"

He flipped to the beginning, "This says it was from a journal written in 1736." Flipping through, he tried to find more, but the rest detailed the history of the region, with no more mention of the canyon or anything relevant.

"I need my team. See what they make of it."

Archer nodded. "Do you need my phone?"

Checking her phone, she shook her head. "Full bars. We're good."

He scanned the other books, but nothing helped. Each of the locals they'd spoken with seemed to have a different take on the canyon, but they all settled on one thing: Don't go near it.

He flipped through the rest of the journal, but couldn't find anything else on the canyon. Dozens of entries on the weather. Bleakness and dust, with the occasional promise of unremitting rain.

"Hey," Lana said into the phone.

Bodie, Noah's brother, answered, "*Hey, Lana. We're about to take off. What's up?*"

"Perfect timing. Meet us at the hotel, and we'll leave first thing in the morning?"

"Sounds great. Bennett and Adair should be there in a few hours, maybe less."

"Perfect. I could use your brain, if you've got a sec."

"What's up?"

"I think..." She curled onto the couch and leaned into Archer's side. He wrapped an arm around her and kissed the top of her head before continuing to scan his book. "There are some stories about this place, and it seems to me the blur and attacks are primarily defensive. Like something is protecting the canyon."

"From what? Ryan checked the other side, and it is an old tear, but no activity on their side. He said it's closed but thin, like, he could feel the static electricity in the area, but it doesn't look like anyone without control over the veil should be able to cross. From what we can find on researching our side, there are next to no natural resources in the area. No reason anyone would want that canyon."

"Exactly. It's bleak. Remote. Inhospitable. No one would *want* to live there."

"Except for someone that wants to be left alone."

"And has a hell of a security system to ward off intruders."

"We'll grab some extra reading material on defenses and privacy preferences."

"I knew you'd follow. See you soon, Bodie. Have a good flight."

"Take it easy," he said before hanging up.

Archer's breath lurched in his chest as he ran the conversation through his head again. "It sounds like you know what's in that canyon."

"A theory."

"What do you think it is?"

"You wouldn't believe me if I told you. I don't even believe me. A few hours ago, I would have said they were myth, but if they're real, that's how they survive. Illusive, protective, hiding in the bleakest parts of the world and repel anyone that so much as glances their way."

"Lana. You're killing me here. What is it?"

"Let me..." She sat up and teased her fingers in her hair. "I need to figure out how to tell you what I think this is—without giving up the whole gig."

"How did you plan on working together if you didn't think I'd figure it out—" He ground his teeth together, regret hollowing out his gut. "Once you've got your team, you're ditching me."

Lana reached for him, but he tightened his fist and shook his head. Her brow dropped low, her tone grave as she said, "This thing almost killed you once. I can't let you, or anyone else, go near it again. I was born to protect. I chose to risk myself for—"

"Don't."

"It's not the same. You're an expert in your field—but this is my world. I was born with a certain set of abilities that enable me to survive what you couldn't possibly."

Archer rose to his feet and moved to the window, staring blankly at the quaintly cobbled street below. "I'll get you and your team to the COP. Then you do this mission your way, and I'll do it mine. I know how this thing operates. I've seen it. Felt it."

A sad smile softened her typically amused expression as Lana moved to stand next to him. She wrapped her arms around his middle and leaned into him. Unable to resist, he hugged her back.

"I'm sorry," she said. "If any human could handle this mission, it's you. But this is precisely why I exist, to complete the missions that humans can't."

He buried his face in her hair and closed his eyes. "Anyone ever tell you how stubborn you are?"

"You'll like my family." She chuckled softly.

Radiant heat glowed in his chest at her simple words, which he suspected she didn't even realize the significance of. Not "would," but "will." "We're not going to come to an agreement on the op, not tonight. How about this? Until morning, it's just you and me. Let's go have that date, and we won't talk shop. Tomorrow, your team will be here, my squad, and we'll drive together to the COP and hash it out then, whether we fight together or go our separate ways." He held tight, an ache burning in his gut as he realized how little time he had left with her. Worse, she still didn't trust him.

And there wasn't a damn thing he could do to even the playing field.

Back down or dig deep.

"I like that," she said against his chest. "Maybe you'll even kiss me at the end of our date."

"Let's not get ahead of ourselves," he teased as he released her. Fingers laced with his, she backed away with flushed cheeks.

Fatal flaw, but he wasn't one to raise the white flag. He chewed the edge of his tongue to block a knowing smile.

She slipped into the back bedroom while he searched for the best place to take a date around here. After nearly an hour, not nearly as long as it took his youngest to get ready, Archer looked up to see Lana coming out of the bathroom.

In a suede miniskirt with ankle boots, and an embroidered white top that draped lazily off her shoulders, she walked with an extra swing in her hips.

Breath caught in his throat, he rose to his feet and couldn't find a single useful word in the entire English language. "I..." Nope, nothing. He closed his eyes and laughed at himself.

A grin teasing at her lush lips, she grabbed the keys and nodded toward the door. "Let's go. I'm hungry."

Like a drooling moron in thrall, he grabbed his coat and followed her out. "There's a chill in the air tonight. Don't you want a coat? Oh yeah, you don't mind the cold. Is that an Alaskan thing, or a whatever you are thing."

"Both, I suppose. I'm not fond of the cold, but I didn't bring a coat that goes with this outfit."

He laughed and locked up behind them. "I had that same problem." Realizing he was still in jeans and a t-shirt, he halted. "I don't have anything nicer than this."

Turning, she stepped close and rested her hands on his chest, her touch burning into him. "You're perfect exactly as you are." Rising to her toes, not as far to go thanks to the spike in her heels, she halted a breath away. "Are you going to kiss me yet?"

Half a frigging mile behind her, his brain went haywire and sent him the dumbest signals. "Not yet."

Lowering, she huffed and turned on her pointy heel.

"Wait." Catching up to her, he spun her. Wrapping one hand around her waist, sliding under her top in a desperate search for skin, he groaned at her soft warmth.

While she looked up at him with flushed cheeks, biting the edge of her bottom, his heart leaped into his throat, his throat burned raw, and his legs melted.

On fire, he embedded his other hand into her hair and pulled her close, longing clawing at his insides.

Fuck. At the last second, he shifted his hold and nuzzled against her neck instead. Lips touched softly to her neck, he inhaled her subtle scent, doubt eroding his confidence.

Not that she would doubt, confident in all things. But he was terrified. He wanted every part of her, head-to-toe.

Maybe it was because they hadn't yet, but he'd never craved something as simple as a kiss like this, like a kid in a damn candy store... or, more aptly, like a horny teenager in a porn shop.

Maybe this was a bad idea. Just kiss her. He wasn't a stupid kid, but he sure as hell felt like one.

In full argument with himself, he squeezed his eyes closed.

Nope. She'd lose interest in him in a day. Not that she'd said it, but he'd gathered pretty quickly that she had no interest in anything after the mission.

Yeah, she wanted him while they were together, but he... fuck, he was such a sap, but he wanted her so much more than a night or two. And she'd be out of his life the second this op was over.

Teasing her hands under his shirt, she traced the grooves of his abdomen before tucking her hands into his waistband to secure him against her, her touch tempting his last thread of control. He pulled her hips tight against him, stilling her hands before he embarrassed himself like the aforementioned horny teenager... instead of a porn shop for the immature, he was skin to skin with the woman of his dreams, and utterly hopeless.

Rock hard, tightening to the point of pain with her hands drifting so close, he thought he might detonate without her. "I..." he murmured, trailing off as he caught himself considering saying something stupid.

She nipped the edge of his jaw. "Let's skip dinner."

"Not yet," he managed to say, kicking himself the moment the words rose from his throat.

Lana licked her lips and smiled. "I like you," she whispered as she stepped back and laced her fingers with his, pulling him with her toward the stairs.

Taking a long, slow breath in and out, he willed away the throbbing erection and parked his tongue between his teeth. Fucking idiot. If his squad knew the dumbshit moves he was pulling? If this didn't work, he'd never hear the end of it.

14

Lana watched as Archer leaned back in his chair, watching out the window at the comings and goings of the idyllic small town. If the place wasn't so close to such a nasty big bad, it might be a nice place to invest in a summer home. As enjoyable as the man across the table. And nearly as tasty.

"If I kiss you, will you tell me what you are?" he asked across the table.

"You can fuck me, and I still can't talk about it," she said with a snarky grin and folded her arms over her chest, knowing he wouldn't disappoint.

Tongue parked between his cheeks, he responded deadpan, "That's my line. Drives my family nuts."

She grinned wider, loving baiting him as much as she enjoyed... pretty much everything else with him. At this point, he'd better be the world's best kisser, or, with how desperate she was becoming to taste those wicked lips, she suspected she'd feel that way no matter what. Like a dry turkey sandwich and stagnant water after a week on a bad op with zero food or drink.

"Wait, that came out wrong." He laughed and shook his head. "I mean, the *can't talk about* it bit."

"I assumed so," she teased. He was too easy of a mark. "Am I getting under your skin?"

"Yes."

"Tell me how you really feel," she teased, leaning back in her chair with a smug grin.

"Not going to lie. I am completely off balance around you."

She considered for a moment, relishing the unreserved honesty. Did he not have a clue how adorable he was? Flummoxed, a smile brightened her from deep in her chest and radiated to her cheeks.

"Aside from your super-powered badassness, what do you do with your time? You like fishing, sort of. Spending time with your family. You seem to like your team."

"Yeah, my team's the best," she said. The team would get a kick out of the Echos in general, but would totally click with Archer.

His stubbled jaw was nearing full beard, bringing out those infinite blues she was drowning in. Most guys were timid about eye contact, but he held her look, seeing more than she was prepared to share.

"Tell me about them," he said, accepting a decaf from their server and cradling the mug in his hands.

"Hmm. Where to start. Quinn's my cousin, and our fathers are... like us." She ached, not being able to describe how meaningful it was to accept the gift, thrilling, like finding the answer to all the questions you'd never thought to ask. He'd appreciate how taking on the demon hunter DNA was so terrifying and risky, and when the pain reached its pinnacle, you feared you wouldn't survive it, but you dig deep and make it happen.

Which, she had little doubt, was why Missy had turned it down. "About five years ago, we were on a mission more impossible than the one you and I find ourselves in. Bennett got hurt, bad, and Quinn was taken from us. Disappeared for months, but I knew she was okay."

"One of your abilities?"

"No, just a hunch. I don't know, I feel like if one of my team was killed, I'd know. Hard to explain. We have good intuition, but nothing tangible." She linked her feet with his under the table, a reassuring warmth washing over her when he completed the connection and locked with her.

"How did you find Quinn?"

"Luck. She turned up at our family tavern, not a clue who she was, who we were, but she was completely in love with Ryan."

"Ryan. He's on your team too, right?"

"Since that day. He's like us, for the most part. Anyway, it was so strange, seeing her so happy in a way I'd never seen before. But I'd expected her to be different, finding her mate, you know?"

"I think so. Walker was seeing this guy for a while—before his fiancé. They're great together. Anyway, this other guy, Walker was always bragging about what a catch he was. But he was an asshole when he was with him. Short-tempered and, I don't know, unlikeable. Quoting these obnoxious references they shared."

"Exactly. But it wasn't like that. It was like Ryan was the missing piece to our team."

"And you mentioned Astrid, she gets airsick and just had a baby?"

Lana grinned. "Good memory. Yeah. She and Quinn found each other in college. Astrid married Bodie a few years ago. Noah's brother. Which is how I met Noah."

"Are they all married?"

"Bennett married Adair and I've never seen him so content. Vann and I are the last two standing."

"Vann. What's he like?"

"Quiet. Strong. Unshakable."

"Sounds like a good guy to have on your team."

"Without a doubt."

"I wish you could say more. It's driving me nuts, trying to figure out how this all fits together."

She leaned back in her chair and watched him across the table. The night outside was dense, the candlelight in the center of their table casting an isolating glow between them. "Oh, I'm sure you know more than you realize."

"So far I'm going with hereditary superpowers."

"I like that. Quinn would get a kick out of it. She's a diehard superhero fan."

The server slid the check on the table.

Lana snatched it up first. "My turn."

He released the thin piece of paper, and said, "You know, I get a stipend for meals."

"And I have a healthy savings account."

While she signed the check, he watched, studying her with an honest interest that knocked her on her ass. Keeping secrets was no fun when the other party was trustworthy and actually cared.

"What about your sister? Doesn't she run the tavern? And how do you have time to tend bar when you're so busy fixing things?"

"It's one of our favorite spots to scheme, so the team's there a lot too and everyone pitches in now and again. It's a good way to unwind. So, Mr. Private Detective, what else did you find?" Her gut wrenched wishing she could lay it all out, knowing he'd understand.

"Actually Brock does the dirty work." Teasing his finger over the rim of his mug, his eyes hooded, he asked softly, "How old are you?"

"You know how old I am."

"How old will you get?"

"As old as I can."

"Fuck, Lana, I'm not trying to uncover any secrets. It's purely personal, wanting to know more about you."

Did she say wrenched? Try constricted, as if a kraken had gotten a hold of her. "Don't."

"What do you think is in this canyon?"

"Something you've never seen. Something I've never fought."

"What have you fought?" Cobalt blues simmering, jaw clenched tight, he studied her with a charged intensity.

"More than you." Her knee kangarooed under the table, needing him to stop before she let every secret pour out of her mouth. Jerking up from the table, she rushed out the door and inhaled a crisp gasp of evening air.

Strolling out behind her, Archer laced his arms around her, threatening the last of her resolve. He didn't want to kiss her? Fine. If he kissed her with half the force he looked at her with, she...

Nope. Not going there.

Her parents would be so proud of the sweet date night, of her not jumping in the sack with the man the first night. Okay, so neither would want to hear what she was thinking when he licked that drip of vodka from the corner of his lip before dinner, or how she liked watching how his throat bobbed and showed off that Adam's apple when he gulped his water. Or that their game of footsy under the table equated to an enticing game of foreplay and had induced a giggle fit.

Archer slipped off his jacket and secured it around her. From behind, he nuzzled into her and chuckled under his breath, "If not because you're cold, wear it so I don't look like a selfish ass."

Toasty from his proximity more than the coat, she turned into him and laughed softly. "Well, if it makes you look good, I'll let you be the one to freeze."

He faked a massive shiver, pure ornery sparking in icy cobalt eyes. As a cluster of laughing strangers approached, Archer looped his arm around her waist, pulling her out of the way of the door so the incoming diners could pass. Enveloped in his arms, heat zinging through her, she rose to her toes and clutched her fingers around the back of his neck, needing that taste no matter what it cost them.

Before first contact was made, a shrill cry for help bounced from building to building and ended things in an instant.

Shit.

Spinning on her heel, Lana took off at full speed.

Muffled cries echoed out from a darkened courtyard three blocks down.

Fuck. Five vampires. Two victims—the couple from the gift shop.

The courtyard was walled off by three shops, with leafy vines covering most of the trellis that masked it from the street.

Lana kicked open the metal gate. A clang rang out as hinges busted and the gate hit the ground.

The two vampires that had been casually sipping coffee at a wrought-iron tea table stood abruptly, the table teetering before crashing to the ground, the delicate mugs shattering as they dropped onto the brick patio.

The third lunged for her.

Lana kicked out at the first, the spike of her heel slicing into his chest. Extra glad she'd worn her long spiky heels, she dug and hoped she hit heart.

Hands desperately clutched over the wound, he stumbled backward.

Pulling a knife from the sheath hidden under her skirt, she caught the next with her elbow and made straight for the vampire that had her teeth embedded in the woman's neck, smiling as she released the human. Perhaps looking forward to a fight?

Ha. Idiot. Lana flashed a wink, and the vampire snarled, dropping her prey off her lap.

Moments after her arrival, bootsteps thundered behind her.

All five vampires turned, surprised to see a civilian.

Archer dove into the fray without question, immediately identifying the threat. Fists swinging, each blow backed by power and confidence, he got the job done. No fancy moves, no ceremony, he must have realized how easily he could lose the upper hand.

Lana wanted to lay back on one of those cushioned chaise lounges to watch the show. Brawling without a care for himself, making every hit count, he smashed through three vampires as effectively as a demon hunter. Would it be bad to whimper and drool in the middle of the fight?

A cry behind her changed her plan. Whirling around, she saw the vampire sneaking up from behind her, the woman backing away after delivering her warning.

Lana jammed the knife into the vampire's throat.

The woman held her hand on her neck, pallor washing over her, not from the minor flesh wound, but from the moment catching up with her.

Lana flipped the knife in her hand to steady her grip, checking back on Archer.

One foot bashed a vampire's chest. He quickly followed up with a left hook that knocked it to the ground.

A downed vampire popped back up and ran for Archer.

Lana sent her knife flying.

As Archer turned toward his next attacker, the knife embedded to the hilt in the vampire's temple.

The vampire behind her leaped to tackle her. Lana ducked out of the way and spun a roundhouse kick to the face. The shatter of bones echoed down the alley, her head wrenched unnaturally to the side, and the vampire crumbled to the ground.

The woman shuffled toward her husband, who sat stunned at the edge of a bench.

As his wife neared, he rose to his feet, his body shaking from the fright, and embraced her as the quiet settled over the courtyard.

Lana said in a calm, soothing voice as if talking down frightened children, "My secrecy is critical, so I can continue my work to stop them. Please do not tell anyone what happened tonight."

The couple nodded synchronously and shuffled toward the exit.

"Go straight to your hotel. You're probably already feeling sleepy from the bites, and you'll want to sleep it off."

The woman's voice quavered as she stopped and rested a hand on Lana's forearm. "This won't... we won't be come like them, right?"

Lana took her hand in comfort and shook her head. "No. You will be fine. Go get some rest."

A whispered thanks, and the couple rushed together down the street.

Archer stood surrounded by bodies, his hands on his hips, a baffled expression on his face. "So...?" he asked.

She held up her index finger and her phone from the pocket of her skirt. "Give me a sec."

He nodded quietly, checking again that the vampires weren't getting back up. Give it a few hours, and they would be.

Glaring at her phone, she pinched her lips together. "Um, Archer? Translate for me? You got to witness my terrible Russian."

"Yeah."

Handing him the phone, she hit send. Without asking questions, he held the receiver to his ear.

"*Da, zdravstvuyte,*" someone answered.

"Ask if they can send someone for a pickup," Lana asked.

Without questioning her, his accent flawless as a local, he relayed the conversation back and forth.

The coroner's accent was thick, but they seemed to understand each other well enough. "*Certainly, what sort and how many?*"

Lana answered and Archer translated, "Five pointy-toothed ones. Cremation needed within the next four hours or so."

"*Of course. Thanks for being here. We don't get enough of you around here.*"

She cringed. "I'm so sorry about that. The last few years have been busy, and we haven't gotten together with the other teams to coordinate in too long. I'll see that we cover this area more often."

Archer stood unmoving, translating the last of the call. As soon as he hung up, handing her the phone back, he tilted his head and repeated slowly, "'Greatly appreciated. Thank you, hunter…?'"

Lana didn't answer, but instead cleaned her knife on one of the vampire's shirts and stowed it back in its sheath. Checking she was free of splatters, as this could be a messy job, she smiled and joined her hand in his. "Let's get back to the hotel."

Fingers combined with hers in a steady grip, he nodded and said hoarsely, "I have so many questions, I don't even know where to start."

The coroner's car sped past as they neared the hotel.

Inside, Archer dropped the keys on the dining table and leaned against the kitchenette cupboard at the far end of the room. Adorably. He folded his arms over his chest, the edible biceps deliciously complementing the curiously frustrated expression.

Lana kicked off her boots before walking fully inside and glared at the heel, the blood caked on and the finish ruined. Scowling, she carried it to the sink and scrubbed off the sticky vampire entrails. Gross.

Once the leather was acceptably clean, she laid the shoe on a towel and scrubbed her hands while Archer watched at her side. With a fresh towel, she smacked her hands dry and tossed the towel over the faucet.

Turning to Archer, she found him watching with that quiet curiosity. She planted herself between his extended legs, her bare feet curling into the plush carpet. She looked up at him and rested her hands on his abdomen.

He tipped his head in a slight nod. "Those were vampires."

15

"Yes," Lana said, drawing out the word as she tried to read him.

"And?" Archer's expression lit up as he seemed to be catching on, but his brow was low with calculation.

"And?" she asked, savoring the tease as he put it together. Relief teemed through her that he had earned a window into her secrets, her grin widening.

"The guy on the phone called you 'hunter.'"

She smiled and rose to her toes, walking her fingertips up his abdomen as she closed the short distance between them.

A smile teased at the corners of his lips, and he finally let out a subtle laugh. "Here I was, thinking you were some sort of super soldier or something."

"Maybe I am?"

"Tell me," he said, wrapping his arms snugly around her waist, and she couldn't help but sink into him, resting her cheek against his chest.

"I'm a demon hunter."

"Is that like a vampire slayer?" His voice vibrated over her body.

"Sort of, but not. I slay a lot of vampires, they're our bread and butter, you could say. But they are only one sort of threat that we handle."

"They didn't turn to dust like in the movies."

"Reality is not nearly as glamorous. Sometimes it's disgusting." She eased back in his arms and ran her fingers through hair, triple checking that she didn't look a total wreck, free of blood splatters.

"That's why you called the coroner?"

"Few know about us, but the arrangement with coroners began centuries ago to save us a lot of time digging, and to prevent them from going public with conspiracy theories."

"Anyone else know about you?"

"Nope."

"Not even the people you rescue, like those in the alley?"

"Usually not. Even a small wound from a vampire can have an amnestic effect. If they do remember us, then they remember the attack, and to protect us as much as we protected them. There are a handful of humans who know out of necessity, like coroners. Ryan's Coast Guard team had to know, as the waters around Alaska were teeming with demons and it became more dangerous for him to not tell them. We have a few contacts around the globe who help us keep tabs on things."

"But you kept it from *me*?"

"Telling anyone is an absolute last resort, but, honestly, I was hoping you'd figure it out. I've been dropping hints."

"What, do you guys police your secrets or something?"

"Yeah. The deal with coroners is strict as hell. Like a doctor's confidentiality agreement on steroids and under threat of death."

A subtle laugh rattled his chest and bobbed his Adam's apple. "If I blab, I'm dead?"

"Theoretically."

"Got it." His hands slipped under the hem of her top, his thumbs tracing the top of her hips, but his expression remained curious, concentrating as he tried to catch up. "What else do you hunt? You mentioned a werewolf friend."

"Werewolves are particularly vicious if the feral monster side of them takes over, but for the most part, they're a lot like me. Half-demon, half-human—well, sort of. Baddies from the other side have snuck across since the beginning of time, but in manageable numbers for humans to fight off. A few thousand years ago, the king of the demon realm accidentally created a massive tear in the veil that separates our realms."

"That can't have gone well."

"It really didn't. A lot of scary monsters came across, and humans have a lot of myths that are rooted in fact. So, the demon realm king's lover got stuck on this side after the, er, disaster, and she bred with a human to create hunters to protect humans. Demon hunters descend from her, except for Ryan."

"Wow. Shit." He exhaled swiftly, his hands mindlessly tracing the curve of her waist.

A knock at the door jarred through her, and she pulled away.

His gaze jerked up, his posture stiffened in alert.

Archer took her hand to stop her, but she shook her head.

"I appreciate the chivalry, but as you see, I don't need protection."

"I know. But, you're sure vampires didn't track you here, after what happened?"

"Vampires selfish creatures and don't like risking their hides for a little retribution." She checked the peephole and saw Bennett waiting in the hall. She glanced back at Archer and winked.

Grinning, she opened the door and jumped into Bennett's arms. He spun her in a circle before releasing her. "Selfish creatures?" he accused.

Lana grinned and pinched him in the side. "Am I wrong?"

A moment later, Adair strolled up the stairs and shook her head with a smile. "He still hasn't learned it's not polite to eavesdrop."

"Maybe. But way more fun this way."

"How was England and the time with your little siblings? And don't think I didn't notice that you didn't send pictures like you promised."

"I sent dozens, you just haven't checked your email."

"Email? I believe I made it clear; I only have one of those for bills and crap. Show me now." She grinned and dragged him inside.

"The twins are adorable and Mom and Dad were nervous wrecks, leaving them for so long, but they did great. I think they enjoyed getting to hear tales of their ancestors and of their future. Apparently, Mom and Dad don't want them to turn out like me, so they're attempting to shelter them." Bennett grinned as he followed Lana into the hotel room. "I'll bore you with the pile of pics later."

With movements inhumanly fast, graceful, Adair slipped her arm around Bennett and leaned into him. "Bennett is already taking his pent-up parenting out on the poor kids, planning their trips to BC without his parents present to shelter them. Honestly, I'm starting to see why Bennett... rebelled so hard."

"My parents were old when I was born and don't move with the times well, but I had a great childhood, as will Ellie and Nick."

Lana turned to see Archer hadn't budged, still parked in the kitchenette, looking utterly shellshocked, but extra adorable from mussing his hair as he'd tried to make sense of it all.

"Archer, meet Bennett and Adair. Bennett has been my teammate since before we were old enough to even be hunters. And Adair is... his wife," Lana shrugged, unsure how to tell him she had vampire-hunter impossible hybrids for teammates. New to the concept of hunters and the paranormal-reality in general, Archer seemed to be hanging on remarkably well.

"Even I don't know how to explain… either of us." Adair laughed and extended a hand to Archer. "Lana brought you up to speed?" She looked suspiciously back and forth between Lana and Archer, sniffing with an extra drama to let Lana know that she knew that she could not only smell the vampire all over them, but could scent Archer all over Lana. "Must be serious."

Without pause, he shook hands with both and responded politely, "Nice to meet you guys. I don't know what all Lana's told you about the op, but she's told me even less about herself, so forgive me if I'm a few steps behind."

Lana moved to join Archer again, but Bennett held her back and whispered in her ear, "What's the deal? How much does he know and why?"

Adair took Bennett's hand and winked at Lana. "I'll explain it to him later."

Lana shook her head and said flatly, "It's not like that."

Raising an eyebrow, Adair sighed with smug condescension laced with pride. "We'll see." She whispered to Bennett, "And I thought you were getting so good about using your senses. I'm a little disappointed."

He scowled and took a subtle sniff in her direction, and seemed to absorb her expression, sense her pulse as he watched her neck. Laughing out loud, he shook his head. "Oh. I got it."

"It's not—"

"Of course not." Bennett shook his head dramatically. "Do me a favor? Don't make him wait fifteen years," he whispered indiscreetly as he pinched Adair's waist before pulling his wife tight to his side.

Strolling across the room, Lana wrapped an arm around Archer's middle and snuggled up. Whatever Bennett and Adair may be thinking... well, okay, shit, she'd been worried that she was about to fall headfirst over the cliff that held demon hunters more fiercely than most, but, like the demon hunter gift itself, love was entirely a choice.

And, as Archer had put it himself, *not yet.*

"If you must know, I had hinted that I was not your run-of-the-mill Alaskan geologist bartender, and then, well, we ran into some vampires on our way back from dinner tonight. It felt wrong to not explain after he knocked three of them flat with the skill of an experienced hunter. He's known about us for maybe fifteen minutes."

"Bet you've got a lot of questions." Nodding with an impressed eyebrow raise, Bennett unconsciously flicked his tongue over a sharp canine.

Archer stiffened, his eyebrows raising halfway to the ceiling, but he held his ground. "You could say that."

"We're not a typical team," Lana said as she looked up at him. She debated explaining Bennett and Adair, but decided to leave that for now. Explaining demon hunters was complicated enough. But vampire-demon-hunter hybrids? Only their team and a few others even knew of their existence beyond the impossible hypothetical, as Bennett was one of a kind, and subsequently Adair was as well.

He held her gaze and smiled softly. "There is nothing typical about you."

She savored a shared smile before turning to Bennett, then asked, "Have you heard from the others yet?"

"They're on schedule and will be here in about ten hours."

Archer nodded in acknowledgement and said, "The rest of my squad will meet up with us in the morning and your team can ride to the COP with us."

"Do you have uniforms for all of them?" Lana teased.

He chuckled, "No. We'll go with the scientist and consultant gig. But, honestly, it's bare bones staffing there, more of a safe house than a base."

"And they won't wonder why you're bringing in armed civilians?"

"We're taking over the COP. I already ensured it is cleared except for essential personnel who know better than to ask questions." Keeping Lana tucked against him, he looked to Bennett and Adair and nodded. "It's about a nine-hour drive from here. We'll leave in the morning."

Bennett didn't wait around, and started to pull out the sofa bed while Adair set out their bags.

Ten hours. She could handle a quiet ten hours. Right? Lana glanced at the bedroom, then back at Archer.

He shifted his hand from her waist to entwine his fingers with hers.

Enchanted, tingling from head-to-toe with anticipation, she walked with him into the bedroom. She clicked the door closed behind them and leaned back. Folding her arms over her chest, she watched as Archer sat on the side of the bed and kicked off his boots.

For the first time since they'd met, he looked tired. The angle of his jaw was sharper, darker as stubble considered becoming beard. His hair was mussed from roughing his fingertips in it.

"Come on," he nodded to the bed. "Let's get some sleep."

She smiled softly and stripped to her panties, her chest fluttering at the flush of his cheeks growing redder as he watched. Breath held, mouth open in stunned surprise, he didn't budge as she walked closer, sidestepped, and without a word, slid between the sheets and laid on her side to face him.

Movements slow and focused, his breath controlled and uneven, he tugged off his shirt and dropped his jeans, but left the slick-fabric boxer briefs on. Yum. She couldn't help the grin that took over at the sight.

Demon hunters were inherently strong and, well, built. She'd gotten used to the average human build and found a wide variety of male figures to be quite appealing. Tall, short, thick, thin, as long as he had a clever wit and a good soul. And kissing skills.

But, damn, Archer fought every fight as if the fate of the world rested on his shoulders. And, well, it sort of did. By the looks of him, he trained as if every fight would require his peak physical conditioning.

He caught her grinning at him before he turned out the light. "What?" He laughed under his breath and held a hand over his yummy tummy shyly.

"Just enjoying the view," she said with a sigh, adding a dreamy drama to it.

Tucking the edge of his bottom lip between his teeth, he flicked off the light and slipped into the bed next to her.

She leaned in to kiss him, needing to taste every inch of that skin, but he hesitated.

"Lana?" he whispered, a breath away.

"Not yet?" she asked quietly. Before he could answer, she trailed her lips along the sharp curve of his jaw.

Groaning, he yanked her by the hips until they connected under the blankets. "Yes. No. Fuck," he muttered. "I'm not any good at this stuff."

"Let me be the judge of that." She smiled as she kissed the hollow at the base of his neck.

He closed his eyes and bit his lip, breath coming fast and impatient.

Trailing her fingers down his chest, along the grooves of his abdomen, she reached his waistband and teased her fingertips at the edge.

He flipped her over and pinned her underneath him.

Wiggling underneath him, she gripped his hips and pulled him tight against her.

Shock rattled a laugh in his throat. "Still not used to that. Be careful you don't hurt me," he teased, but the words settled sourly in Lana's stomach. In the dim light from the moon, his cobalt blues near boiling, he searched hers. "Fuck, Lana, I want you so bad," he groaned, then pulled away. "You're a whirlwind. Sexiest woman I've ever laid eyes on. Fearless, and not just because you can be. I don't want to mess this up."

Melting more each moment he studied her, she searched right back. "I get it, and believe me, you are absolutely worth waiting for. But the second you're ready, even if it's while we're driving tomorrow, you say the word and I'm game."

He laughed out loud and pinned her in a savory spoon like a stolen scoop of peanut butter in a darkened kitchen. He tucked his arm around her and held her close. "What, we'll just pop in the back seat and tell your friends to face forward and turn the music up loud?"

Caught hook, line, and sinker, Lana smiled pinned up against him in the darkness. She rubbed her ass against his raging hard-on and giggled at the throbbing greeting. "Second thoughts?"

He laughed and nipped her ear. "No. My brain is working overtime trying to make sense of tonight. I want you so bad it literally hurts, and I'm worried I might have to go to the hospital like one of those Viagra commercials say to do, but..."

"But it's been a hell of a night?"

"Yeah, pretty much." He sighed, his voice heavy with sleep. "Vampires. Fuck. So, you're... half human?"

"Demon hunters, vampires, and werewolves are considered hybrids. Like us, werewolves have a demon ancestor that took a human lover. Vampires are more like you'd expect from lore in their origins, and are created by a blood exchange, humans changed by vampires."

"And your friends in the living room?"

"They shouldn't exist, but they do. Every so often, there are prophecies that tell of divergences from the norm."

"There's nothing normal about this."

She chuckled. "From *our* normal. Ryan's father is the king of the demon realm, and, like me, Quinn is descended from his long-lost lover, and it was their coming together and making Skye that saved the realm. And Bennett was the first, and hopefully only, demon hunter changed by vampires, which gave him the power to take down the original vampire that was imprisoned underground."

"Wow. And I thought we had some crazy stories of saving the world."

"Ours sound cool, but I've seen you fight, and you're... incredible. I don't know many humans who could take on vampires, and you took out three of them with your bare fists. Hell, I don't know many demon hunters who would have been ruthless and efficient."

He buried his face against the back of her neck and pressed his lips to her shoulder. "Be careful, or you'll puff up my ego," he teased.

She laughed out loud, snuggling closer. "Maybe you don't flaunt an ego like I do, but you, Archer Belak, are a badass fighter and you know it."

"Maybe."

Bennett and Adair must have been sound asleep, like the rest of the hotel, as not even a creak was awake to break the stillness.

Archer whispered quietly against her skin, "No prophecy for this mission?"

"Not that I'm aware of, thank fucking hell. Prophecies carry a lot of pressure, end-of-the-world sort of fights. But..."

"What?"

She huffed a breath, multifaceted frustration threatening to ruin what was turning out to be a fantastic snuggle. "I usually know what we're up against. This isn't something I've fought before."

"The road to the COP will take us closer tomorrow, enough to let your team scope it out—from a distance."

"Sounds like a plan. I want to feel the air around it and see if that triggers something. Maybe Adair, Bennett, or Bodie will be able to scent something, or maybe Vann will get one of his hunches."

Archer stiffened her in his arms, and Lana knew he was drowning in questions. "Wait, Bodie's... a vampire? Noah's a vampire?"

"No, of course not. Vampires can't be out in the sun, well, they can if they marry a demon hunter. Bodie and Noah are werewolves."

"Shit, this is confusing."

Lana laughed as she snuggled into him, loving sharing her world with him. "You're telling me. Until Bodie, we thought werewolves were only the feral beasts that go around tearing people to bits, but that's just when things go wrong. Werewolves are a lot like demon hunters, mostly, but can shift into wolves."

"If I have bizarre dreams tonight, I blame you completely."

"Hey, you didn't need to follow me into that alley."

"Yes, I did," he murmured against her ear.

She turned in his arms and nuzzled into his neck, drifting to sleep with her lips touching his skin.

16

Death by untamable erection. It might actually be a thing. There was no way any blood was left in circulation to make it to his brain.

Archer shut off the frigid water after a miserable shower and wrapped the plush hotel towel around his waist. There had been plenty of hot water left, but he'd needed the cold blast of relief.

Not that it had helped. Even a dip in the Arctic wouldn't tame things after last night. At three in the morning, Lana had awoken for some reason, and subsequently woke him with kisses along his shoulder, his chest, his abdomen. After she'd tormented every bare inch of his skin, she'd wrapped her body around him and fell back to sleep with her breasts pressed against him. Sleep wasn't an option after that.

Slinking out of the bathroom, clutching the towel in front so no one could see how miserable he was, he tried to sneak back into the bedroom without detection. Too fucking bad, apparently.

At the kitchenette, Sauer and Kerse were fighting over which breakfast was for whom, as they had brought food for an army from the restaurant across the street. Walker and Chan were sitting at the small table with Bennett, asking a million questions about the canyon and what he knew, while Bennett danced around the subject and said he didn't know yet. Adair stood on the narrow iron terrace and sipped from a steaming mug of something as sunrise teased at the horizon. Bootsteps hammered up the stairs.

Chan caught him sneaking into the bedroom and flashed him a wink, but Sauer caught his eye. "Hurry your ass up, we're on the road in thirty."

"Sure," Archer nodded, hand on the bedroom doorknob.

"Hold up," Walker said, chasing him down with a pair of coffees. "For you and your lady friend. You get last dibs on breakfast though."

He secured the towel, glancing down and checking that things were calm enough to not embarrass himself as he let go of his safety grip on the towel, and accepted the pair of mugs. "Thanks," he muttered, twisting the bedroom doorknob with his pinky to avoid spilling any coffee. The door creaked open right as a fist rapped on the front door to the hotel room.

Nope, he couldn't handle more curious looks this morning, definitely not any from Lana's team, and absolutely not while he was standing in a towel.

He dashed into the bedroom and backed into the door to close it.

As he leaned back against the door in relief, coffees unspilled in his hands, he felt the final release of terrycloth, as the towel dropped unceremoniously to the floor.

Decked out in black leggings and sleek black running shoes, topped off with a strappy black athletic tank, her sweatshirt tossed over her backpack, Lana had tugged her wet hair back into a messy pony, the dark locks already rebelling at their confinement. Her grin swelled with amusement as she watched the entire incident unfold.

Gaze scanning up and down with a gleam and a wicked smile, she said, "That's the best sight I've seen... ever. And it's not even my birthday." She stalked close and halted a breath away, pinning him against the door while he stood naked, rock hard, towel at his feet, hands full with precariously overfilled mugs, and utterly helpless in so many ways. "Need a hand?" she murmured, hovering inches away like she was going to kiss him.

Shoulders back, he growled under his breath, "Lana."

"Thanks for the coffee," she whispered as traced her fingertips along his abdomen, then pressed her hips against him, the slick fabric of her leggings cool and slick against his cock.

Watching her lips as she spoke, he couldn't find the words, or the will. What was he waiting for, again?

A breath away, she tugged her bottom lip between her teeth and let her gaze fall to his mouth, tracing the curve of his smile, and undoubtedly noticing his shallow breath as temptation engulfed him.

Half a second before he dropped the coffees and gave in, she slipped her mug from his hand and stepped back.

She took a slow sip and moaned as steam curled over her cheek. "Yum," she murmured, watching him over the rim.

"Sauer made it," he stuttered belatedly, chest rising and falling with breathless desperation.

Lana moved to the window and pushed the curtains open. The rising sun cast fingering amber rays into the dimly lit room. Sharply angled rooftops, close enough to hop from one to the next, told of the heavy cold that could come to this place, but the flowers dotting the streets painted a brighter picture. She stood in the light, cradling the mug in her hands and watched the village preparing to wake.

Her smile faded into the gloom of the distant clouds on the edge of the horizon.

Archer set his coffee on the side table and moved to stand behind her. "Are you okay?" he asked.

She nodded quietly and set her coffee on the windowsill, then turned into him. Gaze trailing up his abdomen, rising, she licked the crease of her mouth and bit the corner of her bottom lip, finally meeting his look. Her apple green eyes had melted into a soft sage. "All flirting aside, no more games. Archer, will you kiss me yet?"

Parking his tongue between his teeth, he clenched and held back. "No."

Without dropping her gaze, she breathed in and out, slow and measured. "I know I take things quicker than most, but it's just a kiss, not a marriage proposal. I'm not asking for white picket fences."

A knot embedded in his throat. Archer struggled to swallow the fiery lump as she nailed exactly why he was terrified to kiss her. "It's not *just* a kiss. Not with you."

Forcing a huffing exhale, Lana pursed her lips together and shook her head, looking past him. "It seemed sweet at first, but now it *hurts*. I don't like being yanked around anymore than anyone else. I'm beginning to wonder if the nice guy thing is just an act, and you're stringing me along to see how easy I am to mess with." She pushed past him and started to stuff yesterday's clothes into her backpack.

Feeling as naked as he was, he gripped his hand in his hair and counted backward from ten. "It's not to be sweet, and it's not to hold anything over you. I would never do anything to hurt you. It's…"

She paused long enough to watch him flounder, then crammed her sweatshirt back into the bag and jerked the zipper shut. Tone clipped, she said, "No. You know what? Pretend I didn't ask. We've got work to do."

Outside the bedroom, the hotel room rumbled with the crowd that had formed, the Echos and her team politely arguing over who got which breakfast, the coffee pot puffing away at yet another round of caffeine for an impatient crew of badasses.

Lana hooked her bag over her shoulder and moved toward the door.

"Wait," he pleaded. Standing with his arms out, naked and entirely at her mercy, he said, "Lana. I fucked this up. Which is pretty much my MO when it comes to relationships."

She paused, fingering the shoulder strap of her bag like she was ready to run, and would, if he wasn't blocking her path.

He continued, a flutter in his chest as her shoulders slumped. Maybe he was being an asshole about it, but he needed to know she was drowning as heavily as he was. "I was so terrified that you'd lose interest in me before I could even find my footing. I didn't know what else to do, but to hope to hell you were baited."

"I'm not a fish."

"Good thing, as I'm a terrible fisherman. Really, I've never even caught a trout in the stocked lake outside of my home town."

The corner of her mouth hooked upward. "You should come out with me sometime."

He stepped closer and took her bag, grateful when she let him, and set it on the floor. "How long from the time I kiss you until you dump me?"

Mouth turned up in a fully arrogant smile, wildflower eyes glinting with fire, she shrugged impishly. "Not until after we've had sex at least once. Maybe twice."

"Is there some sort of thrall that demon hunters cast? I don't know what else to call it, but I am completely under your spell. Once or twice isn't going to be enough."

Lana moved closer and rested her hands on his bare chest, coming up to her toes. Lips parted, she watched, waiting. "Let's test it out and see how many times we can go. Did I mention I've got great stamina?"

"Fuck it," he groaned. He cradled her face in his hands.

Without pause, he took her mouth with his.

On impact, exhilaration blasted through him.

His pulse kicked up beyond measure, thrill pumping through him as her pouty lips touched his. Pacing himself, so desperate he wanted to dive in and never look back, he kissed her lower lip, delicately exploring until he knew the precise contours of her.

She gripped her hands around his hips and tugged his body against hers. Impatient and thorough with every touch, she didn't hold back. Plunging into his mouth, stroking, devouring, she told him without words that she was as eager as he was, and rushed him with a passionate enthusiasm.

Fingers curling in her hair, he slanted, taking her deeper, sweeping his tongue over hers and pulling her into him. Completely absorbed in her, their matching coffee-spiced breath, the heat of her touch, the world around them blurred to oblivion.

Whimpering against his mouth, she delved again and again, completely undoing him as she blended skill with affection.

The connection unbreakable, he scooped her up and cradled her against him. Arms wrapped around his neck, she nibbled at his bottom lip before exploring again.

Nothing but her on his palate, overwhelming his senses, he lowered her to the bed and kissed her again and again, light to deep, tongue and teeth and mouths sparring and merging.

She clung tight to him, hands everywhere on his body, gripping his arms, his waist, fused with him. "You are really good at this," she whispered with breathy surprise against his mouth before kissing him again.

The smooth, cool fabric of her tight clothes stroked against his bare skin as she tangled her legs around him, pressing her core to the solid ridge of him.

When she reached between them, grasping his dick and massaging, he throbbed and nearly came at her touch. Jarred in astonishment, he froze, aching to thrust in her tight grip.

Sealing his eyes closed, his mouth dropped open breathlessly, and he stilled his hips.

An unfamiliar laugh from the next room shattered the moment.

He shifted her hand off of him and whispered against her mouth. "We've got ten people out there waiting for us."

"We can be quick." She grinned wickedly before nipping at his ear and sucking and tugging the lobe between her teeth.

He groaned at the magmatic sensation. "Fuck, you're killing me."

A knock thundered at the door. Bennett said softly through the bedroom door, "Hate to interrupt, but we're rolling."

Voice barely above a whisper, Lana closed her eyes and said, "Shit. Thanks. We'll meet you outside in five."

Archer scowled and looked between her and the door, knowing she couldn't possibly have been talking to him, but her voice was too quiet to have been heard by anyone else. "Were you talking to me, or...?"

She grinned and nipped a kiss. "To Bennett."

Dropping next to her on the bed, Archer puffed out his cheeks and pinched the bridge of his nose. "You're saying he heard all of that?"

"He's used to it."

"He's used to you making out with some guy while everyone else is prepping for an op?"

"No, of course not. I don't usually bring guys that I'm dating around my team."

"I assumed you socialized with them."

"They're my best friends, but that doesn't mean I bring guys around them. What if they like him, and I don't?"

"That's not reassuring." He swallowed heavily and asked, not wanting to know how much of his horny, insecure mutterings she may have overheard when he thought he was alone. "Is that a demon hunter thing? Can you all hear that well?"

Lana grinned mischievously. "You'll never know."

17

LANA SNUCK OUT THE door before Archer could even get dressed. She gripped her backpack tight and followed the others out. No wonder he'd made such a big deal out of it.

That was... something else. Like nothing else. Life was a chemistry experiment, and she'd met good kissers along her journey, but Archer was...

Quinn held back and walked out with her. "Everything okay?" she asked.

Lana couldn't find her voice, but answered with a curt nod.

Halting in the middle of the narrow stairwell, Quinn turned and dropped her hands on her hips. "Is it Archer?"

She nodded again, pinching her lips tight between her teeth.

"Oh, Lana, I'm so sorry. You fell for him, didn't you?"

Eyes burning with stupid wet stuff accumulating at her eyelashes, Lana nodded again and tried to push past. "We've got work to do."

Quinn blocked the way. Lovingly, but firmly with her hands on her hips and a pouty smile on her face. "It's scary. I know. But that's a good thing. I'm glad you have some time to figure it out before the mission's done and you have to decide whether or not you'll go separate ways."

"How is that a good thing? I need space to think." She wiped the leaking from her eyes before it could stain her cheeks. "I'll ride in another truck so I can have some breathing room." She moved to get around Quinn, but her tenacious cousin held her ground.

"Nope." Quinn shook her head. "Don't do that to yourself. You're not looking for thinking space, you're looking for pushing-away space."

"The mission comes first. I can't focus if I've got feelings and shit to deal with."

"You can multitask like the best of them. Let it happen. Those feelings are a good thing. When we meet our soulmates, it's different. It's supposed to feel different. Don't squander that feeling. I've never seen you like this over a guy."

"Our duty is so much more important than my personal life. I'm not my sister."

"What? Okay," Quinn said. "I love Missy, but you two couldn't be more different."

"Don't I know it."

"I thought you'd finally forgiven her for not accepting this life."

"Not accepting? It's not like she said, 'no thanks.' She was too scared to even try."

Tone dark and as thick as her magma red hair, Quinn fired back, "She had good reason to be scared. You remember that night you became a hunter. That awful moment, right before it's over. It's so intense, the pain is more than you can bear. It's that moment other hunters warn you about, that all that training and coaching couldn't possibly prepare you for, as you have to suck it up and push through to the other side or you won't make it. Not everyone survives that."

"I know," she growled.

"You know Missy better than anyone. She's fun and outgoing like you are, but she's also sweet and homey like your mother. Do you honestly think she would have survived the transition?"

"But she wasn't even willing to try."

Quinn hissed, "Because *she knew* she wasn't meant for this. She's never been a fighter. You *are*. You always were and always will be. Remember when we were kids, and we got lost on that hike?"

"At least be honest with Skye if you're going to test her survival skills on the fly."

"Oh, hell no, but it did work. We were tired, cold, hungry, and we knew we wouldn't make it home before that storm hit. Bennett, you, and me, we saw it for the adventure it was, and did what we had to do to get home so we could tell tales of our bravery. Missy refused to hike with us ever again. She never understood what it meant to be a demon hunter. But you do. When the battle is at that tipping point, you've got nothing left, and you know, without a doubt, that you are going to lose, what do you do?"

Archer's bootsteps steadily thumped down the steps behind her, stopping behind Lana. He rested his hands on her shoulders, gentle and familiar. He answered for her, a smile shining through the aching rasp of his voice. "You exhaust the last of the fuel in your tank. It's risky, pushing past your limit, but sometimes it's the only way."

Giving him a soft smile, Quinn waved and said, "I'll meet you guys outside."

Lana turned and saw the uncertainty swimming in Archer's cobalt eyes.

She folded her arms over her chest and glanced down the stairs, then back up at Archer. "Few can find the strength and courage to push through when all hope is lost. That's how you operate, isn't it?"

"I can always find one more mile." He stepped down to her level, and then one more. At eye level, he turned to reach for her again, but clenched his fists and dropped his hands back down. "Look, if I'm nothing more than an amusing fling for you, tell me now." Before rounding the bend at the bottom of the steps, he looked back up and said, "If you're willing to give us a shot? I'm in."

At the cars, Lana watched as Archer took the last seat in Chan's SUV, with Vann, Adair, and Bennett sitting in the row behind. Lana hiked up her backpack and piled in the backseat of Sauer and Kerse's SUV next to Ryan. Quinn and Bodie were already on the move in the front car with Walker.

"Not riding with Quinn?" she asked.

Ryan shook his head, "Bodie's having a rough time, being away from Astrid and the baby so soon."

"I feel like such an ass for not thinking of it. Of course he is. Although, Quinn will be much better company than I would be right now."

"She's got a gift for cheering people up."

"I don't think any of the rest of us could have brought you out of your shell."

Sauer fired up the engine, and they took off for the long drive.

Ryan settled into the seat and glanced her way. "You did. Remember when Quinn was taken, and I tried to push you all away by telling you the awful shit I'd done?"

She nodded.

"A few words and a hug from you, and I was officially on the team, knowing I had your trust before I'd even earned it."

"You were meant to be with us."

"Yeah. Fate. It may have worked out in my favor, but I think we're all burned out on prophecies," Ryan said, settling deeper into his seat.

"I hope to hell we don't have to take on any more. Most teams never have to deal with any, and we're stuck with two."

"Three."

"What?" Her heart stopped, her limbs filling with lead as his next words threatened her footing.

His dark irises sparking with flint, he smiled. "Quit your worrying. We were reading a dusty old book from Molly's collection, and there was a line about..." He glanced to the front seat and whispered, "Peace for our Montana friends' people when one of them joined with one of us."

"Seriously? What did Astrid think?"

"She didn't say a word, but I could tell, she's going to read until she's memorized and comprehends its full meaning."

Lana beamed, a lightness glowing in her chest as she imagined the relief on reading that foretelling in light of the bloody history werewolves had endured.

"She's probably looking for a line about a canyon while she's at it," Ryan said with a snarky eyebrow raise.

Nailing Ryan in the ribs with her elbow, Lana rolled her eyes. "Stop it."

"Hey, I haven't actually talked to the guy, so I can't say for sure, but the look on his face coming out of that hotel, and the look on yours? Maybe you haven't figured it out yet, but there's a pattern."

"To his and my expressions?"

"For our team. There's no other team like us, and already, our kids are looking to set the stage for an incredible future for. Depending on how this pans out, I say we send Vann out on any recons involving badass single women."

She shook her head, teeth gritted to sand. "Nope. I am in charge of my own destiny, and I'm sure Vann would say the same."

With a chuckling eye-roll, Ryan folded his arms over his chest and settled back. "You are Quinn's blood, that's for damn sure. In case you missed the message, it's a choice to accept your fate or turn your back. Even though Skye doesn't even understand the concept yet, she's thrilled about the entire idea of it, thanks to Sunshine for filling her head with stories about how fate brought her into this world."

From up front, Sauer grabbed the radio, a laugh in his husky tone. "Chan, how's the mood in your rig?"

"Glum."

"Want to pull over a sec?"

"Sure thing," she answered, pulling to the side of the rural road, the forest still thick around them.

It wouldn't be long until they were in the gray, but Lana knew they had hours of driving ahead.

Sauer and Kerse hopped out simultaneously and Kerse swung open the back door, "Ryan? Can we borrow you?"

Uh-oh.

Out the back window, Lana watched Archer throwing his arms up in the air as Ryan took his seat in the SUV, Kerse grabbing the last seat next to him, and Sauer standing unyielding and unamused. Poorly attempting to read lips, Lana wished to hell she could see what they were saying. Vampire hearing would be handy at times like this. She cracked the passenger door open and held her breath as she strained to hear them.

"Stay the fuck out of my personal life." Archer shoved Sauer in the shoulder, but Sauer held his ground.

"Not this time," Sauer growled back.

"Get back in your rig and get moving. That's an order, Captain." Archer stood tall and gritted his teeth.

"Sir. As this pertains to your personal life, and your head's too far up your ass to figure it out, I'm overriding your orders."

Archer paced a few steps, then turned back. "That's right. *My* life. And I'm done with you all conspiring to fix it."

Sauer's response was so soft she barely caught it. "Twenty-four hours. Then I'll leave you alone."

"Fuck. Fine," Archer muttered. He stormed close and jumped in the driver's seat of Lana's SUV.

She closed her door and slipped into the front passenger seat.

Without a word, while Archer brooded quietly in his bubble through the drive, the bright village reduced into scattered homes idyllically nestled in the woods. The forest thickened until it was too dense for even a gentle breeze, then thinned to bare-boned toothpick trees, then barren, and they were back in the gray stone terrain.

Beyond, the escarpment became an impassable wall, seemingly built by tectonic forces to keep people out. As if understanding sun wasn't welcome, the gray layers of clouds choked out the sun and hazed over the horizon.

"The air feels thin," Lana said, realizing there was no longer even an unbeaten path, rather an endless field of shale.

Archer let out a controlled exhale and nodded. "It does everywhere in the gray, but in the canyon, it's suffocatingly humid. Out of focus, like I forgot my glasses."

"Why such a difference, do you think?"

"Don't know. Something's haunting that canyon."

"I don't believe in ghost stories."

He glanced her direction, a glimmer of a smile in his cobalt blues. "But vampires and werewolves are totally normal?"

"Ha ha. Most ghost stories turn out to be something from the demon realm."

"I got a call this morning while you were in the shower," he said, puffing his cheeks out as if afraid to even say it. "Timeline shortened. We have less than thirty-six hours until the airstrike."

Air whooshed from her lungs. "That canyon is huge. It could take hours to even find the source, let alone disable it. After it repelled bullets like you described—"

"Not my idea. Jameson was furious, and says to lie low at the COP and move in after the dust has settled."

"We can't risk it. Whatever is haunting this canyon, those defenses are retaliatory."

"I know. A few shots, and we were nearly blasted back to the trucks. My ears are still ringing. The damage could be... fuck, I don't even know. Bad." He grabbed the radio and said, "Chan, Walker, you copy?"

"Yeah."

"Walker, head to the COP and get some drones in the sky, then join us at the canyon. Chan, let's head for the canyon and see if we can't provoke it enough to see just how bad of an idea the airstrike will be."

Despite the late morning sun behind the clouds, the sky grew darker. "If we hunters can cross into the blur, maybe we can get a head start and you and the Echos can follow by drone until it's safe to come closer."

Archer set the radio down and slipped his hand into hers, his other hand tight on the wheel to keep them on course over the rough road. "As much as I hate waiting by the sidelines, you're right. My squad can't get in there. I just hope to hell you guys can."

She didn't say it out loud, but she hoped so too. Noah and Simmons were so thrown by this thing, they were willing to synthetically create a werewolf army. If they hadn't been pulling the bodies of their dead friends out of there, would they have been able to go further in?

As they drove over the grinding rocks beneath their tires, engine whining to keep traction over the loose shale, Archer murmured, "I'm sorry if it felt like I was pressuring you."

"I'm sorry if *I* was pressuring *you*," she said, aching at his words. "You weren't wrong. I have my exit plan mapped out before I even finish a first date. My parents were childhood sweethearts and seem to think the world revolves around that innocent love that grows with you. It's... a lot, too pressuring, growing up hearing every day about how demon hunters mate for life, and that you're not a complete person until you find your soulmate. Most demon hunters never find their soulmates, and, fuck, I am perfectly willing to dive into a dangerous fight, but romance for hunters is much less predictable. So, naturally, I don't stay long enough for feelings to sprout."

"Did I mention the only thing to do in my hometown is get married and have kids?"

"You understand."

"Painfully so. Unfortunately, it rubbed off on me and I tend to look for serious, which I don't have time for. Or, inevitably she's looking for something in a partner, and I'm not it."

"What could she possibly be looking for that you don't have?"

He huffed a laugh and blushed. "A lot. She's either in the market for some badass alpha, like out of some romance novel that magnanimously puts her on a pedestal above all else, or a sugar daddy so she can do her thing while living off my combat pay."

"Ouch. Although, nice use of 'magnanimous.'"

"Thank you," he said with a sweet grin. "Honestly, I don't know how the other guys manage it. Meeting great partners that are happy to hold down the fort when we're off the grid for so long, going months without any news, and still be their partner and lover when they're home. Not easy to accomplish."

"Missy, my little sister, got married about three years ago. She'd been my ally until she met Vince, refusing to settle and enjoying fishing as much as I do, but suddenly it all changed. They've got this little guy, and everything is rainbows and unicorns that plume from new love and life, and the happy parents are convinced that everyone should be like them. She's pregnant with her second, and she is glowing." Lana gripped her fingertips in her hair and stared out the window. "My dad is a hell of a hunter, but he doesn't talk shop around the house, and my mom is supportive, but she prefers to not hear how close she comes to losing him when he comes limping home from a dangerous op. My grandfather lived to be three hundred, but didn't settle down and marry until he was a hundred and twenty. I miss him so much. When my dad would get on me about the more domestic requirements of demon hunter life, my grandpa was always reassuring me that life was about more than getting married and procreating."

"Makes sense, finding relief where there's freedom."

"He always told me I could be whatever I wanted to be. That fate was only another path, and I could refuse it."

"Think that's why your sister felt she could decline to become a demon hunter?"

She turned her head and flashed a halfhearted glare. "Don't be logical."

"Sorry," He grinned adorably, watching the road ahead and giving her hand a squeeze.

Silence was easy, comforting even, and they drove another two hours before speaking again, or maybe it was four. Few landmarks and little to look at, not to mention the lack of sun, and the constant gray above and below were so mind-numbing, that it would be impossible to tell how much time had passed if not for the faded green digital numbers on the dashboard clock.

18

"Is it always this quiet around here?" Lana asked, scanning the endless gray.

Archer gave a subtle nod, then radioed to the other cars. "Report."

Chan's voice resonated back, "Those clouds don't seem to be progressing. We can see your dust up ahead."

Walker answered next, describing their coordinates. "We'll be to the COP in two hours."

"Keep up that lead foot. I want to back up our guests from the air until it's safe enough to go in on foot."

"Will do," Walker answered. "See you in a few hours."

Archer linked his hand back with Lana's, the simple connection lasting most of the ride and not once waning to annoying—as she was accustomed, when handholding surpassed its pleasurable five seconds. Somehow, the easy connection hummed with electricity, but soothed her like a fire in the hearth on a blustery morning. "It's about half a mile to the canyon entrance. There's a lookout we can climb up to and you guys can get a sense of things and decide how you want to deal with it."

"Perfect." She stared ahead, the blur already obscuring the horizon.

Like she was just waking, her eyes couldn't lock on to any particular detail, and no amount of blinking cleared it. Growing like a mountain on the horizon, the escarpment opened to a twenty-foot-wide gateway. A staircase path led to it like an ancient, natural castle made of stone. Lana looked up and refocused, seeing it was nothing more than a canyon.

As they neared the canyon, Archer turned toward a ridge that extended long and narrow from the escarpment at the crux of the canyon. As the path steepened, he backed around and stopped in the center of its gravel talus. He hopped out and opened the back hatch, immediately strapping a sidearm to his waist before reaching for the rest of his gear.

Lana reached around him and grabbed his helmet, rising to her toes and positioning it on his head, gingerly adjusting the chin strap and hooking him in.

Quiet and amused, he watched her but didn't say a word.

Good. Lana wasn't sure what to say herself, but she'd rather wrap him in armor from head-to-toe.

In the stillness of the air, the midsummer heat reflected off the rocks. The clouds seemed to lower and thicken the air.

She pulled on her modified bulletproof vest, smiley face and all—courtesy of Quinn and Vann's creativity a few years back—and fastened it tightly over her sleeveless top.

"Nice," Archer commented, knocking on Kevlar.

Decked to the nines in their respective armor, helmets and bulletproof vests, Lana decided she was keeping her borrowed combat boots. They actually went great with her tactical-style black leggings. Far from any military personnel, Archer had ditched the jacket in the heat, but he still wore his snug black tee and dark camo, with his standard issue cargo pants tucked into his boots.

Pulling her phone from her pocket, she stepped back and snapped a pic.

"Not sure the government would appreciate a candid of me in the gray zone."

She winked, checking that the pic turned out. "I'll avoid cloud storage and will print it myself, but I couldn't resist."

Did he always look at her like that? Like he was bursting with affection, masking the yearning with curiosity?

Biting her cheek, she stuffed the phone back in her pocket and cleared the lump from her throat. Dammit, there'd better not be another prophecy.

Enshrouded in silence, only the tail of dust from the other SUV in the distance breaking up the pervasive gray, Archer stepped close and leaned in, touching his lips to hers.

Knowing the photo was going to haunt her for the rest of her days, she gripped the back of his neck and ensnared him. Their helmets knocked together, blocking them from getting close. Unfazed, Archer tilted to get closer and held her for a lingering, dreamy kiss.

In the distance, the sky rumbled, as if stretching its stiff limbs after a long slumber.

Lana licked her lips and pulled away. She grabbed her axe and nodded beyond. "Let's check it out."

He hooked a sniper rifle with a wide scope over his shoulder and nodded up the hill. Shale shifting under their feet, threatening to send them skimming back down the slope, they dug their feet into the hillside and powered up.

"What do you think?" he asked.

"I don't like this," she admitted. "The air is so thin, I feel like we must be at the top of Mount McKinley, but it's like we're at the edge of a thick mass of it, and I've got one foot on either side."

"Spend a lot of time at twenty thousand feet?"

"Once for fun. But it wasn't as enjoyable as I'd hoped. Pretty, no doubt about it, but it was cloudy and lonely."

"I'll go with you sometime, more fun with two. Brock and I did Rainier a few years ago."

The ground rumbled underneath them, hardly measurable on the Richter scale, she would guess. M ore of a vibration over the surface than a tremor from deep underground. She glanced back to see the others were nearing, their SUV clearer, the hum of the engine just barely perceptible now.

As they crested the apex of the ridge nearest to the canyon, her heart lodged in her throat as she looked into the blur. Hazy, dark, and foreboding, the canyon seemed designed to repel visitors.

Archer pointed to the base of the canyon opening. "We knew better than to go in too deep, but even when you're standing at the opening, you can feel it."

The air stiffened. Lana sucked air into her lungs, but there wasn't enough oxygen in it to energize her like she'd hoped. Her skin prickled in warning. "I can feel it already."

Snaking out from the canyon, a jagged wind rattled the finer stones of the hillside before coating them with the thick blast. On contact, the wind ripped through her hair, her armor, slicing over her skin.

She gasped and laughed a brief, shocked snort of a laugh as she caught her breath, "Does it always do that?"

"Not this far out. I'm not bringing my team any closer today."

Another gust ravaged the hillside. Shale rattled like an angry snake.

Unflinching, despite the gale that could send them tumbling down the slope, Archer squinted as he scanned the blurry canyon entrance. "It knows we're here."

Wind rushed harder. Lana dug her heels in and held tight to Archer's hand.

The slope below tremored violently, the shale boiling in the movement as it thundered close.

In the space of a blink, a hazy fist, twice the size of her head, shot out from the heart of the canyon. With focused aim, like a coldcock, the fist rushed toward them.

Archer shoved her behind him.

Furious, Lana grabbed his waistband and yanked him to duck out of the way.

Too late. The fist slammed into Archer's chest, crushing his ribs on impact. Bones cracked, echoing. Archer screamed a harsh cry of pain, deafening under the endless gust of suffocating wind.

The hit ripped his lifeless form from her grip and down the slope.

Lana lunged to catch him, but the gust strengthened and the rocks shifted underneath her. No solid ground to brace herself, off balance, she jumped down the slope after him.

Convulsing, razor-sharp slate boiled under her.

Grabbing wildly, she caught Archer by the hand and held tight as they accelerated, rocks slicing into her skin as she resisted. She dug her feet in, but couldn't secure her footing in the turbulent terrain.

His eyes slammed open as if waking from one nightmare straight into another, and he clutched tight to her wrist as she held his.

As they skidded downslope, she aimed for a boulder that peaked out of the mess. She dug her heels into the loose shale to slow their descent, hand locked around his wrist.

They crashed against the boulder with a jarring halt.

Archer howled with a furious, helpless roar, his grip on her hand wilting as rocks sliced into his skin.

She pulled him against the boulder with her and sheltered him from the worst of the landslide.

Shale rained around them. His eyes fluttered, breath coming fast as he fought to stay conscious.

The deafening roar stopped as quickly as it had begun. Around them, the hillside calmed, and the rocks settled into their new positions, a few strays scuffing down before settling.

Above Archer's eye, a gnarly gash was caked in dust. Blood streamed over his eyebrow and trailed down his cheek, one of dozens of thick gashes. His chest armor was concave, from the force of the blow he'd taken for them.

"You stupid ass," she murmured, clutching him tight against her.

His lips twitched as she cussed at him, blood trickling into the corner, his voice hoarse and weak as he fluttered his eyes open and answered, "Couldn't help it."

So weak in her arms, she was terrified to move him. Afraid to risk the ground shattering beneath them again, Lana choked back a sob and huffed a clearing breath. Now. No time.

At the base of the slope, their SUV roared to life. Out of nowhere, Bennett came sprinting toward them at inhuman speed, with vampiric grace. He didn't say a word as he reached them, but scooped Archer from her arms and took off down the hill.

Lana chased after them, ignoring the slices in her skin tearing open as she ran, ignoring the throb in her ankle where a rock had crushed her in the fall.

Adair had the back of the SUV open and waiting, a spot cleared for Archer.

"I got him," Lana said as she climbed in, grabbing the medkit and lowering to Archer's side. Her own wounds hurt like hell, but she'd be fine after a decent nap.

Archer wouldn't.

Bennett leaped in at Archer's other side, and Adair slammed the doors shut. She leaped into the driver's seat and tore away from the slope. "How far to the outpost?" she asked, hands tight on the wheel.

Lana took a tremulous breath and answered, "Too far."

She opened the medkit, shaking her head, feeling like a little kid bringing a Band-Aid to a trauma ward. Even if they could evac him in time...

Archer lay ghostly pale in front of her, his skin clammy and cool. He grimaced with each rise and fall of his crushed chest.

At Archer's other side, Bennett moved fast, ripping off Archer's vest. "His pulse is weak."

Under the vest, he looked worse than she'd feared. Broken ribs, shattered sternum, deformed and juddering with each breath.

"Dammit, Archer," she cried. "I don't need you to protect me."

His eyes eased open, and he managed to shake his head, his voice hardly above a whisper, "Sorry. Instinct." The effort triggered a cough. He groaned at the pain. Blood coated his teeth.

Bennett sat back on his heels, his eyes bloodshot and tone filled with gravel as he said, "He's bleeding internally. Punctured lung. Lana, I'm so sorry. There's nothing I can do. Even if we could get help in time..."

Lana had never been so grateful for their vampire speed, that they reached him so quickly. But even they weren't going to be enough. As experts in bringing humans to the brink of death, vampires could easily sense his prognosis... but it didn't take a vampire to recognize it.

"I know." Drawing air in and out of her lungs, she didn't seem to be absorbing any of it. Her own pulse lagged, refusing to beat. Helpless. Useless.

Maybe the world's top trauma surgeons and a ventilator could save him, if he survived the time it took to reach them. But it would be a long shot, even if they were around the next bend.

The worst idea imaginable filtered into her brain, gnawing at her gut, tearing at her open wounds. Closing her eyes, she gritted her teeth and said, "I know you won't, and I don't want you to, but, if you changed him—"

"No," Bennett answered sharply. "You know that would be worse than letting him die."

"I know," she said, her voice thickening. Tears flooded her vision, caking in the dust on her cheeks as they streamed down. Lana traced her fingertips along the dark edge of Archer's jaw. "I should have sensed something. Shouldn't have let you get that close. I'm so sorry."

He leaned into her touch, a tear beading at the corner of his eye. Throat seizing, he struggled to cough, but even that was becoming too much.

Lana leaned down and pressed her lips to his forehead, wishing she could at least take on the pain for him.

She heard Adair radio back to the others for directions, updating the others with Archer's guarded status.

Voice low and steady, Bennett said, "Fuck, Lana, um... I think you can save him."

"What?" she asked, jerking up at the hint of hope.

"You need to do it fast. And... it won't work if you don't genuinely believe he's the one."

Breath freezing in her chest, uncertainty bubbling over, she nodded slowly. "Or if he doesn't feel the same."

Archer grimaced as they slammed down and jostled through a dry ditch, but was too weak to move.

"Now, Lana," Bennett urged. "You don't have time to think it over. Five minutes, ten at the most."

She glanced out the windows. Nothing, not a sign of life in sight. No trees. No miraculous hospital on the horizon, not even the outpost.

She looked back at Archer. He grew paler, cooler with each passing moment.

"I'll give you some privacy," Bennett said, then climbed into the front seat.

Archer's broken chest shuddered with each breath. So strong, remarkably for a human, and she knew it was by force of will more than anything. How could she not do everything in her power to save him?

Lana cradled Archer's jaw, tracing her thumb over his stubbled chin, careful not to disturb his injuries. Knowing the words that her father had drilled into her, as every demon hunter should know how to tie their soul to another. Words she feared she'd never feel right saying. Flowing like lyrics to a favorite song, the irreversible vows poured from deep within her.

Surprised to discover she meant every word, she continued. "I bind myself to you, for there will never be another to possess me as you do. Please say you claim me, as I do you?"

Archer twitched as she asked, but didn't respond.

"Archer, wake up. I need a little help here. Can't exactly do this without you. Will you claim me as yours, as I do you?"

Hoarse, almost inaudible, he seemed to smile as he answered, "'Course."

"Good." She nodded, the floodgates wide open, choking her.

"Speed it up," Bennett warned.

Reciting the words of her ancestors, stumbling as she fired them off as quick as her tongue would allow, she described their origins and their purpose as mandated by the ceremonial words that would ignite the transfer. Why did they need so many words to say one thing?

"My gifts are my own to share with the mate of my choosing. Archer Belak, open and accept my abilities to heal and longevity to live out the rest of our lives together..." The power rose like a fever deep within, boiling and coursing through her veins. She pressed her lips to his. Weak, but here with her, he kissed her back, little more than a flinch. Igniting the kindling she'd built with her words, the connection started the transfer.

Aware of the pain it could cause him, she balanced the flow, feeling her power funneling toward him, delivering the burden slow and steady for him, as she had been taught. His breathing accelerated, and she could feel his pulse pounding faster than his weakened body could handle.

Bennett leaped back over the seats and lowered to Archer's other side. He watched as Lana balanced flooding Archer with more than he could handle, trying to move fast enough to keep from losing him faster than she could save him.

"I know," she growled through gritted teeth before Bennett could warn her it wasn't enough.

"Fuck." With pressured, rapid speech, Bennett said in one breath, "He's strong enough to take it all or he's too far gone to take any of it."

"All? As in...? That's not possible."

"Think about how we got the power to defeat Typha."

"That was different. I can't turn a human into a hunter."

"I shouldn't exist, but here I am. Remember the feeling when Deandra gave us her power, how you're sharing your power to make him your mate now. Before it's too late."

Archer slackened at her side, his breath slowing to a shuddering rattle. She flashed back to the power her demon mother had shared, when the team faced inevitable defeat. That power had flooded her, filling her with a strength and resilience that she'd never imagined possible, as she listened to her ancestor's words float on the air, her power flowing through her.

But she'd been strong enough to take it.

"I'm so sorry," she warned, knowing the flood of power into a human could kill him, but without it, he wouldn't survive. Shifting her focus, she poured everything she had into him, instinctively adding layers to the verse she'd been taught. "Archer, I'm not done with you yet. Hang on with me for the rest of my days. Accept my strength, my endurance, my *everything*."

As she flooded her gifts into him, her strength waned, weakness etching away at her.

She powered on, ignoring each razor-sharp spasm in her veins. As she knew Archer would for her.

Sensing that he was on the brink of collapsing or grasping the power, she pleaded with him to find that last mile.

His cheeks flushed red, his pulse thundering under his skin.

She pushed harder, power surging from her like a winter storm in the Northern Pacific.

Like a grizzly waking from a disrupted slumber, Archer roared. Shoulders, jaw, thighs, abdomen... his body constricted. His bellow shook the windows, the steel of the car quaked from the furious agony radiating from him.

Lana poured the last of herself into him.

As she felt her body fall limp from exhaustion, she collapsed at his side.

"Enough." Bennett set his hand on her shoulder, squeezing gently with reassurance. "It's up to him now."

Struggling to even nod, her vision darkened, and she drifted off, clinging to her husband with the last of her strength.

19

Screaming, flailing out to stop the force from flattening Lana and him both, Archer battled time and again, stuck in an endless loop without defeat or victory. Chest aching, breath shallow as each subtle movement pierced his lungs with a thousand knives of fractured ribs, he lost himself in darkness.

But that voice. Her furious roars at him to stay with her resonated in his memory.

As he felt the weight of her tears wash away the blood on his skin, as she seemed to realize he was too far gone, he knew he was going to die when she pleaded with him to claim her as she had him. What better funeral, to have the love of your life ensuring you knew she felt it too?

But somewhere in the haze of it, that sweet moment when she kissed him goodbye, she cussed and yelled at him. When he could bear no more pain, the relief of his end moments away, she flooded him with elemental fire and ice in a violent cocktail that seemed to rework him down to the DNA. Hell couldn't be so excruciating, having the one that had moments ago sworn to protect you, suddenly casting the worst sort of pain over you, demanding that you take more.

Archer's eyes flickered open, his lashes heavy, an amber light in the corner blinding him to the darkness.

Drawing in a cautious breath, anticipating the thousand searing fractures, he realized the pain was gone. In its place, the scent of Lana filled him. Burying his face in her pillow, a smile tickled at the corners of his mouth, imagining Lana sneaking into the chow hall to find coffee.

A soft knock at the door jarred through him and he sat up, realizing he was at the COP, in his own cot, alone. Tensing his hands in his hair, he took a heavy inhale. He shifted from the bed, expecting jellied legs, but the stone floor was steady under his feet.

His hip didn't pop with his first few steps. From his pack, he grabbed the nearest pants and yanked them on. He needed answers, now. Fisting the nearest t-shirt in his hands, he moved toward the door and eased it open.

Chan waited outside, her dark eyes hesitating as Archer stepped out of the room. With a squeal, she threw her arms around him. Sauer and Walker about knocked him over as they did the same, and Kerse stood back and shook her head, a rare grin brightening her expression.

They all spoke at once, none of them making sense until Kerse asked, "What the hell happened?"

"That's what I was going to ask you guys," he admitted.

They huddled close in the familiar living area of the main house at the COP. What used to be a traditional family home had been purchased and modified by the Army years back, and gradually added to by troops stationed here. Someone had left an Xbox a few years back, others had brought plush sofas and chairs so downtime between ops felt almost normal.

Clearing her throat, Chan said, "As we neared the canyon, we felt the wind pick up, and saw Lana and you go tumbling down the slope in the middle of a rockfall."

Sauer let out a heavy exhale and folded his arms over his broad chest. "While Chan was flooring it to get to you, that Bennett guy and another one, Adair, they leaped out of the moving car and took off faster than we could drive over the rough terrain. Unreal how they moved. We weren't even within a hundred meters of you, when they had you both in the car and were gunning it out of there."

Walker shook his head and added, "You can imagine the guards' reaction when this unmarked SUV comes flying to the gate, demanding in."

"I'll bet," he muttered.

"So, we explained you were with us and you were injured and to back the fuck off. Chan had given us the heads up to have medical waiting, but... you didn't need it." Walker gestured into the bedroom. "Lana too, but her teammates said to leave her alone, that she'd sleep it off. I don't know what's with those guys. You tell us they're scientists, but... they wouldn't let us touch either of you. They carried you both in and spent some time in there, cleaning you up it seemed, and then said to stay out."

Kerse snorted. "Seriously. I thought that Bodie guy was going to sprout fangs and claws when Walker tried to bring medical in anyway."

"No shit," Walker said. "And that Vann guy just stood and glared at us while Quinn shoved us out of the room and, well, she was nice when she said it, but she threatened to 'cut our fucking heads off' if we so much as entered this room before you woke up."

Archer indulged in a long blink, remembering Lana coating him in armor before they headed up that slope, as if she knew something wasn't right. "Where is she?"

Sauer rubbed his hand over his mouth and looked away.

Kerse masked her expression, keeping her hand close.

Finally, Chan said, "They um, they wanted to beat the airstrike."

"What? No. No no no." His watch face was shattered, the leather band scratched to hell, presumably the rockfall had torn it up, but he could just make out the time. "The airstrike will hit in two hours. How long have they been gone?"

"Lana looked nearly as awful as you did, slept through dinner and into night, woke up looking furious and healthy as ever, and then they left."

"What time?" he seethed.

"Midnight."

"Fuck," he muttered as he jammed his feet into his boots. A million horrific visions flashed through his imagination. Of the fist going straight for her. Of the airstrike firing early and burning them to the ground.

"Nope," Chan said, shoving him back as he tried to pass. She must have thought he was still wounded, for the delicate pressure she applied. "We last heard from them an hour ago, when they were entering the canyon. If we go now, we'll get there right as the airstrike hits. They know the timeline."

Walker stood next to Chan and blocked him. "We followed with the drones as long as we could. No blur, no humidity. It was like the storm has been washing it away." At his words, the sky thundered overhead. "Signal zapped as they went in, but... they made it in without a hitch."

His stomach rumbled louder than the storm above.

Sauer gently tapped his fist against Archer's deltoid, the light touch uncharacteristic for the big guy. "Come on, I'll fix you something to eat while Walker checks that the drone reboot worked."

"Drone reboot?" he asked.

"When we lost audio with Lana and her friends, we also lost contact with the drones, so there's still something in there, but I ran a back-door reboot. I'll let you know as soon as I've got visual again."

"The second you know anything—"

"I will," Walker said softly. "We like her, too."

"Okay," he said, exhaling slow and steady, trying to calm the internal freak-out. His stomach growled louder than an airstrike.

No idea what else to do, he listened to his gut. When he'd been a teenager, his parents always joked that he could eat a whole pizza without stopping to take a breath. Now? He was so hungry he could eat a dozen.

"They said you'd be hungry," Sauer said, knocking Archer in the shoulder with a light tap. What, did he have a sign on him that said, *don't hurt him*? "I'll cook. You eat. Then, you've got some explaining to do."

"They tell you anything about... why they're here?"

"Nope," Kerse answered. "I'm not hungry, but I'm not budging from your side until you explain what the fuck is going on. That Bennett is... appealing as hell, but as intimidating as he is gorgeous. There's something different about these guys."

He thought about the strange description, on the fact that he'd fallen for a hunter that worked side by side with vampires and werewolves. Plump drops of rain plummeted from the sky as they walked next door to the shanty.

Sauer grumbled and laughed simultaneously, patting his belly as he said, "Thanks to you keeping us up so late—you know, the whole nearly dying thing, which I'm expecting a full explanation for—I could eat a whole cow on my own right now."

Archer passed the family-sized, rickety dining table that had probably hadn't moved since last century, when a foolish family had settled in the area, convinced they could make their fortune on the piles of shale covering the hills around here. Picked a shitty area to settle.

Halting, he muttered, "It knows they're not like us."

Kerse raised an eyebrow, standing in the doorway while Archer poked his head in the fridge. So quiet she was hardly audible, she said with a cautious lilt, "This is the first time it's rained since the Echos before us were here."

"Nothing leaves the canyon, but it makes sure no one enters to begin with." He closed his eyes and images of a hazy fist crushing his ribs flooded his skull... of the hillside boiling... and the sky overhead, thundering with weather that would unsettle the most seasoned of Midwesterners.

Sauer nudged Archer out of the way and snagged out a pile of beef patties, cheese, and fast-food thin buns. "I don't know what those friends of your girlfriend drugged you with, but you're trippin'. Burger?"

Archer backed out of the kitchen and plopped down at the table. "Yes. Please. Doubles. Lots. I could eat a fucking horse right now." And a mountain of burgers.

Kerse parked across the table and leaned back in the rickety wooden chair. Lips pursed tight, she stared at him. "Was it that blur that got you? I didn't see any burns, so nothing exploded?"

He leaned back and considered. "Sort of. We were up on the ridge to get a bird's-eye view, but... it shouldn't have been able to reach that far. That massive fist swung out from the heart of the canyon, like it knew why we were there. Like it knew Lana was a genuine threat. Stupid of me, but I shoved her behind me and took the brunt of it."

"Aw, so romantic. Why was that stupid? It was you or her, and you're the Echo." Sauer laughed as he flipped the sizzling burgers on the grill. Salty savoriness twirled through the steam, aimed right for Archer's nose and sent his stomach weeping with joy.

Kerse looked him up and down and kept her voice low. "Because it wouldn't have killed her."

Archer's gaze flashed to her, realizing they were going to figure it out, and that he would betray Lana's secrets. Biting his lips together, he shrugged to let her know he couldn't respond.

"Chill." Kerse twitched a shrug. "You wouldn't bring a bucket of civilians into the toughest fight of our careers. These guys are *different*."

"Different. Yeah, you got that right."

Kerse leaned forward and poked at Archer's sternum.

"Hey," he muttered, grabbing her hand and twisting it playfully.

"Ow." She half-glared, half-smiled, her jaw dropping in surprise.

He dropped her hand and realized he'd been too rough, yet he'd hardly applied any pressure. "Sorry."

Cheese sizzled as the corners melted onto the grill, and thick cheddar softened and shaped around the beef patties.

Kerse nudged him under the table and nodded to the original, unused iron stove that still stood in the corner, an out-of-place decoration. Not because the army took to antique décor, but because it wasn't worth the effort to remove the heavy thing when the military had bought the place out. Catching her meaning, he popped up from the chair and braced his hands on either side of the ancient appliance, knowing it would take a whole squad to pack it out.

But it didn't. He lifted it from the ground like it was made of cardboard. "Holy shit," he said, breath whooshing from his lungs.

Sauer backed up so he could see, voice shrill as he said, "What the fuck?"

He lowered it back to the floor carefully, knowing the iron legs would puncture the floor if he dropped it, then leaped back as if it was engulfed in flames.

He stared down at his hands, then brushed off the aged iron finish that had crumbled under his grip.

While he was locked in place, staring at his open palms, Kerse appeared at his side with a knife, smiling like she was about to wreak some serious havoc.

"No," he scoffed, laughing in horror under his breath and backed away.

"Please? I just want to see if I'm right about your recovery time." Mischief gleamed in her pale eyes.

"Healing a shattered sternum overnight wasn't enough for you?"

"Fine," she relented with a chuckle and sheathed the knife in its home on her outer thigh.

Sauer dashed back into the kitchen, returning in moments with a plate stacked high with burgers.

Stomach thrilled at the idea of food before he even got a bite in, Archer sank his teeth into the piping hot triple-stacked patties, separated by layers of melted sharp cheddar and sandwiched in a toasted bun. Best burger in living memory, his tastebuds high-fived each other as he chewed. Within seconds, he had one down and four to go.

Still chewing another bite, Sauer cradled his burger, elbows on the table, and said as casually as if they were at the bar for a lazy night back in Tucson, "Think she can do me a solid and pass along some of that strength to me, too?"

Laughing under his breath, Archer swallowed his bite and shook his head. "Sorry man, but I don't think it works that way. Lana was hurt, but okay... until..."

Sauer shrugged and savored another bite. "She looked like hell, almost as pasty as you when they carried her in."

Archer's appetite suddenly waned as he remembered the flashes of her sobbing over him, of her cussing at him and bringing this unimaginable pain on him. What had she done?

As doubt wash over him, Kerse said, "Finish your snack. Whatever happened, an empty stomach isn't going to help either of you."

Burger devoured, Sauer hopped up from the table and licked the grease from his thumb. "They'll be back soon, so I'll make spare burgers just in case. More in the fridge if you get hungry again."

"Thanks," Archer said, watching as Sauer started another batch. "Not a word to anyone. About anything related to Lana and her team... or whatever happened to me. This can't go in any report, not even in your personal diary where you talk about all your secret crushes." He forced the rest of his burgers down, the dry bun scratching his throat all the way down. Without another word, trusting his squad to keep a lid on it, he wandered outside and dropped to sit on the step, letting the pervasive darkness match the void in his chest.

Whatever she'd done, he'd been the one to benefit. Something filled him, stronger, healthier. But... something wasn't right. A hollowness, as if he was missing a critical part of himself. Okay, now he was going to sound like he'd totally lost it, but it was like his soul was lost.

"What about Jameson?" Kerse asked, strolling outside behind him.

"Not even Jameson," Archer said, rubbing the bridge of his nose. "No one."

What had he taken from Lana? If she'd given anything up, and then walked into the canyon weaker than she'd been before?

Stepping in front of that incorporeal fist, or whatever the fuck it was, hadn't exactly been intentional. Logically, he knew she could take it better than he had, but what was he supposed to do?

Fists tensing and releasing, testing, he looked into the storm beyond. Must be a full moon, the clouds emitting just enough light to see the damp pebbles catching the diffused blue light.

On his last trip here, the region had been drier than the desert. Something had happened, and the clouds were weeping, as if their long-lost lover was gone.

Foot braced against the wooden step, he took a long inhale, his lungs filling to twice their normal capacity, then took off full speed.

The outpost was too small for a real road test, but he took a sharp right at the gate and kept running. Nothing out of the realm of possible, but he'd probably shaved a minute off his mile. Expecting the burn in his thighs after sprinting so fast for so long, he began to realize… it wasn't coming. He could run like this for hours.

He hooked into the motor pool, flicked on the light, and checked that he was alone. Jumping with both feet straight up into the back of the truck, tailgate up, air rushed in and out of his lungs at the sensation, bringing a refreshing chill as he landed soft and steady. Like springs in his feet.

He looked up and grinned, then jumped again, grasping the rafter with one hand and swinging his body up.

Fucking shit, it was like he'd next-leveled his body. Diving off the rafter, he spun a flip and landed on his feet, no ache or throb like he would have felt before. Swinging the door back open again, he searched for the next challenge.

What had it cost her, for him to feel so incredible? He gritted his teeth and took off toward the TOC. "Any news?" he asked.

Walker was punching away at the keyboard, his eyes darting back and forth across his screen. "Almost," he said.

Archer stalked closer and looked over his shoulder, not having a clue what to make of the dizzying lines of code. He checked his scuffed watch face. One more hour until the airstrike was scheduled to hit. He snatched the radio and called, "Does anyone copy?"

20

TWELVE HOURS EARLIER

LANA'S EYES SLAMMED OPEN. Heart thundering in her chest, she sucked in air as she struggled to fully wake.

Darkness saturated the foreign room. From under the door, a soft, amber glow cast long shadows across the room.

Panic rose from her gut.

Archer's screams rattled in her skull.

The tension that had seized through his body as he bore so much.

His soft, steady breathing at her side soothed the terror that gripped her. She turned to her side and found him sleeping soundly.

His wounds were mostly healed. The gash over his eyebrow had been cleaned, as the team must have tended to their wounds while they slept. With enough rest, a demon hunter could recover from most any injury. Not impossible to kill, but damn tough.

She rose to her elbow and pressed a soft kiss to his lips, gently to avoid waking him, but she needed to feel the life in him. Unable to resist, she cuddled close, compelled beyond reason to feel his skin warm against hers. She entwined her arm around his middle and nuzzled her nose into the crook of his neck, inhaling the scent of his skin.

His Adam's apple bobbed as he swallowed in his sleep, his brow wrinkling into a scowl.

She cradled her palm over his jaw and whispered that she was here with him.

Once he woke… she didn't want to explain how she'd done what she'd done, without him having a say in the matter. Yeah, he'd agreed, but he couldn't possibly have understood what he was getting into. An ache clenched under her ribs as she traced the curve of his jaw.

Knowing she had work to do, she breathed him in one last time, finding his scent was subtle as a hunter's, but utterly him, as it always would be. As if anchored by sandbags, her body declined cooperating on the first go. Gravity had shifted, pinning her to him rather than the ground beneath her.

Bladder full and nagging, she ripped herself away and stumbled out of bed. She found a pair of towels folded and waiting on the crate next to their bags. Quietly, she eased open the door and looked left and right.

This must be the COP? More like an old house, dark and quiet as its residents slept. She tiptoed out, hoping she wouldn't wake anyone in her search for the bathroom—latrine—but things were getting dire down there.

As she moved into a minimally furnished living room, she found Vann crashed on a makeshift bed on one of the couches. Lights flickered over his face, the only light in the room, and he looked up from the Xbox. Demon hunters could go for days without sleep, but most banked it where they could. In a strange place with so many unknowns, Vann would get his downtime, but his eyes would be open. "First door on your right," he said as he gestured behind him.

With a quick nod, she hustled to the opposite wall and found the door. She flicked on the bathroom light, relieved to find a cleaner shower than at the FOB, but she still had to manually heat the water. Not even the river of boiling hot steam, followed too quickly by a weak, tepid flow, could dim the memories from that awful drive.

Eyes closed under the spray, she could almost hear Archer's laugh as they'd played in the shower at the FOB.

It had worked. But it hadn't been anything like she had learned.

A typical demon hunter wedding was light. A flowery affair, that, quite frankly, often induced the gag reflex. Hers anyway.

After saying the words, the demon hunter kissed their spouse and imbued them with healing and longevity as their lips met, so they could live out their long lives together, raise their children, and pretty much make a picture-perfect fifties-housewife-or-husband sort of arrangement. And then they ditched the reception and consummated things to seal the deal.

She'd delivered the traditional wedding exchange, but it hadn't been enough to save him. When they'd rescued their demon ancestor a few years back, Deandra had shared power with them, giving them a boost of strength and stamina to defeat her captor. That power had stuck with them. Using that sensation, the knowledge that she *could* pass so much, Lana had shared all of herself with Archer, knowing nothing else would save him, and even that was a risk. The fact that he'd survived it...

Memories of that first kiss fired through her when she closed her eyes again. How angry she'd been that he'd held himself back, but she realized he'd been protecting himself. From her.

She squeezed the last of the conditioner from her hair and flipped off the rickety faucet. The house was silent in a sleepy cocoon. But she knew her team was here, ready to dive in when she was.

The blood-encrusted dust rinsed off her skin, her hair damp with the vanilla mint shampoo that Quinn must have had left for her, Lana felt the weight of her panic to save Archer fade away. But the real fight hadn't even started.

A hollowness seemed to grow stronger each moment she was awake. And away from Archer. If they went their separate ways at this point...

Well, she had no idea what would happen. Nor did she want to consider it, the ache stirring into a throb and would eventually climax to an avalanche-level of shattering.

Or so she suspected, based on the throb under her ribs that threatened to send her to her knees and plead for... something.

Pouting as she wrung out her hair and wrapped her towel around her goose-bumped skin, she tried to shut her brain up.

He'd be hungry when he woke, but would he know why he felt so ravenous? She remembered that feeling vividly, and she had been healthy when she'd taken on her demon hunter DNA on her eighteenth birthday. After the nausea from the pain had faded from her own transition, she'd devoured the feast her family had waiting for her.

Vann was tying his boots by the time Lana came out of the bathroom, and the rest of the team was making their way down the stairs or returning from the chow hall with coffees and handheld breakfasts. Lana accepted a cup from Quinn and her cousin followed her into the bedroom.

Closing them in, Quinn stepped close to Archer and teased her fingers in his hair. "I like him already," she whispered.

"You've hardly said more than two words to him," Lana said as she slipped her panties on under the towel.

"The man made you cry."

"That's usually not a good sign," Lana hissed quietly. She kneeled in front of her bag and searched for her favorite leggings, but remembered they had been ripped to shreds. Instead, she tugged her borrowed cargos on, leaving a final pair of tactical-style leggings to be spared from the ravages of the canyon.

"Because you love him. And he risked his life for yours." Quinn gulped a swig of her coffee as she sat at the foot of the cot and smiled at her new cousin-in-law.

"He's the type that would have done that for anyone."

Tone as impatient as the time Lana had made them late for Ryan's birthday to clear out a vampire lair across the street, Quinn said, "You know the marriage wouldn't have worked if he didn't love you as much as you do him."

"*Wedding*. Not marriage. He's been unconscious, so we haven't consummated it."

"Details. Although, I wonder what will happen if you don't seal the deal? From what Bodie knows of the origins of the ritual, without—"

"I know. It's not binding until we've... sealed it. So there's still time to decide for sure." Lana tugged a lacy bra and fitted tank on. If Quinn was this bad, how were the others going to react?

Quinn eyed her like a foolish child. "I'm not sure that's what that means. I think I would have imploded if Ryan and I hadn't—"

Without pause, Lana shoved her feet in her boots and snarled, "Later. Update please. How long was I out?"

"Nearly fourteen hours. The airstrike is set to happen in twelve hours. Vann and Bodie spent some time with Walker trying to scope it out with drones, but there's something about the canyon blocking the signal, so we're leaving within the hour to set up a signal booster to see if we can get visual."

"The Echos can't go near there," Lana said as panic rose in her gut, looking at Archer as he slept, hours away from recovering enough to even stir.

"Let's get moving before they wake up."

Lana tugged her hair into a knot at the back of her head and slipped out behind Quinn, closing the door with a soft click. Geared up in all black, steel strapped to their backs, the team looked ready for whatever the mission might bring. Positioned as a blockade, with their arms folded over their chests, the Echos stood in front of the exit.

"You want to join the pile of bodies already in that canyon?" Bennett snarled, his shoulders taut, ready to flatten anyone in his path.

Vann stood back, arms folded over his chest, but he didn't utter a word.

Toe-to-toe with Bodie, Kerse gritted her teeth and fired a sideways glance at Bennett. "You're only here because Archer invited you."

Bodie's voice was steady, but there was nothing calm about it. Jaw clenched tight, he reined in a furious darkness that said he didn't lose control. Ever. "Enough people have been killed trying to take that canyon. More than you'll ever know."

Lana swept into the room and made her way to the center. "What is going on?"

Among humans alone, chances were, things would come to blows. Or worse. Hunters couldn't afford to be so reckless.

Ryan glanced her way and shrugged. "Power struggle. I think they're almost done."

"To say the least," Quinn said, her hip cocked out to the side like Lana's.

Kerse dropped her gaze to Lana. "We're not sitting on the sidelines. If you're so keen on getting yourselves killed, we'll all go at first light. *After* the airstrike."

Lana looked over the Echos and lowered her voice, a hitch lurching out before she realized how angry she was. "You saw what it did to Archer. It pushed well beyond the boundaries of the canyon. It's unpredictable, and I don't know that we can protect you if it goes on the offensive."

Chan bit the corner of her tongue and nodded to Lana. "Yet Belak is sleeping calm as a kitten now."

Next to Kerse and Chan, Sauer's bearded jaw pursed tight, his fists balled at his sides, ready to snap. Sauer's voice rumbled. "What did you guys do to him? Is he ever going to wake up?"

Vann finally spoke from his corner, quieting the others with his calm, rumbling voice. "He's going to be fine, but he's been through a lot more than a fall. And he'll need his friends when he wakes."

"You're not going without backup," Walker said. Before anyone could argue, he said, "Set up that antenna when you get close, and I'll follow with the drone."

"Thanks," Lana said, resting her hand on his shoulder as she moved past.

Before they reached the door, Chan cleared her throat and said, "If you get hurt in there, we won't be able to come after you."

Bennett glanced backward and smiled knowingly. "Won't be a problem."

"And if you're delayed, we can't call off the airstrike," Chan added, a thread of worry laced into the urgency.

The team stalked out the door, ignoring the warning.

Lana turned back to the Echos and asked, "Keep an eye on Archer?"

Walker nodded and gave her a soft smile. "We'll let him sleep it off, like your friends said to do for you both." Before releasing her, he added, "And you can tell us what you did to him. When you get back."

Although no more than a few hours, the drive to the base of the canyon seemed interminable. The air painfully arid, Lana rubbed the dust from her eyes that seeped in through the closed air ducts of the antiquated rig. Now and again, she radioed back and forth with the team and the Echos, but for the most part, they stared out at the lonely, trafficless path.

Bodie drove with Lana in a truck they'd found at the motor pool with Walker's antenna in the back, and the others took up the rear in one of the SUVs. As Bodie sprayed another gush of the windshield washer fluid, the dust turned to mud and only worsened the visibility.

Lana squinted through a break in the mud and said, "Annual rainfall rivals the Atacama Desert."

"Even deserts get the occasional deluge," he said, unblinking as he scanned the horizon. "When's the last time it rained?"

"When Noah was here. The clouds are darker, heavier today, than they have been in the years since."

Bodie scowled. "Could be a coincidence."

"Or it knows it needs to pull out all the stops to keep threats out."

He gritted his teeth and laughed under his breath. "Goes to an awful lot of trouble to keep out trespassers. Not many in legend that are so violently reclusive."

As the canyon appeared, hazy through the filthy windshield, Lana considered his words. "I've never heard of any demons that can do... whatever is happening."

"Probably not a coincidence." He attempted another gush of windshield washer fluid to break up the ever-crusting muck. "Have you heard of anything that can control the weather?"

"Typha could. Deandra can influence it. Maybe it's a demon thing... but a humanoid demon could just walk out and say hey, leave me alone." Just ahead, she caught a shiny glimpse of the drone Walker had sent to follow them and send back info. She picked up the radio and said, "Walker, can you see much?"

Cracklier the closer they got, his voice was distorted when he answered, "Visibility is poor, but you're almost there. Wind speeds are picking up."

Blurry as ever, darker under the thickening clouds, the canyon came into view.

The team piled out, steel at the ready, protective gear to the max.

Laced with finely ground sediment, the wind whipped through the open without direction.

Lana grabbed her axe and strapped it to her back, blinking to protect her eyes from the unremitting wind.

They quickly anchored the antenna to a boulder and pushed through the wind toward the canyon. "I like ocean missions better," she grumbled.

Ryan flicked the dust from his hair, looking around as if amused. "Hey, you were on recon for this one. You should have suggested goggles."

Bennett capped his water bottle and wiped a drop of blood from the corner of his lip with his thumb. He passed the drink to Adair and secured his shield tight to his arm. "No disembowelments today. Anything not adding up, and we get the hell out of there."

Vann locked his massive sword behind his back as he stalked through the mess. His voice rumbled as he added, "Tight timeline. I don't want to get fried today."

Daunting was putting it mildly. What had looked almost like a castle gateway from afar seemed to be more of a stone gate. No physical gate, but the canyon entrance was flanked by massive columnar basaltic towers. A lovely sort of formation in other parts of the world. Where the gate itself should be, the blur was most concentrated, and sand swirled in the air in front of it.

They hopped over the first of the ridge-like steps that terraced the talus. Quinn paused before climbing the next step that was as high as her shoulders and glared ahead. "You know, blades won't cut through noncorporeal fists."

Lana leaped over the step and wiped her dusty hands on her cargos. "Yeah. That's going to be a problem."

Climbing up after them, Bennett gave a subtle shrug. "Everything we've ever fought, our parents, their parents... there's not a creature any of us have faced that doesn't bleed."

From the next terrace up, Vann tipped his head as he scanned the silent canyon. "This is a security system."

"It, they, whatever is in here knows a hybrid from a human. It was reaching for me, but Archer got in the way," Lana said.

Ryan reached down from the next terrace to take Quinn's hand and scooped her up so she stood next to him.

Lana cleared her throat, extending a hand up. "I'm shorter," she pleaded.

He chuckled and walked over a few steps and plucked her up and over as he had with Quinn, save the dreamy stars in the eyes. As she adjusted her axe, he said, "Werewolves are isolationists. Whatever's in here is violently protective of their privacy."

Bodie peeled his shirt off and stuffed it into his backpack. "Grammy used to read us this story about a grumpy old troll that wouldn't let anyone in his cave, until one day, this brother and sister showed him kindness by rescuing his puppy. From that day forward he made quilts for the villagers, so they'd never be cold again."

Quinn snorted. "Are you saying this is a troll and we should do something nice for it?"

"Okay, I know it sounds farfetched. I didn't say I was sold on the idea, but if we accept we haven't seen everything that's out there, and look to myth, I'm going with troll. If you consider the cautionary tales, trolls are likely humanoid in appearance, but are larger and ambulate with lumbering movements and live in dense forests or caves. The blur, the security system, I suppose those could account for why few have ever actually seen one." He stood on one foot to unlace his boots. "And they are most certainly not interested in making us quilts. People like happy endings."

Speaking up for the first time since they'd arrived, Adair folded her arms over her chest. "Admittedly, vampires tend to stay around people, so it's unlikely I would have come across a reclusive demon anyway, but how have I not even heard of them in over five hundred years?"

Lana shrugged as she looked into the blur ahead. "We've faced squiddy hydra thing and her minions, Quinn and Ryan have taken a kraken, then there were modified werewolves, and the father of all vampires himself? I don't know why we would question something so simple as trolls. This sounds like a snuggly bunny by comparison."

THE DRONE WHIRRED ABOVE and lowered closer to the team.

"I don't think anyone in there is making blankets." Ryan looked up at the towering canyon entrance and held his hand out for Bodie's backpack.

Bodie nodded a thanks and unzipped his jeans.

Over the radio, Chan's voice lilted as she cleared her throat and crackled over the airwaves, "While I appreciate where this is going…"

Lana laughed and radioed back, "You guys are in for a treat." She flashed Bodie a wink and took his jeans, stuffing them into the backpack as Ryan secured it on his own back, covering his unearthly black sword.

Bodie winked back and in less than a blink, where the man stood, a wolf took his place. Rich brown undercoat the color of Bodie's hair, his luminescent, aquamarine eyes looked up and winked.

The radio hissed and crackled, Walker and Chan's voices both frantically calling out, "—copy?—the signal—" She tried to answer, but the radio flickered off. "I think your bare ass frightened away the Echos," she said to Bodie, and he rolled his wolfy eyes at her.

The drone lurched in place and dropped fast. Bennett sprinted back and caught it before it crashed to the ground.

Vann glanced back and moved toward Bennett. He checked the drone and shook his head. "Not EMP. Signal's gone, but electrically, it looks like it should be functional."

Lana clicked her radio off and on again. "Radio too."

Bennett set the drone behind a boulder, sheltered from the wind.

Adair sniffed the air and whispered, "Smells like goats."

Lana tried to catch a whiff, but smelled nothing but dust. "Why aren't we being attacked? We're way closer than when that fist went after us." She reached back and traced the handle of her axe.

As one, the team spread across the width of the canyon. Quinn shook her head and teased her fingers over the twin swords on her back. "It's never good when they roll out the welcome mat like this."

Spaced apart, the team marched slowly in. A stream trickled at their feet, under and around the rocks on the canyon floor. It narrowed as they reached the opening and flowed in a small creek that was ankle deep at its middle.

Adair and Bennett's footsteps were completely silent over the loose gravel as they flanked the edges.

The hair on the back of Lana's neck stood on end, static electricity tickling over her skin, but there was a more ominous edge to it, like a tornado was about to blast through the region. She rubbed her eyes to clear the blur that she knew wasn't her vision.

Quinn had both of her swords ready to strike, stepping cautiously forward. "Veil material is blurry."

As they drew deeper into the murky shadows, the walls seemed to close in around them, yet nothing moved. The wind eased as they entered the shadows of the canyon. Steeper than ninety degrees, the canyon walls seemed to arch up around them, nearly covering the sky in some areas. The rising sun was completely blocked by the clouds, yet the diffused light bounced from wall to wall, the slick rock smooth as glass.

"Obsidian," Lana said as she traced her fingertips over the canyon wall. "Like the basalt at the entrance, this doesn't belong here."

"So you did pay attention in college," Bennett teased from his position in the lead, glancing back and flashing her a shit-eating grin.

"Mineralogy and petrology may not have been my strong suits... or volcanology, but it doesn't take a geology degree to identify an obsidian caldera."

"Caldera? As in... there's been no volcanic activity in this region in... ever," Ryan said.

"Impressive," Quinn said, nudging him in the side.

"I did my homework," he said with a goofy grin, leaning into his wife.

Lana grinned and kept walking. "A-plus for the hunter. That's why it doesn't belong here. We're in the middle of a sedimentary geologic area, not to mention classic glacial erosion and deposition. There are no other volcanic formations in the region. Ryan, do you see much volcanic rock behind the veil?"

"That's just what I was thinking. Yeah, you do." Ryan adjusted his sword and traced his fingers over the cool, black rock. "Canyons are often the result of fractures in the veil, but with how thin it is here, I wonder if they're using the veil to mount their defense. Remember the first time I traveled from the demon realm back home? Brought a damn lightning storm with me."

Head tilting gently to the side, Vann looked deeper into the canyon and said, "Could something be crossing back and forth? Demons find their way through small tears all the time, but to pass freely..."

The ground shook, no more than as if a herd of bison was running at them, but... it was unsettling. Lana glanced around the canyon before pulling her axe out.

"Not likely. I checked the other side, and it's just lovely, rolling plains, unremarkable and uninhabited." Ryan shook his head. "I've never heard of any but the king and his family can control the veil, but this feels like an instability in the veil, so maybe something—"

The rumbling drew closer, louder, shaking the ground under their feet.

Lana gripped the shaft of her axe, ready to nail anything that got too close.

"About time," Bennett muttered.

At her feet, the creek began to boil, rising, rising, reaching her toes as she trudged deeper into the canyon.

Rip-roaring through the canyon like a hurricane, the wind surrounded them. Bracing her legs, she stepped closer, fighting the wind that threatened to knock her into the deepening water and drag her under.

Bodie braced his feet and stalked slowly up the rustling river.

Shield up and ready, Bennett blocked against the wind and Adair took position behind him.

Lana braced her feet wide and fought against every gust to advance deeper into the shadows.

Sensing it before she saw it, its familiar rush pushed through the air. The fist swung out from the darkness of the canyon.

In the space of a blink, she dropped and rolled out of the way.

Having failed, the fist dissipated, but she knew it would be back.

Roars thundered from deeper in the canyon like something out of the depths of the darkest parts of the world.

Quinn snapped her attention to the others and shouted over the wind, "I don't think it likes uninvited guests."

Bennett growled over the wind, "Then why did it let us in so far?"

Overhead, the sky erupted. Wind and rain pummeled at them from all sides.

Lana fought the wind pushing against her, the team doing the same, searching for the source.

Trolls must bleed—if this was a troll. Whatever it was, she had some serious ass to kick. Furious, she growled and gripped her axe, each step harder than the last few rocky, icy miles of McKinley.

Under her feet, radiating up the walls of the canyon, the earth shook, as if they stood at the epicenter of an immeasurably massive quake.

Where the canyon walls had arched above, sharply angled chunks broke away.

Boulders crashed to the ground from all sides.

"That's why," Vann roared as he pinned himself to the wall, scanning the sky as sharp, car-sized chunks of basalt fell down around them.

Bennett held his shield up to protect Adair and himself.

Ryan roared over the constant rockfall, "Recon complete. Let's get the hell out of here."

"What?" Lana shouted over the echoing crashed all around. The creek rose to her knees, the path beyond and behind rapidly narrowing.

Bodie dove out of the way of a falling boulder and sprinted toward the exit. The others followed close behind.

"Go," Lana shouted to Bennett. "If we get crushed, you can come back with an excavator."

Expression set in a grimace, he hesitated half a heartbeat while Adair took off down the canyon for the exit, then took off after her.

The center of the canyon flooded too deep to see a clear path, the walls crumbling faster than she could run.

Lana climbed above the water level and leaped from boulder to boulder.

Louder than the rest, a blast of lighting struck the canyon. A rock as big as a house crashed into the center of the canyon.

She leaped to the other side and pinned herself to the wall to avoid the hit.

A looming shadow caught her eye. A bulky figure watched from deep in the canyon. Patient, unmoving, the creature didn't flinch or react to the collapse.

Fuck he was huge. Like the vampire demon on steroids.

Another stepped behind him, massive fists clenched, a hateful sneer tainting its furry face.

From the shadows, another peered through the storm to watch.

Through the dust, the storm, and the falling debris, their eyes glowed gold against the darkness.

"Move," Vann said, grabbing Lana and leaping to the next boulder before setting her down, a boulder crushing the spot she'd been standing.

"Thanks," she yelped as she took off down the path.

As the water deluged from above and below, wind pushing at their backs, the mouth of the canyon came into sight. The entry was nearly blocked with rocks, the river rising and gushing over the top.

One by one, they climbed over the boulders that had accumulated at the exit, dropping to the ground and sprinting like hell.

At the base of the slope, Bennett, Adair, and Bodie were firing up the engines.

The rest leaped down the terraced ledges of the talus that were rapidly developing into waterfalls.

Her skin burned as the grit-filled wind lashed in all directions.

Lana splashed down again, sprinting with the team until they reached the trucks.

As they neared the rigs, Ryan tossed her Bodie's backpack, and she snatched it from the air. Without pause, she dove into the passenger seat of the truck.

Bodie didn't hesitate, but took off and glanced in the rearview mirror to see that the others were following.

The engine revved hard as they gained traction over the saturated field of shale. Out the back window, Lana saw the clouds focused above the canyon, darker than midnight.

One on top of another, lightning blasts illuminated the dizzying scene and the ghostly fists that furiously lashed out from the canyon.

Hands gripped tight on the wheel, Bodie continued to check the rearview as he drove hard and fast to get the hell out of there. "I officially don't believe a single rumor that trolls are friendly, or that they're not extremely intelligent."

"Agreed," she said as she stared out the back window.

Under the deluge, the windshield wipers couldn't keep up. Lana squinted to see more than a few feet in front of the SUV. She pulled out the radio and called out, "Echo. Do you copy?" No answer, the white noise snapping and popping with no sign of life on the other side.

"That airstrike is going to be an awful idea," Bodie said as she gave up on the radio.

"I can't imagine the trolls are going to appreciate it."

"Worse, what if they do like it? They must be harnessing a lot of power from the veil."

Distance didn't seem to ease the storm. The sky was black and furious in all directions. A gnawing ache ate away at Lana's optimism. And it wasn't just what they had unleashed causing it.

Archer had to be freaking out, if he'd awoken while they were away. While she treaded helplessly above the surface, she seemed to be sinking into a fathomless abyss, like she was one bad decision away from losing herself entirely.

This was her mission. Her recon. And it was no small amount of luck that her team had made it out in one piece.

After nearly losing Archer, she should have known better...

Fuck. If she'd lost him?

An ache brewed deep in her bones, taking hold as fear and frustration shook her to the core. They'd had close calls before. This wasn't new.

But what would happen to Archer if she died before she'd finished binding their souls?

As if he'd become a part of her, she knew the one cure to the hollowness in her—that had nothing to do with trolls—was Archer, a craving beyond anything she could imagine.

"Trade me?" Bodie asked after the canyon disappeared in the distance.

Lana nodded and he stopped the truck. She hopped out and swapped spots so he could get dressed before they reached the base.

With the airstrike due soon, the COP finally came into view. Without slowing, the team barreled for the gates that opened as they arrived. In the middle of the storm, Sauer and Chan ran to meet them, Kerse standing distant under the chow hall awning.

Archer stood in the center of the base, soaked to the skin and lightning flashing behind him. Hands on his hips, his hair and clothes clinging to every angle of him, he waited.

When lightning flashed right overhead, thunder on top of the burst of light that set the base trembling, he didn't flinch.

Harder than the pummeling downpour hammering the windshield, her heart thundered in her chest. He looked... furious. Powerful. Beautiful.

As soon as she pulled into the truck's spot in the motor pool, she slammed on the brakes, shut off the engine, and jumped out.

Archer strolled in behind the other Echos and stood in the back, arms folded over his chest. His cobalt eyes boiled, but the rest of him was stoically patient.

Chan halted in front of the demon hunters and said, "Tell me that storm is an ironic way of saying you cleared the canyon."

Bennett strolled close and shook his head, rubbing a hand over his face as if fatigue was finally getting the better of him. "Not even close. At least we know what we're dealing with."

At his side, Quinn's shoulders slumped forward. "But not how to defeat them."

Vann quietly rumbled, "Status of the airstrike?"

From the rear, Archer glanced subtly at his watch and finally spoke. "Seventeen minutes."

Legs frozen in place, her brain mushed to nothing, as the fiery waves of Archer pheromones surged in her direction. Out of breath, she asked, "Is there no way to cancel it, until we can find out what effect it may have?"

His voice gruff, his eyes locked onto hers. "Not up to me."

Vann asked again, "Do we have visual?"

"No," Walker grumbled. "Drone's down for the count. Satellite imagery isn't looking promising, but come on," he motioned.

The others took off after Walker. Quinn patted Archer on the shoulder as she passed and said, "Glad you're okay."

Archer gave her a soft nod, but didn't look away from Lana.

The short distance between them a painful crevasse, Lana ached to get closer, but didn't dare. "I can explain," she said.

22

"What happened?" he asked, reining in the fury that seethed palpably through his veins. The cure for the burning ache in his chest stood across the room, but he was frozen in place. Millions of questions burned in his mind. Worry echoed loudest as he tried to understand what was behind the guilt in her expression.

Lana stood dripping wet, the edge of her bottom lip tucked into her teeth as she studied him, her uncertainty threatening to crush him, or to change his life again.

"What do you remember?" she asked, her expression set firmly. There was a weariness under her eyes he'd never seen.

"Pain," he growled, unable to hold anything back from her.

"I'm so sorry." Her green eyes were saturated with regret, and that plump lower lip was rosy when she finally released it to take a deep breath. Chest rising and falling as if the effort required to take even a light breath was overwhelming.

Arms gripped over his chest, his fists clenching tight at his sides, he tried to sort it all out, but he didn't even know where to start. He couldn't shake the memory of the pain that should have taken his life, and when he needed her, she'd gone running back in and risked her life.

Under the surface of it all, there was a… a viciousness he'd never felt, so overcome with the need to rush into that canyon and *hunt*.

More, and so, so much more tantalizing, he needed to cross the garage and sweep Lana onto the back of that truck she stood in front of and… fuck, and plow into her like he should have back home in Tucson. Before they'd sunk so deep. Like some damn primal urge that was entirely hormone and instinct driven. And not at all polite. "I—"

Sympathy eroded, her cheeks flushing in contrast to the pallor, she stomped her foot and demanded, "What were you thinking, jumping in front of me like that?"

"What was I thinking? Lana, in the moment, I'm not about to stop and think about who's tougher. That fist nearly killed Brock. He got out of the way in time, but I was a breath away from losing my best friend. When I saw it whooshing toward *you*, the rocks on the hill below boiling with nowhere safe to land? No way I was going to risk losing you." He shouted, his hands flew in fury.

While his mouth was digging in for a fight, a fucking bizarre urge permeated into his brain cells—and parts further south—and his words stuttered as he lost his flow. He was caught up watching as each breath seemed to shift the heavy weight of the wet fabric of her tank top a margin lower. What the fuck was wrong with him?

"So you… dammit, Archer. You could have died. Were well on your way to doing so."

A bird settled onto the rafter above, ruffling the rain from its saturated wings, but it seemed to sense the threat of explosion and left as quickly as it had arrived, the storm outside less electric.

Archer gnawed on his cheek. He huffed out a breath of air and said, "There were moments that I wish I had."

In absolute contrast to the gray of the stormy sky casting through the windows overhead, her brilliant green eyes flashed as she watched him, as if she could see what he felt, the change in him, the strength, and, in all likelihood, the hard-on that hit the moment she climbed out of that truck.

"Until it cleared," he said. "And I woke from a barrage of nightmares. Alone, only to learn you had gone right back out there."

"Dammit, Archer. That's why I'm here. I hate that I didn't protect you better."

"No, Lana, it's not—" He shut himself up, his words spiraling in his head and seeming less and less relevant as his focus narrowed on one thing.

He clutched his hands in his hair and closed his eyes, but could see nothing but her. "Fuck," he muttered as he opened his eyes.

The guilt in her expression was going to crush him.

He took a breath and said, "Whatever the hell you did to me… Lana, I want you so bad, I can't think straight. I've got a million questions, but more than anything, I need to know you want me even half as bad as I want you."

As if his words triggered something, her cheeks flushed, and he knew.

He closed the distance between them in a blink.

Without hesitation, with the energy she exuded in everything, she launched into his arms and wrapped her body around him.

Exploding on contact, their mouths met. Needing every inch of her as quickly and thoroughly as was physically possible, he kissed her with frantic desperation.

Equally ravenous, she clutched her hands in his hair and closed her lips over his tongue, sucking him in before releasing to stroke him again.

Kiss after kiss, he felt the restlessness inside him easing, but the craving wouldn't relent. Her scent fresh as a storm in the desert summer, her taste exquisite on his tongue, he needed her even more than he had their last morning together when he'd neared the point of explosion.

And he needed both hands.

As if reading his mind, she slipped her feet to the ground and her hands went straight for his waistband.

Fuck, he wanted her so bad, he could come at the slightest touch. And he needed so much more with her than a quick bang.

Everywhere. All of her. To fill his mouth with the taste of her.

He dropped to his knees and ripped at the buttons of her cargos, tugging her pants down and glared at the high cut panties in his way. Sexy as hell, but in the way. "I thought I said to wear a skirt, and no panties," he growled playfully as he looked up at her.

Eyes already glazed over, her breath coming fast before he even touched her, she nibbled the edge of her lip and whispered, "I'll never break another promise to you."

He licked her skin along the edge of lace, the fabric rough against his tongue in contrast to her satin skin. Fingers entwined around the fabric to protect her from the impact, he snapped the fabric and launched the delicate purple lace behind him.

Home free, he grabbed her by the hips and pressed his mouth to her core. With the urgency that he'd kissed her, beyond control but with complete precision, he traced his tongue in a long, consuming lick over her slick center. The taste of her was like nothing else, like everything he'd been craving without ever realizing it.

She clutched her hands in his hair and let out a cry as he sucked. Harder. Wildly.

Until her legs began to tremble. Then he slowed and laved, building her carefully up again.

"Spread your legs wider," he ordered, his mouth leaving her only long enough to utter the command.

She laughed breathlessly and asked, "When did you get so bossy?"

"I'm the highest-ranking officer on post," he murmured, blowing a gentle wind over her sensitized core.

Within the constraints of her dropped cargos, her boots crunched over gravel as she spread for him.

Craving the slick heat he'd tasted, needing to feel every inch of her as much as taste, he thrust his fingers into her and caressed.

Fingertips gripped in his hair, she urged him on. Her tone was sweet, but her words were sin.

As if he could sense what she needed, tuning in to her rhythm as if each kiss, each lick, each crest of orgasm anchored him to her, he shifted his angle and accelerated.

Her tone heightened, breath quickening. Her pelvis pushed tighter against him, and she cried out with victorious *yesses*.

Knowing she hummed on the edge, he increased the pace. Fingers pressed to the sweet spot inside her, he rubbed and felt her tighten around him. Breath coming faster, her voice chanted in soprano whimpers. He closed his lips over her and sucked until he felt the vibration run over her body and into his.

As she neared her pinnacle, he braced his free hand tighter around her hip and covered her with his mouth, sucking and laving, overwhelmed with the thrill of what he could do to her, of how she responded to him, of how her satisfaction drove his, the explosiveness threatening to ignite the building. Her quickening moans rose to a full-on roar as he brought her to climax, sending a rush through him as if she'd been stroking him as he did her.

After cresting her over the edge, he gently released her and rose to his feet. A smug grin teasing at the corner of his lips, he wiped his thumb over the corner, and he savored the taste of her on his tongue.

Her eyes were closed and her smile slack and delicious as she relaxed into his embrace. He wrapped his hands around her waist and pressed against her core, painfully hard, as if the sky would fall if he couldn't have her, completely, *now*.

As she opened her eyes and met his look, her smile widened, and she slipped her hands under his shirt. Palms and fingers spread wide over his chest, she tweaked his nipples before trailing her fingertips down and unbuttoned his cargos with a taunting pace that threatened his ability to make it long enough to even feel her around him.

Shreds of light from outside flashed brighter than if the sun itself had descended upon them.

Instantly on alert, he held her against him and dragged her to the ground with him. Keeping her encased in his arms, he rolled under the truck as a sonic boom shattered over the base. Reflexively, they both grabbed their ears and screamed to block the noise.

Uninterrupted rolls of thunder followed as the ground shifted beneath them. Lana clutched him close, scanning the room, ready to fight back. Minutes went by, explosions clashing with thunder and the ground jarring back and forth with each blast.

The ground stilled. Above, rain on the metal roof returned to the dull roar with thunder and lightning flashes declaring the storm had won.

"You okay?" she asked, palming his jaw in her hand and looking up at him with the sweetest worry that anchored him as much as much as their physical connection.

He nodded subtly, lost to the world as she held his gaze, a storm boiling in her look. Hand palmed over the bare skin of her rear, he groaned and bit down on his lip. "We need to get to work," he grumbled, but pressed her tighter against him instead. Needing to feel her against him, to take her while the world crashed around them, he struggled to catch his breath.

"Yeah," she answered softly, then rolled off him and pressed her back into the rocky floor of the motor pool and pulled her cargos up. Under the truck, surrounded by shattered glass, she opened her mouth to say something, then bit her lips together and crawled out the other side.

She snatched a sweatshirt from her gear in the truck and tied it to secure her pants where he'd ripped the buttons off. Finally, she said, "Now you owe me two pair of pants."

He backed toward the door and flashed her a wink. "I told you to wear a skirt."

23

THE BUILDINGS STILL STOOD, unharmed, but the air felt different, thinner. He pushed into the TOC and saw shifted equipment, a few chairs overturned, and the Echos and demon hunters stared at a single computer screen.

Bennett glanced up and gave him a subtle nod.

Chan's expression was hopelessly dark, but she feigned a smile and asked, "You're okay?"

"Fine. Report?" he asked, scanning the swirling smoke that coated the image on the screen.

Bodie stood back and rubbed his hand over the back of his neck, an ironic chuckle buoying his words. "It didn't care for the airstrike."

Walker pointed to the center of the image. "We saw the flashes from the explosions making their way up the canyon, and tornadoes seemed to form around each, as if the storm spit the explosives back out. A lot of smoke and debris, but less blur."

The storm looked to be ravaging at full force over the canyon, stronger than over the base.

Chan turned to Lana and said, "I think it's time you explained."

Archer stepped to Lana's side and slipped his hand into hers, the fragile state of their relationship scaring the hell out of him. Lana entwined her fingers with his, sending a shiver zinging over his skin as she decisively finished the connection, stirring something deep in his core he didn't know existed prior to this moment.

Ryan looked to the others and said, "I had to tell my Coast Guard crew, eventually. I think this is a pretty damn good reason."

With a nod, Vann added, "I've got a friend in the FBI who knows enough to know when to call me."

Lana gave his hand a squeeze and looked up at him.

Archer caught his breath and said, "This is so much bigger than these guys. No one outside of this room, not even your spouses. Especially not to leadership. I think we all could guess what the military would do with this sort of information."

"I don't doubt it," Walker said, seeming to understand completely. Thank fuck. He knew the Echos would get it. As the best of the best, and the first to get thrown into the worst shit on the planet, they knew when to shut the hell up.

"It's not the sort of thing you can… replicate." A sneer on his lips, menacing as pure predator, Bennett snarled, "Try, and I will hunt you down."

Even Kerse paled at the threat.

Archer glanced at the screen, but dust clouds obscured the image.

Tipped back in her chair by the computer, Quinn smiled with a subtle knowing smirk. "My friends, you have teamed up with demon hunters for this particular mission."

"Um, like, vampire slayers?" Sauer asked, an eyebrow-raising grin brightening his expression.

"So, what, are you guys like, immortal or something?" Walker asked. "I mean, did you make Archer one of you?"

Archer's ears perked up, realizing he didn't have a clue if he was immortal now. A million and one questions multiplied by another few hundred after whatever Lana had done to him. Her thumb rubbed gently over his, her touch sending a fire through his veins and steadying him all at once.

Lana shook her head. "Demon hunters only live a few hundred years."

"And you're all demon hunters?" Chan asked, eyeing Bennett and Adair with their pointy canines and almost mesmerizing allure.

"Close enough," Bennett said with an easy shrug.

"How old are you?" Sauer asked. "I mean, you all look like you're in your mid-twenties or so, but, fuck, you could be a hundred fifty and we wouldn't know it, right?"

Adair smiled subtly, but didn't answer.

Lana spoke up instead, "We're actually not very old, for the most part. I think I'm oldest at forty-one. Or, wait, Vann, aren't you pushing fifty?"

He shrugged and masked a wicked grin. "Thereabouts."

Lana continued, "Anyway, we're all coming due to update our IDs and move on. My family has owned the tavern since before Sitka was Sitka, so we've become a part of local folklore. No one questions us when we laugh at their foolishness when anyone dares to raise an eyebrow in our direction, and we claim our family is huge, and we all look remarkably similar. Actually, it's pretty handy that my sister chose a human life, so they'll see at least some of the Fischers age. And I saw three gray hairs and two wrinkles on my dad before I left."

Curiosity dancing in his eyes, Walker asked, "So it's like, hereditary? Then how did Archer..."

"Long story," Lana said, cutting him off.

Grief burned in his throat as he realized the implications of what they said. Could he tell his family? In a few years, they'd begin to wonder why he wasn't aging... assuming he was a demon hunter now. He leaned down and whispered to Lana, "I'm like you now, right?"

She nodded softly. "Yes. I'll explain everything. Later."

"I mean, if you could do that for Archer, then maybe..." Chan asked, her eyes alight with the idea.

"Not how it works," Vann uttered, silencing them with a dark look. "Archer becoming one of us was extremely unusual."

Bodie growled under his breath and folded his arms over his chest. "Like Bennett said. Don't even try. It won't end well for anyone involved."

"And this is why you all survived the canyon?" Kerse asked, seeming uncaring about the threat or the prospect of power.

Sauer rubbed a hand over his thick red beard. "How *did* you guys get into the canyon, and what set that storm off?"

"That's why we went alone," Quinn said, serious for the first time since Archer had met her. "We got in... but they weren't going to let us leave. If we were fully human, we wouldn't have."

"What do you mean?" Kerse asked, uncharacteristically talkative as she drilled for answers. "Why would it let you get close, if you're the only ones that can destroy it? Wouldn't it want to repel you?"

"I don't know. And it's *them*, not *it*," Lana said.

"You saw?" Archer asked.

"Briefly," she admitted, scowling as if it wasn't adding up. "At least three, but, I need time to think. I'm going to go take a shower. Someone's going to watch the satellite images and see about getting another drone out there?"

Archer leaned in and pressed a soft kiss on her cheek, whispering, "I need to catch up with the Echos. Then you can fill me in on what you saw?"

She nodded and backed away.

While the demon hunters disappeared, Archer looked to the Echos and said, "Data collection. I want to know the complete weather history of the region, including anything that coincides with the storms. I want the latest intel on the latest insurgent activity, civilians nearby, and any political changes. I hope to hell that blast didn't hurt anyone, or set off any other attacks. And as soon as we know the full effects of the airstrike, I want to know about it."

"Got it," Walker said, clicking away at the keys as he connected with another satellite. The others hopped on computers and phones and got to work.

Chan looked up and asked, "Hey. Everything okay?"

"Fine. I've got a lot of investigating of my own to do."

Walker leaned back in his chair and rested the keyboard on his lap. He teased without looking up, "Like, what all you're going to do with all that extra strength?"

Sauer chuckled under his breath. "Or why he and Lana look all disheveled, and why he's still looking at her like he's working up the nerve to ask her to go steady."

Chan tossed a pen at Sauer and rolled her eyes. "Get out of here," she said to Archer. "We'll report in when we know more."

Before he had to listen to any more chuckles or whispers, he stepped out into the storm. Unaccustomed to the torrential rains, the ground was slow to percolate, and the saturated shale had become a shallow lake. Not bothering to cover his head, already soaked to the skin, he stalked across to the main house.

As he reached the door, he stilled, remembering to turn the knob gently, or he could rip it off without effort. To the right of the main door, his bedroom door closed, and he heard Lana talking to someone on his sat phone.

Fuck. He needed answers, and she was holding back. Like why the hell he was the horniest person in history, and if she so much as glanced in his direction, his dick stood tall in full salute? He stormed up the stairs. As if the world was peachy keen, surrounded by books and notes and hopeless research, the hunters laughed and teased each other as they read.

"What am I missing?" Maybe it was a good thing she wasn't here for this conversation. When she was around, he couldn't think past the tip of his dick. Without her... it all came flashing back. The pain. Of her leaving him to fight when they'd promised to be partners.

No one spoke. Glancing at each other, they seemed to silently fight over who had to explain the dirty details. Why this was he "extremely unusual?" Why, after hours of pain with Lana sobbing over him while he was dying, was he stronger, faster, and sharper than ever, but still felt remarkably normal?

What toll had it taken on her? She hadn't said a word about it, but she had dark circles under her eyes. Something was taking a toll on her, and judging by the healthy and hale looks on the others, it wasn't because of their fight in the canyon.

Fury boiling from deep in his gut, he held his breath to restrain the roar that threatened. "Answer me. Did she—" He gripped his hand in his hair, blowing a rush of wind from his lungs. "Whatever she did, I'm like her. If she gave up anything for me... If she lost any part of herself to save me... I need to know how to fix it." He gnawed on the edge of his tongue, wishing he could storm downstairs and feel her skin against his, as if the simple act of being with her would make it all better.

Bodie smiled sympathetically, rubbing his hand over the back of his neck as if unsure how to start. "Honestly, I don't think that's possible, to *give up* power. It's more like sharing."

"I don't know." Vann's voice cracked as he broke the confidence of the room. "She shouldn't have been able to pass so much. I have never heard of that happening." He turned to Archer and asked, "Looks like you stretched your wings a bit. *How much* are you like her?"

Archer bit the edge of his tongue and shrugged. "I could run for a day without needing a break, and I think I could bench press a truck. I survived what should have killed me."

With a giddy grin, Quinn said, "Pretty much. That's... more than she should have been able to share. I think she shared it all."

"And, this won't make any sense. I don't know how to describe it, but... Okay, I've been trained to kill when I have to, but I'm actually pretty pacifistic. But I've got this rage in the back of my mind, like I'm burning for a fight."

Ryan scowled and murmured, "Hunters have an ingrained desire for violence. Let it take over, and that violence could take over. But you're also half human still, so don't ever forget that. We exist to protect humans."

Leaned back in his chair, Bennett said easily, "Near another canyon, not that long ago, someone shared abilities with us."

Quinn's smile turned pensive as she seemed to be working it out. "How would Lana be able to do what a demon did?"

As if realizing the answer, Vann folded his hands over his abdomen and smiled smugly. "Deandra knew we wouldn't win the fight, so she shared power with each of us. It wiped her out, but once she recovered, she was as strong as ever." Vann glanced at Archer, then seemed to switch directions and asked the others, "Sharing is the right term, but it's also more than giving." He looked back to the others. "Don't you feel Deandra in you now? I mean, there was always a connection, but it's stronger now."

Bennett nodded. "Fuck. Yeah. I do. It's like she's always there, not in my head, but like there's a part of her embedded in me that wasn't there before. Adair is too, after I shared myself with her. Of course,

I've got Tromos laced in there, too, so my head's pretty fucked up in general."

"Thanks for including me in that," Adair said, and nudged him with a fluttering eye-roll. "Flattering."

"I'm not part of you now, too?" he asked, flicking the tip of his tongue across a sharp canine.

Archer took a long breath of air and backed up a step. "Am I hearing a consensus coming soon, or do you guys always talk your way around settling on an answer, so you don't have to admit that you don't know?"

Adair smiled at him, the girl-next-door innocence almost fooling him into thinking she wasn't... what she was. "This is pretty typical. But they do usually get around to the point, eventually. I think they're almost there."

"True," Bodie said with a confident nod. "I think we've concluded that Lana shared her power with you. But we're dodgy on the details because it's not something hybrids can do easily. Or, ever, really. Lana seemed to have done what her demon ancestor did for these guys a few years back, in how she shared her power. Normally, she would have shared her healing and longevity as part of the hunter's bond, but not more than that."

"Bond?" Archer asked. A rising flutter lurched inside his chest. The last few days were such a blur, but he played back the words she'd said as he'd lay dying in her arms.

Bodie opened his mouth to answer, but Bennett fired him a shut-the-fuck-up look and said instead, "You were too badly hurt and we were out of time. So, she gave you everything."

"What aren't you telling me?" he asked, needing to hear what he was beginning to suspect. Why he was in the middle of one of the toughest ops of his career, had survived what no one should have, only to come out stronger on the other side, and all he wanted to do was get Lana naked.

Vann said with a knowing look, "She made a poignant, emotional decision that drove the exchange, and his human life was waning when it happened."

The corners of Adair's lips quirked up. "When a vampire changes someone, the progeny must first be drained to the brink of death, otherwise the progeny wouldn't have room for the full dose of demon."

Vann nodded and said, "The chances of that happening under normal circumstances? Impossible. No human should have been able to take all that once. Maybe like vampires in a sense, but hunters aren't built to share like that."

As if threatening and informing without coming out and flat saying it, Bodie's aquamarine eyes flashed darkly as he said, "Hunters are like werewolves, in that we aren't full demons, nor, as Vann said, are we designed to share our power like vampires. It takes so much out of us, we can only share power *once*, and," he looked at Archer, as if threatening and pleading at the same time. "It's based on a bond that's already unbreakable. So, to share so much..."

Bennett kicked him under the table and snarled. Posture stiffening, Bodie glared back and seemed to growl under his breath.

"Stop it," Quinn hissed. She turned to Archer and said, "It's a lot, and Lana should be the one to explain the major details. We're just guessing," she said poignantly to the others, "as she shouldn't have been able to do what she did. But you're special to her."

"Great," Archer muttered. "So, to save my life, Lana shared all of her powers with me. But she couldn't do that for just anyone, and wasted her one share on me. And, she couldn't have done so much if I weren't almost dead, and no one else has done it to this extent before."

"Exactly," Adair answered. "Well summarized. You might fit in with these goofballs after all."

Bennett pinched at her side, and Adair squealed and snatched his hand before he could do it again.

24

Narrowly escaping another confrontation with Archer, as the heat of the aggressive moment in the motor pool faded and she could focus, Lana closed the door and snatched his satellite phone from the charger. Breath whooshed from her lungs as she dropped to the edge of the cot.

No idea what time it was on the other side of the world, she knew her target would take her call and walk her through things. Although he wouldn't agree with how she'd done it, he might be able to explain how she could mitigate the stupidity of it.

"Hey, Dad." She exhaled into the phone when he answered, the nagging tears glazing over her vision the moment they connected.

"Hey, honey, everything okay?" As she'd anticipated, Ross's booming voice was gentle as the wildflower-dappled field behind their home.

"Um, sort of," she admitted, the waterworks already threatening. She squeezed her eyes shut to push it back.

"Mission going okay? Quinn already called to pick my brain and see if I'd heard of anything like what you're facing."

"We've got our work cut out for us. I'll tell you all about it when I get back. Anyway, that's not why I'm calling."

A hollow tunnel sound filled her ear as she heard her mom's melodious voice come over as her dad had shared the call, "Hey, honey. I hope you don't mind if we put you on speaker?"

"Just the two of you?" She grimaced, imagining Missy there with her perfect husband and her perfect little toddler snuggled up.

"Just us. You've got that thing in your voice. Are you okay?" Julia asked.

"I, um. Wow. Where do I start?" She closed her eyes, suddenly wishing to hell she hadn't dialed in the first place. One wrong word, and they'd gush with congratulations. "We ran into a tough situation. Nothing I couldn't handle," she quickly added. "But someone got hurt. A man. I'd been spending a lot of time with him, and he's become a good friend..." Dead silence on the other end, like a cat waiting for the perfect moment to pounce. "He risked himself to protect me, and he wasn't going to survive, so, um, I sort of, um... married him."

"Oh," her mom began, trailing off. Lana could picture the fissure between her eyebrows as she tried to understand.

"I'm so sorry, honey. It worked? He's okay?" her dad asked.

"He's fine. Great." Better than great.

Her mom was immediately in protective mode. "But you don't sound fine. Lana, this is one of the most important decisions you'll ever make, committing to the right mate, so if you have regrets—"

"It's not like that. He was dying, and sharing the traditional healing and longevity weren't enough, so I gave him *everything*. It took a lot out of us both, and then I had the trolls to take care of. And then the airstrike... We've been busy."

"*Everything*?" Ross asked, the skeptical lilt in his tone reminding her of when she told him the truth about werewolves. And why she hadn't even told him about Bennett. "I'm not sure I follow."

"As you taught me, I was sharing myself steadily and taking the brunt of the burden for him. But it wasn't enough. Archer didn't just need the ability to heal, he needed the strength and endurance to pull himself through it. I remembered how it felt when Deandra flooded us with a dose of her power to defeat Typha, and I used that feeling to share all of my abilities."

"That was awfully risky. Humans aren't built to take on so much. You could have killed him. There's a reason we only share so much. I can't even fathom how painful that would have been for him."

"He was already stronger than most humans," she gritted, her jaw aching as she struggled to remember why she'd called in the first place.

Nor did she need the reminder of what he'd gone through. His screams would forever echo in her memories, and she'd never forgive herself for bringing that on him.

"Look, that's not the point. What I really need to know is... He wasn't exactly coherent when it happened, and so we haven't... And I'm not sure I did the right thing for him. Dad, I need a straight answer. None of this soulmate bullshit. Okay?"

That airstrike had been well timed. Instinct had taken over, and she was intoxicated by him, needing to share all of herself with him, needing all of him in exchange. When he was around, she couldn't think straight, as all she could focus on was getting him naked.

"Of course, of course. I'm listening."

"If we don't consummate this, can we go our separate ways? And he can live out a normal life? I guess I'm not clear on what might happen if we don't complete it. Would the power fade, or would he keep it? Would he get hurt?" They'd have to go their separate ways. Indefinitely. It was bad before, but she burned with an overwhelming need to experience all of him.

"Lana. Don't hang up—"

"Don't go there—"

Her dad's words rushed through the line. "You know it wouldn't have worked if you didn't genuinely believe him worthy of being your life partner, and if he didn't feel the same way."

"I know that's what they say, but it's just words shared in a sappy ceremony—"

"Uh-uh. Nope. Don't bullshit yourself. I know you, Lana. You felt it when you shared your power. To share your power at all, it takes a bond more profound than what most humans will ever find. I would imagine that sharing *all* of you, that could only come from the deepest sort of love. That connection you and he must have already shared with each other—"

Flipping her hair out of her face, she shoved her shoulders back and laughed sardonically, "Yes, he's attractive and I enjoy his company. But that doesn't mean—"

Her mother's tone was livid as she boiled over the crackling airwaves. "You listen up right now. We've been patient while you played around. I know you always looked up to your wild grandfather. And we get it, we really do. Falling in love is powerful. Intimidating. But this is serious. I can hear you getting defensive and acting like this is no big thing. You can't share such a huge part of yourself with someone who's only a fling."

Even though they couldn't see, her head shook in denial, and her knee vibrated so fast she feared she might bust through the floor. Her throat clenched shut and she should have hung up when she knew she'd crossed the tipping point. "He was in and out of consciousness, and didn't know what marriage to a demon hunter meant anyway, so he couldn't possibly have understood what I was asking of him. What if... what if, now that he's fully conscious... What if he says *no*?" She rubbed the ache in her chest, having admitted it out loud, but they'd have seen right through her anyway.

And her dad's turn. Tag-teaming was their specialty. "Lana, how long has it been since the exchange?"

"Less than two days. But he slept to recover for most of that, and once I recovered, I left to try to take the canyon." Or get her ass kicked by unfriendly trolls. "And I just got back." And started the bonding process. And would have finished it if the region hadn't exploded.

What was she going to do if he walked in this room right now? She'd probably strip naked and lick him all over. No wonder no one knew what would happen if they didn't complete the bond.

"Tell me, how do you feel?"

She held the flippant "horny" response and stared down at the empty cot, at Archer's glasses on the nightstand. Tears blurred her vision as she struggled to stay upright. "Awful. Like I'm bleeding out and there's no way to stop it."

Where she expected sympathy, her dad's tone was steady. "I didn't think I'd ever see you so overcome by fear. Since the day you were born, I knew you were going to be a fiercer fighter than me, more than your grandfather. You have always been special. Don't you for one minute think that you can run scared from what should be the easiest thing you've ever done."

He swallowed and slowed his pace.

"Lana, if you don't complete this union, you'll live the rest of your life alone and miserable. Like a ghost lost in the ether. If you don't consummate this, yes, he will keep his new abilities, but you will *never* feel complete. Not even a glimmer of hope. You'll begin to lose yourself, your soul knowing that you *quit*. *You* are not a quitter. I can't believe I'm telling you this, of all people, but go have sex."

Speechless, her mouth opening and closing like a wide-mouthed bass, Lana held the phone out and stared. She cleared her throat and asked, "And what about him? If we don't complete it?"

Long pause. She knew he wouldn't want to say it, but her dad admitted, "It'll change him, hollow him out, but I can't say for sure as I've never heard of a human taking so much."

Lana breathed a heavy sigh of relief and crackled, "Okay."

Her dad's tone lightened to the diehard romantic she'd been expecting all along. "But if you do come together, I guarantee, you'll never have a moment of regret. There's a part of you that comes to life when your soul connects with its mate on the deepest of levels."

A lump in her throat, Lana nodded without speaking.

A shred of sympathy in her voice, her mom asked, "Call soon and let us know how it goes?" Julia's blush was palpable, and she quickly amended, "Not the sex. I mean, yes, I want to know that you enjoyed it, but I meant, how you two resolve things?"

"Um, sure," she coughed over a teary laugh, ending the call and clicking off.

Well. That sucked. She set the phone on the nightstand. One of Archer's t-shirts was on top of the pack, so she stripped her clothes off and wore only his shirt before crashing on the bed into a pummeling nap of dream after dream of him. Writhing, moaning in her sleep, she woke to the sound of her screaming his name as he filled her.

Fuck. No wonder she was so exhausted. Her subconscious was doing its utmost to seal the deal to the point she was afraid she might jump him on sight. Without him, her body seemed to want to sleep to heal the wound that was growing from being away from him, but her sleep was fitful, her dreams attempting to heal her in his absence.

Hollow. Yup. She could see why that would be her fate if...

With a pitiful, horny and sexually frustrated pout, she wandered into the living area, and crashed onto the couch at Vann's feet. Blue and green flickering from the TV, his thumbs paddling rapidly over the controller, his gaze was locked onto the screen. Perfect. Vann was the quietest of the team, and his silence was exactly what she needed right now.

"Congrats," he said, the rich rumble of his voice quaking over her last hope of ignoring the problem at hand.

"Smartass," she grumbled and curled her feet up on the sofa.

Clicking the Xbox off, he tossed the controller aside and leaned back, folding his hands over his abdomen. "You did the right thing."

"I know."

"Were those your parents on the phone earlier?"

"Yes. They weren't helpful. I got an earful."

Quiet as a serene little clam, Vann didn't budge.

"I mean, I know it wouldn't have worked if I wasn't in love with him or if he wasn't in love with me. But come on, that doesn't mean I had intended to marry the guy. Or, at least, not so soon."

Nothing. Not a peep. But definitely an amused smirk.

"And how can I really know that he's the only one on the entire planet for me, in such a short time? Yeah, he's nice to look at. And he's easy to be around. Great kisser. Amazing kisser. If there were an Olympic event for kissing, he'd be an all-time greatest gold medalist. But what if the sex isn't any good? You can't know if someone's worth spending the next two or three centuries with if you don't know if they're any good in bed."

Tipping his head back, Vann let out a riotous laugh.

"What's so funny?" She groused, shriller than she'd intended, hoping to hell she didn't wake the entire house in her panic.

"Lana Fischer waited until marriage. How chaste of you." He eased his laughs and wiped a phony tear from the corner of his eye.

She nudged her foot against his hip and scowled.

He grinned with pure devilry. "I think it's a sign. Just go talk to the man. And, honestly, if the sex isn't any good, you have centuries to experiment and figure out how to make it incredible."

"We're still on a mission, you know." She snorted, wishing she hadn't topped it off with the infantile eye-roll, but knew that he'd get it. "We have other things to worry about."

"Lots to worry about, but plenty of time to kill. The Echos are compiling data about the canyon before and after the airstrike, the status of the surrounding regions and civilians, and hopefully getting adequate drone and satellite imaging so we can find a way back in. Astrid's been burning the midnight oil on her end. The rest of the team is banking some rest while we wait. We'll hit the books tomorrow morning with what we've brought, but I think we could all use a break after today's setback. Not much to do right now."

"Trouble, that's what you are," she said with a snarky scowl.

"Go find your husband," he said, gesturing to the stairs.

"Fine," she huffed. Why did she call her parents? Was she crazy? She'd known it would go exactly as it had. Well, not exactly. Their belief in love overcoming all wasn't a surprise.

Ending by telling her to have sex was new, as they were typically telling her to wait it out and get to know the man first.

And she'd proven her own point.

First guy she got to know first, and she married the poor bastard.

25

Not a sound peeped in the house except Lana's feet creaking over the stairs, the team recovering from their defeat while the Echos sorted out the status of the canyon and its inhabitants. The light from Vann's video game darkened as he shut the machine off and pulled up the blankets on the sofa to get some sleep. In the upstairs loft, she found Archer curled up in a plush chair, his scowl etched deep in his brow as he dreamed.

Diffused lightning illuminated the room through thick curtains. Like an eerie lullaby, the rain hammered a heavy hum on the roof.

Lana moved silently around the book-littered table and lowered to the ottoman at Archer's feet, the brushed microfiber fabric smooth against her bare legs. Even in sleep, his lips were utterly kissable, soft and serious.

She should let him sleep, but suspected his sleep was as restless as hers had been. Unable to resist, she palmed his cheek and traced her thumb over the curve of his bottom lip. As if he'd been expecting her, he smiled and leaned into her hand, placing a longing kiss on her palm.

"Hi," she whispered, knowing to give him a minute before expecting alertness.

Eyes fluttering open, he rubbed his hands over his face and sat up straighter. "Hey," he murmured. "You okay?"

"I'm fine," she answered, sitting back so she could explain without the blinding thrill that threatened her resolve if she touched him. "I owe you a full explanation."

"Yeah, you do," he said, reaching for her.

She shook her head and tucked her hands in her lap. "I can't think clearly when you touch me."

"And I can't think at all when I'm not touching you. Whatever you did, you're a part of me now. I close my eyes, and all I see is you." He laughed under his breath as his cheeks flamed red. "I'm surprised I wasn't humiliating myself, jerking off in my sleep... seriously, I've had some... um, well... these dreams are... really vivid. You are really here, right?"

A fiery rush flooded her veins, burning deep in her core as she recalled the dream that had awoken her so abruptly. "I am."

A tempting smile teasing at his lips, he squinted dreamily as he said, "The last few days have been the strangest of my life. I throw you behind me to save your life and don't remember much after, but pain. I was going to say that it was the worst pain imaginable, but I could never have fathomed enduring so much, and, fuck, it will haunt me to the end of my days. Then I woke to find you've ditched me to fight the fight we were supposed to fight together. I'm stronger than a damn ox, faster, and I'm not even sure when my stamina tops out. Most of all, I am completely, utterly, obsessed with imagining you naked."

"That should go away with time."

He chuckled and said, "What will? Not the naked part, as that's plagued me since you sat on my couch back in Tucson with me and your skirt slid up so I could see that upper curve of your thigh." He shifted forward and framed her legs between his, wrapping his hands around her thighs, his hands warm against the chill of the stormy night.

"Slacker. I've been there since I heard your voice on the phone before I left Montana." As his hands kneaded her thighs, his fingertips sweeping under the cotton of the borrowed shirt, she stilled his grip and said, "I still need to give you that explanation. Before we take this any further."

"Fire when ready," he said with a wicked grin that threatened to dissolve her resolve.

"So. To, um... So you wouldn't die, the only way to save you... There's this traditional demon hunter ceremony, with words passed down from generation to generation, and the hunter and their chosen mate express their willingness to bond, to... according to my father anyway, to, um, unite their souls."

"Bond? Unite souls?"

"Marriage. Like, the forever kind. No divorce. No separation. Partners until death literally do-us-part, well, even then, I think there's still no moving on."

He scowled and stilled his hands, staring beyond her at that blank wall. "We got married?"

"You said '*I do.*' I mean, you didn't exactly say those exact words, but you agreed when I asked if you would claim me forever."

"What, exactly, did I say?" Arms folding over his chest, he leaned back in his chair.

"You were too weak to say much, but I distinctly remember you saying, 'of course.' Bennett and Adair witnessed."

Laughing under his breath, he parked his tongue between his teeth. "I'm delirious, and the woman of my dreams asks if I want to claim her. What did you expect me to say?"

"It's not about the words, it's about the intent and the feelings and... and—"

"Yeah, I got that."

Sapped of the last of her energy, again, Lana reached for him, then drew back as she realized what she was doing. As if curling into his lap would solve all her problems. "I didn't want to get married either. But it was the only way to save you. And now we're stuck in this together. I bound my soul to a man that couldn't possibly know if he wants to marry me."

"Who said I didn't want to marry you?" he asked, a smile teasing at the corners of his mouth.

"You did," she fired back.

"When did I say that?" he said with a laugh, sitting back up and grabbing her legs, tugging her toward him.

The ottoman shifted under his control, and she was ensnared in his grip. Studying her, as if he was waiting for those three little words, as if he could sing them from the rooftops without a moment's hesitation, he waited with patience that melted her into a puddle. Not one of those rainy-day puddles, but a damn monsoon that threatened to wash her downriver.

"Just now," she said pitifully.

"I don't believe I did."

"It's too soon. We can't possibly know already."

His thumbs traced over her bare legs, holding her soft in his gaze, seeming to wait for her to decide if she was going to run away scared or kiss him senseless. "Lana, you were ready to flee when things hinted at getting serious between us. I've made it clear that I'll do whatever it takes to hold on to *us*. But I'm not 'claiming' you, without knowing you want to claim me, too."

The hope in his stormy cobalts shattered every worry in her mind that had passed, telling her exactly what she needed to know. Why did he have to be so... *everything*?

"A mutual claiming then?" she asked with uncertainty, wrapping her legs around his waist, the connection saying what her words weren't ready to express.

"I'm serious." He cradled his hands around her jaw, seeing right through her. "What do you do when the fight's more than you can handle, and you begin to doubt that you'll see it through?"

"It wasn't life. It was me that put you in that position. If you want out of this, now's your chance. If we consummate this, there's no going back." She swallowed a lump in her throat, not daring to tell him the rest.

"Define 'no going back?'"

"You've seen my married teammates. Quinn and Ryan can't seem to exist in the same room without touching each other. Bennett and Adair have this *knowing* with each other, as if they're on this other plane of existence that only they exist on."

"They seem perfectly functional when apart."

"They are. I'm not talking about codependency. Hunters can survive without their spouses and live comfortably apart when things work out that way, but together... It's like the world makes more sense. Bodie's doing fine without Astrid here, but he's stronger and happier with her. You and I can still go our separate ways. If that's what you want."

"Fuck, Lana. What happens now? If we had a preacher and our families, right here, and you had the choice to spend the rest of your life with me by your side, or politely decline and decide I'm not the one, what would you do?"

"That's not fair."

"No, it's not. But it's what we've got." He tipped her chin, so she looked him in the eye. "I couldn't have said marriage was the next step for us, but I'd been keeping you at a safe enough distance that you wouldn't see how hung up I am on you, knowing I'd scare you away. Lana, if I hadn't gotten hurt, and you walked away when this op was done, my heart would have dried out and crumbled into dust."

Her chest rose and fell, a glimmer of hope threatening to choke her. Before she'd spoken the words, her soul had already recognized its mate.

His gaze still holding hers, he refused to let her go. "Tell me I'm wrong. That you could have walked away."

"I would have," she admitted.

Releasing her, Archer leaned back and looked away, his cheek pulled tight as he chewed the edge of his tongue.

She crawled onto his lap, straddling him and framing his face in her hands.

He looked up at her, the ache in his expression burning a hole in her heart.

"And I would have lived the rest of my days a hollow casing of my former self. Of what I could have been. In this role, I've seen the toughest of the tough, the baddest of asses. It comes naturally for us, fighting, conquering. Sometimes too much, and I've seen hunters lose control. But power didn't come naturally to you. You see a wall, and you climb over it or bash through it. You'll work to exhaustion to get it done, and you'll lay down your life if that's what it takes." She lowered her palms on his chest, and waited. "I would have walked away, but I would have regretted it every day for the rest of my life."

Breath releasing, the corners of his mouth turned up in a slow, easy smile. He scooped his hands around her rear and tugged her against him. He teased his lips over the corner of her jaw, nipping at her ear.

Lana tipped her head back as he trailed kisses along her neck.

"It doesn't come naturally to you, either," he murmured against her skin. "You said so yourself. Your sister wasn't built for it. Few are,

I would imagine," he said as he tugged her earlobe between his teeth, sending electric shocks radiating from the intimate contact. "And I would never have pegged you for modest."

"Kiss me," she asked, pointing to her lips, a soft laugh vibrating under her breath.

"No," he teased, passing his lips over her collarbone, lingering in the hollow at the base of her neck.

She leaned into him, savoring every touch, but knew he'd be disappointed if she didn't push it a little. She pressed her chest against his and captured his mouth with hers.

Without pause, he granted her the kiss she'd craved, melding with her as she did him. Hands grasped around her bare hips under her borrowed shirt, he took the kiss deeper, slow and intense, as if they had all the time in the world, but he didn't want to wait another second.

The world a blur, the air in the loft warm despite the afternoon storm, Lana indulged, holding nothing back.

Fingertips teasing over her skin, he raised her borrowed shirt and cupped her bare breasts. Helpless, heat burned at his touch, and she leaned in. Knowing her mind before she did, he trailed open-mouthed kisses along the top of her breasts, settling over a tight nub and pulling her in.

Breathless, she released a soft moan as he sucked her harder. "Wait," she whispered, barely able to find her voice as her consciousness was otherwise occupied. In what was probably the stupidest thing she'd ever said, her body screaming at her to shut up and finish it, she said, "Let's get through this mission. And if you still want me forever, let's do this right."

His mouth everywhere, searching, tasting, he stopped mid-kiss at her words and murmured against her skin, "*Now* you want to wait on sex?" He chuckled under his breath, the loving amusement in his tone melting her straight down to her toes. "You're killing me."

"I don't want to, but... I need you to be sure." She sat up straight and pulled the t-shirt back down. "We'll call it an engagement."

"Fuck that. Lana, I want you so bad. Forever. You *are* my wife. It's done and I'm so sure. I don't need to wait."

"Now who's the impatient one?" she teased. "There's this instinct to hurry up and consummate, so I might actually explode waiting, but... Archer, I made this decision for us. I want you to have time to take it all in before accepting."

He nipped a kiss and looked her in the eye, his cobalt blues thick with amusement. "Lana?"

"Yeah?" she breathed, lost in him.

"Bet you a thousand bucks you can't wait two days."

"Think you're that irresistible?"

"You said so yourself. I'll wait a hundred years if I have to, but I sure as hell don't want to."

She shifted to climb off of him, knowing what would happen if she stayed. A snarky grin teasing at his lips, he laced his arms around her before sliding the borrowed shirt over her head. Lips turned up in a wicked grin, he said, "I'm holding onto my shirt for now. Until we're married, I don't have to share."

Completely naked atop him, she squealed and grabbed for the shirt as he held it out of reach. "I'm not going downstairs like this."

Smug, he chewed the edge of his cheek and leaned back, resting his arms behind his head. "Should have thought of that before you stole my shirt."

Downstairs, she heard footsteps shuffling as the house began to stir. "Archer," she growled low.

He watched her squirm, naked and helpless on his lap, and tamed a smug grin. "Yes?"

With a huff, she jabbed him in the tummy. "I misjudged you. I thought you were a nice guy."

"That's what they all think," he said casually. "Nice doesn't mean I don't take what I want. And I want you naked."

Heart thundering in her chest, she utterly, completely knew that he wasn't going to be the shy lover she'd anticipated. She rolled her eyes adoringly and muttered, "Whole new side of you."

Gently, caressing, he watched her expression as he slid his hand low and rubbed her center. "It's only consummating if I come inside you, right? Like, the old-fashioned sort of sealing the deal?"

Halfway there, burning at his words, at the heated look in his eyes as he watched her response, she managed to whisper, "Yes."

"Yes, what?" he asked, dipping his fingers deep inside her, cupping her with the base of his palm.

"Stop making me talk," she hissed, teetering on the edge of control.

"Yes, what?" he insisted, massaging faster.

"Yes, the bond is only complete when you come inside me."

"Good," he murmured. "Lay back."

She wouldn't last two minutes if he got his mouth on her again. A smile tugged at the corner of her mouth, and she dared him with a knowing look. She shifted off and kneeled in front of him. Looking up, holding his gaze, she said, "Payback."

She tore the buttons off his cargos like he'd done to her. Watching her, a curious and wicked grin teasing at his lips, he didn't argue as she slid his cargos down his hips.

Muffled voices stirred downstairs. Footsteps came and went. "Lana," Archer warned as she grasped his cock.

"I'm not nice either," she said, licking her lips and watching him grow breathless as she squeezed him tight in her grasp.

Someone began to come up the stairs, Sauer judging by the heavy bootsteps, but Adair laughed and said, "Who's hungry for dinner? I make killer sausage you'll want to sink your teeth into."

Sauer's footsteps eased back down, he and the others walking away.

Lana winked at Archer before taking him deep into her mouth. Every time they were together, in whatever form, she came alive as her senses filled with him.

She caressed and pulled. The taste of him, the feel of his silky skin against her tongue, was like nothing else. Like no one else. She needed every part of him.

His breath quickened, his response flooding into her, driving her higher, faster, filling her with a satisfaction as intensely stimulating as if his orgasm was her own.

26

Horny was a concept very familiar to Lana, but never with such a... tenacity. Archer had a point. Had she ever waited two days? And with him? She wasn't kidding, she might actually explode.

Foreplay of every sort was fair game, but *fore* implied something was to come after. Thankfully, the demon hunter version of consummating followed the traditional definition of sex that had old-fashioned lords and ladies lifting skirts and ducking into darkened closets for hundreds of years. Filled with random, sexful thoughts flittering through her brain, she realized there were plenty of same-sex demon hunter marriages. She'd have to ask her great aunt how she bonded with her wife, as they'd clearly sealed the deal and died at ripe old ages, well into their three hundreds...

Okay, now she was getting desperate in her search for loopholes. It was clearly much more romantic than splooge-meets-cervix.

While the others ate dinner, they'd taken turns enduring cold showers, separated to their own research and strategizing, then finally crashed on the cot, snuggled tight and miserably happy. Happily miserable. Whichever.

By three in the morning, she left him sleeping in their bedroom so at least one of them might get some rest—and so she could avoid jumping him.

Her stomach was grumbling anyway. She slipped on her second-to-last pair of pants, her inadequately pocketed leggings, snagged one of his sweatshirts, stole a thick pair of his socks, and slipped on her new favorite combat boots.

Cozy and exhausted, she walked into the darkness. The void of it instantly threw her off balance. The distant storm radiated from the canyon, a pall on the entire region. Within seconds of being out in it, her soaking hair stuck flat to her scalp, and her clothes were plastered to her skin.

Wandering into the chow hall, she flicked on the light, grateful to find it empty. She peered into the fridge and found a stack of sandwiches.

Stomach cheering before the food even reached it, she tore into the first of them, downing varying combinations of meat and cheesy goodness. She brewed a pot of coffee and poured the biggest cup she could manage, tempted to chug right out of the carafe.

For a moment, she stood outside, under the overhang of the shanty, and watched the sheets of rain pummeling the base, the occasional flash of light illuminating the drenched shale. Lowering to the dampened top step, she watched, sipping her coffee, feeling the storm wash the land clean.

When her cup was drained, Lana moved back into the house and climbed the steep staircase, stopping at the large table in the center, already covered in familiar leather-bound journals the team had brought. Grabbing a text on obscure monsters, she curled into the microfiber chair she'd thoroughly sullied with Archer a few hours ago. One by one, Quinn, Bodie, and Bennett filtered in, each studying a different book, sharing ideas now and again, but they all seemed as discouraged as she was.

"How could no one have ever seen a troll before?" she groaned, tossing yet another book back onto the discard pile. "Nothing but rumors, and no more than a paragraph here and there. At best."

Bennett shook his head. "There seems to be consensus that they don't like visitors, but no one has ever actually fought them. No descriptions of the blurry conjured wind-fist, soul-suckingly dry air, the suffocating wind, nor the storms."

Finding humor for the first time in days, Lana dropped her head back on the cushioned headrest and chuckled under her breath. "They're not trolls, they're aliens. Gotta be."

Quinn chortled and snapped her book shut. "And I'm done. Research has failed us and we're making shit up."

Ryan wandered up the stairs, Vann following close behind. Ryan dropped into the chair next to Quinn's, immediately yanking it close so she leaned into him. "We got visual," he said.

Six sets of eyes watched him with curiosity and suspicion, like he was making shit up like the rest of them had been.

Bennett eyed him and kicked him under the table. "And?"

Ryan's smile faded, and he glanced around the table and frowned. "Are you sure there's no beer around here?"

Curled up in her cozy chair, Lana laughed and said, "Not exactly the tavern."

"Anyway," he continued. "Lana. What exactly did you see out there?"

"I'm really thinking trolls. We were in the middle of a rockfall rainstorm, so I couldn't say for sure. They were massive, like, maybe ten feet tall. Built like a trio of hairy bricks. Burly. Gold glowy eyes."

Bennett folded his arms over his chest and tipped back in his chair, the wood not daring to creak under his nimble movement. "Get them out in the open, and I think we could take a trio of bigfoots."

"Bigfeet," Quinn corrected with a shit-eating grin.

Vann considered, then countered, "Or is it bigfoot, like the plural for moose or fish?"

"And more than three," Ryan commented casually.

Quinn sat bolt upright and glared at him. "More?"

"Probably," Vann said from the spot he'd claimed at the corner of the table. "We finally got a decent look from the drone that Walker and I rigged. At least twenty heat signatures, but could be more if some were too close together to differentiate."

Bodie tossed his book on the table and rubbed his hand over the back of his neck. "Fuck," he muttered. "I was wondering what all I was smelling. They need to take a dip in that stream more often."

"Blurs, inhabitable ground, and unpleasant wind," Lana said. "Plus a little *je ne sais quoi* that discourages tourists. A foul odor. Noncorporeal shadow-wind-fists that can crush a human. Not an ideal spot for a honeymoon."

Lana wrapped her arms around her knees as the rain picked up outside, her hair still damp from her last coffee run. The rain was so saturating, she doubted her hair dryer would do the job, if she'd had room in her bag to even bring it.

Adair nodded to Vann. "And the airstrike? Did you see the damage?"

He tilted his head with a subtle shrug. "The canyon walls were pretty damaged from them driving us out of there, so tough to say for sure what was them and what was the airstrike. Water level is still high. So, even without the airstrike, things would be pretty impassable."

Ryan added, "Walker says the airstrike would have been precise, as the military doesn't want the canyon damaged or they'd block their own path. Walker estimates they deflected only half the blasts."

Bennett flicked his tongue over a sharp canine and grinned with his typical headstrong desire to go in swinging. "They're deflecting because they don't want to get hurt. I guarantee they bleed. There are seven of us. If we need to sneak our way in and take out one at a time, then that's what we'll do."

Steady bootsteps resonated up the steps, jarring her concentration. "Eight," Archer corrected. Feet wide at ease, arms folded over his chest, he was irresistible.

This must-consummate instinct was murder. His t-shirt seemed to fit better, his sculpted build even more defined the more she looked at him. The set of his jaw seemed more determined, darkened by the edge of unshaved shadow. Wet from another cold shower, his hair rebelled and tweaked up in the front. In the black t-shirt and dark camo, the dog-tag chain over the smooth skin of his neck and bulging under the snug shirt...

Okay, Lana was officially a fan of uniforms. Maybe she could just lick him all over for the next century? Or, well, now that she knew how effective that mouth was, that those lips were as wicked as they looked, with a hint of pout and a shy smile that grew to be more arrogant the more she got to know him... she could survive off oral escapades for quite a while.

Biting her lips together, she looked up at the ceiling. The wall. Her book. At anything but him.

Ryan nodded to Archer. "You ready for something like that? I mean, we don't know what all you're capable of yet. We assume you're full hunter, but what if you're not, and we bring you into the thick of it?"

Archer gave a sharp nod. "I'm getting a pretty good handle on what I'm made of."

Worry gnawed in her gut, threatening to expel all those sand-wiches from her belly. Lana dared looking at him again.

His bloodcurdling screams of pain still rang in her ears, his lifeless form unmoving as she gave everything to bring him back. Again reminding her of what she'd done to him, and what could happen to him. "You're not on the team," she said hollowly.

Expression pained, Adair fired a look at Lana. "Neither am I, but we need fighters. Lana, you gave him this power. Let him stretch his wings."

He flipped his head back toward her and asked, "We have wings?"

Bennett shook his head and said with a sigh, "No."

"Damn," Archer muttered, an adorable smile teasing at his lips.

Bodie raised his hand. "They're right. We could use the help."

Lana looked over and folded her arms over her chest, realizing she was outvoted. She watched as he crossed the room toward her, mesmerized at how he moved, with extra grace and power that was already becoming so natural for him.

Archer squatted down at the side of her chair and looked up at her, the blue of his eyes boiling, his dark lashes hooding his gaze with the edge that had made him one of the top warriors on the planet. Quietly, he whispered, "Maybe you're not ready to be my wife, but are you ready to be my partner?"

She glanced up to see the others quickly averting their eyes, well, all but Quinn, who looked on and flashed her a sap-happy wink.

Heart in her throat, she floated, turning back and letting herself sink into his swimming cobalts.

"I can't lose you," she murmured, knowing the team would hear, but at this point, not caring. They knew who she was, and probably were all thinking how she must be freaking out right now. As she was.

"Well, we're in a bit of a pickle," he said, a lopsided grin on his face that set off the little butterflies that resided in her tummy. "When we started out on this mission, we agreed to be full partners. You shook on it."

"I did," she whispered.

"I wasn't born for this like you were, but I've been waiting my whole life for this."

She leaned in and touched her lips to his, melting at the blazing contact. Her eyes were heavy, and the little butterflies threatened to make her cry as she whispered, "I'm not ready for you, but I need you anyway."

Bennett cleared his throat and said, "As no one questioned my suggestion to sneak in and take out one at a time, I'm assuming it means we're in agreement."

Taking the obvious hint, Ryan adjusted his posture and said, "Sure. So far, we've managed to piss them off enough to block the entrance to their own home and bring floods over the region. Maybe you can run fast enough to get out of there in a hurry, but the rest of us were lucky as hell to not be pummeled, squashed, and drowned. An average demon hunter probably wouldn't have made it out of there. And, as I am fairly certain they draw power from the remnants of veil in that old tear, no fucking way I'm risking moving any of us through the veil to get into the heart of their lair."

Archer scooped Lana into his arms and dropped into the fluffy chair, cradling her in his lap and keeping his arms around her, while the team debated their next move.

A grimace scrunching his brow, Bodie rubbed the back of his neck and said, "Vampires, werewolves, and most every demon stupid enough to cross to this side *all* know to be afraid of hunters. Either trolls are as unfamiliar with hunters as hunters are with trolls, or..."

"Or the reason there aren't any hunters, nor any decent records about trolls, is because hunters have never survived a run-in with them," Vann said, puffing his cheeks out as he glared at the useless stack of books on the table.

Lana smiled as ideas pinged in her brain. "You know? We always meet the enemy in their territory. As Bennett so graciously demonstrated, hunters tend to barge in, swords drawn, for guts and glory."

"It's usually effective," Quinn said, brow dropping as she seemed to be following Lana's train of thought. "But it's entirely unfair for us, never getting home field advantage."

"We've got miles and miles without a civilian in sight. And trolls seem to be very adept at *defense*," Lana said.

Archer traced his fingers over her abdomen mindlessly. "This base is prepped for anything. If they only deflected half of the airstrike, I wonder if they can deflect our firepower when they're outside of their cave?"

Bennett snorted and leaned his elbows onto the table, rubbing his hands over his face. "How are we going to convince the most isolationist monsters we've ever encountered to come out and play?"

27

THE ODDEST TWITCH VIBRATED through his fingertips, compelling him to reach for Lana. Helpless to resist, he laced his fingers with hers. Ryan and Quinn had seemed like a pair of magnets, constantly touching, even in casual, subtle ways. Bennett and Adair were similar, but there was an easygoing independence to them, as if they had all the time in the world to stand side by side, yet when they looked at each other, there was a sensuality that said they were entirely in tune with each other's every move.

Archer was beginning to understand how the whole bond, power transfer, soulmate thing worked. Maybe. It was crazy, but... before, he'd been drawn to Lana unlike anyone else.

Now? Well, fuck, it was like the world was going to come crashing down if he couldn't scoop her up and kiss every inch of her skin, inhale her tempting scent... and plunge into her, feel her tighten around him, her wicked grin blossom as she —

Lana nudged him in the ribs and set the binoculars down. From the lookout on the northeast corner of the COP, he could just make out the edge of the storm, thicker closer to the canyon, and fading. The FOB probably hadn't seen a drop.

Sauer finished securing a .50-caliber machine gun, ready to blanket the trolls' approach, and then stepped back to admire his work.

Archer calmed his thoughts and bit down on his tongue to remind himself where he was. Yeah, he'd bet that she wouldn't last two days. He wasn't going to last two more hours.

At the opposite corner, Kerse and Walker were setting up mortars and loading sniper rifles.

He cleared his throat and tested his earpiece. "These guys get close, and I want every Echo in a rig, ready to drive until you see nothing but dust in the rearview. We don't know how powerful these guys are outside the security of the canyon."

A few begrudging acknowledgements bounced around the squad, but no one argued.

"So these things are... demons? I'm not a biblical sort of person—" Sauer began.

Lana laughed, the sound washing over Archer like a warm shower. "It's an antiquated name. Monster hunters would be more appropriate. Big bad dudes from another realm. Although there are others, like us, that are half-demon, half-human. The ancients assumed those that came through the veil were evil raining down upon them. Not all of them are out to kill people, but there are enough violent ones to keep us busy."

"Huh," he said, nodding. "And... *trolls*?"

"Apparently," Lana answered with a sheepish shrug. "A lot of myths, and even children's stories that began as cautionary tales, are rooted in truth. The stories describe trolls as hermits. There are, of course, many iterations of troll tales, but the consensus seems to be that they are big, lumbering sorts that live in dense forests or in caves."

Thunder rumbled beyond, and the lookout tower shuddered under the magnitude of it. Archer cleared his throat and looked in the direction of the canyon.

Sauer unfolded a camp-style chair and plopped down. "They blasted our shots back at us when we went after them, and they sent half of our airstrike shots back into the atmosphere. I'm not sure swords are going to do much. Or why we're bothering with guns, as they haven't done much so far."

"There's a chance they might not be able to draw power from the veil this far from the tear."

Sauer nodded, his bearded scowl lowering. "If we figure out how to get them to come out of their hidey hole."

Lana leaned up against Archer's side.

Arms folded over his chest, he rubbed the back of his fingers against her damp skin. A web of lightning bounced from cloud to cloud, illuminating the entire sky for a brief moment, followed immediately by thunder that rattled the rooftops. "From Scandinavian folklore, right? Weren't trolls afraid of Thor and his storms?"

"Yeah," Lana said softly. "Maybe the storm and damage from the airstrike are why the drone could finally get close."

"Then why set off the storm?" Archer asked.

Sauer plopped his feet on the ledge and leaned back comfortably in the chair. "I am terrified of spiders. Like, deathly afraid."

Archer snorted a laugh. "Don't I know it." He nudged Lana and bit his lip impishly as he riled Sauer. "You've never heard anyone scream as loud as Sauer did when he saw a tarantula in my backyard. He won't sit out there now, until the rest of us have thoroughly inspected every nook and cranny."

"That monster was as big as my hand. And these hands aren't small," Sauer said with a shiver. "Point is, if I wanted to scare someone away, I'd send spiders after them."

Her laugh light against the gusting wind, Lana said, "Wouldn't you be afraid the spiders would crawl back toward you?"

"Yeah, but if I was more scared of the intruders than the spiders, it would be worth it."

"Aha. So maybe trolls do know about hunters, and they *are* afraid of us," Lana said with a delighted lilt to her voice.

Sauer smiled knowingly and rubbed his hands over his beard. "You throw a bunch of spiders in my house, and I'm out."

Lana grabbed the radio and said, "Vann. You still working on the visuals with Walker?"

"Yeah. What's up?" Vann asked.

"How are our pals in the canyon holding up?"

"Looks like they're huddled on high ground, under the cover of a ledge."

Lightbulb flashing in Archer's mind, he pictured the canyon and all its legends, what Bodie had explained about trolls and their violently hermit lifestyle. "Ever throw a punch at a bully, run, and see if he follows?"

"Someone get bullied a lot as a kid?" Bennett interrupted over the radio.

"I've got a few names I'm looking up next time I'm home," Archer joked. "Seriously though. Give us a few hours to equip the drones, and we can drop flashbangs sequentially from north to south. Howitzer should be able to fire past the target and tear down the canyon walls. Scare them, crush their home, so they have no choice but to come after us. If they try to scatter, we funnel them in with more flashbangs and Howitzer blasts."

Kerse snarked over the radio, "Cattle drive?"

"Bingo," Archer said.

Bennett seemed to be enjoying this way too much, and added, "Hang a few pics of Archer's face, and they'll come straight for us."

"Thanks," he grumbled.

"No really," Chan said, almost sympathetically with a lilt in her calm voice. "Archer, you've slipped through their grip twice. If they are forced out, they're going to come straight for you."

"So we lay out some of Archer's clothes along a path leading right here, like breadcrumbs," Ryan said with a wave from his post on a far rooftop.

"Very funny," Archer said, rolling his eyes and muting his audio.

Sauer leaned back in his chair and folded his hands behind his head. Feet up, he nodded to Archer and Lana. "Run along now, children. I've got work to do."

Archer snorted and kicked his foot lightly against the leg of the folding chair. "Now I see why you called lookout. The rest of us get to arm this place to the teeth, while you put your feet up."

"Hey, you guys have all that super strength and energy. We mere humans need to rest before the fight."

Archer huffed jokingly, but couldn't help but consider Sauer's words. Everything about him felt stronger, more efficient, each breath taking in more oxygen than before. Maybe in another hundred years, it will have sunk in that he wasn't human anymore.

After opening the hatch to climb down, he enveloped Lana in his arms, compelled to feel her close to him, desperately needing the connection. As his hand splayed over her abdomen, he burned at the feel of her soft skin under his palms.

The edge of her lower lip tightened in her bite as her gaze rose to meet his before she pulled away and lowered out of the lookout. No more than a rung of ladder down, and she let go and leaped to the ground. He glanced down to find her standing with her hands on her hips, a tempting grin brightening her expression as she waited.

Thrill surged through him at the challenge. He skipped the ladder entirely and dropped out through the hole. On impact, he landed on one knee, his fist on the ground supporting him, fuel pumping through him as he scanned the terrain, ready to run.

He popped to his feet and looked her way, grinning mischievously as he realized what he'd done. Instinct had tensed each muscle in sequence as he readied for the fight.

Lana's delighted laugh danced through the stormy air. "Badass landing. You look like a superhero."

Gravel crunching under him, he stalked toward her, arrogantly tugging her pelvis against his. "I thought I was going to land on my feet like you did."

"That's how Ryan always lands. I thought he was doing it to look cool."

"Entirely unintended. You've got more of this subtle badass to your landing, like you could stop and file your nails while enemies surge toward you."

"That's always been more my style. Vann gets this back-the-fuck-off look, and I'm not sure Bennett stops long enough for me to tell; he just goes barreling into the fight."

"What about Quinn and Astrid?"

"Astrid has this grace, like a ballerina, almost curtseying. Quinn has more of a baseball-style attack stance, braced and ready to tackle."

"I think I'm getting the hang of this."

"You're a natural," she said, rising to her tiptoes in the middle of the storm and touching her cool lips to his. "If I hadn't made the choice for you, even knowing the risk of the change, would you have chosen this?"

He rested his cheek against hers and held her tight against him as a gale-force wind threatened to flatten the base. "In a heartbeat. I get a few centuries with you, and I can do more than I ever could in the military. Plus, did you see my abs?"

She tilted her head back and laughed out loud. "I absolutely noticed." She nuzzled closer. "This is how I know you're mine. How could anyone *not* choose this?"

He brushed a stray lock of sopping wet hair from her face and his voice lowered. "Does your sister know how much it broke your heart, when she didn't choose the life you did?"

Lana shook her head and rested her palm on his chest. "I don't know."

"Have you told her?"

"Emphatically and loudly. When I got back home and found her still human, I spit a record-breaking string of expletives at her. There was some throwing involved as well. It wasn't pretty."

"Does she know you're *still* hurt?"

"Of course not." Lana huffed and pounded her head against his chest, then snuggled up and squeezed her arms around his middle. "It's been nearly twenty years. We've had some great times since."

"But it's always there, isn't it?"

"She's got a great rhythm. Genuinely happy. So I'm working on it. But her children will carries the DNA, and he won't have the choice with the way she's raising him. We spend our lives preparing, before taking on the traits."

"Except me."

She laughed against him and burrowed tighter. "You, my amazing... husband, fiancé, whatever... you, are one of a kind. You might not have trained to become a hunter, but you were made for this anyway."

He kissed the top of her head long and firm as he breathed her in, holding her without pushing.

Ryan hollered from the rooftop beyond. "Archer. Get your ass up here. I need a hand."

Releasing Lana, he flashed her a wink and sprinted toward the house. Without slowing, he jumped straight up to the rooftop, grabbing the edge and thrusting himself over, adrenaline surging through him at the ease of it. He puffed under his breath, knowing he was grinning like an idiot.

Ryan laughed and flicked water from his hair. "You know, these guys all grew up knowing what they were. I came from a different demon, and my mom wanted me to have a normal childhood. Not that growing faster and bigger than the others was anything close to normal, but I didn't know why until I really grew into it and Sunshine couldn't put it off any longer."

"Your dad was king of the demon realm, right?"

"He *is* the king of the demon realm. Pure demons are immortal. Anyway, I didn't know anything about him, or who I came from. I had a great childhood, but a rough start to demon hunting life. Eventually I joined the Coast Guard," he said as a rumbling sound that had nothing to do with the storm shook the outpost.

Archer glanced down and saw Chan backing around in a truck with crate after crate of weapons in the bed—some they'd brought, and others kept at the base for just such an occasion — and a howitzer on its trailer.

At the base of the house, Quinn said to Bennett, "Ready?"

He grinned and nodded for Chan to step back. "Let's do it," he said.

Each grabbed a side of a crate of rocket launchers, stacked on a few crates of grenades, and enough ammunitions to keep firing all night. Across from Ryan, Archer leaned down and grabbed the first crate by the side. Crate by crate, they stacked an arsenal on the platform fashioned on the roof.

Even rooftops and lookouts were closer to the fight than he wanted the squad.

As the others moved on, Ryan continued to set up the post. "Gotta say, having demon hunter power was always a boon when shit got tough, before I met Quinn and the team. Like a safety blanket, or, I guess, a reminder that I could handle anything—even the shit I couldn't."

Archer asked, "How'd that go, working in the civilian world? Coast Guard, right?"

"Yeah. I didn't know why we were so busy, until the whole prophecy started unfolding. The ocean is filled with monsters of all kinds, way more than on land. I got lucky, working with a great crew, an amazing captain, and it was a good time in my life. But when I joined these guys and the ocean calmed down, it was tough to keep up a civilian career, when the fight I needed to be fighting was somewhere else."

"You're saying I need to rethink my career?"

"You can do whatever you want. I'm just saying, it's not easy."

"I'm getting the feeling this life was a bad choice for Connery and Simmons." His gut wrenched, imagining how they'd watched their squad mates get crushed by an unknown enemy.

"That was different. They were werewolves trying to help humans fight demons. Werewolves are badass fighters, a lot like demon hunters, but they're not bound by duty. Most live perfectly peaceful lives, usually someplace remote, with their pack."

"But if they hadn't been trying to fit in with humans, to fight as humans, they could have done more."

"Exactly. Bodie and Noah are fighters, defenders by nature, and the quiet life doesn't suit either of them. But, fuck, if the military had realized they had werewolves?"

"That would be a fucking disaster." There wasn't a person outside his squad he'd trust with the knowledge he now carried.

"Anyway. Not to bump your stress level up just yet. You've got plenty on your mind right now."

Archer glanced down to see Lana leaned against a pillar outside the chow hall, a steaming cup of coffee in her hands as she looked across the base. His heart lurched in his chest, realizing it was more than his job that needed changing.

His family would get a kick out of her. An attitude bigger than the plains, but a small-town girl at heart.

It had been hard enough keeping so much from them as an Echo, but at least they'd known vaguely what he was up to.

28

HANDS WRAPPED AROUND A piping hot cup of joe, Lana leaned her shoulder against the pillar outside the chow hall and watched two of her favorite guys on the planet working on the roof of the house. The storm was strong as ever, wind whistling around them, but they stood strong as they drilled the weapon into place.

Lana flipped her hair from one side to the other, but the sopping locks were irretrievably uncooperative. She took a slow sip of coffee as she captured the image in her mind. When she'd first come outside, they bore matched expressions of worry, soaked to the skin in dark t-shirts, Archer in his camo and Ryan in his navy cargos.

Ryan didn't make friends easily, but Archer was the kind of guy no one could resist. Well, she couldn't, anyway. His small-town roots and self-effacing humor balanced the cold, efficient soldier.

Neither were strangers to end-of-the-world drama on the horizon, steady in the preparations, the waiting, and undoubtedly in the heat of the fight. A smile on each of their faces, a joke and a laugh that was muted by the pummeling rain that flowed from the gutterless roof over her head, Archer and Ryan chatted easily while they worked. Archer tightened double checked the roof would hold if the wind kicked up, that the crates were secure but accessible, then rose to his feet, and looked ahead in the direction of the canyon. While Ryan flipped the cordless drill in his hand and tucked it into his belt, Archer glared at his soiled hands and tugged his sopping wet shirt over his head. He meticulously wiped the grime from his fingertips.

The front door squeaked behind Lana, and Quinn came out. Coffee in hand, she leaned against on the opposite post and immediately followed Lana's line of sight. "Nice view."

"I know, right?"

"Still no sex?"

"Would I be drooling this hard if we had?" She sighed dreamily as Archer knocked Ryan on the shoulder.

"Uh-huh," Quinn answered absentmindedly as Ryan looked down and smiled adorably at his wife.

Lana felt the moment Archer spotted her, her heart thundering under her ribs as she looked up to find him biting down on the edge of his tongue to hold back the smitten grin that utterly melted her. Smitten. An entirely new experience, and a new favorite word.

"You're getting twitchy. Think it's safe to wait until after the fight?"

Lana huffed a breath, sending steam from her coffee whipping through the storm-filled air. "Probably not."

"Would it change anything?"

"I need to know that he's sure."

He strolled casually down the steep roof, feet angled to combat the slick shingles and launched over the side, landing ready to attack as he had before.

A delighted laugh bubbled up in her belly, brightening as he flashed her a wink and rose to his feet. Raindrops plump as gumdrops jetted from the darkening sky, streaming over his skin. Gaze locked on hers, he stalked toward her.

As he neared, Quinn mumbled, "He looks pretty certain to me."

Halting a breath away, a step below so their eyes met, he slipped her coffee from her hand. A gulp and a gasp, and he handed back the mug. He said into the radio, "Timeline and status updates."

With an easy cadence, Sauer reported in first. "On lookout. Aside from that storm, calm as a kitten in all directions."

Walker and Vann were working on programming the drones while Chan set up the flashbangs, Kerse and Bodie were rigging the base to blow.

From the TOC, Walker added, "Brock's taking care of blocking any surveillance for us, says to give him another six hours, so he only has to hack one satellite."

"Finish your tasks and everyone get some food and rest."

Lana leaned against the railing and watched as Archer ensured everyone knew their role, so the op would go off without a hitch.

He clicked on the radio one last time. "Rendezvous at the TOC in five and a half hours."

Ryan came up from behind Archer and added, "Assuming we piss these trolls off enough to come for us, if they move as slowly as some of the legends say, it could be days until they reach us."

Quinn shrugged. "Unless that's another story that myth got wrong. Big doesn't mean slow. My dad is big and lumbers, and he's fast."

"We'll be ready, either way," Ryan said, strolling up the steps and smacking a kiss on Quinn's cheek. Without pause, he encircled her in his arms and tugged her backward into the chow hall, trailing smiling kisses along her neck.

Lightning flashed brighter as night closed in. Lana caught the envy in Archer's expression, understanding pinging through her. How many times had she watched her cousin disappear for a private moment with Ryan, and how many times had the jealous bug bit her on the ass?

She bit the edge of her lip and tipped Archer's gaze back toward her. Brighter than lightning against the saturated clouds, his cobalt eyes held her spellbound.

He fingered his hands in her hair, his thumb massaging the back of her neck as he closed in and took her mouth with his.

Without a word, he scooped her into his arms and carried her through the storm to the house.

At the door, he released her mouth long enough to open the door. Rain pummeled against the windows, cocooning the house against the storm.

Lana knew what he was thinking. She knew she could deflect.

In the dim amber light of their bedroom, he lowered her to her feet.

No more than a breath, light and delicate, he touched his lips to hers before lowering to one knee.

Heart tripping so fast her head filled with clouds and her legs with lead, she bit down on the edge of her lip and shook her head.

"Uh-uh, not this time," he said with a subtle laugh. "When we get home, my entire family is going to ask how I proposed. We can't say I was bleeding out on my deathbed when you ordered me to marry you and took my vaguely conscious, incoherent response as a yes."

She tipped her head back in laughter, and he took her hand to steady her.

"Come on, let me do this right."

"Can't wait another few days, huh?"

Half laugh and half snarl, he looked desperately up and her and shrugged. "I feel like I've overdosed on Viagra and the only way I will ever feel whole again is to fuck you. As soon as possible."

A laugh rumbled from deep in her throat, and tears pooled in her eyes. "This is the worst proposal in history," she said with a hysterical laugh. "We're better off with the dying story."

"Stop laughing so I can get the words out. We're on a time crunch here. The sooner you say yes, the sooner we can get to the good bits so I don't walk into battle with a raging hard-on, while silently hoping your top magically flies off in the heat of battle, so I can watch you fight and scope out your tits at the same time."

She laughed out loud and shook her head.

"I'm sorry, but that's my latest bizarre horny fantasy. It's like I've got porn streaming in my head all day, and you're the star."

Laughter rumbled through her.

He chuckled softly and tugged gently at her hand. "I'm focusing now."

She swallowed another laugh and bit her lips together. "Okay, I'm ready."

With another head shake, he pinched the bridge of his nose and swallowed a laugh. "Serious. I can be serious."

Heaviness coated her ribs as she watched him balancing laughter and the gravity of a proposal worthy of mating their souls. She lowered to her knees and steadied his jaw in her hands.

Thumbs tracing the rough edge of beard that had thickened over the last few days, she captured his look. "I like your proposal. There is no one else, in this realm or the next, that I would rather share my soul, my power, or my life with."

He leaned into her touch and kissed the palm of her hand. "You've expanded my world in so many ways. I could live out my extended life without you, but I sure as hell don't want to. Please be my wife."

She touched her forehead to his, heat radiating off him and warming her to her toes. "Yes," she whispered.

He smiled and tugged her tight against him, her soaked top pressing against the bare skin of his chest. Languishing and feverish, his lips joined with hers.

Thrill quaked through her as she waited, needing to hear him say the words, more magic than the spell she'd cast to bind her soul to his.

Breath warm over her skin, a tremor to his voice, he said, "I love you. I need you. I want to share my life with you."

She brushed the tip of her nose across his. "I love you, too."

He growled and ripped her top over her head, dispatching the bra with a quick flick and tearing the buttons on her cargos again.

A laugh tickled in her throat, but was silenced as he scooped her up and sat on the cot, setting her on his lap. Hands on her breasts in an instant, he pinched down hard on one and suckled at the other, her breath rushing from her lungs at the aggressive attentions.

Her back arched, and she leaned in, craving more. A rumble echoed from his chest and he took more, tightening his grip and taking her in his teeth.

He released her long enough to toss her onto the cot and ripped her pants the rest of the way off her. Her lace panties were shredded in an instant.

As he spread her legs, he bit her inner thigh and licked.

Sensation rocketed through her. With a hoarse voice, her brain equally raspy, she said, "I honestly expected you to be sweet and shy."

Breath hot against her skin, he murmured, "Maybe it was a ploy to pique your interest."

"No, you're too honest for that. You're sweet with a spicy—" Before she could finish, he licked the flat of his tongue over her clit and sent shocks vibrating through her.

"I didn't get to be in the military's most covert unit, and now the world's, without an aggressive side." His lips soft and full over her center, he kissed her delicately. "I can do gentle, if you prefer." Attentive and luxurious, he lavished over her most sensitive area in the sweetest way possible.

As her body relaxed against him, sensation slowly burning into her veins, he gave her a final, delicate lick, then shifted hard to uncompromising. Thick and curled, plunging deep into her, he fucked her with his tongue. A howl on her breath, she gripped the edges of the cot to steady herself.

Unsteady as he traced a circle around her, her body bowed. Unpredictable, seeming to know exactly how to keep her unsettled and swirling, he shifted over her clit and drove his fingers inside her. Hand palmed over her inner thigh, he steadied her as he plunged in and out. Her breath quickened as he flicked his tongue over her, his fingers inside her matching the rhythm of his tongue.

Lightheaded as she indulged in the dirty decadence of his touch, she could glide on the erotic sensation all night. As he caressed, reading her like an open book and adding intriguing twists, he covered her clit with his mouth and sucked. Hard. Fast. Unrelenting.

Wetter than the sweat beading between her breasts, hotter than his mouth over her, sensation scorched through her veins and she arched her back off the bed. Orgasm vibrated over her in wave after wave of exquisite sensation. Archer reached up and grasped her breast, tightening his fingers over her nipple.

White hot electricity burst from her core straight to her throat and she cried out to temper the fire that engulfed her.

Breath coming fast as she lay still, in shock, as he released her, she wrapped her hands around her middle and laughed deliriously.

He covered her body with his, grabbing her hands and pinning them over her head, and the hard ridge of him pressed against her core. "Fuck, you are so amazing," he whispered.

"You," she murmured, licking her lips as she rode the feeling of being looked at like that, after feeling like that. "I am... really, really looking forward to another few centuries of fucking you."

He laughed with his lips pressed against her neck. "Please tell me you're ready."

"I'm ready," she said. "I've been working out exactly how I'm going to claim you. But you already claimed me."

He cradled her in his arms and rolled her on top of him. "I get teased for being patient and not playing around, but it gives me plenty of time to create some intricate fantasies. I've got enough to fill the next few centuries."

She flipped her hair out of her face and tugged his cargos down over his hips. Hard and long and throbbing with impatience, his dick sprang free and smacked him on the abdomen. She laughed and gripped him tight in her hands.

He hissed, "Patient, but it'll be a miracle if I make it five seconds. You are way too much for me, and I'd like to not humiliate myself before—"

She grinned and shifted over him. Teasing her hips over him, she rubbed her slick center along his hardness, up and down and ground into him.

He gasped and tightened his hands around her hips. He didn't push, he didn't say anything, but looked up at her and watched with sweet patience.

Biting her bottom lip between her teeth, she hovered at the tip of him, taking him into her no more than an inch. Fuck, she was so wet already, and he was so patient, when she knew he must be ready to take charge like he had with his mouth.

Slow and torturous, she took him fully inside her, sliding up and down as she adjusted to his thickness.

He groaned at her deliberate, agonizing movements.

Squeezing tight around him as she withdrew, taking him deeper each time she sat back down on him, she settled and began to rock.

Breath caught in her throat, heat radiating up from her core like she was stepping into a whirlpool of a spa, she bit her lips together to regain a sense of control, but she was already sinking into scorching, slow motion ecstasy.

Quietly, with a fascination that stirred her arousal deeper, he watched her surfing along the wave of her peak as she fought to keep from crossing the tipping point so quickly. Something in his look, so sincere, tipped her over the edge. While she moved over him, tightening around him as she fell into a dizzying vortex, a subtle smile raised the corners of his lips. He held her gaze and whispered, "I love you."

Unblinking, as if he'd been waiting for this exact moment, his words shattered her. Heat burned deep in her core and she couldn't hold back the tide anymore.

The ground shook beneath them, the walls threatening to collapse the building itself as the howitzer blasted a round toward the canyon.

His hands grasped over her hips, his grip tightening as she clutched her fingers over his abdomen. Grinding, faster, her soft moans grew into victorious roars. Surging, beyond control, she felt him focusing every subtle movement to sustain her climax.

Another blast to send the enemy on the move. Ignoring the world around them, trusting in the others to manage the op, she focused on her husband, on the way he watched her move over him, her response. A smile teased at her lips as she sailed over the crest, her breath shuddering as her climax slowed to a resonant hum.

Archer gripped her hips and suddenly shifted their pace, driving her fast and hard over the top of him. Needing him to feel as utterly overcome as she had, sensing the urgent pace he craved, she grabbed him and rolled them to the side.

The cot couldn't take the rough movement and collapsed under them. He laughed as they crashed to the ground, and he rolled her beneath him.

Quickly finding a new rhythm, like a pummeling jackhammer, he pounded into her again and again. He wrapped his hand around the inside of her thigh and drew her knee up, deepening the angle as he filled her with each stroke. Harder, deeper, he groaned as his body tensed as he drew closer to his climax.

Voice hoarse as he accelerated, holding her with him, he met her look and murmured, "Tell me you love me."

She laughed and clutched her hands around his backside, pulling him tighter against her. "I love you," she said breathlessly.

Sweat thick on his brow, his muscles tensed as he slowed his movements, he smiled and pressed a soft kiss on her lips, then quickly built to a faster, intense rhythm. Lana's smile fell to desperate pants as the pace quickened. Heat pooled in her core as he pounded faster, massaging and challenging her with each thrust.

Sensing him nearing his peak but holding back to bring her to another, she tightened around him to bring him over the edge.

Groaning as she moved with him and squeezed around him, he braced her with him and carried her over the edge again. Her pulse quickened, her vision tunneled to anything beyond him, and they climaxed together.

Collapsing atop her, still inside her, he held her close in his arms and she nuzzled into his neck. "I love you," she whispered against his skin.

"I love you, too."

Head on the hard ground, she turned to glance around at the destroyed bedroom. She giggled under her breath, their slick, bare skin vibrating together.

Archer opened his eyes and sat up, glancing around in the dim light of their bedroom. "Oops," he mumbled.

She sat up and wrapped her limbs around him, pressing her breasts against his back. The tremulous uncertainty that plagued her was gone. In its place, she felt anchored, settled, yet the strength of the demon inside balanced her. Her pulse steadier, her muscles more responsive, she could walk a tightrope while carrying a car if she was so inclined.

In the distance, the thunder seemed to heighten, but she realized it was the hum of drones rising across the base and moving toward the canyon. She trailed kissed along his shoulder, reaching her hands around his middle to find him already hardening at her touch. "Plenty of time," she murmured against his skin.

As she squeezed him tight in her hand, he groaned and his words came out in a laughing growl, "You mentioned stamina?"

"Uh-huh," she whispered, stroking him, loving how he hardened again, his entire body responding to her touch. "I've never been with another hybrid. I wonder how many times we can go before we wear out?"

He flipped her over and pinned her backside against him. Lowering his hand to stroke her, he whispered in her ear, "I will never get enough of you."

29

Archer crashed on his back as Lana landed on top of him.

When he'd woken from the change to find Lana had gone, he'd known something was different. Had felt powerful. Alive. But a piece of him—a big fucking chunk of him—had been hollow from expected fulfillment unfulfilled.

Since then, each kiss had brought him closer to filling the gap, building hope that things would be okay.

The complete acceptance, love and sex and all the good stuff that went with it... he was fueled with an unstoppable power.

At the five-hour mark, he'd left Lana sound asleep on what was left of the bed, and checked that everything was a go. Drones launched. Outside, the Howitzer fired again and again, shaking the reinforced walls of the house and everything in the region.

Knowing everything was running smoothly, he'd ensured everyone took turns banking sleep as they could, alternating herding duty, and climbed back in with Lana.

Breasts pressed against him, she nuzzled into his neck and mumbled, "Food."

"We should have spent our honeymoon at a hotel so we could call for room service and not have to stop," he said with a smitten grin, surprised when she moved against him and he ached as blood surged south. Again.

A knock at the door softened things real quick. Chan's voice was light and filled with amusement as she said through the door, "If anyone is still alive in there, it's time."

"There goes my nap," Lana said, sitting up and glaring against the light.

He checked his barely readable scuffed watch and grimaced. "Fuck. I guess they don't move slow. If they're in range already, they move faster than we can drive."

"Come on," she said, grabbing his hands to boost him up. "After-fight sex is just as fun."

He grabbed his pants from the pile of rubble surrounding them, but remembered the buttons were ripped off. Scowling, he stood and walked to grab his backpack and pulled out his last pair of wearable cargos.

Lana laughed as she pulled up her lacy black panties. "Payback. I'm down to one pair of pants now, thanks to you."

He cautiously buttoned and then tugged a t-shirt over his head.

Trolls.

Huh.

What was he going to tell his family? *I got married in the middle of an op, by the way. Yes, I met her at a bar, but that was just so I could bring her out to kill trolls with me. Oh, and she's made me part demon, and I'm probably going to quit my job to fight evil at her side for the next few centuries. But, hey, we waited until marriage to get it on, so there's that.*

Yeah, that was going to go great.

"Hey," he said, standing up and resting his hands on his hips, an alarm ringing in his head, louder than if someone had triggered an air raid warning. "Babies?"

"And...?" she asked with a panicked grin tugging at the corner of her mouth.

"You said it wouldn't happen on a mission, right?"

She let out an exhale and shook her head with mirrored relief. "No. I ovulate about once a year. And, as a full demon hunter, which I think you kind of are, you should be able to tell when you're firing active rounds."

He scowled and glanced down. "Huh. I have no idea how I would even know. You're sure about you though?"

"Positive. I mean... Never mind, I'll tell you about the single known failure another time, but there's no reason to think that would happen to us."

"Don't scare me like that. I mean, I want them eventually, but holy shit, this is new and terrifying. We can wait a few decades, right?"

She palmed her tank top and stepped over the rubble of the bed to reach him. Hand on his chest, she looked up and gave him the sweetest damn grin.

He tipped his forehead against hers and let out a sigh. "I'm not sure how to tell my family. If I can tell my family. If I can stay in the military—or if I even should. There's just so much."

"Did you talk to Ryan about how he handled being in the Coast Guard after joining our team? You should talk to Noah, too, before you decide anything."

"Fuck, that will be so awesome to see him again. I still can't believe he's alive. From the sounds of things, the military probably wasn't a good idea for him, or he'd still be in? But Simmons... what the hell happened?"

"Noah pulled through, in the end, but he messed up—really, really, tragically fucked up. Simmons got lost to the feral. Werewolf stuff. He's building a cabin, so we should go visit, maybe pitch in on getting it done, and I think it would be good for you both."

He stuffed his feet in his boots and nodded weakly.

As if a herd of bison stampeded toward them, although still miles off, the ground trembled.

Together, they walked outside. Unstable clouds threw sheets of hail mixed with rain, each icy ball pinging off the roof and coating the ground in a layer of white gravel.

The lightning parted, creating an aisle of flash-free skies between the COP and the canyon.

Loose shale shifted as the earth rumbled, steady and rhythmic, growing stronger.

Judging by the earthquake headed their way, they'd succeeded in pissing off the troll, and they were aimed straight for the COP. Every corner was guarded by one of his Echos. Sauer hopped off the Howitzer and climbed up to the rooftop of the house, settled in the folding chair, and comfortably stroked his beard, enough weapons surrounding him to blast them with nonstop firepower, for herding or attacks. Kerse wore a dark cap over her pale hair, dressed head-to-toe in black and face painted to match the dreary sky, lying prone on the TOC roof, her sniper rifle aimed and ready. Chan and Walker flanked the gate, armed and loaded with grenade launchers.

Casually moving up behind them, Vann nudged his side. Archer glanced over and saw the offered earpieces.

He accepted the earpieces and handed one to Lana. Voice quiet over the noise of the night, he said, "Report."

Sauer's husky laugh warmed the airways as he said, "Good of you to join us, Belak. Only you would pick such a romantic honeymoon."

He rolled his eyes and asked, "Kerse? What do you see?"

Tone serious despite the smile he knew marred her standard grim expression, she said, "Nothing more than shadows, but they'll be here soon."

Chan came on next. "You're going to want to check out the latest drone footage."

Vann nodded toward the TOC. "I'll show you," he said, as if he'd been waiting patiently all night, and wouldn't hurry until the first blows were exchanged.

Quinn came out from the motor pool, carrying Lana's massive axe and a pair of modified body armor vests she must have snagged from the armory. She was prepped for the fight in her own black sleeveless top, cargos, and her own bulletproof vest that matched Lana's that had gotten shredded.

As Quinn caught up to them, she tossed the axe and Lana snatched it from the air with a grin. "Thanks. I wondered where I'd left it."

"You were distracted when we got back," Quinn said, walking alongside Lana as they followed across the courtyard toward the TOC. "And I am hopeful you two have nailed things down and are now distraction-free?"

Archer glanced back to see Lana grinning widely as she read the inside of the vest, then turned to show him. In bold sharpie, a smiley face and the name *L. Belak* was written on the inside. Quinn handed him one just like it, with *A. Belak* written next to his smiley face.

Okay, fuck, he considered getting a little misty-eyed as Lana proudly secured hers and strapped her axe to her back. She nudged him playfully with her elbow, her glassy eyes matching his.

"Ready to take on anything. Even the unfriendly sort of trolls," she finally answered. Bright and eager as ever, more so, perhaps, Lana strutted behind him with Quinn in her preferred tactical-style leggings, her stolen combat boots, and an athletic tank under the vest, her dark hair in a tangled ponytail, and her massive axe ready at her back.

Drenched after the brief walk, they stepped into the TOC. Ryan and Bodie stood in front of the projected image from the drone footage. From the speakerphone, he heard Brock saying, *"You wake Archer's lazy ass yet? I've got a lot of hell to give him. Trolls and demon hunters and a shotgun wedding."*

He laughed and said, "Glad you're up on the latest gossip. What do you have for me?"

Brock answered, *"There's the newlywed. You guys stirred a hell of a lot of interest around that canyon. When the dust from the airstrike settled, the satellites were able to make out the forms of two dozen of these things looking very cranky."*

"How do you know they were cranky?" Lana said with a laugh.

"Ha," Brock said, laughing along. *"I'm presuming they were cranky. They deflected a good number of the blasts, as you guys saw with the craters outside the canyon, but I think the effort was more than they could handle. There's no more blur, no hazy shadows."*

Archer scanned the drone footage and watched as one of the trolls came sprinting toward it, leaped twenty feet in the air, and the image went suddenly dark. Holy fucking shit. Archer swallowed the knot in his throat and asked, knowing his voice was hollow and cracking. "And the flash bangs?"

Vann said under his breath, "The good news is, it worked. We pissed them off alright."

With a proud grin, Quinn said, "Judging by the constant little earthquake, I think they are very pissed, very fast, and want revenge."

Despite the sweat beading at his brow as he realized the team was accustomed to very different combat than he was, Archer found a stunned laugh tremble under his breath. The number of times Lana had tried to warn him that the Echos were out of their league flashed in his mind. Yeah. She, uh, wasn't wrong. Even without their other-worldly security system, the trolls would have flattened them.

Brock hemmed and hawed as he said, "*I suppose if that's the good news, maybe you'll think the bad news isn't so bad?*"

"What?" Archer asked, dreading the response. What could be worse, at this point, than fast, furious, oversized and powerful trolls headed their direction?

"*Another goddamn military distrusting fuck-up. Jameson's been keeping his cards close to his chest. He sent another goddamn Echo team to infiltrate the insurgent camp and just now thought to mention it. Sent them months ago. Deep cover; they're posing as insurgents and made it inside. Bad news is, they didn't report in, and intel doesn't have a fucking clue where they are.*"

"What?" he said again, teeth gritted tight as he realized how epically bad this was looking. No wonder Jameson didn't fill him in on any of this. Archer would have said it was a fucked up plan that would only get more people killed.

"*The military thinks the airstrike was a complete success. I was able to scramble the images before intel got ahold of anything with the trolls, but they can see the canyon is calm as a kitten now. Insurgents are moving south thanks to the noise from the airstrike, thinking we're moving in on their camp. They're armed to the teeth and have also gone on the offensive. There's a ranger bat suiting up as we speak, to meet the insurgents at our end. You're on the clock.*"

If the troops arrive before the trolls were cleared? "We're fucked," he muttered, shaking his head as dread surged through him. "How long do we have until shit hits the fan?"

"*Four, maybe five hours.*"

Chan's voice came through his earpiece, as the whole base had been in on the conversation. "Our furry friends will be here in seven minutes."

Bodie tipped his head and shrugged. "We know they can only deflect so much firepower."

Stepping away from the image, Ryan fingered the handle of the sword strapped to his back. "The veil's holding solid. Storm's unchanged. This far from the canyon, they shouldn't be able to cause too much damage to it."

Vann switched cameras to the other drone and showed twenty-six trolls pounding the ground, aimed straight for the COP.

Lana grimaced. "They do look cranky."

A quirk in his smile, Vann nailed Archer with an amused look. "Watch out for any conjured fists. I suspect they'll be aiming for you first."

Archer shrugged and backed up a step. "I'm a lot tougher than when they last saw me."

30

Closer. Harder.

The saturated shale rumbled under her boots as twenty-six sets of troll feet pounded toward them on the rampage to end all rampages. When Lana had first thought they might be up against trolls, she'd thought, "Nice, we can handle a few little critters." Even if they were ten-foot-tall critters, no problem. But these guys... yeah, not what she'd expected.

In a wide line spanning the courtyard, her team stood waiting for the fight to begin. Every time they went into a fight, they knew it might be their last. They knew they might not all make it out alive. Had some close calls over the years, all of them.

But dammit, she had a lot of looking forward to do.

Pessimism wasn't her thing.

Lana reached back and traced her fingertips along the leather-bound handle of her axe. Twenty-three years of fighting, and the thrill never waned.

Fear. Excitement. The rush that came with the impending fight.

Her heart thundered in her chest, fueling the adrenaline harder into her veins.

Another two or three-hundred years of this? With these guys, and her new favorite teammate? She was fully on board.

Archer stood at her side, sidearms strapped to his hips and a fully automatic assault rifle ready in his grip.

She tipped her head up and laughed, letting the rain freely stream over her face, licking a plump drip that had settled on her lip. "Ever hold a sword before?"

He huffed a laugh and glanced back and forth at the others. "Before now, I'd never even seen a real sword up close."

"Many hunters have tried to incorporate guns and other explosives, but they're rarely as effective, and some monsters look at us like we're throwing lemons at them. And you don't want one thrown back at you."

"Yeah," he muttered, shaking his head, his focus unshakable.

Vann and Ryan both wielded broadswords, Ryan's inhumanly black blade from the demon realm, and Vann's passed down through generations. Quinn preferred her twin swords strapped to her back à la Deadpool, but she mixed it up now and again. Were Astrid here, she'd have her sleek swords strapped to the sides of her long legs. For a while, Bennett had ditched the shield as he adjusted to his vampire speed, but he'd adapted it to be more streamlined, and Adair preferred her knives. Under the roof of the chow hall, Bodie had already ditched his shirt and started to untie his boots.

Archer's brow scrunched together and looked at the odd man like he was watching a farce for the first time. "Um..."

Bodie flashed him a wink and a wicked grin before lowering his jeans over his hips.

"So..." Sauer echoed through the com.

Lana raised her eyebrows up and down and said, "This is my favorite part."

Archer rolled his eyes and grinned at her, no weird jealousy. She winked and grinned back.

At the far end of the courtyard, Chan looked back and her eyes popped open. "You guys have some weird ways of getting ready for a fight."

As the rumbling drew nearer, the enemy close at the gates, Bodie set his neatly folded clothes next to the door of the chow hall and stepped out into the storm. Within the space of a step, he shifted into the wolf and stalked into the line with the rest of the team.

"Well that's something you don't see every day," Sauer said with a rumbling appreciation. "Archer, can you do that?"

He laughed and looked up at the tower, shaking his head. "Nope, sorry."

"They're here," Kerse's voice resonated sharply over the airwaves.

The sky above darkened, the storm letting up as the trolls seemed to block the clouds above them.

"Confirm their count," Archer said.

"Twenty-six strong."

Sauer's deep voice piqued high as he squealed under his breath, "They're fucking huge."

"Range?" Archer asked.

"One hundred fifty meters," Kerse answered. "One twenty-five. Damn, they're fast."

Sauer asked, "You sure you don't want me to fire?"

"Kerse?"

"One hundred meters."

"Sauer, see if you can knock a few down, but don't let them escape," Archer said, his voice steady as he calculated.

Shots blasted across the distance, debris flying in the air where the shots landed. The ground rumbled harder, faster as they came with an added fury.

Closer. Closer.

"Slowed a few. Not much," Sauer said, a growl on his voice.

"On my signal, open the gates," Archer commanded. "We've got Rangers coming in from the south as we speak, insurgents heading into the canyon from the north, and a missing Echo squad. Finish it quick."

Lana gripped both hands on her axe at her back and brought the weapon around her, holding it defensively in front of her. She glanced at Archer. His expression was set firm, his jaw strong and eyes sharp, unflinching.

The ground rumbled harder, tremors climbing her legs that had only a smidge to do with trepidation. Lana took a steady inhale.

"Twenty-five meters," Kerse said.

"Now," he said evenly.

Hands gripped firm around the iron gate handles, Chan and Walker pushed hard and fast.

As the outside came into view, charcoal gray fur camouflaged to match the bleak terrain, the massive creatures funneled through the opening. Or, funneled was too gentle of a term. Chan and Walker leaped back out of the way as the trolls' broad shoulders slammed through the gateway, sending debris flying.

Up close... yeah. Trolls were no laughing matter. If even one of them survived this, these dudes definitely needed a thorough write-up for the reference books.

The rank smell radiated off them. Mangey fur... almost like ferals, but twice the size, and their gold glowing eyes were something out of this world. "Bodie, I think these might be cousins of yours," Bennett said, flashing a shit-eating grin at the wolf.

Bodie snarled under his teeth, but his wolfy grin showed he was working on a comeback for when he shifted human again.

For a brief moment, she almost felt bad that they'd picked a fight with creatures that just wanted to be left alone. They looked awfully cranky. More than cranky. Snarling, teeth-baring, growling, I'm-going-to-pummel-you-to-dust expressions, they looked ready for war. And loving it. She would swear a few were even smiling. Maybe they needed to get out of their cave more.

Keeping clear of the line of fire, Chan and Walker took off toward the house and climbed the ladder, taking position at the towers, SAWs and mortars ready.

"Short range, fire," Archer said, holding his ground as the enemy drew near.

Blasts shook the earth, lighting up the sky as the Echos opened fire on the trolls. The heavier stuff aimed at the rear so none would double back. Good fucking thing. Lana's eyes widened as she watched half of the explosions ricocheting off in all directions.

A few trolls slowed and dropped, reducing their numbers by at best, five.

The rest closed in.

Bennett sprinted into the fray ahead of the rest.

Lana turned to Archer, heart thundering under her ribs as he aimed his weapon, fearless and ready. "Love you," she mouthed.

He flashed her a wink and said the words back.

Axe gripped tight, she sprinted into the thick of it.

Trolls. What the fuck. The smallest of them was twice her size, their legs thick as tree trunks, arm span wider than they were tall.

The first of them slammed a fist—real and corporeal—at Bennett. He raised the shield and slammed back. Shockwaves blasted out.

Stunned, the troll recoiled, quickly swinging from the other side.

Bennett juked under and drove his sword into the creature's side.

Roaring, the troll lashed back with one hand, gripping its side with the other.

And Lana knew everything she needed to know.

One of the trolls aimed straight for her. Three times her size and probably thinking he'd step on her and be done.

She sprinted toward it and dropped to her knees at the last second, skidding over the wet shale as the block of a fist swung hard, air whooshing over her head as she ducked under the blow.

Slamming her axe, she nailed it in the hamstring and bounced back to her feet.

Leaping into the air, she used the weight of her weapon to spin her in a three-sixty, slicing into the thick neck of the next troll.

He slumped to the ground. Dense, burgundy blood pooled onto the saturated ground, a dark river flowing out from the wound.

She glanced back to see Archer had emptied the assault rifle already and dove into the fray, swinging with his bare fists. Like a prize fighter, a fearless brawler, he pummeled a creature twice his size. The troll grabbed his abdomen and stumbled to the ground, heaving as he struggled to draw a breath.

Not stopping to gloat or dwell, Archer kept moving.

As the trolls' numbers chipped away, Lana felt the rain collecting overhead, the storm starting to funnel inward.

The air thickened and the hair on the back of her neck stood erect. A sonorous hum, deep and furious, rose as the trolls moved toward each other to form a circle.

Lana rubbed her eyes as the air seemed to blur around her. She sucked breath in through her mouth, oxygen waning from the atmosphere as heat radiated off them.

She scanned her surroundings. The team gripped their weapons tighter, encircling the trolls as they all sensed the change.

She moved to stand next to Archer. He rolled his neck and pinned his shoulders back as he readied for the next attack. Furiously unafraid, his gaze narrowed and his jaw flexed fast. Voice thick, he whispered into the earpiece, "Echos: Run."

Without hesitation, the Echos grabbed their weapons and were on the move. Walker and Chan leaped away, out of sight as they skidded over the far side of the house. Kerse and Sauer climbed down from their perches and took off at a sprint.

Energy pulsed from the trolls. A vortex sucked air from all around, blasting steadily outward in all directions.

Lana pushed toward them, but couldn't get decent footing as a hurricane-force wind spiraled outward.

Engines roared from the motor pool as each Echo took a vehicle and floored it out the back gate.

Adair sprinted toward the trolls, but not even her vampire speed was enough to push through the trolls' barrier.

Bodie growled with his lips pulled back, his fur standing on end as he crouched low to hold his ground.

Wind swelled thicker and spun faster.

Lana's hair tugged at its binding, sopping strands of hair slicing over her cheeks. Her grip tightened on her axe, feet digging into the shale, every effort focused on holding her ground.

Shield in front of him, Bennett shoved against the barrier, making a margin of progress. He roared over the growing rumble of the wind.

Quinn shouted to Lana, "I don't think they're sewing quilts in there."

Lana tipped her head back and laughed out loud.

Archer came to stand next to her, feet braced into the ground, standing sideways to deflect the wind. Half laughing and half growling with disbelief, he hollered over the deafening wind, "Is it always like this?"

"Like what?" she asked, looking up at him with a curious grin.

"I figured it would be easier, being stronger and faster."

The wind spun faster around them.

She shook her head and laughed dryly. "We're half human, and a good number of our enemies are full demon. It never gets any easier."

A gust spiraled through the air, and a rush of wind walloped in her direction and sent her flying backward in the air. She gripped her axe and spun her body into a backflip. Landing on her feet, she roared and dug her boots into the wet shale.

Down on one knee, Archer dug his fingertips into the rocks to combat the force sending him back.

Pride thundered in her chest as she watched him adapt so naturally to the fight. He glanced back at her, a wickedness in his grin, as if he knew what was coming next.

The wind stopped. Silence, still and penetrating, the pressure in her ears shifting.

A shadow rose from the trolls and concentrated into a fist as massive as a troll's head.

Aimed straight for Archer, the fist came rushing for him.

Lana ran to reach him.

Rising to his feet, Archer balled his fist at his side, bracing his feet into the rocks.

The fist closed in fast.

Anastomotic lightning gathered, flashing and uniting in a spiral overhead.

Lana screamed for him to get down, but he didn't hear her over the thunder.

Holding fast, core braced and his shoulder strong, Archer slammed his own fist back.

The bare skin of his knuckles met the shadow of the trolls' combined force as he punched back.

The shockwave blasted in all directions.

The rocks at his feet turned to dust and shot into the air, swirling around him.

Dense gray fog expanded from the blast, spinning in a dizzying, blinding funnel. Archer disappeared into the thick of it.

Lana roared and ran in after him. Rocky shrapnel sliced over her skin as she pushed into the darkness.

In the center, Archer had become the target.

A troll lifted him in the air and threw him backward.

Lana shrieked and ran for him.

The team sprinted into the fray.

Archer's body slammed into the wall of the chow hall, and he dropped to the ground.

Lana skidded to the ground as she reached him.

Without pause, he pushed to his knees.

She threw her arms around him and nuzzled into him.

"I'm okay," he said, pulling back and holding her look. Already bruising, blood pooled in the corner of his mouth, he smiled and kissed her softly. "Let's finish this."

Taking a heavy breath, thrill fueling into her veins as she realized he was exactly the man she knew him to be, a hunter in every sense, a smile twitched at the side of her mouth and she nodded. "One more mile."

She popped to her feet and grabbed his hand. He groaned but let her pull him up, and she readied her axe as they stood side by side, smacking the handle against her palm.

Wind eddied around the trolls. The trolls threw fists of dust and wind ahead of their block-like corporeal fists as the team came at them with blades, strength, and speed.

With Archer at her side, she ran into the thick of it.

Turning back toward them, a trio of trolls lifted their arms to the sky. Lightning coiled above. Electricity hummed in the air, and a bolt split, aimed at them both.

Could Ryan control the veil like this, if he didn't care how badly he thrashed it? There was no way these things could cause such a storm, without shredding into the veil.

Lana dove to the side, Archer to the other.

She ran to one side of the trio while he flanked the other.

They threw a fist at Archer, and he slammed his fist back at it. Again, he threw their strength back at them with his fearless hit.

The trio recoiled.

Archer slammed his body into one. Leaping, he spun and nailed the nearest with a blunt kick. Massive and pissed, the troll flew backward in the air toward Lana.

Ready for it, she spun her axe and rode the spinning force, slamming her blade into its chest.

Again, he passed her another and she finished it.

The team weaved through the remaining trolls. Bruised and depleted, but not one of them shied away from the fight. Adair sent a knife flying, the blade embedding to the hilt between the eyes of the center troll. Bennett blocked a conjured fist with his shield and drove his sword into the abdomen of the nearest. Wolfy teeth sinking into the thigh of one, Bodie dove through troll legs, while Vann followed and sank the final blow into each the wolf wounded.

Weapons lashing out with unstoppable fury, the team fueled the last of their energy into the fight.

Archer juked around the troll that tore his direction. He spun at the last second, nailing it in the back with his fist and sending it flying in Lana's direction.

One by one, the last of the trolls dropped lifeless to the ground as the team finished them off.

A final troll remained in the middle of a team of hunters, all bleeding and bruised, a few dazed and flirting with unconsciousness.

Alone, pissed as hell with his eyes glowing bolder than the sun, the troll seemed to draw on the last of his energy and pulled down the sky.

Wind rushed in all directions.

Lightning struck the ground in a dozen hits.

Archer ran for the troll, drawing its attention away from Lana.

Fist aimed straight for Archer, the troll was out for revenge.

Lana rushed from behind it, axe overhead as she sprinted toward it.

Waiting, anticipating the blow, Archer threw his arms out, making himself an easy target.

Lana leaped into the air and spun in a three-sixty with the weight of her axe. Blade strong and true, she slammed it into the neck of the troll.

Beneath her feet, the troll stumbled.

She sliced deeper, wrenching her blade back. It collapsed under her feet, and she leaped off, landing on one knee.

Dazed, her breath shallow, Lana looked across at Archer. Limping, more bruises and lacerations than clean skin, he smiled and hobbled toward her.

Aching from head-to-toe, deep to the bone, Lana rose to her feet and met him halfway. Stunned, smiling, he pulled her close.

She melted into him. He enveloped her in his arms and she touched her lips to his.

The air around them quieted, and a natural, subtle, misty breeze stirred the air.

31

Archer's earpiece buzzed madly, shattering the brief moment of relief. "Repeat," he said, holding his fingertips over the earpiece to be sure he heard right, already heading toward the gate to get moving.

"The insurgents are nearing the base of the canyon," Chan thundered back.

"The Rangers can handle it," he said.

"They've got hostages," Chan said quickly. "The Rangers are still an hour south of you."

"Hostages?" He hissed, his heart stopping dead in his chest.

"The other Echos. Cover must have been blown. All six are bound, gagged, and marching south at gunpoint."

Vann tipped his head up. "Need a hand?"

The Echo's rigs rumbled closer and halted outside the base. Sauer and Chan piled out of their rigs and climbed in with the others, leaving the engines running for the team.

Archer glanced back at the other hunters and said, "We got this. You guys need to clear out."

Lana blew him a kiss and said, "Time to decide."

He ran back for her and halted in front of her, cradling her cheeks in his palms, his wounds from the fight already beginning to heal. Thumbs brushing over her jaw, he leaned down and touched his lips to hers. Impatience rose around them as the timeline chipped away to nothing. "I will always choose you," he murmured. Releasing her, he backed away and climbed into the front passenger seat next to Chan.

As the Echos took off, Archer looked back.

The team gathered their equipment and quickly piled into the other SUVs, driving out and heading toward the nearest town.

"I need confirmation the base is clear," Walker said through the earpiece. "Count off."

The Echos and hunters all reported in as they drove off in different directions. As the COP shrank in the distance, from the bench seat behind him, Walker punched in the final code.

Bright as day, the COP ignited in a massive explosion. Fire and smoke engulfed the base. As quickly as the charges had detonated, the base was obliterated, not even a post left standing.

A memory as distant as a fading nightmare, the drive to the canyon bore a sense of finality. He knew his time had come, and was grateful for everything he had gone through, for his friends, for the fight that had to be fought. But it wasn't his fight anymore.

No blur. No gloomy cover. Only the dissipating clouds in the sky when the canyon finally came into view.

At the base of the talus of terraces, the stream now a lazy, sinuous flow, the Echos slammed to a stop and took position around the base of the canyon.

Kerse and Sauer climbed to their perches, sniper rifles strapped to their backs until they dropped to their abdomens and aimed into the darkness.

At his side, ducked behind a boulder, Chan raised her sidearm at the ready. Walker skirted the edge of the escarpment, approaching from the side.

Brock's voice rumbled in his ear, humming with the echo of the drone that lowered from above. *"Eyes in the sky. Two hostages bound in front, the other four are surrounded by insurgents. Thirty-two sporting good old-fashioned AKs."*

"Good of you to join us," Sauer voiced back.

As a unit, each knowing their role, brothers and sisters that knew each other's minds, they set things right.

Flying toward him like a stone, a lone grenade with his name on it, and Archer made his decision.

RAUCOUS LAUGHTER FILLED THE warm air as the tavern filled with Coasties on shore leave. Fishermen toasted over the latest catch. Locals shared platters of fresh seafood, fries, and late summer fruit pies.

Lana filled a trio of beers to the brim and scooped them onto the bar, sliding them across toward her thirsty patrons. There was no place like it in the world. Wood floors older than her father, a fire roared in the ancient hearth, and a dazzling summer rain tapped against the paint-sealed windows.

Missy tugged her dark hair into a messy bun and pulled her apron over her baby bump. She bopped her hip into Lana's and grinned. "Thanks for covering for me."

"Anytime," she said, smiling at her little sister. Not so little anymore, she supposed. Lana now looked like the younger sister, as Missy had sprouted a dappling of grays that said the tide was beginning to turn. One day, Lana would look like the daughter, then the granddaughter, and eventually would bury her human sister.

"You've been quiet since you got home," Missy said, her sweet voice lilting with concern.

"It was a hell of a mission," Lana said softly.

Her dad appeared in his server's apron and slapped his hands down on the bar. "I'll say," he said, winking at his girls. "Trolls? Really?"

Lana rolled her eyes and poured a river of tequila over a line of shot glasses on a tray and passed it across. He grinned and took the tray, disappearing into the crowd.

"Exciting fight?" Missy asked as she sprayed water into a trio of glasses filled with ice.

"I think so. Not your type of place," she said, swallowing the lump of regret. She took a breath, and added, "Actually, there was this adorable village with flowers in every window. You would have loved to see it."

Missy smiled and flashed Lana a wink. "You've been smiling to yourself when no one's watching. I wish I could have seen it."

She bit the edge of her tongue, unsure how to respond. Three weeks since she'd left him, watching as he'd driven off to another fight. "What?"

He'd called every day since, but the distance had been killing her.

And... damn, her dreams had been filled with creative fantasies she knew he'd be game to try, and her days had been filled with wonderings on what he would think of building a house outside of town, maybe after a long honeymoon on a sun-drenched beach.

"You, falling in love. Typical, you rushed into it, and I get to find out after the fact," Missy said as she passed a pair of fish baskets to a pair of diners at the bar.

Lana sucked in a slow breath and leaned back.

"When does his flight get in?" Missy's expression dazzled with amusement.

"Tonight," she promised. Her phone should buzz any second with a text announcing his flight was taking off.

Their dad stepped up to the bar and leaned his elbows on the time-worn wood. "Your mom's got everything all prepped and the table is even already set, so you can bring him to breakfast tomorrow," he said with a matching dazzle.

Missy leaned back and glanced over Lana's shoulder to the door, then back to her sister and their dad. "Lana?" she asked.

Lana ignored the rumble of more boots hitting the tavern floor behind her as another ship must have come in. "What's up?"

Missy's expression was light, but her eyes were heavy with something. "I don't regret my decision."

Ross's moss green eyes were heavy, and he took a deep inhale. Clearly, they'd been talking behind her back. Lana's heart clenched in her chest as she glanced at her dad, then back to Missy.

A frog in her throat, Missy said, "But not a day has gone by that I haven't berated myself for not talking to you first. I should have told you that I wimped out."

Tears blurred her vision as she watched her sister biting her lip, anticipating Lana's response. She grabbed her sister and tugged her in for a hug. She rocked her back and forth and said, "You didn't wimp out. Deciding this life wasn't for you, this life that you were raised to believe was the *only* way? Turning down all the perks that go with it? Missy, I would never have had the guts to do what you did."

"You're not mad still? I was too afraid to tell you. Lana, I always knew what I wanted. You might take after our grandfather, but I am our mother."

"I *was* furious. I realize now, I should have known, and I should have been a better sister and paid more attention. You've made a fantastically sweet life here. This tavern is the heart of our family, and you've courageously filled it with so much love and life."

Missy stepped back and brushed a drip from her eyelashes. "You think so? I mean, it's all I ever wanted."

"Yes. You're my little sister, and I always want the best for you. You're happy and I'm happy for you." She grinned as an idea took root in her mind.

"What?" Missy asked with a familiar tone of suspicion, reminiscent of the many times Lana had gotten them into trouble.

"I get lots of babysitting time, so my favorite little nephews can decide on the path that makes sense for him. When the time comes."

"Deal," Missy said with a sniffle. "Kai's already a homebody like me, but..." She rubbed her belly and rolled her eyes. "This one is already taking after his Auntie Lana, I'm afraid. He thinks my uterus is a trampoline. But yes, I want them both to grow up knowing they can be whatever they want to be."

Ross cleared his throat and winked at Missy, glancing behind Lana knowingly.

Missy sniffled and looked toward the door. The corner of her lips quirked up, then back to Lana. A laughing lilt in her tone, she said, "And what about you? When do I get a little niece or nephew to spoil?"

Strong arms enveloped Lana from behind, tugging her back against him.

Lava flooded her veins and thrill burned over her skin as she leaned into Archer. She traced her fingertips over his arms and leaned into him.

"Going to be awhile," he answered for her.

She turned in his arms and rose to her toes.

He splayed his hands on her back under her top and pulled her close. "I caught an early flight."

His cobalt eyes flashed with delight, a grin spread wide on his yummy lips.

A million words danced on her tongue, but he touched his lips to hers and answered them all with a kiss. The world around them faded to a soothing roar as she sank into him and his mouth mated with hers.

Keeping her close, his warm breath mingling with hers, he whispered, "I love you."

"Love you too," she answered. "Doing okay?"

He chewed the corner of his tongue, a smitten grin on his lips as she linked her hands with his and leaned back to watch him. "I am," he answered. "My funeral's tomorrow," he said, his chest rising and falling. Fingers linked together, his smile hesitated. "Killed in action. But the rest of my squad, and the other Echos, all made it out safely."

Her brow fell. "Your family, your squad—"

The corner of his mouth turned up wickedly. "Are the only ones who know the truth."

Relief washed over her, and she moved in to wrap herself around him and never let go.

"Hang on," he said, laughing under his breath. He glanced at her father and sister and said, "Um. Hi. Archer Belak."

Her dad grinned the sweetest, glassy-eyed look.

After shaking Archer's hand and babbling a giddy greeting, Missy jumped up and down and squealed. "Missy. Nice to meet you."

"Heard a lot about you," he said, grinning as he tucked Lana against him. "Great place you've got here."

Missy beamed and glanced around. "Thanks."

Her dad cleared his throat and said, "So you really are, completely... like us?"

Lana felt him shrug at her side. "Apparently."

"Huh. That's.... a first."

Grinning wide, Missy said, "I smell a prophecy completed."

Lana shook her head. "That sounded rather hunterly of you."

"Hey. I may not have chosen it for me, but I can't imagine you choosing anything else."

Archer cleared his throat. With a wicked grin, taking her hands, he backed up a step and said, "My family promised to keep my secrets on one condition."

"And what's that?" she said, suspicion warm and fuzzy in her belly.

He lowered to one knee behind the bar with her and took a heavy inhale.

She tipped her head back and laughed. "You already did that."

He took her hand and flashed her a dreamy look, that wicked smile still teasing at his lips. "My whole family got on a video call during the layover on my way here and concluded I had bungled it, so I am to try again."

She tamed her laugh and bit the corner of her lip.

"Lana Fischer. Love of my life. Keeper of my soul and my heart. Will you claim me, as I do you?"

She went to answer, but he shook his head.

"I know you're in a hurry to get this marriage going, but I need to make sure you're certain," he said playfully.

She rolled her eyes. In her peripheral, she realized the entire tavern was watching. Her sister leaned against the bar next to their dad, both of them grinning like idiots.

"I'm a forever sort of guy. I will fight by your side. I will have your back. I will love you as long as we walk this earth."

She pulled him to his feet and bit her lip in a watery grin. "I love you. I want you forever, always by my side. Marry me?"

He laughed and held her hand, sliding a simple band over her finger that held a river of blue and green gems on a bed of platinum. "That's my line," he murmured with a grin. "They're going to make me do it again."

"They want a wedding, don't they?" she asked.

"There's this cabin a few miles north of my hometown, on the lake where I never caught any fish. Big wedding. Your family and mine, your team and my squad. Flowers and dancing and champagne."

"Do I have to throw a bouquet?"

"That's your call. But I've got three unmarried siblings that will be sorely disappointed if you don't. We're pretty traditional." Lacing her arms around his neck, he wrapped his hands around her waist and hovered a breath away. "Say yes?"

"Yes," she whispered against his mouth and melted into him in a grounding, highflying kiss that sent cheers erupting through the ancient tavern.

THE END

Carrie Thorne is the author of kick-ass romance novels, specializing in white-hot chemistry, healthy relationships, and a mix of action and dreamily falling in love. Whether it's a sinuous flow down a lazy river or evil bad dudes hot on heels, Carrie's stories will draw you in and ruin your sleep. Happily ever afters are for everyone, and kindness is everything.

She's also an introvert who loves people, travel, fitness, video games, food, and is a true Pacific Northwesterner who lives for rain and outdoors and trees and mountains and ocean, and... she's a total dork. At home, she's lucky to have two creative and confident kids, a witty veteran husband she fell at-first-sight for, and a tiny pup snuggled at her side. In addition to writing romance, Carrie has been a nurse practitioner, a Martian and Earthling geologist, a banker, and she is usually elbow-deep in a DIY project in which she bit off more than she could chew.

Where is she now? Depends on the weather. Cozied up by the fire with a steaming mug of black coffee, or stretched out on the hammock with a frothy IPA in the shade of her forest. Either way, she's working on the next great love story to conquer your TBR list.

www.CarrieThorne.com